Heiress of War

Elle Winters

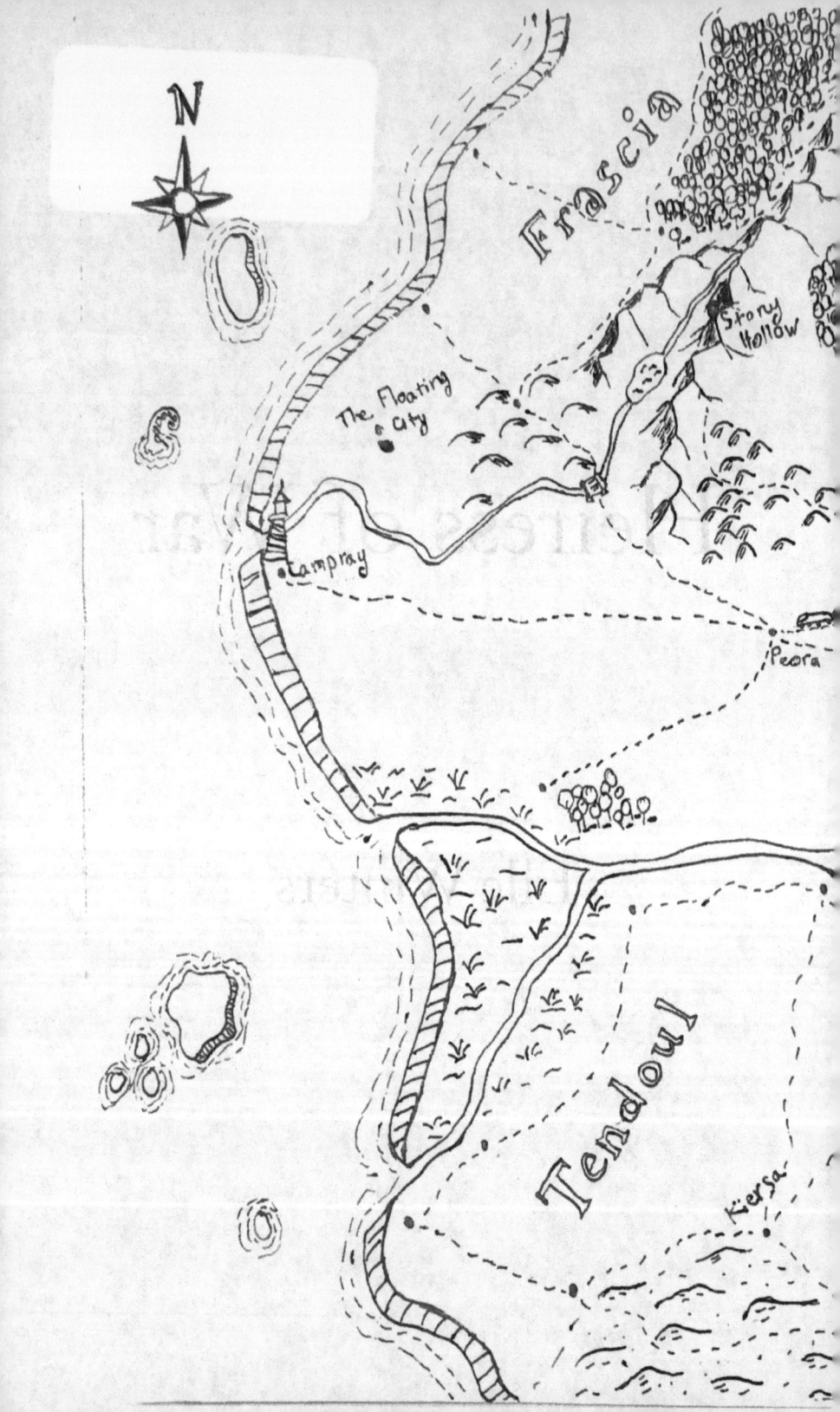

First paperback edition January 2026

Cover by AK Westerman, AK Organics Abstracts
Maps by Elle Winters

ISBN 979-8-9937456-0-2 (paperback)
ISBN 979-8-9937456-1-9 (ebook)

For Matthew,
I wouldn't have been able to write this without you.
We're better together, always.

1

Cora was certain there was no better smell than cinnamon sugar. The scent wafted down the cramped sidewalk to where she stood in line. The seconds ticked by, growing in number as the man in front of her shuffled forward. Cora leaned around him to check the line. She knew Theo was already waiting for her. He could wait.

A sleek black car zoomed by next to the line, mixing the smell of exhaust with the scent of Alma's churro cart. Cora scowled at it as it rumbled away across uneven cobbles.

Alma had set up her cart at the edge of the old Night Market. Cora could see a few of the brightly colored stalls set up in front of stone buildings older than the concrete beneath her feet. Just a few blocks down, the car screeched to a stop in front of a club, the flashing neon lights reflecting off the door as it swung open.

Cora turned her attention away, uninterested. The line shuffled forward again and a warm voice called out to her.

"Cora, where have you been lady?"

Cora smiled easily, savoring the sound of Alma's gently rolled r's. "Studying for exams."

Alma clucked her tongue. "Those professors better give you good grades."

"If they don't, I'll send them your way."

"I'll set them straight for you," Alma rested a hand on her hip. "How many churros you need tonight?"

A small shadow moved behind Alma, catching Cora's attention. She smiled slowly. "Better give me three."

Cora strode away from the cart with three paper-wrapped churros. She moved closer to the Middle Ring, sparing a glance up at the top of the old stone wall. The little shadow had been right next to it, away from the market and the rumbling club.

Cora slowed, frowning at the statue in front of her. Ancient as the wall itself, and so weathered it was hardly recognizable in the evening light. A phoenix perched on a stone pedestal, its wings pointed to the sky—the symbol of the fire goddess Elidi. And behind the statue hung a bright red poster, visible even in the shadow of the wall.

Tired of losing jobs to androids? The poster read. *Join the People's Employment League today and fight for your right to work!*

"Are you still putting up these posters, Mila?" Cora asked.

A small girl, eight or nine years old, came out from behind the statue. She held a roll of tape and several sheets of red paper.

"They pay me for every poster," she shrugged.

"But do they bring you churros?"

Mila's eyes lit up. She snatched the pastry out of Cora's hand, scattering cinnamon sugar everywhere.

Cora laughed and brushed crumbs off of Mila's shirt. "You better get home before your mother drags you to bed."

Mila threw her arms around Cora and gave her a squeeze before bounding off into the darkness. Cora brushed sugar off of her head scarf and jacket. She glanced up at Elidi's shrine, frowning again. She glanced up, then sighed softly. She broke off a small piece of churro and laid it at the statue's feet.

"Accept my offering, great goddess," she murmured.

The holo-bracelet on her wrist chimed. She glanced down at the message typed across the screen.

Where are you? The match is about to start

Cora held the bracelet up to her mouth. "Just save me a seat, I'll be there soon."

She turned her back on the shrine and took a big bite. Totally worth it.

Just save me a seat, I'll be there soon.

Theo swiped his thumb across the screen, erasing the message.

2

The Dragon Slayer was mostly empty, other than a single table of city Watchers in the corner. The old wooden stool beneath him groaned as he shifted. It was likely as old as the tavern itself.

"Are you having another tonight, Theo?"

Theo slid his empty glass forward. "Not tonight, Sloan."

Taller than Theo, with a mane of thick red hair and a meticulously trimmed beard, Sloan took up most of the space behind the bar. Sloan wiped a few drops off of the otherwise spotless surface. The wood gleamed in the dim light, despite the countless nicks and scratches along its edges.

"Where's your girl?" he asked

Theo gave him a hard look. "She's not my girl."

Sloan cocked his eyebrow.

Theo glanced away, lowering his voice despite the lack of other patrons. "You'll send her down when she gets here?"

"Sure thing."

Sloan slid his hand under the bar and a panel in the back corner slid open. Theo gave him a little wave before walking into the elevator. The panel slid closed again and the elevator descended. Theo hummed along to the soft music playing over the speakers. It took a full three minutes to reach the bottom.

Sound washed over Theo as he left the elevator. He stood at the top of a bowl shaped cave, staring down into an arena. Small puffs of dust hung over the sandy floor of what was once a dragon training den. He could still make out dragon perches on some of the walls, high above the cave floor.

People filtered in through a series of tunnels connected to the cave, most of them walking at least half a mile to reach the arena. Not for the first time, Theo silently thanked Sloan. Only people the burly barkeep really liked used the Dragon Slayer's elevator.

Cheers drowned out blaring music, until all Theo sensed was the pounding beat in his chest. It grew stronger the closer he got to the stands. The grainy voice of the announcer was indistinguishable as it echoed around the cavern. Theo wrinkled his nose, dodging a cloud of musky smoke.

Finally, he found a pair of seats about halfway up the stands. He tapped the screen of his holo-bracelet, calling up a small holo-graphic keyboard. He quickly sent the seat numbers to Cora.

Bass vibrated through Theo's seat and pounded through his bones. It infected him, setting his knee bouncing with anticipation. Cora slipped into the seat next to him just as the duelists entered the arena.

"Did I miss anything?" she asked, offering him a churro.

"No. Is this what took you so long?"

Cora shrugged and dusted her fingers against her pants. "Not this guy again. Hasn't he had enough of losing for one season?"

Theo gazed back at the arena floor, where a stocky man attempted to flourish his sword for the crowd. The slim sprite opposing him watched with a bored expression.

"He probably owes one of the gangs money," Theo guessed. "Only reason to keep coming back."

Cora grunted noncommittally. She kept shifting back and forth, neck craning.

"You couldn't have found us seats behind someone shorter?" she groaned.

Theo nearly laughed. He hadn't noticed the seat next to him was behind a tall elf woman. He silently traded seats with Cora.

The bell rang for the match to start. Theo couldn't look away from the disaster unfolding before them. The swordsman was no match for the sprite. Even without the advantage of flight, the sprite was barely exerting any effort. The swordsman couldn't land a single hit. The sprite darted around him, punching through his guard to score ten points. Then twenty. The match ended when she reached thirty points. The swordsman slumped into the box just off the arena floor, head in his hands. Theo's gut twisted for the guy.

"That was brutal," Cora said.

"Whoever sets the roster has it out for him. There's no way he should have been paired with that sprite."

Cora shook her holo-bracelet awake. She sighed as her clock flashed awake.

"Do you have to go already?"

Cora nodded. "I told you I only had time for one match tonight."

"Yeah, yeah, have to get your beauty sleep and all that." T

4

tucked the end of her blonde braid back under her head scarf.

"What is it tomorrow, kissing babies?"

"No, kissing babies was last week. Tomorrow is raising money for orphans."

"Ah yes, how could I forget about the orphans? And then you'll be volunteering at the soup kitchen?"

Cora shoved his shoulder. "Actually, I have to get ready for a welcome party."

Theo stood, rolling his wide shoulders. "Well, I can walk you out. I should head home, too."

He led the way out of the stands, making an opening for Cora in the crowd. She nodded her thanks once the crowd thinned. He walked slowly so that she could keep pace as they made their way up to the elevator.

"How's your mom doing?" Cora asked, slightly out of breath.

Theo slowed a touch more. "She's doing alright. She's been calling Isla and the kids nearly every day."

"It must be hard having them in another city."

Theo's hands clenched briefly. "Yeah, but at least the train line is finished. I keep telling her to go visit."

"You wouldn't go with her?" Cora asked, swiping long strands of hair out of her face .

"I've got too much work right now."

Cora didn't press, and Theo didn't elaborate. They went back to chatting about the match as the elevator ascended. Humid night air pressed around them as they left the Dragon Slayer. Theo walked with her until they approached the Middle Ring.

Cora turned to him, her smile warm. "Well, I'm off to help some orphans. Have a good night, Theo."

"Night, Cora." Theo smiled back. "Oh wait, I didn't ask who the welcome party was for."

Cora's smile fell slightly. "The new Chancellor of Galta."

Theo gaped at her. He fought to keep the surge of anger out of his voice. "It's been, what, a month since they 'reorganized' their government? Is that even enough time to clean the blood off the streets?"

Cora winced. "My parents invited him. Something about

5

creating ties with the new leadership before their other neighbors swoop in."

Theo swallowed, forcing his fists to unclench. "Just tell him about your work with the orphans. It'll charm the blazes out of him."

"Will do. Good night, Theo."

She gave him a wry smile before disappearing into the night.

Cora wove further away from Theo, meandering down streets at random. After six years of nightly wanderings, she could map most of Narous. She knew every route from home to the Dragon Slayer, and knew her way to Theo's work, their favorite restaurants, and the weekly markets that moved around. She both loved and hated crowds. They came with both the ability to disappear, and the risk of recognition.

Cora skirted the busiest streets, only getting close enough to glimpse the nobility in their flashy clothes, with their haggard attendants and sleek-bodied androids. She wove down streets packed with stone houses next to glass and steel shops. She edged around the Night Market, slipping down narrow alleys until she reached a familiar metal gate.

It was set into thick stone blocks, the hinges rusty. It shrieked as Cora pulled it open enough to slip through. She needed to get Theo to oil the hinges again. She tapped the light on her holo-bracelet, giving off a cold blue glow.

Just inside the tunnel beyond the gate was a waterproof box. She changed in the dim light from her bracelet, carefully folding her street clothes into the box. She had learned the hard way that a good rain could flood the tunnel.She pulled on the loose pants and shirt waiting in the box for her. Not quite pajamas, but just as soft and comfortable. She couldn't remember how many sets she had anymore.

The last thing to go into the box was her head scarf. She did her best to smooth the impossibly long braid now hanging uncovered down her back. It was going to be a pain to brush before bed.

Cora snapped the lid closed before heading further into the tunnel. She kept the light on, barely needing it. She knew every

6

bump and crack in the floor. The tunnel ended at a dusty wooden door. She paused, listening.

Silence met her.

She eased it open and slipped into the quiet hallway. The door closed behind her, blending with the rest of the trim.

She moved on soft feet, slipping past the servants' quarters up to the main hallway. She passed the kitchen on her way, snagging an apple from the hanging baskets. Cora straightened her back and tossed her hair over her shoulder. She quit skulking and became once more Her Royal Highness Cora Catarina Maria Bjorn, Crown Princess of Liskow.

No one bothered Cora as she crossed the palace to her room. She typed a message out to Theo.

Made it home. Off to get my beauty rest.

Her holo chimed just as she reached her bedroom door.

Tell the Chancellor I said hello.

Cora smiled, pushing open her door.

A tall blond man rounded the corner and smirked at her. "Where do you sneak off to at all hours of the night?"

Cora arched an eyebrow at her twin brother. His Palace Guard uniform was unbuttoned, his hair mussed. "Were you just waiting at your door to harass me?"

"I have much better things to do than wait around for you."

"I'm sure," Cora replied dryly. "How is Liana?"

Arik ran a hand through his hair, as if suddenly conscious of it. "The Countess of Kleo is very well, thank you."

Cora didn't comment further. She entered her room, Arik not far behind.

"Where were you anyway?"

"Where I always am at odd hours of the night."

It was Arik's turn to look skeptical. "I checked the library."

"Well, I did just get a snack." Cora held up her apple core.

"You didn't show up on any of the monitors."

"I think Nolan is making you paranoid." Cora kept her voice light. "Soon you're going to be checking for assassins under my bed."

7

"Very funny."

"Why were you looking so hard for me anyway?"

Arik's eyes tightened. "Just doing my Internal Security internship proud."

Cora's head whipped towards him. His tone was casual, but his words held an edge sharp as a knife.

"And I need snacks to take back with me to Liana."

Cora gestured to one of her desk drawers. Arik searched through the stash of packaged goods, setting a few aside. She closed the drawer, careful not to jostle the scented candle she had left burning on her desk.

"Do I want to know what you're doing with the Countess of Kleo in the middle of the night?" Cora asked.

He looked up and waggled his eyebrows. Cora tossed her apple core at him, shuddering. Arik laughed, scooping up his pile and heading for the door. She followed, snatching up a dropped package.

"Next time, find your own snacks!"

"Thanks, Cat!"

Cora shook her head, closing the door behind him. Her holo dinged again, projecting a reminder above her wrist.

Welcome Committee—9 am

Hair and makeup—6 am

She played absently with the candle. Her fingers wove through the flames, the fire nothing but a pleasant warmth against her skin. She'd never known the pain of heat, thanks to the gift of the Bjorn clan. But as her mind drifted to the Galtan delegation, she had the sinking feeling she was about to get burned.

2

Callan shot up, panting. He frowned at the white sheet tangled around his legs. He had just been hiding, shots ringing around him.

His legs swung over the side of the bed, feet sinking into plush carpet. The remnants of his nightmare faded as his surroundings crystallized. He rose, thoughts still fuzzy, fumbling for the light switch.

The hotel room came into sharp focus as his eyes adjusted. He allowed his heart rate to slow. It was a dream. Or a memory. Either way, he was no longer fighting for his life. He shivered into the bathroom and turned the hot water full blast. Callan washed away the last remnants of his dream, letting it swirl away with the suds. By the time he finished, the entire bathroom was steamed.

He wiped the mirror clean, regarding the face staring back at him. Callan Byrne, Hero of Galta. He slid his finger along the scar cutting through his left eyebrow. It had been months, yet his fingers still found it. Blue eyes scanned his chin and determined it wasn't worth shaving just yet. He ran a comb through his dark hair and called himself presentable.

He dressed with similar precision. His pulled out his clean uniform, freshly pressed by one of his men. He wore no regiment number, only the new symbol of Galta on his shoulder. His eyes lingered on the insignia. He had chosen it himself. A brilliant red phoenix on a background of gold. A nation rising from the ashes.

Callan checked the time and frowned. He sat to lace his boots just as a knock came at the door.

Daen entered without waiting for permission. Callan nodded to the lieutenant.

"Are you ready, sir?"

"Almost."

Callan stood, checking that the bed was neatly made. Satisfied, he swept past Daen and into the hallway. The rest of his men were already waiting for them. He gave them a quick inspection before declaring them presentable. He ignored the elevators, instead leading his men down the stairs at a brisk clip.

They wouldn't take vehicles, a decision finalized just the night before. Callan's men created a bubble around him, clearing a space in the crowded streets. He looked up at the palace as they moved. Half of the building stared out from slits in the stone walls. Guards patrolled between stone parapets, gleaming steel spears on their shoulders. The other half of the palace towered in a blinding spire of glass and steel. From what Callan had seen of Narous, the rest of the city was much the same. A jumbled mash of ancient relics and modern wonders.

People gathered on the streets as Callan and his men passed. He smiled and waved, sharing a look with Daen. The captain had mapped a long, circuitous route to the palace. The crowds only grew. His men soaked in the attention, waving and winking at pretty girls.

"The Hero of Galta!" someone shouted. "The Oppressor's Bane!"

People along their route took up the shout, until the titles were a chant following Callan all the way to the palace gates. They were met by two men in palace uniforms. One was a lanky young man with blond hair. Callan immediately recognized him as Prince Arik. The other was older, with close-cropped dark hair and a shadow of a beard. He inclined his head as Callan and his men approached.

"Welcome, Chancellor Byrne," he said. "I'm Nolan Harcroft, head of Palace Security. This is His Highness, Prince Arik."

Callan bowed politely. The prince gave the barest of nods. Callan's fingers twitched briefly, then he motioned for his men to bow as well.

"If you'll follow me." Nolan gestured toward the palace.

Callan followed them inside, keeping his pace measured. No need to appear too eager.

Even this early in the morning, the palace was noticeably cooler than the city. Daen wiped a bead of sweat away from his eyes. Loren, Daen's second, sagged slightly at the pleasant change of temperature.

"Your honor guard can wait here," Nolan said.

He pointed to a room with a handful of tables and chairs and a coffee bar. A couple of Palace Security guards already occupied tables, snacking or scrolling the holonet. Callan and Daen exchanged glances.

"I prefer to stay with the Chancellor," Daen replied gruffly.

Nolan frowned. "Very well. The rest of your men can stay here."

Callan gave Daen a small nod, and the rest of his guard filed in. Nolan barely waited for them all to enter the room before leading the way again. Prince Arik let out a sigh, like he was used to Nolan's brisk pace.

They stopped outside a set of intricately carved wooden doors. Callan's eyes roved over scenes of dragons flying over rolling hills. Their scales gleamed with polish. The doors swung open before He could take in anymore.

The inside of the room was just as beautiful as the doors. Long stained-glass windows depicted more dragons, breathing fire. Tall bookcases nestled between the windows, the same wood as the doors. To one side of the room stood a heavy desk, its edges carved with sailing ships that seemed to ripple in the mottled light from the windows. Nolan pivoted away from the desk, addressing a trio settled on a couch on the other side of the room.

King Adalric and Queen Eira perched together, their hands intertwined. King Adalric was the spitting image of Prince Arik, only thirty years older. His blond hair was heavily streaked with gray, but his eyes held the same sardonic twinkle. Queen Eira was more guarded in her expression. Her hair shone red in the sunlight, in the longest braid Callan had ever seen.

And sitting in a chair nearby, was the Crown Princess Catarina.

Her hair was just as long, if not longer, than her mother's. It spilled into her lap in golden curls. Heavy makeup, as was fashionable on the holonet, obscured much of her face. Black-

11

lined eyes that couldn't decide if they were gray or green. Those eyes. They took him in like a general assessing a battlefield. Alight with intelligence, but guarded as a fortified keep.

Callan found his mouth suddenly dry.

"Chancellor Callan Byrne of Galta, Your Majesties."

Callan swept himself into a low bow. He had to clear his throat twice. "I'm honored to be here, Your Majesties."

"We're honored to have a leader of Galta attending the Allies Council again." Queen Eira's low voice was warm.

"It's been too long since our countries have met. You'll find the new Senate of Galta is eager to restore our old alliances."

"As long as you're not as stuffy as the last Galtan ambassador," King Adalric said. "That man was a bore."

Queen Eira elbowed her husband sharply.

Callan chuckled. "I make no promises," he said, raising his hands. "But I hope you don't find me too boring."

King Adalric rose and clapped Callan on the shoulder. "Well, my boy, what do you think of hunting?"

Cora wasn't expecting the Chancellor to be so...young. News from Galta had been patchy during the conflict, more so than she originally thought. She recalled Devita—her "public relations specialist"—advising her to focus on her studies. Whole lot of good it was doing her now.

"I find it hard to believe this guy led a revolution," Arik murmured. They hung back while Father chatted with the young Chancellor. "He's barely older than we are."

"They expect us to lead a country, too."

"They expect *you* to lead a country."

Cora pursed her lips. Arik certainly hadn't been dragged to every meeting the past few months, or pretended interest over every research facility and project within fifty miles of the capital.

The council chamber wasn't far from Father's study. Cora took a steadying breath outside the door. She let her eyes run over the dark wood, the carved bears marching across a wide plain. The doors swung open to reveal a rectangular room flooded with cool light. A long oval table gleamed with polish, cushioned chairs

12

surrounding its length.

As expected, Lord Baeros was early. His cane leaned against the arm of his chair, gleaming like ebony. Silver hair brushed his shoulders, the top half pulled back from pointed ears. His deep brown eyes did not match the smile painted onto his face.

"Your Majesties," Lord Baeros rumbled. He bowed to them from his seat.

Mother's mouth tightened at the corners. "Always good to see you, Lord Baeros."

Cora and Arik shared the briefest glance. They both caught the edge of sarcasm in her tone. If Lord Baeros caught it, he chose to ignore it. Instead, he brushed an imaginary crumb off his Manufacturer's Guild pin. Cora still hadn't gotten a straight answer as to what exactly his plants manufactured.

She acknowledged each council member politely, noting that Ambassador Faizan from Tendouli had shown up. Cora made a point of greeting her warmly. The woman responded stiffly, sitting with impeccable posture. Cora fingered the edge of her agenda, but didn't bother opening it. They wouldn't stick to it anyway.

Cora noted each person that filtered to their seats. Every race was represented at the dark wood table, a calculated move by her parents. Chancellor Byrne and his guard were the only humans at the table she wasn't related to.

Cora felt eyes on her. She glanced across the table to find Chancellor Byrne watching. His blue eyes burned into her, sending heat across her cheeks.

Father rose, cutting off the pleasantries. Chancellor Byrne looked away reluctantly, leaving Cora slightly breathless. She barely registered that the meeting had started until Lord Baeros began talking.

"First of all, I was sent a fleet of crown-funded androids to put on my assembly lines. I was told they would streamline production and reduce waste. They would even reduce costs! By replacing half of my workers." Lord Baeros paused as a murmur swept the room. "Then the other half of my workers quit in protest. Now I was not only behind on my orders, but also at half capacity. Here I am thinking it can't get any worse. And what message finds its way

13

its way into my inbox? My government contracts have all been terminated."

"The *old* contracts were terminated," Mother cut in coolly. "Because *new* contracts were sent to you as soon as the *experimental* androids were recalled. And if memory serves me, those new contracts included better state protections for your workers."

Lord Baeros looked like he had sucked on a lemon. "And yet my work force remains at half of what it should be."

"Then perhaps you should consider your employees' requests for better pay."

Lord Baeros reddened. He made to open his mouth again but was cut off by the Tendouli ambassador.

"And what will become of these automatons?" Her accent made each syllable ring crisply across the table.

Minister of Innovation, Lillin Kilgore, responded. "They will be analyzed and re-purposed." She pushed her glasses atop her thick black curls. "Most of them have already been reassigned to sanitation."

Lord Baeros regarded the dark-skinned elf with barely concealed loathing. He made it abundantly clear that she was a traitor to elf-kind by supporting the "usurpers."

Ambassador Faizan frowned. Her shimmering orange wings, folded so carefully still against her back, buzzed. "Very well." She managed to sit up even straighter. "Then I must inform you that Tendoul will no longer be trading with Liskow."

The room froze. Cora fought to keep her expression neutral. Mother revealed nothing on her face, while a storm brewed in Father's eyes.

"Surely the Tendoul Elders wouldn't want to dissolve a centuries-long alliance over this," he rumbled.

Ambassador Faizan's expression was hard. "The Elders would rather maintain a *millenia*-long relationship. We will not anger the gods by treating with automatons."

Mother laid a hand on Father's arm. She pulled out her most charming smile. "Perhaps we can continue this discussion after the meeting? There are other items on today's agen—"

14

"No." Ambassador Faizan rose. Her wings snapped open, then closed again. "We have been tolerant of many of your so-called advances. Horseless wagons, floating barges, lights with no fire. But you go too far. You will bring the gods' wrath down upon your heads, and Tendoul will have *no part of it*."

Cora watched, stunned, as the ambassador stormed out. The council doors banged shut behind her, echoing in the now silent room.

Mother exhaled slowly through her nose. She cast her eyes around the room, focusing on the far end of the table. "Ivar, please tell me you have some good news."

Father's cousin—and Minister of Justice—Ivar Bjorn drummed his fingers on the table. Once a star knotball player, he still had the burly build of an athlete. Thick eyebrows pulled down over brown eyes as he cleared his throat.

"Not entirely. The protesters—excuse me, People's Employment League, have gone to ground since the last demonstrations. The city Watchers are analyzing the latest vandalisms for patterns, but they remain inconsistent. We have, however, identified one of their leaders."

Ivar tapped the screen of his holo-bracelet a few times, and an image rose from the center of the table. A young woman smiled wickedly at them, rotating slowly in place. Her hair was deep blue, while pale green scales shimmered across her cheekbones.

"Thalassa Mellis." Ivar glowered at the woman's picture. "She's on the run from the Eastern mer tribe for larceny, conspiracy, and high treason. We've uncovered several payments to a bank she's linked to."

"Why would she care about employment rights in Narous?"

Cora swallowed as all eyes in the room swung to look at her. She shoved her shaking hands under the table.

Ivar's smile didn't reach his eyes, and when he spoke, it was with forced patience. "As far as we can tell, she doesn't. We believe she was hired on to their cause."

Cora fought to keep from shrinking into her chair. Mother drew Ivar's attention away from her.

"Is this criminal in custody yet?"

"No, Your Majesty. This is an ongoing case."

The discussion moved on, Cora struggling to focus on the conversation. She felt Ivar's eyes on her. She chanced a glance at him, finding contempt blazing in his gaze. It disappeared quickly when her parents spoke to him.

As the meeting began to close, Chancellor Byrne rose from his seat.

"Before we finish today, I'd like to thank King Adalric and Queen Eira for allowing New Galta a seat at this table." Mother and Father acknowledged him with inclined heads. "As a symbol of our gratitude to our friends and allies, I have a gift for you."

Chancellor Byrne motioned to his captain, who pulled a bundle of wrapped cloth out of his coat. Chancellor Byrne took the package and set it in front of Father. Father's eyes lit up as he unwrapped the gift.

Inside was a phoenix statue about the size of Father's hands. It was painted in brilliant reds, the tips of every feather dripping gold. The phoenix's wings were spread, as if leaping into the air.

Chancellor Byrne bowed as Cora's parents thanked him for the gift. His eyes flicked to hers over the table.

"I hope our friendship will continue for years to come."

Callan didn't get a chance to speak with Princess Catarina. A tan woman in tall heels swooped in after the meeting adjourned to whisper in the king's ear. He nodded, motioning to Queen Eira and Princess Catarina. They swept out of the council chamber with polite goodbyes, leaving Callan sitting at the table. He pushed down the disappointment, making to rise himself.

"I've heard quite a lot about you, Chancellor Byrne," a gruff voice said.

Callan twisted as Ivar Bjorn slipped into the chair next to him. He shook the man's hand, recalling his name from the information packet he read on the way to Liskow. The Minister of Justice, one of King Adalric's closest living relatives, and if Callan remembered correctly, fifth in line for the throne.

"All good things, I hope," Callan replied.

"Interesting things, certainly."

Callan sized up the aging minister. A few inches taller than Callan himself, with broad shoulders and a broadening midsection. He kept his graying hair slicked back from his head, not a hint of facial hair to be seen on his face. Thick eyebrows shaded calculating brown eyes.

"I suppose that depends on what you find interesting." Callan took a long drink from the water glass in front of him.

The room emptied, leaving only Daen and a man in a city Watcher's uniform with them.

"What I find interesting is how a twenty-five-year-old nobody became the most powerful man in Galta."

Daen shifted behind Callan. He flexed his hands, eyes darting between Ivar and the Watcher stationed behind him.

"Is there a question you're trying to ask me, Minister?" Callan kept his tone neutral.

Ivar pulled a folded piece of paper out of his coat and tapped it on the table. He considered for a long moment before tossing it in front of Callan.

"Let me know if you want to repeat that performance."

Callan fingered the paper as Ivar and his man left. He waited until the door closed fully, then stood and tucked the paper into his pocket.

Dr. Grayson Moore shook the last drops from his water bottle. He looked down the path at his team, counting heads. He tossed his empty bottle into his pack as he waited.

Dr. Lander trudged up the trail, one hand up to keep her hat in place. "Did you see that last scat pile?"

Gray nodded. "I think we're close."

The crisp mountain air filled his lungs, feeding the energy coursing through him. Today was the day. He could feel it. He kept an eye on the slowly ascending interns. Most of them had never been on a research trip. His only graduate student rotated between hiking and flying, earning her nasty looks from the others.

The interns huffed up one at a time. Ophelia lagged, notebook out again. The sprite's wings fluttered sporadically as she muttered to herself. Gray edged around the other interns, meeting her. She tapped her pencil against the page, eyes focused beyond him.

"Habitat is right for small mammals, but there isn't much cover for deer and boar…"

"They've already moved into the valley by this time of day," Gray interrupted. "They tend to forage up here in the mornings and evening."

Ophelia nodded, pencil racing across the page. She snapped the notebook closed, tucking it into her back pocket. Her pencil went into her messy pink bun.

She blinked a couple of times, glancing around. "How far are we?"

"Almost there. If our hunch is correct."

"Well, what are we waiting for?"

Ophelia bobbed past the other interns. They scowled at her back, dragging themselves to their feet.

Gray only laughed, catching up. The ground sloped downward and trees appeared, growing denser the further they went. He noted a clearing in the trees. He wasn't able to see into it, but his gut pulled him in that direction. He forged through the underbrush, leaving a trail for the others.

They stayed close together, careful to step over roots and brambles. Gray occasionally paused to consult his compass, adjusting their path as needed. The birds grew quieter the closer they got to the clearing. He slowed, making as little noise as possible. The trees thinned, and another sound replaced the birds. He crept forward, approaching the edge of the trees cautiously. His breath caught as he stopped. The rest of the team huddled nearby, eyes wide.

Dragons lay curled over burrowed nests. Gray counted a dozen nests in total, each guarded by at least one parent. Gray's eyes roved over each individual, taking note of color and spot patterns. He carefully set his pack down and pulled out paper and pencil. He rifled through the sheets until he found the one he was looking for. He wrote methodically, recording each individual with an identifier and a quick description.

His team shook off their awe and followed suit. Ophelia took out the tablet and snapped pictures. Dr. Lander eased next to Gray, grinning.

"We finally did it!" she whispered.

Gray grinned back, eyes shining. "Yes, we did."

Dr. Lander squeezed his hand before turning back to her own papers. The team worked as quickly as possible, recording what they could observe from their position. Once a paper was complete, it was handed over to Ophelia to scan into their digital record. Gray leaned against the tree behind him, watching the dragons. He breathed deeply, heart swelling.

"Who are they?" Ophelia breathed.

Gray sat up straight, following the pointed finger.

A group edged into the clearing, weapons drawn. The dragon nearest them growled, smoke rising from her nostrils. Her lips pulled back, baring rows of serrated teeth. Several gun barrels pointed in her direction. The dragoness shifted, tail curled protectively around her eggs. The group split, flanking the dragon. Her head whipped back and forth as her growl intensified.

"We need to leave," Gray hissed. "Everyone, grab your packs."

"What is going on?"

Dr. Lander shared a grim look with Gray. She pivotedturned back to her intern, hands shaking as she struggled to zip her pack. "You heard Dr. Moore. Get your packs on."

The dragoness bellowed, drawing Gray's attention. A long gash shone red along her arm. Gray's fists clenched around the strap of his pack. The other dragons hunched over their eggs, growling and hissing. Gray counted a dozen men that he could see. Eight of them harried the dragoness, while the rest circled, keeping their eyes on the rest of the nesting dragons.

"Why don't they just roast these guys?" Ophelia whispered.

"Dragon eggs need to be kept extremely warm," Gray replied. "And breathing fire takes a tremendous amount of energy. Even with their mates bringing them food, they don't have any fire to lose."

A poacher across the clearing cried out. He backed away from another nesting dragon, clutching his arm. Another poacher shouted something Gray couldn't make out, and a rifle went off. The dragoness shrieked as blood dripped down her wing.

"Let's go," Dr. Lander murmured.

Gray started. He'd been too absorbed in the scene in front of them to hear her approach. He looked behind her to see the other interns already gone. Ophelia was still next to him, watching the poachers in mute horror.

"We're right behind you," he told Dr. Lander.

The older biologist nodded, chasing after her students. Gray laid a hand on Ophelia's shoulder, opening his mouth to urge her away. The dragoness roared, shaking the ground beneath them. She charged after the poachers, exposing her nest.

A man approached the silvery eggs. He knelt next to them, caressing the surface. Gray stared at the wondrous ovals. They were small enough to be carried in one hand. The poacher reached to the side and grabbed a large rock.

Then he smashed the eggs.

A strangled cry came from Gray's left. Ophelia trembled, eyes glued to the massacre. Gray crept toward her, sending the rest of the group on their way.

He gripped Ophelia's shoulders, forcing her to look at him. "We need to go."

"But that man, he just…" Her voice broke. "Those babies."

"I know, Ophelia. But if we stay, they will turn those guns on us."

Ophelia faced the nest, tears rolling down her face. She climbed to her feet, still trembling. Gray gave her a little push to get her moving. But she was frozen. He followed her gaze.

"There's one left. We can save it."

"Ophelia, no!"

Gray reached out too late.

The sprite burst through the trees, wings beating furiously. The man squinted up at her, hand halfway into a sack at his side. Ophelia dove, eyes focused on the egg. The man calmly drew his hand out of the sack and reached for his belt. She stretched out her hands to snatch the egg.

A flash of light temporarily blinded Gray. The man's knife slashed through the air, and Ophelia screamed. She crumpled to the ground next to the egg, wing bloody. The man took a step toward her, knife still out.

Gray didn't think. He burst through the trees at a sprint, barreling into the man. Muscle memory kicked in, and he rolled quickly to his feet, the man dazed on the ground. He pulled Ophelia up and half-carried her back the way they had come. They didn't stop moving until they were out of the trees.

Gray paused for breath, letting Ophelia slump on the ground. She was pale, wing limp against her back. She clutched her arm to her chest.

"Is your arm hurt too?"

Gray gently felt along her arm. Ophelia let it relax with an exhausted smile. She had the egg. He gaped as Ophelia's grin widened. He shook his head in bewilderment, helping her back to her feet.

"It might not hatch." Gray warned.

"I know. But at least those bastards don't have it."

Gray shook his head again, a slow smile creeping over his face. "Don't tell the others, but you're my favorite intern."

Father motioned to Mother and Cora. Cora forced herself not to hurry, exchanging polite goodbyes as she followed her parents out of the council chamber. Indira clicked along next to the king.

"How long ago did the message come through?" Father asked.

"About an hour, My Lord." Indira glanced at the screen of her tablet. "Dr. Moore said he could come straight from the hospital."

"Hospital?"

Indira tucked the tablet against her side. "One of their team was injured."

The tiny mer woman kept pace with Father easily, despite her four-inch black heels. The hair carefully piled on top of her head was equally black. Indira's hair lost its green sheen long ago, just as the scales on her arms and cheekbones were only visible when the light hit them. She was due for a trip to the coast soon.

Indira opened the door to Father's study for them. Cora settled herself on the couch, pulling her hair out of the way so she could sit. Indira frowned at the fireplace behind Father's desk. A fire danced behind the grate.

"I'll send for someone to put that out," Indira said, reaching for her tablet.

Father waved her off. "Leave it. I can't stand the chill."

Cora's brow wrinkled. Father was cold more often these days. Indira excused herself, leaving Cora and her parents alone.

Father strode to the fireplace while Mother settled herself behind the desk. He pulled a smoldering coal out. He turned it over in his hand, the faint red glow deepening the lines on his face.

Mother wrinkled her nose. "You know I hate it when you do that."

"Hmm?"

Mother sighed. "The fire, Adalric."

Father glanced down, seeming to notice the coal for the first

22

time. He dropped it back into the fire, wiping the soot on a handkerchief in his pocket.

"Who is Dr. Moore?" Cora asked

"We've been working on a special project," Mother said. She sifted through a stack of papers on the desk, hardly glancing up. "The head of the team, Dr. Moore, is coming to report on a breakthrough."

Cora waited for some sort of elaboration. It never came. Her holo chimed, breaking the silence. She opened the message and sighed audibly. It was from Devita.

Mother swiped across her own holo, tapping into Cora's to see the message. "What's wrong, dear? Devita's just preparing for the Anniversary Gala."

"I don't see why I need a public relations specialist. All she does is put me on every holo stream available."

Mother set down her papers to give Cora her full attention. "Catarina, the image that you cultivate now will carry with you when you assume the throne. Given the current climate, and the ah, *biases* of certain segments of the population, it is prudent to cultivate a favorable image. Especially leading up to the anniversary of our monarchy."

Cora glanced at the stained-glass windows at the far end of the room. Her eyes traced the dragon's spread wings, each scale vibrant as a gem. They were depictions that had been a part of this palace long before her family ever set foot in it. She knew some of the books on Father's shelves were just as ancient, although she couldn't pick them out from where she was sitting.

A knock at the door interrupted her musings.

Indira entered, leading a man who appeared to be in his late twenties. His hiking boots left dusty footprints on the rug. Dirt streaked a sun-tanned face and caked itself into short brown hair. He swept onto one knee with the practice of a courtier.

"Dr. Moore," Father rumbled. "Please, stand."

Dr. Moore brushed his hair back as he stood. "I apologize for my appearance, Your Majesties. I came straight here."

"Dr. Lander said you ran into some trouble."

Mother's eyes flicked to the soiled rug. Her lips tightened at the

23

corners, nothing more.

Dr. Moore shifted on his feet. "One of my interns was injured at the nest site."

"Are they alright?" Cora asked.

The words were out before she realized. Dr. Moore started, noticing her for the first time. Mother's eyebrow rose slightly, and Cora flushed. She didn't need her mother to elaborate—she was here to observe.

"She will be, Your Highness," Dr. Moore replied. He glanced between Cora and Mother. "Thank you for asking."

"But you found them?" Father pressed. He moved to stand next to Mother, a hand on her shoulder.

Dr. Moore broke into a grin that crinkled the corners of his eyes. "We recorded a dozen active nest sites. I haven't gone through all of our data yet, but we confirmed eight breeding pairs."

Father squeezed Mother's shoulder as she beamed back at Dr. Moore. Cora fidgeted in her seat, trying to keep up.

"Excellent work, Dr. Moore." Mother sat up taller in her seat, her celebration passing. "In gratitude for your work, your entire team is invited to the Anniversary Gala. We'll announce the discovery that night."

Dr. Moore bowed deeply. "Thank you, Your Majesty. It would be an honor."

"Indira." Father twisted toward the corner of the room. "Have Dr. Moore give you the coordinates of the nest site. I want the entire area cleared of tourists. And have that young man who wrote my last speech draft one for the gala."

"Of course, Your Majesty," Indira said. She gestured to the door. "If you'll follow me, Dr. Moore."

Dr. Moore bowed once more before Indira escorted him out, leaving Cora alone with her parents.

Father grinned wolfishly at Mother. "Let's see those superstitious banshees on the council spin this."

"Adalric," Mother chided. "Don't confuse conviction for superstition."

Father waved his hand, too smug to hear the warning in her tone. Cora saw fire in her mother's eyes, the kind that only lit when

24

he disrespected the old religion.

"What exactly are we celebrating?"

Cora's parents seemed to realize she was still in the room.

Father crossed the short distance and put warm hands on her shoulders. "Wild dragons, Cat."

Cora's mouth parted. She glanced between her parents in awe.

Father laughed, giving her shoulders a squeeze. Mother allowed herself a wistful look before returning to business. Her eyes locked onto Cora.

"You better not leave Devita waiting."

Gray gave King Adalric's assistant all of the data he had available. He watched her meticulously copy it into her tablet. When she was finished, she smiled up at him.

"Thank you, Dr. Moore. Your research truly is incredible."

Gray smiled back politely. "Do you know how soon the nest site will be secured?"

Indira glanced through her notes. "We should be able to get out there within a few days."

"Just…" Gray glanced back at the carved study doors anxiously. "Please make sure they get there quickly."

"Is something wrong, Dr. Moore?"

"Poachers," Gray said darkly. "They injured one of my interns."

Indira's mouth pressed into a line. She nodded solemnly to Gray. "I understand. I'll make sure securing the nest site is our top priority."

Indira's tablet lit up with an alert, and she excused herself.

As the sharp clicking of heels faded away, Gray allowed himself to process what had happened. Years of study and a lifetime of dreaming had finally paid off. Wild dragons survived the purge. Gray was *right*. He laughed aloud, then let out a small whoop. He didn't hear the soft close of the study doors. He spun around, starting when he found Princess Catarina watching him with amusement.

"Sorry, Your Highness. I suppose that isn't appropriate behavior."

"I won't tell if you won't."

Gray laughed, passing a hand over his face. He inhaled deeply, sobering. "I suppose I should be thanking you."

"Me?" Princess Catarina frowned.

"My research partner told me you were influential in getting our project funded. Without you, we never would have found the nest site."

Princess Catarina glanced behind her at the study. "You're giving me too much credit. Really. My parents did most of the work."

"Still, thank you, Princess Catarina."

Her frown deepened.

Gray sensed it was time for him to leave. He bid the princess a polite goodbye, then left her to her thoughts.

By the time he made it to his apartment, he was intimately familiar with each and every sore muscle in his body. His leaden feet barely cleared the last stair to his doorway. He tossed his keys onto the dining room table, where they were promptly swallowed by the mounds of paper strewn across it. His boots landed in a basket of shoes, while his socks crested the peak of his laundry hamper. He ignored the notifications blinking on the tablet still sitting on his nightstand and headed straight for the shower. The rest of his clothes sailed with near-perfect aim to join his socks, but it proved too much for his mountain of dirty laundry. He veered away from the toppled mass. It could wait.

Gray allowed his mind to rest. He breathed in the steam from the shower and let the heat ease some of the soreness in his muscles. He wanted to stay in there longer. Wanted to let the relaxation carry him into his bed and off into a deep sleep.

But his mind flashed back to the nest site, to Ophelia rushing the poachers. He twisted the faucet off, jaw clenched. It had been close, too close. Like the night he lost his parents. Guilt solidified in his stomach.

No longer ready for bed, he clanged back down the staircase of his apartment building, legs screaming in protest. His car seemed to protest too, the brakes squealing at every intersection. He'd have to wash the dust out of them.

It took him longer to find a parking space than drive to the hospital. Driving up and down each line of spaces did nothing for his mood. By the time he made it through the doors, his jaw was tense and aching from clenching it.

He walked through the brightly lit maze of the hospital. The scent of antiseptic stung his nose. Soft beeps and whirrs emanated from androids as they rolled by, carrying tools and medicine in their spindly arms.

Finally, he found Ophelia's room. He paused in the doorway, taking in the bandage snaking around her left wing. Dr. Lander sat in a chair next to the bed, eyes rimmed with red.

"Hey, Dr. Moore," Ophelia called softly.

Gray gave her a smile.

Dr. Lander started, head whipping toward the door. She passed a wrinkled hand under her eyes before smoothing back gray-streaked hair. She forced a smile. "Oh, Dr. Moore. How was the meeting at the palace?"

Gray sat in a second chair next to Dr. Lander. "Good. Our entire team has been personally invited to the Anniversary Gala."

"No way!" Ophelia grinned.

Dr. Lander put a gentle hand on Ophelia's arm. "You might not be released before then, Ophelia."

Ophelia deflated.

Gray looked between the two women, brows furrowed. "How long do they think she has to stay?"

Dr. Lander bit her lip, refusing to meet Gray's eyes. "You know, I think I'm going to get myself some coffee. I'll be back in a minute."

Ophelia folded her arms, watching as Dr. Lander left the room. The monitor beeped softly as Gray waited for her to speak. Her face was pale and drawn, her light pink hair limp around her shoulders. The baggy hospital gown swallowed her, so different from the hiking pants and flannel shirts he usually saw her in.

"I will never fly again."

Gray exhaled slowly. He waited for her to continue, but she didn't. She betrayed no hint of emotion, just kept her round brown eyes trained on the blanket draped over her legs.

She shrugged her right shoulder. "I made the choice. I don't regret it."

She finally met his eyes, and he saw the truth of her words there.

Gray nodded slowly. "Still, I'm sorry. No sprite should be grounded."

"I'll live. But, Dr. Moore, could I ask you something?"

"Of course."

"Will you take the egg?"

Gray stared at her. Ophelia gushed about her responsibilities and having no time, but he wasn't listening. All he could hear was his grandfather's words.

"You have the blood of a Dragon Rider, Grayson. You are almost certain to bond if you can find a dragon..."

Once, all he'd wanted was the chance to be a Dragon Rider. But that was a long time ago, in the part of his life he'd labelled "before." In the "after," he wasn't so sure. Was he even worthy to try?

"Dr. Moore?"

Gray blinked, refocusing on Ophelia. She stared at him expectantly, her eyes huge under the bright hospital lights.

"Yes." Gray's voice was husky. He cleared his throat. "I can take the egg."

4

Cora barely heard Dr. Moore's farewell. She kept circling over the way he thanked her. As if she had championed his research, let alone known about it in the first place. The real question was, whose idea was it to give her the credit, Mother or Devita? Cora watched as Dr. Moore disappeared around a corner. An ember flared deep in her belly, filling her with foreboding.

If dragons were still alive in Liskow, how long would it take for people to look for Dragon Riders again? Cora knew better than to voice her concerns. She tamped down the ember, forcing it down to an ignorable glow.

She made her way down to the media room, or more appropriately, Devita's Lair. The room was painted a bright white. Large lights and bounce boards illuminated furniture in neutral colors. Behind the lights sat a staging area, with a changing screen and hair and makeup station. Jean and Anya, Cora's personal stylists, were already waiting for her. As she settled into the chair, Devita emerged from the changing area, tablet already open.

"Ah, there you are, Your Highness."

Devita towered over Cora. She wore sleek black pants and a crisp white blouse. Platinum hair swept across her brow and into a low tail, making her skin appear deeply tan. Dark brown eyes sat under brown eyebrows plucked to perfection. Devita motioned curtly to Jean and Anya, who sprang into action touching up Cora.

"Today we'll film your promo for the tricentennial gala," Devita continued, not bothering to wait for a greeting. "We need to get it circulating around the holo streams."

"I haven't prepared a speech."

Devita tapped her tablet, and text appeared on the prompter behind her. "I already have one for you. You can read through it now."

Cora suppressed a sigh. She scanned through the text as her hair was set and arranged. She had to pause as Anya applied thick black liner around her eyes. Cora squeezed her fingers together, staying perfectly still as they fussed over her. Finally, Jean applied his final touches and Anya stepped back. Cora read the last few lines of the speech, her lips pressing into a line. It was the same flimsy platitudes she always uttered.

"Is this really what I should be saying for the tricentennial? It completely ignores the current issues."

Jean and Anya exchanged a glance and took a small step back.

Devita lifted one eyebrow. She forced a smile, stepping closer to Cora.

"Your Highness." She spoke each word slowly, deliberately. "Your people look to you as a beacon of stability. Besides, this is a celebration of our country, of your family. Politics can be set aside."

Cora stared at her, arguments rising and falling in her mind. Eventually, she gave Devita a curt nod.

Devita's smile turned smug. She motioned for Cora to get out of her chair. Anya and Jean stepped in, making adjustments to her outfit.

Devita frowned. "It looks like we need to send a note to your nutrition team." she typed quickly on her tablet. "Your diet needs some adjusting."

Her eyes lingered on Cora's hips, then trailed to her waist. Cora's hands tightened, her knuckles white. She sat in front of the blinding lights and delivered the speech. Devita made her do it eight times. Cora performed as instructed, tweaking the speech at her direction. The words bled together until they were nonsensical.

Devita dismissed her, and Cora forced herself not to rush from the room. Heat blazed in her belly and across her neck. She marched straight through the castle without stopping. She burst through the kitchen door, startling the head cook.

Helen took one look at her and motioned to a stool next to the

30

spacious kitchen island. Cora dumped herself into it, shoving hair out of her face as she did. Helen set a large piece of cake in front of her.

Cora tapped her fingers to her chin, then lowered her open hand in Helen's direction. *Thank you.*

Helen nodded, returning to the pot she was tending.

Cora stabbed her fork into the cake. She chewed forcefully, feeling the heat dissipate as the cake disappeared. By the time she had scraped the last of it off the plate, she was calm again. She downed the glass of milk Helen offered, thanking the cook.

She sat watching the bustle of the kitchen for a few minutes, breathing deeply. The servants mostly ignored her, other than some respectful nods. Cora waved to Helen as she left, but the cook didn't notice.

Her holo chimed as she walked down the hall. She sighed softly. Back to work.

Cora left the palace at her first opportunity. Her day was filled with more meetings and a stack of homework. She hadn't even started on review for her final exams, but she needed a break. The duel was a highly anticipated match-up, but mostly, Cora wanted out.

She messaged Theo as soon as she left the tunnel. For the millionth time, she silently thanked him for setting up their private holo channel.

She checked the time, smiling as she realized that she could grab had time for a churro on her way. Alma greeted her with enthusiasm, warming Cora through.

Mila was nowhere to be found, but there were more red posters around. Cora's churro was long gone by the time she took the elevator down. She checked her holo again for Theo's seat number. She climbed the stands, huffing. Her legs weren't built for the long stairs. She grinned as she spotted Theo, shimmying her way across the packed rows. She froze as she noticed who was sitting on Theo's other side.

"Cora! This is Gray!" Theo shouted over the crowd. "Gray, this is my friend, Cora!"

31

Dr. Moore reached a hand across Theo for her to shake. Cora shook it, then quickly sat down. She hoped Theo's long frame blocked enough of her face. Of course he would start a conversation with a total stranger.

Theo leaned over towards her. "Gray is a wildlife biologist. He's trying to prove wild dragons are still alive. Isn't that crazy?"

"Basically impossible."

Gray made no sign that he heard them. He slowly munched on popcorn, watching as the arena floor was prepped for the match.

Theo leaned back, speaking loud enough for them to both hear him. "If there are wild dragons still out there, why wouldn't we know about them already?"

"Poachers." Gray said. The word dripped with disgust. "Dragon parts are valuable. There are a lot of claims about what kind of properties they have. The most lucrative is the claim that certain parts were blessed by the gods, granting anyone who consumes them power."

Cora could have sworn she felt a breeze blow across the back of her neck. She shivered and rubbed her fingers together. "Exactly what kind of power?"

Gray studied her for a long beat before going back to his popcorn. "If anyone knew, it was the Dragon Riders. That secret died with them."

Theo brushed a dark curl out of his eyes, and Cora fought to keep from staring. He'd let his curls grow out a bit more than usual. The black coils were glossy under the arena lights, bouncing slightly as he moved his head. She longed to run her fingers through them, just to see if they were as soft as they looked. Her eyes drifted along his warm brown skin, along the sharp planes of his cheek and jaw, down the straight nose.

She felt someone's attention on her, and her gaze cut across to find a pair of knowing blue eyes watching her. She ripped her attention away from both Theo and Gray, sinking into her headscarf to hide the flush blotching her face.

"So, poachers are killing dragons for their parts and somehow keeping it a secret?" Theo asked, oblivious to her scrutiny.

"Dragons are elusive to begin with," Gray said with the air of a professor beginning a lecture. "They're solitary hunters with speed and camouflage. The most sought-after prize is dragon eggshells. My hypothesis is that poachers locate nest sites, then destroy the eggs before they hatch."

"Why don't they just pick up the shells after hatching?"

A shadow passed over Gray's face. Cora's embarrassment evaporated, replaced with a yawning pit deep in her gut.

"Because they claim that the shells can't be harvested after hatching." Gray took in their horrified expressions and nodded grimly. "If I can prove the wild dragons are out there, I can petition to make them a protected species. Then maybe a new generation of dragons can actually survive."

A rush of empathy flooded Cora, squeezing her heart. She caught Gray's attention, meeting his eyes fully.

"I hope you find them."

The crowd roared, making it impossible for him to respond. He gave her a nod instead, understanding gleaming in his eyes. They all turned back to the match. Cora let herself relax as she tracked the duel.

Before she knew it, they were calling a break. She blinked, glancing at the scoreboard high above the arena floor. Fifteen minutes to give the duelists a rest before the match went into overtime.

"Man, I forgot how good Don was," Theo said. "It's been so long since I saw him duel."

"Do you know him?" Gray asked.

Theo opened his mouth to respond but was cut off by an oily voice coming from a couple of rows below.

"Well, well, Theodore Sturn. I can hardly believe my eyes."

The man speaking reminded Cora of a bulldog. Stocky, with beady eyes and an underbite. Beside him were two others, differing in height, but with equally massive arms.

Theo sat very still. The tendons in his forearms stood out starkly as his hands clenched into fists. His voice was deceptively casual.

"Hello, Rolph. Still haven't found a dentist, I see."

Rolph chuckled, eyes glinting darkly. "Witty as ever, Sturn.

33

When am I going to see you in the ring?"

"You know I don't do that anymore."

Cora eyed him sharply. When had Theo ever dueled in the arena?

Rolph's beady eyes locked onto Cora. "Did you finally get yourself a girlfriend?"

Cora's face flushed. She inhaled, prepared to retort when Theo stretched with exaggerated casualness. His arm slung over the back of her seat, and his fingers tapped against her arm twice. Cora bit back her response at the old signal. Let me handle this.

"You might not be familiar with the feeling, but women actually enjoy my company."

Rolph's cronies snickered. The stout man glared at them, cutting off their laughter. The five-minute bell rang, and the crowds began trickling back to their seats.

"I'll see you around, Sturn."

Cora tracked Rolph until he was lost in the crowds.

Theo exhaled, relaxing. He didn't move his arm.

"You know that creep?" Gray asked.

"Unfortunately," Theo grumbled. "From before I went to tech school. Rolph didn't have the grades for any trade, if I remember correctly."

Gray perked up, facing Theo more fully. "You work with tech?"

Theo nodded. Cora became acutely aware of just how long Theo's arm was. His fingers kept brushing her waist whenever he moved.

"Would it be too much to ask for you to take a look at my tablet?" Gray asked. "It was damaged in the field, and I really need the data off of it."

"Sure, I can do that for you. You can drop it off to me whenever."

Theo gave Gray his work address, but Cora wasn't paying attention anymore. She hadn't realized how much he talked with his hands. Heat climbed up her neck. She shifted away from his hand but only managed to bring herself closer to him.

The duelists entered the arena again. Cora took the opportunity to lean forward, exhaling slowly a few times, until her cheeks cooled.

She sat forward for another round, barely keeping track of the points. Her mind turned over, replaying Theo's conversation with Rolph. The crowd roared, jarring her back to reality. The score was tied *again*. Gray stood, stretching.

"I have to call it a night. It was great to meet you both," he said, extending a hand.

Cora shook his hand briefly, then chewed the inside of her lip as he shook hands with Theo. She waited until he was out of earshot before rounding on Theo.

"What was all that about with Rolph?"

"Just an old rivalry. Nothing too important."

"It seemed pretty important."

Theo eyed her, fingers tapping against the back of her chair. "My brother and I used to duel. It was how we earned money before trade school."

His tone made it clear he didn't want to elaborate. Cora didn't push him. She checked the time again, finding a reminder waiting on her holo-screen. SheCora groaned. She forgot about the meeting with her professor. His office hours were so gods-burned early.

"Skies," she swore. "I have to get back."

"I can walk you out," Theo said.

"You really don't have to."

Theo was already on his feet, offering her a hand up. Cora took it, telling herself she didn't notice how warm and gentle his hand was. He kept a hold of her until they reached the elevator. They walked side by side through the half-empty Dragon Slayer, Theo's knuckles bumping against hers. He held the door open for her, his citrus and mint scent wafting over her.

The night air hit her face like a frigid lake, clearing her head.

"I'm going to regret staying out this late when my alarm goes off." Cora chuckled. "But thanks for inviting me."

"Anytime. It's nice to have you out in the real world."

Cora smiled wryly. "Unfortunately, *my* real world involves getting up at the crack of dawn to be covered in layers of makeup and stifling fabric."

Cora waved over her shoulder, then slipped into the dark night.

Theo watched Cora leave, hands in his pockets. He nodded to the palace guard across the street, who nodded back. The guard was dressed in plain clothes and meant to be inconspicuous, but Theo knew every guard in the rotation by now. There were only a few, taking turns protecting his princess. Theo didn't bother watching the guard follow her; he knew the routine. Cora was in safe hands.

Theo took his time walking home, hands thrust deep in his pockets. The lightness he felt from his time with Cora ebbed away with every step. Eventually, he climbed the porch steps, lingering in front of the door.

He knew she would be awake. She was always up late these days. He steeled himself, pushing inside.

"Theo?" Her voice was soft and hoarse.

Theo left his shoes by the door, taking the hallway to the kitchen. He didn't understand why she chose the hard wooden dining chairs over the comfortable sofa. She had a tablet in front of her. At least she had pushed the box to the side for the night.

"Mom, why are you still up?"

"Oh, you know I don't sleep well when you're out." She waved her hand dismissively.

Theo didn't comment on the dark circles under her eyes. He filled two glasses with water and sat across from her. Mom sipped at her water while he noted how thin she looked. She barely resembled the woman she had been growing up.

"Did you have a good time?" She gave him a wan smile.

He nodded, glancing down at the table around the open box. Mom had spread out the mementos carefully. He glanced down at the picture in front of him, sighing. It was the last time they had all been in a picture together. Theo gently held it between his fingers. He knew the company insignia on his father's uniform so well he could have drawn it with his eyes closed. His eyes traced Dad's smile, the curly black hair they shared. He put the picture down without even a glance at Lane. Theo's heart still ached when he tried looking at his brother's face.

"Have you heard from Isla recently?"

"Yes." Mom helped him place objects back in the box. "Apparently your nieces are becoming quite a handful."

Theo closed the lid on the box, placing his hand on top of hers. Her eyes were shining when she stared up at him. She forced a smile, patting his hand.

"Why don't you go to Campray and visit her?" Theo kept his voice gentle. "I'm sure the girls would love to see you."

Mom shook her head. "Oh, I couldn't leave you here by yourself."

"I'll be fine for a while. Isla would be thrilled."

"You want me to leave?"

Theo sighed, passing a hand over his face. "I don't mean it like that, Mom. I just…" He took a breath to keep his emotions in check. "I can't sit here and watch you waste away. You need to get out of this house."

Mom powered off her tablet, avoiding his eyes. She pushed away from the table hard enough to rattle her glass of water. "I think I'm going to go to bed."

"Mom."

She didn't turn back, climbing the stairs on quiet feet. Theo slumped forward, head in his hands. He glanced at the box, a weight in his stomach. With a growl, he pushed the box to the far end of the table and stood. It was probably best if he went to bed too.

5

Cora fought to keep herself from slamming the door. She stood outside her professor's office, fuming. She clutched her textbook, the edges digging into her skin.

"Your parents and I have decided to give you a private exam," Dr. Pointer said, staring at her over the rim of his glasses. *"So you can have fewer distractions, and ah…*adequate *time to study."*

Cora shoved her textbook into her book bag. She wasn't at the top of the class, she knew that for sure. But she already had *adequate* time to study for the final. She didn't need an extra three days. She threw one last glare at the office door behind her. Dr. Pointer valued his job too much to stand up to his sovereigns.

She paced down the hallway, fuming. This was too much, even for Mother.

Her holo dinged, interrupting her internal tirade.

> Family Dinner – 7 pm

Cora's lips pressed into a line. Mother would be getting an earful. Tonight.

Theo swore, picking his screwdriver off the floor for the third time. The thin metal kept tumbling from his fingers. He swiped his hand across his pants, certain there was no grease on it.

A bark of laughter echoed from across the room, and Theo jumped, dropping the screwdriver again.

"Burn me," he swore.

Theo resisted the urge to throw the screwdriver across his workstation. He buried his face in his hands, exhaling slowly.

The clock hanging above the employee entrance ticked steadily, the sound piercing through the dull chatter beyond Theo's workstation. It taunted him, counting down to the day he hated most. He counted thirty incessant ticks before snatching back the screwdriver and jamming it into the panel he was working on.

Sharp footsteps clipped closer. Theo half-expected to see a blonde head round the corner as he turned. Instead, a middle-aged head of dark hair poked in, worn and frayed around the edges.

"How's it going, Steve?"

Theo's manager shrugged, leaning against the side of his desk. "Same as usual. Having trouble?"

"Stripped a screw."

Steve nodded, surveying Theo's stagnant repair pile. Something about Steve's scrutiny made him glad he'd taken Gray's equipment home to work on.

Steve's lips curved down into a frown. "Your annual personal day is coming up."

Theo swallowed, throat suddenly tight. "Tomorrow."

"I've never asked what it's for, and I don't care. I just want to make sure it isn't going to interfere with your workload. I need every member of our team tightening up turnaround time."

"Are you trying to ask me to give up my personal day? Because I've had this day off every year since you hired me."

Steve bristled, crossing his arms. "We all have to make sacrifices now and then, Theo."

Theo's fist curled around the screwdriver. He fought to keep in a biting reply. He swept his eyes over Steve, trying to distract himself. It wasn't like Steve to be so callous. On more than one occasion, Theo had come back from his personal day to a short note and his favorite drink, left on his desk by Steve.

Theo's brows drew together as he took in Steve's wrinkled shirt. Usually, his button-ups were straining around the midsection, but his shirt hung loosely around his middle. Dark circles stained the skin under his Steve's eyes, and his dark hair was dusted with more gray.

"Is everything alright, Steve?"

Steve heaved a sigh, glancing around the warehouse. No one

39

was near Theo's workstation, but he scooted closer. He reached a hand up to loosen his tie as his voice dropped to a murmur. "Keep this to yourself, alright? I've got a friend who's a city Watcher. He's been doing undercover work attending PEL meetings."

Theo's brows rose. "The Watchers are that concerned about the PEL?"

"They're taking them very seriously," Steve said gravely. "My buddy's been going to meetings for months with nothing to report. But things are changing. People at the meetings are getting restless. They're frustrated. A lot of them can't get work. And they keep calling for the PEL to take action."

"What kind of action?"

Steve shook his head. "They won't say anything specific. My buddy thinks they know the Watchers are at the meetings, so they won't say." His Steve's voice dropped even lower. "But it all started when the Galtans showed up."

Theo's heart dropped clear to his toes. He knew exactly what kind of action the Galtans inspired. A memory flashed through his mind, a headline from the Galtan uprising. Of what happened to the Galtan royal family.

"Has anyone been arrested?"

"No grounds yet. But just in case, I want to make sure our most sensitive equipment gets repaired first."

Theo followed his gaze to the dented android at the top of his pile. He nodded in understanding. "I'll make sure it gets done next. I don't mind coming in during the knotball game. After my personal day."

"Alright, just make sure it gets out of here as soon as you get back. We won't be repairing any more for a while."

Steve gave him a pat on the shoulder before disappearing into another workstation down the line. Theo stared at the limp android, the silence in his station giving way to the sharp ticking of the clock once again.

Cora could hardly focus on her homework. Every time she opened her textbook, her professor's words echoed in her ears. Then she would inevitably begin rehearsing what she was going to say to Mother at dinner. Maybe if she made Mother angry enough, she'd be banned from public speaking for a while. She wished.

She rested her head in her hands, holed up at her favorite table in the palace library. Bookcases stretched high above her head, surrounding her table like sentinels. Soft light filtered through the frosted glass window behind her, dust motes dancing in the golden beams. She was deep enough into the stacks to be out of sight of the solitary librarian, and utterly alone, save for the silent palace guard a few rows over.

She watched the dust motes floating in her quiet haven, struggling to remember the last sentence she read. Every so often, her holo would project a reminder in her face. Appointments, assignments, fittings for the upcoming gala. The sun sank lower into the sky as she tried to study, then eventually gave up and opened the holo-net instead.

Another reminder pinged.

Family Dinner

Cora groaned. She contemplated faking an illness. Her mother wouldn't believe it. She gathered her books as slowly as she dared, taking the extra time to drop everything off at her room. She took a few minutes to make sure she was presentable, then decided she'd procrastinated as long as she could. She trudged across the family living quarters, following the scent of fresh bread.

Mother hadn't brought many things from the rural town she grew up in, but she had brought her own mother's recipe for bread. Cora used to watch her make it every day to offer to Elidi. Now, she only ever saw the loaf her mother baked monthly for family dinner.

Cora pushed open the door into her parents' set of private rooms. She left her shoes in the front entryway, pushing them into line with her toe. Her socks squished into the thick carpet beyond, through the formal sitting room. Voices carried from the family room beyond.

"There she is!"

Father filled his thick armchair, ice clinking in his drink as he waved her in. Mother sat in her own chair next to him, while Arik sprawled across a settee meant for two. And taking up half of the other settee was Chancellor Byrne.

Cora froze.

"Catarina," Mother said firmly, breaking her stupor. "How was your appointment with your professor?"

Cora worked to keep her fists unclenched. She took a deliberate breath in and out, then pasted on a thin smile. "Great. He cleared some things up for me."

Mother didn't notice the tightness in Cora's voice. Or chose to ignore it. She gestured across the rug to Chancellor Byrne. "You've come just in time to save Callan from more of your father's hunting stories."

"Nonsense! Callan is enjoying my stories, aren't you? Yes, have I already told the one about the manticore? Had to be at least eight hundred pounds..."

Mother stared pointedly at the open seat next to Chancellor Byrne. Cora suppressed a sigh and settled next to him. Mother pressed a drink into her hand as Father continued his story. Arik caught her eye, mouthing the words along with him.

"And then I drew my hunting knife..."

Cora smiled into her drink. Only water, pity. She kept an eye on her mother, waiting for an opening to interrogate her as to why there was a guest at *family dinner*. Chancellor Byrne, of *Galta*, no less.

Her opportunity never came. Mother only waited until Father paused to announce that dinner was ready. Cora followed her family into the dining room, acutely aware of Chancellor Byrne just behind her. Her eyes focused instantly on the extra chair at the table. Right next to hers. Cora perched on her seat, back straight. She refused to meet the intense stare emanating from her mother's chair.

"What does your family think of your new position, Callan?" Mother asked.

Callan cleared his throat, flustered. "I'm not sure. My father died when I was young, and my mother passed just last year."

"I'm so sorry." Mother reached over to place a hand on Callan's arm. "I lost my own mother when Catarina and Arik were young. I know how challenging it can be without that support."

"Thank you. I think my mother would be proud of the new Galta we are building."

"How is that going?" Father asked from the other end of the table. "I heard senate elections were a nightmare."

"Adalric," Mother said sharply. "No politics at family dinner."

Father let out the smallest of sighs. Cora shared a glance with Arik across the table. Almost in sync, they began enthusiastically filling up their plates. No staff served them during family dinner. The food was brought from the kitchens, and then the Bjorn family was left to themselves. Cora's mouth watered at the sight of the gleaming roast chicken and vegetables. Mother's bread lay at the center of the table, flanked by a dish of butter and a bowl of jam.

Callan followed their lead, passing dishes around the table. They sat in silence for a long few minutes as everyone ate.

Arik caught
Cora's eye across the table. He stared at her pointedly, head tilting toward Callan. SheCora returned the stare, nudging his foot under the table.

"What do you think of Liskow, Callan?" Arik asked.

"It's beautiful. More rural than I was expecting, given what I'd heard of Narous."

"What's Galta like?"

Callan turned to her, eyes growing distant. "It's small, compared to Liskow. Our major cities blend into each other, but there's so much going on. It's...loud, compared to here."

"I hope your men won't get bored while they're here," Mother said, smile polite, but eyes sharp. "Without the excitement of Galta."

Cora stabbed at the food on her plate. So much for keeping politics out of family dinner.

"There's plenty of excitement in Narous," Arik replied smoothly. "If you know where to go. You just have to be willing to walk for it."

"You must be talking about the duels down in the old dragon caves." Father chuckled. "I went to a few of those when I was younger."

Mother clucked her tongue disapprovingly. "Why anyone would want to sit and watch people fight each other is beyond me. Weren't those outlawed years ago, anyway?"

"Dueling to the death is outlawed. The people would have rioted if they'd been outlawed altogether. And the city would have lost a significant amount of taxes from all the betting."

Callan glanced toward Cora. "Have you ever been to see these duels?"

"Can't say that I have." Cora took a long, deliberate drink of water.

Arik shook his head, laughing softly. "Cat's not the type for duels."

"What's that supposed to mean?"

"You can't stand to watch a knotball player get injured, let alone watch people *purposely* hurt each other. You wouldn't last the first round."

"A lady shouldn't be worried about going in the first place," Mother sniffed. "Besides, Catarina is too busy with her studies." Mother turned to Callan, her voice dropping as if Cora wasn't right beside her. "Catarina's professors push her so hard. They had to extend some deadlines for her to keep up with their course loads."

Cora's knuckles turned white around her fork. She busied herself with her food, face red. Callan shot her a glance that she refused to meet.

The conversation moved on, leaving Cora to stew. She had lost her appetite, but she forced herself to continue taking bites, just to limit how much she had to talk. By the time dessert was over, she was ready to bolt.

Mother stood from the table. "That was a lovely dinner. Thank you for joining us, Callan."

"Thank you for having me."

"There are games in the sitting room." Mother feigned a yawn. "I'm afraid I'm ready for bed."

Mother stared across the table at Father, still seated.

He stretched as he stood. "Arik, are you up for a game of dragon snap?"

"Adalric."

44

Father stared at Mother, brows furrowed. She raised one eyebrow. Slowly, Father's mouth softened to a small *O*.

"Right. Good night, kids. Don't stay up too late."

Mother and Father quickly exited, leaving Cora alone with Arik and Callan. The room let out a collective sigh.

Arik leaned back in his chair, unbuttoning his uniform jacket. "You know they're expecting us to go play games, right?"

Callan glanced between the siblings with a shrug. "I can stay for a while."

Callan followed Arik and Catarina back to the sitting room. He resisted the urge to keep glancing at her. He'd noticed her shoulders slowly curling inward throughout dinner, until her chair seemed to swallow her. Even without her parents hovering, she seemed shorter than before.

Callan tamped down a flare of indignation. He took a seat at the low sitting room table across from Catarina. Arik pulled a chair closer, a deck of cards in his hand.

"Have you ever played dragon snap, Callan?"

"I've played a few times."

He had, in fact, played it nearly the entire way from Galta. Callan accepted the cards Arik dealt, arranging them face down. Catarina did the same, avoiding the casual glances he sent her way. He couldn't tell if Arik noticed his sister's silence, or if he chose not to comment on it. Arik corrected his card placement, then launched into the game.

Callan was confident in his grasp of dragon snap. Arik demolished that confidence. The prince beat him three times before leaning back from the table.

"I should probably call it a night." Arik said with an exaggerated yawn.

A silent exchange passed between Arik and Catarina. Callan watched from beneath his lashes, gathering the cards back into a neat pile. Catarina scowled as Arik stood.

"Don't stay up too late, you two," he said with a wink.

Catarina's eyes followed her brother. Callan kept shuffling the deck of cards, waiting for her to break the silence.

"We really don't have to keep playing." Catarina said.

"Don't you want a chance to beat me, too?"

That earned him a half-smile. She met his glance for the first time since dinner. "Don't feel too bad. Arik and Father beat just about everyone."

"Something tells me you let them beat you."

A flush bloomed across Catarina's face. The sight of her pink cheeks, pale green eyes shining, stirred something in his chest. He knew he was staring too intently, but he couldn't look away.

Catarina glanced down at her cards. She cleared her throat pointedly. "You go first."

"What if I make a bet with you?"

"I'm not really one for gambling."

"Hear me out." Callan waited until he captured her eyes again. "Whoever wins the round gets to ask a question, any question. Loser has to answer."

Catarina took a long moment to answer. Her eyes searched his. She could look as long as she liked.

"Deal. It's still your turn."

Callan lost the first hand. He stared up at Catarina expectantly.

"What are you hoping to accomplish here?"

"As in, this room, or…?"

She arched an eyebrow at him. "In general."

Callan gathered up the cards again to keep his hands busy. "An end to border disputes, for one. Better trade, for another. Galta's been on the bad side of the largest power on the continent for decades now. It's had an effect."

Catarina frowned down at her cards. "You grew up poor?"

"As dirt. My dad died when I was young, so it was just me, my mom, and my older brother. He left as soon as he was old enough for a better job."

"I'm so sorry. I can't imagine losing any of my family."

Callan shrugged. He glanced away from her sympathetic gaze. "He was in the military. When the border saw battles every week, we knew he might not come back."

"A friend of mine lost his dad at the border, too."

A softness passed over her features that stirred something hot

46

and angry in Callan's gut. He looked down at the cards splayed across the table, smirking. "My turn to ask a question."

Catarina double-checked the cards, then leaned back in her chair. She gestured for him to continue.

"Did your father actually fight a manticore?"

Catarina laughed, a genuine sound from deep in her belly. Relief washed through her, a subtle relaxing to her shoulders. She shook her head as she calmed. "We've never been able to prove if it's true or not. Believe me, Arik and I have tried."

"I do believe you."

The words were more sincere than he'd intended. Catarina sobered, dealing the next hand while throwing glances at him. He let her catch him staring.

"That's game," she announced, displaying her winning hand.

"What's your question, Princess?"

"Why did you want to be chancellor?"

"I wanted to make a difference."

Catarina lifted an eyebrow skeptically.

His lips turned up in amusement under her scrutiny. "What?"

She shook her head. "I just don't know why anyone would willingly choose to be in politics."

"Maybe it's different when you're born into it, but I never had a choice before. Never had a voice, or a chance to change how things were done. I watched as people like my dad were used as cannon fodder over petty trade disputes. Saw my neighbors working themselves to death, barely scraping by. So I found a way to *do* something about it. I gave my people something to fight for. Gave them leaders to look up to."

Catarina's face was unreadable. Her eyes searched Callan's again, probing into his very soul. He laid himself bare under that gaze, hoping she'd find what she was looking for.

"I've never met anyone half as passionate as you are," Catarina said softly. "It's refreshing."

"Anytime, Catarina."

They stared at each other for another moment before Catarina glanced at her holo. She exhaled slowly and stood.

"It's getting late. I should go."

47

"I'll walk you."

They left their cards for some silent staff member to clear away. Callan held the door open for Catarina. She passed by, nearly brushing him. The faint scent of lilacs trailed after her.

They walked the short distance to her room, stopping outside her door. He longed to trail his fingers through that long golden hair. Instead, he tucked his hands into his pockets. Catarina lingered in her doorway, staring up at him.

"It was nice talking to you, Callan." She took her time saying his name, as if testing it out. "Have a good night."

"Good night, Catarina."

The door clicked shut behind him as he turned back to the guest wing. His holo chimed quietly as he walked.

How was dinner?

Callan smiled as he read the message. He took a moment to reply.

Better than expected.

6

Gray's fingers tapped against his leg as the elevator rose. He couldn't remember the last time he was so *nervous*. Part of it was the ringing fear that he was overstepping. He'd already come to see her once. He knew it was her last day in the hospital. And yet, he couldn't get her out of his mind. And he happened to know her favorite restaurant. More like he'd filed away the name of her favorite restaurant when she'd mentioned it during field work. Just in case.

The elevator dinged, depositing him in a white corridor. He counted the room numbers as he went, wrinkling his nose at the burning smell of hand sanitizer permeating the hallway. A handful of nurses offered polite smiles or nods as he passed. He returned them, shifting the bouquet he held. He stopped outside Room 301, fingers tightening around the takeout bag hanging at his side. Now or never. He tucked the flowers out of the way to rap his knuckles against the door.

"Come in!"

Ophelia's eyes widened as he entered. Gray paused, a sheepish smile spreading across his face.

"Are those for me?"

"Yeah." Gray eased around the bed, making for the lone chair next to it. "Although I'm just now realizing I probably should have brought something to put them in."

"They'll be fine."

Ophelia reached her hands forward eagerly. He relinquished the flowers, watching as she brought them close to her nose. She practically melted into them as she inhaled.

She fixed large brown eyes on him. "How did you know pink was my favorite color?"

"Lucky guess."

Ophelia followed his gaze to the pale pink hair that reached just past her shoulders and laughed. It brought a bit of color to her cheeks that made Gray's heart flip. She was naturally pale, but between the blood loss and the fluorescent lights, she'd been ghostly the last time he'd seen her. Now, the color had returned to her lips, sitting like two rose petals against her teeth.

He was staring. Gray shook himself, setting the bag of takeout on the narrow table next to her bed.

"Is that what I think it is?"

"I know how awful the food is here, so I thought I'd bring you something decent."

Ophelia abandoned the flowers on the table to rip open the bag. He could've sworn he saw tears come to her eyes as she scanned the contents.

"Is this from The Aerie? How did you know that was my favorite restaurant?"

Gray rubbed the back of his neck. "I thought I heard someone talking about it in the field. I guess it stuck."

She shot him a knowing glance before peering back into the bag. "You brought enough to feed an army. Why don't you have dinner with me?"

"Oh no, I wasn't trying to invite myself to stay."

"You're not inviting yourself. I'm inviting you. Sit."

Gray obeyed as she spread the meal across the tiny table. She passed him a fork, then dug in without waiting for him to start. He suppressed a chuckle, stabbing his fork into the nearest takeout box. His mouth filled with the tang of chili sauce, followed quickly by a pleasant burn.

"I get why this is your favorite," Gray said around his food.

"It's not as good as the food back home, but it's close."

"That's right, you're from the Floating City. I'd like to go there someday."

"Yeah, well, other than the food, you're not missing much," Ophelia grumbled between bites. "Besides, no wings, no entry.

Unless you're secretly rich and can buy your way in."

"No secret riches, I'm afraid."

"There goes my plan to marry you for your money."

Gray reached across the table for another dish, hoping she didn't notice his ears flushing. He kept his tone light, avoiding her eyes. "You're going to need a backup plan."

"What if I just flirt with you to get an A?"

"Why would you need to do that?"

It was Ophelia's turn to flush. She glanced up at him from under her lashes, and Gray found himself staring again.

"You're that impressed with me, huh?" She asked, fluttering her lashes.

"It doesn't hurt that you're the only graduate student in my class. Why are you taking a freshman-level class anyway?"

"Like you don't know."

Gray's brows knit together. "Know what?"

"Oh, come on!" Ophelia threw her hands up, dropping her fork with a clank. "Why do you think your class is almost entirely women?"

"Uh…" Gray froze, something about her tone making him feel like a cornered deer. She watched him expectantly, her fingers tapping against the edge of the table. "Because they're interested in apex predator behavior?"

Ophelia passed a hand down her face. "So brilliant, and so oblivious. Is this why you're still single?"

Realization finally caught up with him. The lightness he'd felt a moment ago dissipated. "No, it's not. Well, maybe, but not the main reason, no."

They continued eating in silence for another minute. Gray contemplated if it was time for him to leave.

"So, what is the reason?"

Ophelia's voice was so quiet he almost missed the question. He glanced up to catch her looking under her lashes again. He had to swallow twice before answering.

"I'm half-elf." Gray shrugged. "I know it's getting more common, but there's still not that many of us. And you never know how the genetics are going to work out. Will you live as long as an elf, or maybe half that? Longer than any human, that's for sure." Gray sighed, Ophelia watching him the entire time. "I don't want to choose someone to spend my life with, then spend most of my life without them. Watch them grow old and die while I'm still the same as when we met. But I also hate the idea of leaving someone behind for decades, or even centuries after I'm gone."

"I'm mixed, too," Ophelia murmured. "A little of everything, but mostly sprite. Coming from a city that celebrates sprites above all else…" She heaved her own sigh. "I was less than dirt to them."

"They don't know what they're missing."

The words slipped out of him without a second thought.

Ophelia's eyes shone before she swiftly swiped at them. He glanced at her bandaged wing, at all that it meant for her to lose her flight. He wanted to say more, but Ophelia beat him to it.

"How's the egg?"

"Good. I snagged a portable incubator from the lab and candled it. It seems healthy, from what I can tell. I'm going to have to take it somewhere with a real incubator though. The portable ones aren't meant to be used for long periods of time."

"Doesn't the university have an incubator you could use?"

Gray chewed on his lip, considering how much to say. He wasn't ready to share his family history just yet, or the budding hope growing inside him. Not yet.

"I'm not sure the university is equipped to handle a baby dragon," Gray sighed. . "Especially considering how classified our research is."

"So, where will you take it?"

"Home." The word sat heavy on his tongue. "After the gala. Are you coming with us?"

Ophelia's face fell. She shook her head, pink hair swaying. "I'm not allowed to do any physical activity for a couple of weeks."

"It won't be the same without you."

Her lips quirked up at that. Gray smiled back, rising to take the empty takeout boxes to the trash. He lingered, Ophelia's eyes tracking his every movement.

"Tell you what," Gray said. "I'm not sure how long I'll be out

52

of town, but when I come back, why don't we go to the Aerie together? You can tell me all about the city I'll never get to visit."

For a beat, the only sound was the humming of the lights. Ophelia studied him, a soft crease between her brows. Gray held his breath.

"I'd like that."

Cora rubbed her neck as she left the library. She needed to stop falling asleep on top of her textbooks. Or textbook authors needed to make their books more interesting. Bits of text floated through her mind, jumbled and out of order. She shook her holo- bracelet awake and groaned. It was nearly midnight.

She barely registered the footsteps behind her. She jumped when a long arm fell around her shoulders.

"There you are!" Arik kept his voice low. "Come with me."

"Where?" Cora yawned.

"You'll see."

Cora allowed herself to be steered through the halls. They passed only a handful of servants and palace guards, then no one. The thick carpet beneath their feet turned to stone, and the air carried a distinctive chill. Cora blinked. Arik had led them to the oldest wing of the castle. A wing that was never used.

"What kind of trouble are you getting me into?"

"Relax, Cat. No one cares if we're here." Cora doubted that. When they had tried exploring these halls as kids, their nanny gave them a thorough lecture.

Arik led her around three corners before stopping at a set of double doors. Like Father's office, these were carved with scenes of dragons. Cora counted nine of them, teeth and talons exposed as they flew. Next to each of the dragons was a scratched-out spot— right where a tiny wooden Dragon Rider would have sat.

Arik dropped his arm from around Cora's shoulders and put his hands on the door. He threw a grin over his shoulder and shoved.

"Let's start this party already!"

Cora followed behind Arik, pausing just inside the doorway. Nine stone chairs lay in an arch at the far side of the room. Behind them was a wall of windows overlooking a vast stone balcony. She knew that three centuries ago, there had been no glass or railings, leaving the room open to the air. Open to dragons. She didn't take the time to look at each chair, but she knew the stone was carved with the house sigil of each of the Nine Guards.

The one and only time she had been allowed in this room, it was only her and Father. He had lectured her about the crimes of the Nine Guards, then moved on.

Tonight, however, the room had a small gathering. Cora picked out a handful of Arik's noble friends, Liana, and…Callan. He stood in front of the massive hearth at the side of the room. The blazing fire cast shadows over his face, deepening his scar.

Cora realized that she hadn't moved. She forced her feet forward, smiling politely.

"The birthday prince and princess have arrived!" Liana cried.

She threw her arms around Arik and kissed him, earning whoops from his friends. Cora checked the date and time on her holo again. It was after midnight.

"Surprise." Arik laughed, arms around Liana's waist. "I thought we should have our own celebration."

Cora cocked an eyebrow. "Couldn't wait until after the game tomorrow?"

"You know my party is better than the stuffy event Mother planned. Besides, you only turn 21 once!"

Cora shook her head, laughing. Leave it to Arik to throw a pre-birthday party. Someone pressed a drink into her hands while someone else tapped a portable speaker, filling the space with music. She drained her glass, then found herself moving to the pounding beat.

Her earlier exhaustion melted away as the music swept over her. She found herself spinning between partners, each of Arik's friends taking a turn twirling the birthday girl.

Then she found her hands in Callan's. They danced for two songs, spinning and laughing. The music slowed, and Cora begged for a break. Callan handed her a fresh glass, gesturing away from the hearth. They sat on the cool stone floor outside the makeshift dance floor, taking a long minute to catch their breath.

"I'm surprised this is still here." Callan gestured to the room behind them.

Cora shrugged. "I suppose Njal liked the reminder of his conquest."

"The Dragon Riders don't deserve to be remembered."

Cora lifted an eyebrow at the icy words. Callan shifted until he was directly across from her. It gave her a chance to study his face. Light skin broken by a long scar on his left side, dark hair cropped close to his head, and a sharp jawline free of a single facial hair. He didn't seem to mind her scrutiny, taking the opportunity to observe her just as closely. Her eyes stopped their roving only to be captured by his.

"They had a gift given from the gods, and they turned it into a squabbling oligarchy," Callan grumbled. "They completely turned their backs on their people."

"There must have been a few good ones," Cora mused. "At least, that's the only way I can explain how they still have supporters."

"And how many of those supporters are elves? Towards the end, they almost exclusively chose elves to join the aristocracy. You know how elves treat their oaths."

Cora did know. She knew how many took their own lives for those oaths after Narous fell to Njal Bjorn.

"You seem to know a lot about the Riders," Cora replied. "Do they teach you about them in Galta?"

It was Callan's turn to shrug. "The Riders had a finger in just about every country on the continent. They come up in almost every history and political science courses. Don't the schools here in Liskow teach you about them?"

Cora glanced away from those sapphire eyes, toward the empty thrones. "Once the Riders realized they'd lost the city, they turned their dragons on the libraries. They had dozens, all across the city, and one here at the palace. Turned to ash within minutes. Then, most of those close to the Riders either died in the battle, were executed, or fled. It didn't leave much behind to teach."

"Typical," Callan scoffed. "Wasting all of that knowledge along with their gods-given gifts."

"Do you practice the old religion, then?"

"No more than the average person. Why do you ask?"

Cora tilted her head. He stared at her with an openness that made her breath catch.

"You keep saying they were gifted. I've never heard anyone say that so casually."

"I suppose you've never heard the Dragon Riders' origin myth, then?" Cora shook her head again, earning a tiny nod from Callan. "The first bond between human and dragon was formed by the goddess Elidi, to fight a great evil. The Riders later swore to be the world's protectors."

"But instead, they developed a taste for power and used the threat of their dragons to subjugate hundreds of thousands."

"They lost sight of their purpose and angered the gods."

Cora pressed her lips into a wry smile. "Agree to disagree."

"I'm sorry," Callan said sincerely, voice raised over a shrill peal of laughter. "I heard your mother was quite devout. I suppose I assumed..."

Cora waved away the apology. She took a long sip from her drink, the glass clinking as it settled onto the stone floor. "If the gods cared about us, you'd think they would be more involved in our lives."

"But they are involved in our lives." Callan leaned forward, eyes gleaming in the firelight. "The old religion revolves around the idea of balance. In nature, in society, even in one's self. If the gods interfere too much, they throw off the balance of the world. So their touches are subtle."

"I can't say that I expected you to be so passionate about religion."

Callan smiled, passing a hand through his hair. The motion made Cora's heart skip. Even self-conscious, he was beautiful.

He nodded toward her empty glass. "Would you like another drink?"

"No, thank you. Two is about my limit. Besides..." Cora glanced over at Arik and his friends, laughing at some joke she hadn't heard. "Someone needs to be sober enough to get all of them home tonight."

"Your brother certainly knows how to throw a party."

"That he does."

"You don't seem thrilled about it." Callan's eyes probed her face.

The corners of her lips lifted into a wry smile. "Yes, well, you'll find that being in politics makes it hard to find real friendships." Cora stood abruptly. "We should probably get back to the party."

Callan shot to his feet after her. He grabbed her hand, tugging her back to face him. "I'm sorry, I didn't mean to…" He sighed, reaching his other hand into his pocket. "I wanted to give you something. Consider it a birthday present."

He flipped over the hand he was holding and placed a small statue in her upraised palm. It was a phoenix, identical to the one he'd given Father. Cora ran her fingers over the cool surface, taking in every meticulously painted feather.

"My mother made this statue for me when I was little." Callan's voice thickened. "To remind me that hope rises from ashes. After our conversation last night… I hoped it would remind you of me."

"Callan, I don't know what to say." Cora swallowed around a lump in her throat. "Thank you."

Callan smiled at her, eyes crinkling under long, dark lashes. Cora found herself leaning closer to him, just as he leaned toward her.

A yell near the fireplace broke the spell.

Cora whirled, tucking the phoenix into her pocket. Arik's sleeve was on fire. She sprinted across the room, snatching up his discarded coat as she ran. His friends stared in a drunken stupor, stumbling back from the heat.

Arik was still laughing, completely unaware. Cora flung the jacket over his arm, wrapping it tightly. Arik glanced down at his sleeve, then at her, realization finally dawning across his face.

"I think it's time to call it a night," Cora said firmly.. "

Liana threw her arms around Arik's neck. Tears leaked down her face, smearing her makeup. "Are you alright? That was horrifying! Let me see your arm."

Cora redirected Liana away from Arik's makeshift bandage.

57

"No, Liana! We need to leave it wrapped until the medical staff can check it."

Arik shot her a grateful look. He leaned down and whispered something to Liana that Cora chose not to hear. Liana nodded, swiping at her tearstained cheeks. She called to the rest of Arik's friends, and they began filing out, wishing the twins a final happy birthday.

Callan was the last to approach. "Do you want help taking him to the medic?"

"No, thank you." Cora smiled gratefully. "I can take it from here."

Callan lingered another moment before bidding them both good night. Cora waited until the door shut completely before unwrapping Arik's arm. His shirt was ruined, but the skin underneath remained perfect.

Cora scowled at him. "Nice going."

"No one saw anything," Arik waved his hand dismissively. "And even if they had, they won't remember it tomorrow."

"At least if you *had* blown the family secret that has been kept for *three centuries*, I could finally have something to hold over your head."

"Thanks for protecting my perfect image, Cat."

Cora pursed her lips, pivoting away from her brother to survey the room. Abandoned glasses lay scattered, while the sharp scent of spilled alcohol flooded Cora's nose. "I assume you already told the staff to come clean up when we were done?"

"Why would I need to tell them? It's their job to come and clean."

Cora stared at Arik, mouth hanging open. He poured the last of his drink on the fire, then dropped the glass on the mantel.

"You do know they don't clean this part of the palace every day, right?" Her eyebrows pulled together. "Who knows how long it will be before some unsuspecting housekeeper finds this mess?"

"Relax, Cat." Arik draped an arm over her shoulders and steered her toward the door. "It's their job. If they can't clean up a little party, they shouldn't be working here."

She was nearly dragged off her feet as he Arik swayed. They

58

stopped several times on the way to his Arik's room. Each time, Cora was sure Arik would pass out in the hall, and she'd have to leave him to sleep it off on the patterned carpet.

She supported him all the way to his bed, where she gave him a gentle push. He curled up on top of his covers, clutching a pillow as he started to snore. Cora pulled off his boots and set them next to his bed. She crept out of his room as quietly as she could.

Cora trudged down the dim hall. As she went, she typed out a message to housekeeping. That taken care of, she Cora slipped into her room, nearly ready to pass out herself. She stopped at her desk and pulled the phoenix from her pocket. She ran her fingers over it again. She pressed a tiny kiss to the top of its head before setting it gently on her desk.

Theo flipped the switch, bathing the repair shop in light. The soothing hum of electricity was soon joined by the commentators on the holo-net. Theo pulled up the main feed for the knotball match, then settled in at his workstation. It was a rare day for him to be completely alone in the shop. While the rest of the city took a holiday, Theo soaked in the solitude of the shop tools and his thoughts. He had a growing pile of projects to finish.

Theo picked up a knee-high android with dull eyes. The owner claimed it had just stopped working one day, but there was a large dent where it had been kicked.

Better it than the family dog.

Theo removed the dented panel with deft fingers and set it aside. He cast glances at the holo-feed as he examined the inner workings of the android. The wiring that loosened from the abuse was easy enough to fix. He watched the royal family enter the stadium. His lip quirked up at Cora waving to the crowd. He grabbed the dented panel, testing it with his fingers.

Might need that mallet.

He looked back at the feed as the royal family entered their private box. The cameras zoomed in as Cora settled next to a man Theo didn't recognize.

"… Callan Byrne, known as the Hero of Galta. Sources are saying he has made quite the impression on the royal family," one of the commentators drawled.

Cora fiddled with the ends of her braid, sitting entirely too close to Callan. He said something that had her glancing away coyly. Callan leaned toward her, eyes burning with intensity.

A pop startled Theo. He tore his eyes from the feed, gingerly uncurling his fingers from the access panel. He didn't need the mallet after all.

Theo listened with half an ear as he continued through his pile of projects. He saved any loud projects for when the feed cut to the royal box, drowning out the commentators' gossip. By half time, he'd made his way through most of his pile. At this rate he'd be done before the game was even over. He leaned back in his chair and stretched.

Hopefully they got halfway decent entertainment this time.

Theo waited, but the field remained empty. The crowd stirred restlessly as the lull dragged on. The screens in the stadium went black. They fuzzed, then filled with the symbol of the People's Employment League. A small crowd of every race filed onto the field, carrying banners and signs. Near the front, a woman held a microphone.

"Only last week, hundreds of people were informed they no longer had jobs at this stadium." Her voice reverberated through the stadium. "Ushers, concessions, lighting, sound, even security were laid off. Only to be replaced by machines. Hundreds of people who rely on the sporting season to feed their families are out of work, thanks to our government. Well, we say *no more!*"

A few scattered cheers echoed through the crowd. The woman raised her fist in acknowledgment.

"Stop giving our tax dollars to soulless corporations making soulless automatons! Give the people back their jobs!" There was an ominous pause as the woman stared directly at the king. "Or we'll take them back ourselves."

Smoke filled the field, curling up towards the stands. Sprites flew over the crowd, throwing smoke bombs into the air. People screamed as they exploded, deafening and blinding the crowd. Spectators streamed toward the exits, coughing.

The feed zoomed back in on the royal box. Guards ushered the royals to the exit. Callan looked up and yelled something Theo couldn't hear. He could only watch helplessly as Callan threw himself over Cora. Steaming liquid exploded over the box,

61

drenching empty seats and splattering bodyguards. Theo heard a scream, angry red welts covering a guard wherever the liquid touched the man's skin.

The feed abruptly cut off, leaving Theo staring at a blank screen, numb.

Cora slid into the Dragon Slayer, taking extra care to go unnoticed. The old tavern was packed to the brim and buzzing with conversation. She stretched onto her toes, trying to see through the crowded space. She spotted Theo at the bar with Gray and paused. She didn't want to make small talk tonight, but she forced herself over anyway.

Theo gave her a sharp look as she sat next to him. She greeted them both, then ordered herself a drink. He glanced over at where Gray was talking to Sloan, then leaned close to her.

"Should you be here?"

Cora's fingers tapped against the top of the bar. She had spent several hours in her room while the palace buzzed like a hornet's nest. The morning replayed in her head until she thought she might explode.

"I couldn't stay at home any longer," she replied defensively.

"At least at home you'd be *safe*."

Cora eyed him, subtly pushing his drink away. "Are you alright?"

Theo waved his hand dismissively, reaching for a handful of nuts. She glanced over at Gray, who shrugged. Cora opened her mouth to speak again, but Theo stood abruptly.

"There's finally a break in the line for the toilet," he announced. "I'll be back."

Cora handed his mostly empty glass to Sloan, ordering him a water. Gray studied her curiously. Her fingers found the ends of her scarf. Gray shifted to take Theo's vacated stool, moving himself closer to Cora. He leaned in slightly, his voice only loud enough for her to hear.

"It's smart for you to cover your hair. Common women don't wear it that long."

"I'm sorry?" Cora asked, genuinely confused.

62

"You know, if I hadn't met you in person, I don't think I would have recognized you." Gray paused to sip his drink. "Your Highness."

She stilled, the color draining from her face. She shoved her hands into her lap to keep them from shaking. "What are you talking about?"

Gray laid a gentle hand on her shoulder. "Relax. I didn't mean to frighten you."

Cora stiffened, looking pointedly down at the hand on her shoulder. Gray lifted his hands in a placating gesture, then dropped them back down to the bar.

"I won't say anything," he promised. "I just don't like pretending to be ignorant." He took another drink, eyeing her. "And I'm more than a little curious why the princess would run around the city on her own."

Cora calmed, leaning forward on the bar. She shot him a glance as her own drink arrived. She took it but didn't drink. "That isn't really your business, is it?"

"Forgive me, Highness."

Cora sighed, releasing the tension in her shoulders. She faced Gray more fully, sizing him up. She took a long drink. "Out here I'm just Cora."

"Understood." Gray took a beat before asking, "Is there a story behind the name Cora?"

"I was named after my grandmothers." She kept her voice low, leaning closer to be heard over the din of the tavern. "Catarina Bjorn never liked that her name was second. When my uncle died and Father took the throne, she convinced them that Cora was too common for the crown princess. Everyone has called me Catarina since."

"But out here, you can be Cora."

She put her back to the bar, not letting herself consider what that meant. Her life on the streets of Narous was a fantasy, a glimpse at what might have been. A voice whispered that her time out was nearly over. The hinting, the meetings, the touring of government facilities—it was the beginning of the end.

She'd once walked straight to the city gate, determined to slip out into the night and never come back. Instead, she'd stared at the Watchers posted there, knowing they'd recognize her immediately. It wasn't the consequences of running away that kept her rooted across the street from the gate; it was the disappointment she pictured on Mother's face.

Her heart squeezed, sucking the air from the room. She glanced around to distract herself. She spotted Theo staring at a screen near the far end of the bar. His face was red, fists clenched at his sides. Rolph stood across from him, expression smug.

"That can't be good."

Cora and Gray exchanged glances. They left their bar stools, Gray pushing through the crowd and opening a pocket for her. They worked their way in between Rolph and Theo.

Cora laid a hand on Theo's arm. "What's going on?"

"Are you really going to back out in front of your girlfriend, Sturn?"

"I don't know what kind of rivalry you've imagined between us, Rolph," Theo said darkly. "But I owe you nothing."

"You owe me a lot more than you think."

Gray pushed forward a step, his shoulders nearly touching the two men. "This isn't the place. Let's just all take a step back and calm down."

Rolph glared at Gray, then beyond him at Theo. He pointed a thick finger. "He's right. This isn't the place. We'll settle this in the ring."

"Like hell we will."

Cora tugged on Theo's arm, heart pounding at the rage in his eyes. "Why don't we get some fresh air."

Gray stared Rolph down as Cora guided Theo toward the door. Together, they herded him out onto the street. Theo breathed deeply, fists clenching and unclenching. Cora and Gray gave him space to calm down.

"That son of a *kraken* put me on the fight roster. He must've paid someone to forge the consent form." Theo ran a hand through his hair, mussing the dark curls. He slowly focused on Cora and Gray, as if just realizing they were there. His eyes settled on her, and his skin paled. "You need to go home, Cora."

"No, *you* need to get home. Let me walk you." She stepped forward.

"No." The word was sharp. "Please, Cora. After Rolph, and this morning... Just, please."

She tried to keep the hurt off of her face.

Gray laid a hand on her shoulder, smiling reassuringly. "I can make sure he gets home."

"You'll message me when he gets there safe?"

Gray nodded, giving her shoulder a little squeeze. Cora gave Theo one last stare before bidding a reluctant good night. She felt Theo's eyes on her back as she started the long trek back to the palace.

Theo stared at Cora's retreating form. His head pounded while his stomach twisted into itself.

Gray came up beside him, following his gaze. "She'll be alright."

"Rolph thinks she's my girlfriend."

"And?"

"And if he finds out who she is, we'll all be in deep dragon shit."

"So what are you going to do?"

"I'm going to have to fight him."

They started down the dim street, Theo leading the way. Gray stayed quiet, letting him brood. It wasn't long before they stood in front of a narrow two-story house. Theo rested a hand on the closed front gate, staring past the neat flower beds to the single light on.

"Look, Theo, I won't pry," Gray said. "But clearly this is about more than just a fight. How bad is this?"

Theo's nail picked at the faded wood. He pushed aside the memories fighting to flood his senses. "My brother was killed over a fight, Gray."

Gray let out a long breath. He took his time answering. "What can I do?"

Theo tore his eyes away from the house to stare at Gray. He couldn't remember the last time anyone had offered him help so

65

freely. He had to clear his throat before he could speak.

"Keep Cora out of it."

Gray nodded in understanding. Theo turned back to the house, steeling himself. He pushed open the gate and strode the short way to the front porch. He waved to Gray at the door, then went in before he could lose his nerve.

He followed the sound of soft voices to the living room. Mom had the news streams playing while she repaired her favorite tea kettle. Theo's stomach dropped. He had promised to fix that last week.

"You're home early," Mom said.

Theo sank onto the couch next to her, silently taking the kettle from her hands. He finished the repair and set the kettle on the low table in front of them. Mom watched warily, picking up on his mood.

Theo twirled a screwdriver in his fingers. "I got signed up to fight."

Mom shot up straight, eyes wide. She gripped the arm of the couch with white fingers. "Absolutely not."

"I can't get out of it." Theo focused on the tool in his hands.

"No!" Mom pushed herself off the couch. "You promised me, Theo."

"What do you expect me to do?"

"Don't go! Just don't show up!"

Theo shook his head, finally meeting his mother's eyes. "I can't do that."

"Why? Because you have some sort of reputation to uphold?" Mom's voice was near breaking. "No reputation is worth your life."

"If I don't show up, the Red Gryphons will come looking for me. For us."

"And if you fight and win?" Mom's eyes shone. "They'll take you, just like Lane."

He had to glance away, fighting a wave of grief. His fist clenched around the screwdriver he still held. "I know this guy, Mom. He won't leave me alone until I fight him."

"Theodore, please. Don't put us through this again."

66

Theo stood and wrapped her in a hug. His shirt grew wet where her face was buried in it. He squeezed her, as if he could stop her shaking.

Rolph was going to regret what he did. Theo would make sure of it.

8

A persistent pinging sound woke Cora from a dead sleep. She shot up, heart racing. It took her a full minute to realize it was a reminder on her holo-bracelet. She read the message three times before comprehending what it said.

Meeting with Mother. 20 minutes.

Cora forced herself to swing her feet over the side of her bed and head into her bathroom. She washed her face before the water warmed, embracing the frigid spray. Stray hairs poked out of her braid like porcupine quills. Was it really worth it to brush out all the tangles? Better than listening to Mother comment on it. She had to clear her brush several times before she could braid it again.

She didn't have time to pick an outfit Mother would approve of. She threw on loose pants and a cotton shirt, frowning at the Tendouli label. Mother might not notice. But she would notice if Cora was late. She pushed her feet into the closest set of shoes and rushed out of her room.

Cora nodded to the palace guards at the end of the hall. Martin and Greta were on duty today. They both nodded back to her. Martin passed her a donut.

"You look alert this morning," Greta commented, eyes twinkling.

"Don't tell Arik. He'll start expecting it."

The two guards chuckled as she waved over her shoulder, donut already half gone. She wiped the last crumbs off against her pants, grimacing. Maybe Mother wouldn't notice.

It wouldn't matter if she did notice. Mother would forget all about it once Cora finally had it out with her about the meeting

68

with Dr. Pointer.

Cora made her way deeper into the palace, resolve hardening. The halls here were rough stone, noticeably cooler than the newer sections of the palace. There were fewer guards and servants, although she still said a brief hello to the ones she passed.

She stopped outside a set of wooden double doors carved with a meadow scene. Trees, flowers, and waving grass stretched in front of her in deep mahogany. In the middle of the meadow, a dragon curled up under a weeping willow. Cora pushed open one door and slipped in.

Sunshine streamed from the glass ceiling, bathing the room in gold. Plants filled the entire space, broken by winding paths of paved stone. Sweat beaded on her forehead as the heady scent of flowers and wet dirt wafted through the space. She paused under a small tree, the shade offering little relief from the stifling heat and humidity.

Flowers grew in complementary colors, marking the way to shrines for each of the gods. Blue and purple blooms for the god of the seas, shaped like sea creatures themselves. Yellow and green flowers for the goddess of the earth, most incredibly rare. White and pink blossoms for the god and goddess of the skies—a whole swath of puffy flowers like miniature clouds. And finally, orange and red flowers pointing to Elidi, the goddess of fire.

Cora knew where her mother would be. While the pathways to each god's shrine were neat and lovely, the path to Elidi's shrine was exquisite. Red stones led down twin beds of fire lilies. Dwarf fruit trees spread just behind the lilies, paper lanterns bobbing from their branches. The sweet smell of lilies mingled with fresh bread as Cora entered the shrine.

A short stone walkway brought her inside the cave-like building. A tile mosaic of a red-headed woman took up an entire wall, a phoenix perched on her arm. Twin braziers flanked a stone dragon across from the mosaic. Mother knelt before the statue, head bowed. A small loaf of bread lay at the dragon's feet.

Cora used to watch Mother bake a loaf of bread every morning. It had been years since then. And even longer since the last time she'd been inside this shrine.

69

Mother's head lifted at the sound of Cora's footsteps. A smile touched her lips but didn't reach her eyes. "Catarina, there you are."

"It's been a long time since we met here."

"I'm sorry, my day is completely full getting ready for the gala. This was the only time I could talk to you."

"It's fine. I understand. I actually wanted to talk to you, too."

Mother motioned for Cora to join her on the floor. Cora sat cross-legged on the cold stone. Mother stayed kneeling on the red velvet cushion she always brought with her.

"The announcement you recorded for the gala is doing very well. In fact, it's had the best response of any official holo- stream to date. Devita suggested that you make the opening speech at the gala, and I agree." Mother fixed Cora with a calculating stare. "Now, I've already spoken to your professors, and they've agreed to give you another day on top of what they've already granted you. That should clear your schedule to memorize the speech Devita is writing."

"I don't need extra time, Mother." Cora managed to keep the frustration from her tone. "I'm ready for my finals without it."

Mother continued as if Cora hadn't spoken. "That being said, she also has some ideas for your dress. I know you already picked out the gown you wanted to wear, but Devita found something more appropriate, and a wizard of a tailor to make some modifications in time…"

Mother blazed on, unaware that Cora's eyes had wandered to the mural behind her. Elidi's stare pierced her like a challenge. Her resolve faltered.

"What did you want to talk to me about, Catarina?"

Cora faced her mother again, putting on a bland smile. "Nothing. I'll get the speech from Devita and start working on it."

Mother gave her another half-smile and patted her knee. Cora excused herself, the eyes of the goddess boring into her back as she slipped out.

Cora retreated to her favorite table in the library. She slumped into the hard wooden chair, burying her face in her hands.

Coward, a voice whispered in her mind.

She didn't know why she expected anything different this time. Her determination never lasted in front of Mother.

"Are you alright?" a low voice asked.

Cora's head whipped up to meet a set of bright blue eyes. Callan leaned around a bookcase, his brows lowered. Cora inhaled sharply, her pulse pounding in her ears. She had the urge to smooth the crease between his brows with her fingers.

She waved her hand dismissively instead. "Yes, I'm fine."

Callan eased closer, setting a book on the edge of her table. Cora tracked the movement, aware of every step he took towards her.

"I'm a great listener," his voice was like velvet brushing against her skin. "If you need to talk about anything."

"Thank you," she breathed. He was close enough to warm the air between them. "I should really start memorizing my speech, though."

One of his hips leaned into the table, his hand coming to rest on the surface. His finger brushed against hers, soft as a whisper.

"I could help, if you'd like."

Cora's eyes drifted to his lips. They were full, and so much closer than she had realized. She huffed out a nervous laugh, her hand drifting away, just a bit.

"I'd hate to bore you," she countered.

"Not a chance."

Callan leaned in, eyes lidded. Cora stretched closer, heart thudding as the distance between them narrowed. His breath brushed across her face, the smell of him flooding her nose. Pine and clean sheets wafted over her, snapping her eyes open. Wrong, so wrong.

A throat cleared behind Callan.

Cora leaned back in her chair, hand sliding into her lap.

Irritation flashed across Callan's face, there and gone. Slowly, his head turned away from her. "Yes?"

A man in his early thirties, with close-cropped blond hair leaned around a bookcase. "The senate meeting is about to start, sir. We need to set up the holo- stream."

"Thank you, Daen. I need another minute."

Daen nodded once. He glanced knowingly between them before backing away.

Cora's face heated. She put on a polite smile. "You should go. I'll see you at the gala tomorrow?"

"If you need anything before then, you know where to find me."

His eyes smoldered as they crossed her face. She felt them like a brand across her skin. It wasn't until he followed after Daen that she realized she'd been holding her breath. She sat for a long moment, staring after him.

Devita was going to have a field day with the rumors flying after this.

But she found it wasn't the rumors that were bothering her as she left the library. It was Callan's smell, still clinging to her skin. She wanted citrus and mint.

9

Cora had to admit, Devita had impeccable taste in dresses. She kept running her hands over the cream-colored satin, smooth as silk beneath her fingers. A tasteful neckline fell off her shoulders, the sleeves ending at her elbows. It hugged her torso, flaring out at her waist and down to the floor. A panel of pale gold fabric split the skirt, framed by embroidered red bears. A line of red bears also marched just under her neckline, all of them framed by gold filigree. The only change Cora had advocated for was fewer petticoats. Devita grudgingly relented, taking her from a cupcake topper to a skirt that swished gently as she moved.

"Have you gone over your speech?"

Cora's finger pinched her skirt in annoyance. As if she hadn't spent the last day practicing it.

Devita stared at her expectantly. The public relations specialist cut an impressive figure in a one-shoulder black dress. The skirt slit a little above her knee, revealing long tan legs and shiny black heels.

"Yes, I memorized it yesterday."

Devita arched one perfectly plucked eyebrow. Cora stared back. Devita held out a hand, a single gold bracelet glittering on her wrist.

"I'll be standing by to read it over the earpiece." Devita pasted on a smile. "Just in case."

Cora bit her tongue to stop the retort she wanted to say. She managed a thank you, untangling her fingers from her skirt to shove the earpiece in.

Devita motioned to the side. Anya materialized, smiling at

Cora. She gently tilted Cora's chin up and applied a deep red lipstick. Cora didn't dare to move until Anya declared her done. Devita gave her the briefest glance, murmuring into a tiny microphone clipped to her dress.

"Good luck," Anya whispered.

Anya gave her hand a quick squeeze before disappearing again. Cora turned to face the doors into the ballroom. She breathed in, then out, willing her stomach to settle. Devita stood up straight, done harassing whoever was on the other end of her conversation.

The doors swung open, and Cora stepped through. She stood at one end of the cavernous ballroom, on a balcony overlooking the floor. The dark wood gleamed under the light of five chandeliers. The matching wood of the balcony was criss-crossed by long scratches. Cora couldn't help imagining the countless dragons that had once perched above dancing Riders.

She stopped on the addition arcing out from the original balcony, the wood a shade lighter than the rest of the structure. To either side of her was a set of sweeping double staircases, all of it connected by a wooden railing that had been added along the entire length of the balcony. A small, squat android was quietly whirring beneath the railing, a microphone plugged into its power port.

"Friends, it is my honor to welcome you to the tercentennial gala. Over the past three hundred years, my family has watched over Liskow and its people…"

Cora barely registered the words she said. She had practiced her inflection, each word flowing as if she hadn't memorized it just yesterday. She saw Devita from the corner of her eye, watching from the shadows further along the walkway, one hand on her microphone. Cora delivered each word exactly as written. Her earpiece remained silent.

"We are so proud of the nation Liskow has become. We love all of its peoples and cultures. Together, we can continue to bring Liskow into the future and create a home for every citizen."

Cora stepped back from the microphone as polite applause filled the ballroom. Music floated from a small orchestra at the opposite end of the balcony.

Devita appeared at Cora's side, a genuine smile on her face.

74

"Well done, Your Highness."

Cora nodded, handing back the earpiece. Devita melted into the shadows as Cora glided down the stairs. She was quickly met with praise for her speech. She nodded and smiled, swiping a drink from a passing android. It was long gone before she finished her first round of small talk.

A dark red suit cut through the crowd, and Cora found herself once again staring into piercing blue eyes.

"That was some speech." Callan smiled down at her.

Cora resisted the urge to snort. "It was something, wasn't it?"

Callan chuckled. Cora's heart did a little flip at the way the corners of his eyes crinkled when he laughed. Her mind pulled her back to the library, the way his hand felt against her skin. And the way her heart protested at his sudden closeness. Wrong, wrong, wrong. Hot shame flooded her, and she twisted to set her empty glass on a passing tray.

She froze, staring down at the humming android holding the tray. Cora glanced around the room, remembering that she took a drink from an android server. There were too many shoulders and torsos in her way to see through the room. Maybe it was the same one.

"Are you alright?"

Cora's eyes snapped back to Callan. "Yes, I'm fine. Just thought I saw someone."

"Is there some sort of protocol to asking the princess for a dance?"

"Not that I'm aware of."

"Then, may I?" Callan bowed, one hand out to her. His eyes danced, locked onto her face.

Cora couldn't stop the flush washing across her cheeks and neck. Why was this room so blazing hot?

She placed her hand on top of his waiting palm. "This is your last chance to save your toes."

"I think I'll manage," Callan replied.

Cora was all too aware of the heads that turned as he led her to the dance floor. Other couples already swept around the open space in the center of the room. He put his free hand on her waist, pulling her against his chest. Her brain fuzzed for just a moment before she remembered to lean her torso back. They made graceful arcs across the floor, her skirts swaying along with them.

"Where did you learn to dance like this?" she asked, slightly breathless.

"I had a few lessons before we came to Liskow." Callan raised a brow at her expression. "I am a very thorough researcher, Catarina. You can't attend a ball if you don't know how to dance."

He spun her, earning a few appreciative murmurs from the watching nobles. He led her to the center of the floor as the song reached its crescendo, then dipped her low to the ground as the final strains played.

Callan lifted her slowly, his hand lingering on her waist. Cora's hair clung to the back of her neck. She pushed stray curls off her forehead, acutely aware of all the eyes on them.

"Are you up for another dance?" he asked.

Cora stared up into those intense blue eyes. The dance floor, that had seemed so open before, pressed in on her. Callan's head tilted, his eyes never leaving hers. Cora shivered.

"Not right now." She forced herself to smile. "Later?"

Callan bowed to her again. Cora bobbed a swift curtsy, then fled the dance floor.

She angled toward the far side of the room. A series of long tables stretched against the wall, full of food and beverages. Cora seized a glass of water, draining half of it in one long gulp. She pivoted to face the room, lifting her heavy hair off her neck. She shouldn't have been talked into leaving it down.

Just to the side of the dance floor, Callan was swarmed by nobles. One of them clapped him on the shoulder, gesturing toward the dance floor. He smiled politely, completely at ease. She envied his ability to adapt so easily to politics.

The sharp click of heels brought Cora's attention back to her side of the room.

"Now that is a fine piece of manhood," Lady Stellana said, nodding toward Callan.

Shiny dark hair swept off a heart-shaped face to reveal pointed ears. Jeweled flower clips dotted the silky waves swaying down her back. Her midnight-blue dress glittered like stardust, perfectly accenting her chestnut skin. Large almond eyes framed a straight nose, and her long neck led down to curves Cora could only dream of.

"I'll take your word for it, Stellana." Cora pointedly turned back to refill her water.

Stellana cut her a skeptical glance. "Perhaps not, considering the last date I set up for you didn't end well. Lord Wyatt seemed quite bruised by your...rejection."

Stellana nodded across the room. Cora followed her motion to where Wyatt was very purposefully not looking at her. Cora smirked, remembering how she'd slapped him. He'd had an imprint of her hand on the side of his face for days afterward.

"I suppose his expectations were skewed after his...date with you," Cora replied, sipping her drink daintily. "He thought I wanted the same thing he gave you."

Stellana's deep red lips pressed into a line. "There's nothing wrong with having a little fun, princess. Forgive me for thinking you'd enjoy yourself."

Stellana was swept onto the dance floor before Cora could respond. She set down her glass, no longer thirsty. She swept through the ballroom, occasionally pausing to greet someone in passing. She managed to spot Arik at the side of the room, hands in his pockets.

"How is Stellana?" Arik asked casually.

"Same as ever," Cora replied. "You should go ask her to dance."

Arik made a face, earning him a laugh. His face straightened, his hand tapping the side of his leg.

She followed his gaze to where Liana was standing, nodding politely to a young man. Cora didn't know his name, only that he hung around with Wyatt and his friends. He was carrying a very one-sided conversation while Liana shot glances over at Arik.

"Why don't you go save her?" she nudged his shoulder. "She's clearly waiting for you."

Arik tapped at his ear. "I'm still on duty."

"When has that stopped you?"

"It's stopping me tonight."

"Testy."

"I can't drink, I can't dance, and I have to sit here and watch someone else flirt with my girlfriend."

Cora leaned against the wall next to him, frowning. "Why are you on duty? Usually Mother and Father are practically throwing people at you to be dazzled by that signature charm of yours."

"Yeah, well, as future Protector of the Crown, Nolan suggested I get used to being on duty at events."

Cora punched his arm softly. She forced lightness into her tone. "That's still years away. You should be sweeping your girlfriend off her feet."

Arik shot her a skeptical look. "Don't act like you don't know."

She did know. If her parents' frequent talks of stepping down hadn't tipped her off, then the way they kept shoving her into the public eye certainly did.

She would be queen by winter, if she had to guess. And Arik would be her Protector.

"I shouldn't keep distracting you," she muttered. "See you later."

Arik grunted in reply, staring daggers at the young man with Liana. Cora left him to it, heading back into the crowd. She kept her pleasantries brief and slipped away, retreating to the balcony. The sounds were softer above the crowd, the air cooler against her face. She pulled her hair over her shoulder, letting her back breathe. She found a comfortable section of railing and leaned on it, watching the couples swirling across the dance floor below.

Cora was finally feeling relaxed when the soft click of heels came from her left. She stifled a groan. She knew whose footsteps those were.

"Hiding out, are we?" Mother asked lightly.

"Only a little. I needed a break from the crowd."

"You probably get that from me. You certainly don't get it from your father."

Cora followed her gaze to where Father had gathered a small crowd. His eyes danced, even from the second floor.

"He has always been the life of the party," Mother said fondly.

"Even at a simple village harvest festival."

"I forget sometimes," Cora murmured. "That you were raised in a small town. Was it strange, coming to live here?"

"It was like coming to a new world." Mother's voice was distant. "I was suddenly a princess and had duties and expectations. I was far away from home, and completely out of my comfort zone. But"—Mother put her arm around Cora—"I had someone I loved dearly at my side. And we figured it out together."

Mother stroked Cora's hair softly, kissing her forehead. "It's time we head back down."

Cora swallowed a sigh, straightening. She followed her mother back down the stairs and into thick of the party.

Callan was buzzing after his dance with Catarina. He could still feel where her body had pressed against his. Her long golden hair flowed like a maiden from a fairy story. It took everything in him not to carry her off to a dark corner and finish where they'd left off yesterday.

The courtiers swarmed almost immediately after she left. They smiled and nudged him, trying to subtly pry into his relationship with Catarina. He kept his replies vague and noncommittal. If everything went as he hoped, no one would even have to ask.

He extricated himself from the vultures as deftly as he could. He only made it a few strides from the dance floor before he was stopped again. The man had dark, thinning hair and a neat mustache. He was tall, lean, and clearly kept up on his exercise. He moved with an easy grace as he held his hand out to Callan.

"I've been hoping to meet you, Chancellor Byrne," the man said, his voice smooth. "I'm Elred Torben, Minister of Information."

"A pleasure, Lord Torben."

"Such an interesting case, your Galtan revolution. A country that has been in repeated cycles of turmoil for decades pulls together within a matter of months."

"Our people were tired of the *turmoil*, as you put it." Callan painted a polite smile on his face. "They just needed to be organized."

"You mean they needed you to lead them."

Callan shrugged, hands sliding into his pockets. "I did what they needed from me."

Torben smirked, grabbing some sort of finger food from a passing tray. He leaned closer to Callan, the skewer with bits of meat and vegetables spinning in his fingers. "You must have a great deal of charisma to have pulled that off. Certainly more than has been seen in this palace in a long time."

"Your princess is charming enough."

Torben slid a chunk of meat off his skewer with a scoff. "A product of her mother, with a fraction of her cunning. A lapdog with no teeth." He illustrated his point with a stab of the skewer. "There are a growing number of those who would like to see the kind of change you just had in Galta."

A flicker of anger passed through Callan. His jaw tensed, eyes burning into Lord Torben. "Should I count you among those?"

"Simmer down," Torben muttered. "I would like to see change of a far less bloody nature. In fact, I think our dear Princess Catarina could benefit from a partner experienced with change. A leader risen from the streets, a consort of the people. If you could make that happen, I could see it benefiting both our nations greatly."

Callan caught a drink as it passed by, contemplating Torben's unspoken offer. He swirled the pale liquid in the glass, fixing the lord with an intense stare. "I'm still trying to work out how this would benefit you."

Torben picked at his nails with the empty skewer. "Let's just say, I prefer the princess stay right where she is, head firmly attached. I find her leadership far more palatable than some of her cousins' would be."

Callan took a long sip, eyes never leaving Torben. Lord Torben met his gaze calmly, but his empty skewer continued twisting in his fingers. Callan watched the spinning bit of wood, the way Lord Torben's fingers nearly strangled it.

Slowly, Callan held out his hand. "It was a pleasure, Lord Torben. I look forward to speaking again. Soon."

Torben shook his head with a knowing smile. He melted back

into the crowd, leaving Callan alone. He managed to avoid being ensnared again on his way to the food tables. He had only just sampled some of the food on his plate when he heard the distinct click of heels approaching him.

"My, aren't we popular tonight?"

Beside Callan stood a breathtaking elf woman in a midnight-blue dress. She shifted her weight to one hip, exaggerating her generous curves.

Callan's eyes shifted away as he swallowed. "A little too popular for my taste."

Her red lips curved down into a pout. She sidled closer, leaning forward until her cleavage was on full display. She reached forward to rest a hand lightly on his arm. "You wouldn't deny a lady's attentions, would you? I've been waiting so patiently to introduce myself."

He made a point to stare straight into her eyes. "It's a pleasure to meet you…"

"Stellana."

She thrust a hand forward. Callan took it, kissing the top of her hand lightly. He released it quickly.

"You don't have to act so stiff," Stellana purred. "I won't bite."

"You seem the type that would enjoy biting."

Stellana laughed, a genuine, guttural sound. "Oh, I like you. It's too bad someone else has already caught your eye. A bold choice, I must say."

"I've always appreciated a challenge."

Stellana leaned in closer, nearly brushing her entire body against him. She spoke only loud enough for him to hear. "A word of advice, Chancellor. If you want to survive in this court, you'll have to get better at playing the game."

"And what if I don't like games?"

"Then you need to be prepared to have the things you care about taken away from you."

Callan followed her gaze to the balcony above. Catarina stood up there, chatting with Queen Eira. Callan hardly noticed as Stellana slipped away. He watched Catarina speak to her mother, shoulders falling just slightly. He tapped his holo, pulling up the message that was already typed and waiting. He glanced at Catarina once more as she made for the stairs, then hit send.

Gray fought the urge to tug at the collar of his tuxedo. Where Dr. Lander had even found tuxes for everyone on such short notice, he didn't know. She'd also helped their female interns find dresses and had managed to find a high-necked bottle-green gown for herself. Her ashy blonde hair was pulled into a bun, streaks of gray visible at her temples.

Dr. Lander twisted over her shoulder to hurry the interns along. Gray hung back to count heads as they crossed the street, searching for a fifth person for the hundredth time already. He'd check in with Ophelia later.

They joined the throng pressing against the palace gates. Most of those on the street were bystanders gawking as people checked in for the gala. His group was one of only a few on foot. It took several minutes to get through security at the front gates, then they were walking up the long drive to the palace itself.

"I told you not to wear heels," Dr. Lander muttered behind him.

Gray suppressed a smile. Marta, their youngest intern, grumbled something he couldn't hear. Dr. Lander *humphed*, then called for their interns to hurry along.

The palace seemed somehow bigger than the last time he had been here. Flowers dripped from light fixtures and lined railings. The din of many conversations filled the halls as they followed the crowd to the ballroom. Dr. Lander remained poised, but the interns stared in open awe. Images of bears were scattered throughout the decorations, the symbol of the Bjorn clan. But underneath, Gray's eyes were drawn to the hidden dragons.

Carved into railings, etched above windows, flying in the background of paintings. Even the wide hallways were built to accommodate dragons. And the ballroom. Gray's breath hitched when he entered the space. His eyes immediately went to the balcony that circled the entire room. A perfect perch for dragons. He could pick out the bricked-over archways where dragons had once flown in and out. Maybe even his grandfather's own dragon. Gray tore his gaze away, swallowing around a lump in his throat.

A few curious glances were thrown at Gray and his team, but they were mostly ignored. He led his team to the farthest end of the room where a few tables were set up. A handful were already occupied by elderly guests. Gray's team took an entire table to themselves, the interns still doe-eyed.

The room quieted as they settled into their seats. He looked up to see Cora come to the front of the balcony. Her speech was polished but lacking the warmth he had come to expect from her. He clapped politely when she finished.

"So, what now?" Marta asked.

Gray exchanged a glance with Dr. Lander. They'd already given them the "best behavior" speech before entering.

"Now, you go have fun," Gray replied. "And remember you're representing the team, and the university. And if you do something embarrassing while drunk, Dr. Lander and I will record it and put it on the holo-net."

Gray watched the interns pair off, heading for the dance floor. He leaned back in his chair, fingers drumming idly on the tablecloth.

Dr. Lander watched him, eyes sharp. "Are you doing alright, Dr. Moore?"

"You know you don't have to call me that. I was your student just last year."

Dr. Lander smiled. "I know, Grayson. I just like to remind you of what you've accomplished."

"Isn't this event a reminder? Our team was personally invited, after all."

"And yet you look like you're at a funeral."

Gray sighed, eyes rising back to the balcony. "You know how I feel about events."

"Yes, I was shocked you came to your own graduation."

Another reminder of what he'd lost. Who he'd lost.

Gray flagged down an android server, taking two drinks from it. He placed one on the table in front of Dr. Lander.

She leaned her head on one hand, glass untouched. "I can handle the interns if you don't want to stay."

Gray paused, drink halfway to his mouth. He raised his

eyebrows at her. "You're sure you want to babysit?"

"Dr. Moore, I've been handling interns a lot longer than you. They'll be fine."

Gray set his glass down. He passed a hand down his face, stubble biting into his palm. "I'm going out of town for a little while."

"I know."

"You do?"

"I know what Ophelia gave you." Dr. Lander's eyes bored into his. "And I know who your grandfather is. I can handle things here while you go home."

Gray nodded. His voice was thick when he responded. "Thank you. I'll have holo access, so I'll be working remotely."

Dr. Lander smiled, resting a hand on top of his. She squeezed gently before leaning back and motioning to the door. "Go on, get out of here. I'll check in with you in a few days."

Gray gave her a grateful smile. He didn't linger. He skirted the dance floor, avoiding couples exiting. He passed by Cora, giving her the tiniest of nods. She met his eyes briefly, returning the greeting before moving on. The walk back out of the palace and through the grounds felt much shorter than the walk in.

The city streets were as busy as the palace itself. Music blared, songs overlapping each other. People danced while food vendors took up nearly every corner. Gray stopped long enough to snatch up some street food, eating as he walked. Before long, his jacket was undone, and his bow tie lay untied around his neck.

He wove through the crowds until he reached his apartment building. The stairwell blocked out nearly all of the noise from outside, giving Gray a reprieve. He climbed to the top floor, avoiding a couple locked together halfway up.

His apartment was just how he left it. The table was still three-quarters covered by papers, but he'd managed to finally put away the last of the laundry he'd washed. He changed out of his tux and into his typical uniform—jeans and a short-sleeved shirt, topped with a hiking shirt. This one was a navy blue, which he left open, the sleeves rolled to his elbows. He left the tux on the bed. He'd have to ask Dr. Lander what to do with it when he got back.

Out of the closet came a duffel bag, into which went clothes, toiletries, and the mountain of paperwork from the table. Gray zipped it closed, glancing over at his nightstand. The field incubator hummed softly, the egg nestled securely inside. He picked it up gently, one finger tracing the glass. The egg was the color of fresh cream, dotted with chocolate-brown spots.

Gray flicked off the bedroom switch, then clicked on the incubator's light. A concentrated beam hit the egg, illuminating the inside. He studied the webs of red crossing the middle, barely visible around the curled-up form inside. The dragon wiggled, nearly jostling the egg out of its position.

Gray turned off the incubator light, shoulders relaxing. The baby was still alive. And nearly ready to hatch, if his guess was correct. The small bar at the base of the incubator was at one-third battery. Enough to get him home to Stony Hollow.

His holo chimed, breaking into his thoughts.

Hey! I've got your equipment all fixed up. It's ready whenever you are.

Gray blinked at Theo's message. He'd nearly forgotten about the equipment. He shook his head, setting the incubator next to his bag. He needed that equipment to finish his research. Gray double-checked his bag before grabbing his boots.

I'm ready. Send me your address.

Cora made the rounds through the ballroom, stopping to exchange the same handful of pleasantries with important courtiers. As she went, she caught the same android server from the corner of her eye. She stepped back to a quiet corner of the room, finally able to see more of the serving staff.

They were all androids. There wasn't a single living server crossing the ballroom.

Disbelief washed through her. She wanted to believe that Mother hadn't thought this through, that there was some chance for a mistake. But Mother never made uncalculated decisions.

Cora's disbelief shifted into outrage, then outright fury. She snatched a glass from a passing server and downed it. She slammed her empty glass down on its tray, rattling the other drinks.

The seething fire that had been building inside her flared. Her eyes roved the crowded room, locking onto Mother. Cora wove through the sea of dresses and suits, gaze fixed on her prey. She murmured polite excuses as she wove and ducked while an inferno built behind her navel. She reached her mother's side, cheeks as red as the embroidered bears on her gown.

"Androids, Mother? Are you *serious*?" It came out as an infuriated hiss.

"Catarina, darling, you're flushed. Are you alright?"

Cora batted away the hand Mother lifted to her face. She was attracting curious glances, but she didn't care. "Instead of hiring extra staff, you 'repurposed' the androids *here*. And you *still* wonder why there are protests every night."

Mother's lips pressed into a thin line. She gripped Cora's arm, her fingertips digging into the skin. "We can have a conversation about this when you are *sober*," she snapped. "For now, I think it's best if you call it a night."

Cora opened her mouth to retort but was cut off by a smooth voice.

"Is something the matter, Your Majesties?"

Cora's cheeks heated further as Callan drew close. She hadn't noticed him approach.

Mother's face rearranged into a smile. She stood a little straighter, her grip on Cora tightening. "Catarina isn't feeling well, I'm afraid."

"I'm sorry to hear that." Callan surveyed her, stopping briefly on the arm captured in Mother's grip before flicking over to the queen. "I'd be happy to escort her to her rooms."

"Thank you, but I'll see to Catarina myself. Enjoy the gala."

"Please, Your Majesty, I'd hate for you to have to leave your guests."

Mother's smile hardened. "I really do appreciate your chivalry, Chancellor, but this is a family matter. It will only take a moment."

Cora shifted on her feet, eager to be out of the sweltering ballroom. The courtiers around them subtly shifted away, pretending not to listen. Her cheeks burned even as her indignation cooled. She caught a glimpse of a photographer trained on her and resisted the urge to groan. She would be all over the holo-net tomorrow.

Mother pushed her toward the exit right when Cora spotted them. Black-clad figures moving at the edges of the room. There was a chorus of soft thumps, then a loud hissing as smoke billowed across the ballroom.

Guests cried out and sputtered as the visibility dropped to nearly zero.

"Catarina!"

Mother pulled her closer, wrapping her arm around Cora. Cora fanned the air in front of them.

The smoke thinned, revealing dozens of armed figures in dark clothing. A shadow emerged directly across from them, trailing tendrils of smoke as she moved.

Cora instantly recognized Thalassa Mellis.

"Quite a party you have here," the merwoman drawled. She twirled a large knife in long fingers. Waves of long, dark blue hair were bound loosely at her neck. Her eyes were a dark gray, hard as the floors her boots clicked against. "I see you *updated* the staff this year." Thalassa's eyes never left Mother. "What a fitting way to commemorate your family's rule. Three hundred years. That's an *awfully* long time."

Callan eased closer, placing himself between Thalassa and Mother. Her eyes flicked to his face. Her voice rang through the hall.

"Let's show these people a real party!"

The crowd surged, jostling Cora. People pushed for the exits with cries of panic. More screams burned her ears as renewed smoke thickened the air. She tugged on Mother's arm, trying to pull her toward an exit. Mother stood frozen.

"You people make me sick," Thalassa spat.

Thalassa tossed her knife, catching it in a backhanded grip. She lunged forward - toward Cora.

She heard someone call out her name. Thalassa's eyes locked on her, frigid and dark.

Callan was there, shoving Thalassa off balance. The mer's lips

lips drew back in a snarl. Cora hardly breathed, pulse pounding in her ears.

Callan stayed between her and Thalassa. He was larger and stronger, but she was incredibly fast. They tussled, knocking into Cora and Mother. Mother gasped next to her, but she couldn't tear her eyes away. Callan shoved Thalassa back.

A loud bang shook the chandelier above them.

Thalassa shot them one last withering glance before darting into the thickening smoke. Callan took a step after her. Something glinted in his hand, but before Cora could see what it was, Mother's hand slipped off her arm.

"Mother?" Cora turned.

Red poured down the front of Mother's dress. It leaked from the corner of her mouth.

Cora reached for her mother, slamming to her knees on the floor next to her. Mother's eyes were unfocused as she reached toward Cora's face.

"Catarina," she whispered. "I'm so...tired."

"Mama, no," Cora croaked. "You have to stay awake."

Cora shook her. Mother's eyelids fluttered, fighting to stay open. She took a wet inhale, coughing blood. Cora's vision blurred. She clung to her mother, unmoving as someone tripped over her skirts.

"Cat!"

Cora's head snapped up at the sound of Arik's voice. He knelt down across from her, purposefully looking away from their too-still mother.

"Cat, we need to go."

His words were slow, deliberate. It took her a moment to process them.

"We can't leave her."

Arik glanced down, swallowing hard. He fixed his eyes back on Cora. He laid a hand on her arm. "We can't help her now."

Her vision swam as fresh tears poured out. She shook her head, fingers digging into wet fabric. "No. *No.*"

"Catarina." Arik waited until Cora met his eyes. "I need to keep you safe. We *have* to leave."

She trembled but allowed Arik to gently pry her fingers out of Mother's dress. He pulled her to her feet, wrapping an arm around her.

Callan emerged from the crowd next to them. His eyes raked over Cora, snagging on the front of her dress. "Are you hurt? What happened?"

"Our mother is dead." Arik's voice was emotionless. "Catarina needs to leave immediately."

A sharp *crack* echoed. Both Arik and Callan flinched.

Cora's eyes widened. "Was that…?"

"Gunfire," Arik confirmed, pulling her away. "Hopefully from the palace guards."

Arik half carried her to the nearest hallway, dodging shattered glasses and smashed canapes. Three palace guards were waiting, weapons drawn. Cora only recognized one. It took her a long moment to remember his name—Jace. They were grim-faced as the twins and Callan joined them.

"Take Catarina to her rooms, quickly."

They nodded, forming a ring around her. Arik gave her a squeeze before backing away.

"Where are you going?" She couldn't keep the tinge of panic from her voice.

"I'm going to make sure that Nolan got Father out. Get to your room, Cat. You'll be safe in there. Callan, make sure she gets there in one piece."

Callan nodded grimly, placing a firm hand on her back. Arik gave her a long stare before Cora and her honor guard rounded the corner. She had the sinking feeling her brother was saying goodbye.

Her dress suddenly felt too heavy, as if it were trying to drag her down with every step. She swore the halls narrowed the further they got from the ballroom. The further they got from Mother. A suffocating numbness settled over her, making the world slow.

She barely registered as something warm and wet splashed across her arm and neck. But then there was empty air at her elbow where a guard had previously been, and she snapped back into focus.

"Shit."

Callan practically shoved her around a tight turn. Cora clawed at her dress, pulling it away from her feet.

"They're everywhere," the guard on her left spat.

"It's like they know exactly where we're going."

Cora blinked slowly, trying to remember his name. Before she could recall, he let out a little gasp and fell. More red swam in front of Cora, her stomach rolling.

A firm yank on her arm sent her down another hallway.

"Deepest hell," Jace swore.

"Easy. Don't let them rattle you." Callan's voice was low, steady. "They're trying to make us panic."

They rounded one last corner and came to a stop. Cora sagged against the wall. It took her a moment to realize this was her hallway. All she wanted was to crawl into her bed and curl into a tiny ball. She took a step toward her room.

A deep rumble sounded, accompanied by a tremor and shattering glass. Callan and her guard exchanged looks.

Jace wrenched open her bedroom door and herded her inside. "You need to get out of here, Your Highness."

He pulled the firearm from the holster at his waist and checked the magazine. It was only half full. Had he been firing at the intruders? She couldn't remember.

Cora glanced around her room, hugging herself. "What about you and Callan?"

"We'll hold them off. No matter what you hear, just keep going."

Callan's voice carried from outside the doorway. "I need a squad of men in the royal family's wing. Now."

She couldn't hear the response from his holo over another tremor, this one closer.

"But—"

"Catarina." Jace's voice was sharp. "This is my job, one that I'm doing gladly. Besides, we both know you have an escape route. Now get out of here."

Jace slammed her door shut. Three loud bangs rattled the door as she stumbled backward.

90

She raced into her closet, clawing at the back panel. It ground open, scraping against her hands. Too long since she'd used this one. She stumbled down the corridor, tripping over her hem and debris. Muscle memory was the only thing that allowed her to recognize when she connected with her usual tunnel. She pulled open her waterproof box, rifling through the clothes. Could she get out of this gown on her own?

Several muffled bangs reverberated down the corridor, jolting her. She yanked out a jacket and threw it on over her dress. She smacked her holo- bracelet, but the light wouldn't shut off. Shaking, she ripped it off and threw it into a dark corner. Cora dashed out into the night.

She raced down several blocks, taking corners at random. Her lungs burned within minutes, but she ran until she felt like passing out. Cora stopped on a quiet side street, gasping for air. It took a painfully long time to ignore the sweat trickling down her back and get her bearings.

"Shit."

Instinct had taken over. She was on one of her usual routes from the palace. The back of her neck prickled, and she swore she heard footsteps approaching. She backed into the shadows, bumping into the wall behind her.

Get a hold of yourself. Where can you go?

"Are you okay?"

Cora jumped, whirling toward the small voice. A skinny girl holding a roll of tape stared at her with large brown eyes.

"Mila!" she sobbed.

The girl squinted at her, taking a tiny step forward to get a better look. Her eyes widened, then swept over Cora's ruined gown.

"Cora? Why are you dressed like a princess?"

She knelt, grasping Mila's shoulders. "Mila, I need your help. I need to get to Theo's house. Do you know where it is?"

Mila nodded quickly. "My mom used to deliver their mail. I've been there before with her."

Cora sighed in relief, staggering to her feet. Mila slipped her hand into hers and pulled her down the dark street.

10

It's for me." Theo waved his mom away from the door.

Grayson Moore entered the house and shook Theo's hand. "Thanks for letting me come by on such short notice."

"No problem. I have your tablet in the kitchen."

Theo led Gray down the hall, motioning for him to take one of the seats at the small table. Gray took in the scattered tools as he sat. He fingered a delicate-looking brush, wrinkling his nose at the lingering scent of rubbing alcohol.

"Was it hard to fix?"

Theo shook his head, sitting across from Gray. He brushed his arm across the table to clear some space for the tablet. "It just needed a good clean. I think you should invest in a good case. It'll keep dirt and debris out of it."

Gray nodded absently, already typing his passcode into the device. He breathed a sigh of relief as pages of data loaded in front of him.

"Thank you, Theo. Really," Gray said earnestly, his eyes shining.

Theo rubbed the back of his neck, flushing.

Before he could respond, a sharp knock sounded on the kitchen door. Theo frowned, leaving Gray to scan through the data. He opened the door to a small figure shivering on the doorstep. Her jacket was entirely too big, the blonde hair escaping from the hood pointed in every direction.

"Cora, what are you doing h—"

Theo's voice choked off as she edged into the light. Splatters of red mixed with her smeared makeup, matching the deep red-brown stain on the bottom half of her dress.

"Is that *blood*?"

Cora pushed past him without answering, eyes wild and unfocused.

Theo grabbed her shoulders, leaning down until they were at eye level. "What happened? Are you hurt?"

Cora swallowed. When she spoke, her voice was tiny and hoarse.

"No, I'm not hurt. At least, I don't think I am."

"Theo, are you seeing the news feed?" Mom asked, entering the kitchen.

She stared at Cora, eyes sliding up and down her frame. Mom hesitated only a moment before snapping into action.

"Dr. Moore, could you grab the blanket from the sofa, please? Theo, pour her a glass of water." Mom was already at Cora's side. "Sit down, dear."

Gray followed her orders without question. He returned with the blanket, which Mom wrapped around Cora before guiding her into a chair. Theo pressed a glass of water into Cora's shaking hand, his fingers lingering around hers. They were almost as cold as the water.

He watched her gulp down the water, staring at the red matted into her hair. He longed to reach out, to smooth back the wild hairs from her face. To wipe away the tear tracks on her cheeks. Instead, he shoved his hands into his pockets.

"What did you see on the news?" Gray asked.

Mom chose her words carefully, eyes never leaving Cora. "The palace was attacked. The prince and princess are missing."

Cora looked up timidly.

Mom smiled warmly at her. "Well, the prince is missing."

"Cora," Theo said gently, moving into the chair next to hers. "What happened?"

Cora's eyes unfocused, the color draining from her face. Her voice was a whisper. "They came out of nowhere. They… My mother… They killed her."

Mom's hand flew to her mouth. Gray swore softly. Theo's knees hit the floor next to Cora as he pulled her into his arms. He pushed back the hood of her jacket and smoothed her hair with one hand, the other wrapping tight around her. She shook as she sobbed into his shoulder.

"I'm so sorry, Cora," he murmured. "You're safe now."

Cora shook her head against him. "No, they're searching for me. I didn't know where else to go."

Theo glanced over at his mom. Her lips pressed into a thin line. She came next to Theo and tugged Cora to her feet.

"Let's get you cleaned up, sweetheart. Then we'll figure out what to do next."

Cora nodded numbly. She wiped at her cheeks, further smearing her makeup. He watched them go upstairs, his heart a crushing weight in his chest.

Gray stared at him thoughtfully, arms folded across his chest. "She can't stay here."

"I'm not kicking my best friend out."

"That's not what I meant." Gray glanced at his bag slung over the chair. "I was already planning on taking a trip home. I could leave now, and she could come with me."

Theo began putting away his tools and cleaning supplies, avoiding Gray's eyes. His gut tightened at the thought of Cora leaving. His fingers brushed against his wet shoulder, and his stomach twisted tighter. His mind flashed back to a night years before. He remembered the door bursting open, his mother's scream, and the overwhelming grief that followed.

"Cora should decide for herself."

Gray nodded, glancing up the stairs. "I'll talk to her after she's had a moment to herself."

Theo nodded, unwilling to voice the thoughts swirling through his head. Because he knew that if he opened his mouth, he'd admit that he didn't want to let her out of his sight.

For the first time since that awful night, Theo was ready to fight again.

Cora sat on a stool in Naomi's bathroom, her back to the mirror. Naomi wiped her face gently. She had to rinse the washcloth often. Cora didn't want to see what she looked like, so

94

she stared straight ahead while Naomi worked.

"Thank you," Cora whispered.

"There's no need to thank me." Naomi waved a hand, spraying drops of water everywhere. "You're practically family."

"You've only just met me."

Naomi stared into her eyes, face serious. "You brought Theo out of a dark time in his life. In all our lives. Your friendship brought hope back to our family. You are as much my blood as he is."

Cora's eyes welled up with tears again.

Naomi pulled her into a crushing hug and kissed her forehead. She pulled back to nod toward the shower. "You get cleaned up, and I'll find you some new clothes."

Cora nodded, and Naomi left her. She worked quickly, eager to shed her ruined dress. She tried to detangle the snarled mass of her hair but gave up when the water only made it worse. When she finished, she found a towel and a pile of fresh clothes waiting for her. She caught the faintest hint of lavender as she pulled them on. Cora had never been so grateful for a simple shirt and pants.

Naomi knocked at the door, poking her head in. "Ah, good. Those do fit."

"Yes, thank you." Cora fingered her dripping hair. "Do you have a comb?"

Naomi bustled in, gesturing for Cora to sit again. She retrieved a comb from a drawer and started working at the long blonde locks. She pursed her lips. "What are we going to do with all this hair?"

"Do you know how to cut it?"

Naomi glanced up sharply. "Are you sure that's what you want?"

She nodded. "Please. I don't even know how to do it on my own. I just…can't handle it right now."

Naomi stroked her hair, wordlessly pulling a pair of shears from another drawer. "How short?"

Theo's mouth dropped open at the sight of Cora coming down the stairs. She wore no makeup, and his sister's old clothes, but what shocked him was her hair. It no longer fell past her hips in the braid he knew so well. It swung over her shoulders, brushing just under the neck of her shirt. She looked like...*her*.

Cora paused at the foot of the stairs, catching his stare. "This seemed easier."

She fidgeted with the ends of her hair, avoiding his gaze.

Theo snapped his mouth closed, realizing he was making her self-conscious. "It suits you."

Mom watched them with a knowing gleam in her eye.

Theo gestured to the living room, refusing to look at his mother. He drew the curtains over the single window, leaving the only light source the tall lamp in the far corner. Gray stood next to the dark fireplace, perusing the photos cluttering the mantel. Mom settled into her rocking chair near him. She tapped her holo-bracelet, shutting off the news feed projected on the wall. Cora settled onto the faded sofa, leaving the only open spot next to her. Theo was unable to stop himself from draping an arm over the couch behind her as he sat.

"So, what now?" Cora asked.

"I was already planning a trip to visit my grandfather," Gray said, veering away from the mantel. "You can come with me if you want."

Cora twisted the ends of her hair again . "What about my family? Naomi said Arik's missing. And Father-"

Her voice cracked, and she swallowed hard. Theo recognized the grief in her eyes, felt it deep in his soul. The arm resting over the back of the couch drifted lower, his fingers brushing against her arm.

"Hey," Gray knelt in front of her, eyes soft. "I'm not going to force you to do anything you don't want to do. But I know from experience that sometimes you need space to clear your head."

"You can stay here as long as you need," Mom cut in.

Cora sat in silence for a beat, considering. She took a shuddering inhale, and nodded.

"Where does your grandpa live?" she asked.

"Well, that's the thing," Gray hedged. "It's not exactly down the street."

"How far is it?" Theo asked.

Gray dug around in his pack, extracting a paper map. He spread it across his lap, angling it so they could all see. "It's a small mountain town, northwest of us." Gray tapped a spot on the map. "There are only so many roads, and a huge parcel of private land, but at this time of year I can make the drive in about seven hours."

Cora perked up, staring at the shaded area Gray was pointing to. "I know what that is. It's the Bjorn hunting cabin. I have the passcode to the gates."

"Won't there be security? Guards, cameras?" Theo interjected.

Cora shook her head. "Guards only go up when my father and brother have a trip planned. There are one or two exterior cameras, but I think that's it."

Gray and Theo gave her a skeptical look, so she continued, somewhat defensively. "The cabin isn't just for my immediate family. It's for the Bjorn clan. Many of my relatives value their privacy, so security is limited."

"What are the chances another family member will be there?" Gray asked.

"This time of year? Pretty low." Cora looked over the map again. "It will be much quicker to cut across my family's property than to go around."

"If you think it's a good idea, then I'm in."

Mom caught Theo's eye. She motioned her head toward the kitchen as Gray and Cora began discussing logistics. He reluctantly followed her out of the room, murmuring an excuse.

Mom stopped him in the kitchen doorway. "You should go with them."

His brows lowered. "I can't."

"Why not?"

"Because I'm supposed to be dueling Rolph tomorrow night."

Mom shook her head, eyes clearer than he'd seen in months. "She needs you, Theo."

"Mom, if I don't show up tomorrow, the Red Gryphons will come here."

"Then it's a good thing that I've decided to visit Isla after all."

He fought to keep his voice from cracking. "Are you sure?"

Mom nodded. She put a hand on his face, stroking her thumb over his cheek. "You have carried the weight of this family for far too long, honey. It's time that you did something for you."

Theo stared down at his mother's glistening eyes, a warmth like a soft hand brushing over his shoulders. It stoked a fire in his belly, urging him back into the living room.

He pulled Mom into a firm hug. "You'll leave first thing in the morning?"

"I'll take the earliest train."

Theo nodded into her hair. He squeezed her one last time before striding back down the hall, that warm hand still on his shoulder, urging him on.

11

The streets were chaos. People kept running in between cars, some throwing rocks at cars and people alike. Smoke rose from multiple streets while yells and screams pierced the night. Gray's hands clenched the steering wheel as he skirted Watcher blockades.

I should have tied down my bag, Gray thought, cursing himself.

He could hear it sliding around in the trunk, banging into his newly repaired equipment. Hopefully the equipment and the egg would survive all of the sharp turns.

"This is insanity," Theo grumbled from the front seat.

"Yeah," Gray grunted, slamming on his brakes as a person darted in front of the car. "We should be out of the worst of it now."

Cora shrank against the back seat, flinching every time a set of headlights illuminated the inside of the car. Gray kept one eye on her in the rearview mirror, his hands unclenching as the streets grew quiet.

The Outer Ring rose from the darkness, casting them into shadow as they neared. They followed the weathered stone wall to the closest city gate. Gray idled in line behind several other cars.

"Why are we stopped?" Cora asked softly.

"The Watchers are searching cars."

The tension in the car heightened the closer they inched to the front of the line. Gray forced himself to relax. He spoke quietly, a polite smile painted on his face, as they pulled up towards the Watchers.

"Remember, we have nothing to hide. If we don't act suspicious, they won't suspect anything." Gray's window slid down, and he greeted them warmly. "Good evening, officers."

"Sir," the nearest Watcher replied.

He had three companions, one of them in a different uniform. Gray recognized it as a palace guard uniform.

Shit.

"Roll down your windows and unlock your car."

"Is something going on?" Gray hit the buttons to comply.

"Just a routine inspection."

They all sat rigid as the Watchers poked around the back of Gray's car . A tiny, sharp inhale from the back sounded as the palace guard peeked into the car. The woman stared at each of them for a long minute before stepping back.

Gray and Theo exchanged a glance, waiting for her to expose them.

"You're free to go."

Gray flashed them another smile. "Have a nice night, officers."

They rolled through the city gate and down the road, picking up speed. Gray let out a sigh of relief.

Theo twisted around in his seat, reaching back to touch Cora's knee. "Hey, we did it! We're out of Narous."

"Yeah."

Gray glanced at her in the rearview mirror. Cora was frowning, eyes troubled. She caught his eye in the mirror.

A silent understanding passed between them, leaving him absolutely certain. They shouldn't have made it through that inspection.

They drove for nearly three hours. Gray struggled to stay focused on the dark road in front of him. They passed through the foothills an hour ago, the road inclining nearly the whole way since. There were no lights this far into the mountains. Trees crowded on either side of the narrow dirt road, making it feel like they were driving through a tunnel.

"The turn-off is on your left."

Gray slowed, nearly missing the tiny track away from the main road. The small road branched, and Cora instructed him to keep left. They soon approached a small wrought-iron gate. Gray

100

Gray stopped, glancing around for cameras or guards. There were none.

"This seems like very little security for the royal family."

Cora shrugged, opening her door. "I don't know of any security threats on the property since it was built."

She hopped out and trotted to the gate. She entered a code into the keypad, and the gate swung forward. Gray eased the car through, then waited for her to get back in.

"This is the staff gate. It should take us around back to the kitchen."

They drove for another couple of minutes before the trees fell back, revealing a large clearing and an even larger building. It wasn't the kind of cabin Gray was expecting. It was a two-story, with clean lines and large windows. Behind the cabin was a small garden with a pond. Small solar lights stuck into the ground lent a soft glow to the walkways. There were no lights on inside.

"At least it seems like nobody's here," Gray said.

"Just to be safe, let's park at the staff bungalow."

"There's a *staff bungalow*?" Theo muttered.

It was a few dozen yards away from the cabin, tucked into the trees. The gravel crunched softly under their feet as they walked up to the cabin. Gray slung his bag over his shoulder, unwilling to leave the egg unattended. He'd have to check the battery level inside. Cora entered the passcode again at the door, swinging it open for them to enter.

They kept the lights off, following Cora to the other side of the kitchen. Gray made out a massive gas stove, a gleaming double-door refrigerator, and a deep pantry. The white countertops nearly glowed in the dark, making it easy to navigate the dim kitchen. They passed through a short hallway and into a large room.

A semicircle of couches and chairs faced a massive stone fireplace. A pair of long, curved horns was mounted over the mantel. Gray suspected they were from a dragon. He moved on quickly, dumping his bags next to a couch.

Theo was already kneeling at the hearth when Gray turned around. Within minutes, a fire was crackling behind the grate. The flames cast dancing shadows over the room, obscuring the framed

101

photos scattered across the walls.

Cora sank onto the floor in front of the fire with a sigh. "I always forget how cold it gets up here."

"Do you need a blanket?" Theo asked.

Cora pointed to a chest under a long window. Gray followed her finger, tossing blankets out blindly. Theo caught them both, draping one over Cora before taking the other.

Gray took one for himself back to a couch. He lay back on the thick cushions and settled under the velvety fabric. "This might be the softest blanket I've ever felt."

Cora chuckled, pulling her own blanket close. "You can take it with you when we leave."

"What if someone notices it's gone?"

"I'll blame it on Arik."

They sat in silence for a few minutes. Theo added more wood to the fire, and slowly the room warmed.

Gray's eyelids started to droop. "So, how exactly does a princess become friends with a prize fighter-slash-mechanic?"

Cora and Theo glanced at each other.

"Chance." Cora shrugged.

Theo quirked an eyebrow. "Or fate."

Gray chuckled, eyes half closed. "That's very specific and definitely answers my question."

Theo laughed. "Well, you see, I bumped into a wide-eyed blonde lost in the lower city. And when I asked if she needed directions, she asked bold as day if I knew where to watch a duel."

"A duel on your first night out?"

Cora shrugged again. "It was the most rebellious thing I could think of at the time."

"Ah yes, the poor royal slumming it with the peasants."

Cora smacked Theo, earning a laugh from Gray.

"And we've been friends for the last six years," Cora finished. "The end."

"You seem to have a habit of picking up strays, Theo." Gray's eye cracked open enough to see him shrug. Gray smiled, settling back onto his pillow. "I meant that as a compliment."

They fell quiet again. Gray's breathing started to even out, and his mind began to drift. He wasn't sure how long he dozed before soft voices drifted over to him.

"Why *did* you sneak out, that first time?"

There was a long pause. Gray could picture Cora's frown as she chose how to answer.

"The night before I did, I woke up to someone shoving a pillow over my face," she whispered. "I was afraid to sleep in my own room. I found a secret passage by chance and followed it."

Gray rotated his head, eyes half open. Theo had his arm around Cora while she leaned into his side.

Gray was drifting off again when Cora spoke, voice still low.

"Why didn't you ever tell me about your brother? Or that you used to duel?"

Theo took a long breath before responding. "I suppose for the same reason we never talked about why you came out every night."

A loud pop from the fire broke the moment. Gray heard the shifting of blankets as Cora and Theo broke apart.

"There are beds upstairs. Should we wake up Gray?"

"Let him sleep. I'd rather stay by the fire anyway."

There was soft creaking as someone settled onto the other couch, then a couple of thumps as chair cushions and pillows hit the floor. Gray drifted off into a dreamless sleep.

Jace's aim was impressive. He picked off the few black-clad figures brave enough to turn the corner.

Callan hadn't grabbed a weapon. He fended off a knife-wielding figure with his fists. Between blows, he relayed his position to Daen. It was only a few minutes before his men arrived, driving back the last few harrying them.

"Where's the princess?" Daen's eyes scanned the hall.

Callan whipped around to Jace, who gestured at the door behind them. H threw it open, nearly sprinting inside. The room was empty. He raked a hand through his hair, ready to tear the place apart stone by stone.

Calmly, Jace strode past him, into the closet. Callan followed close behind. He stared over Jace's shoulder at the gaping hole in in the wall.

"Into the city."

"You're acting extremely casual about this situation," Callan growled.

"Relax, Chancellor. Princess Catarina only has a few places she goes. I've already notified Nolan, and he's sending teams to find her right now."

Callan breathed in slowly through his nose. He nodded and stalked back out of Catarina's room. Daen was waiting for him in the hall, brows lowered. He didn't comment on whatever he saw on Callan's face, merely showed him the message on his holo.

Callan scowled. "Tell her I'm on my way."

Callan left his men to help with cleanup as he headed deeper into the palace.

Thalassa Mellis leaned against the stone wall, arms crossed. Callan's fists clenched as he approached. He breathed deeply through his nose, forcing his voice to be steady.

"What was that?"

Thalassa quirked an eyebrow, then busied herself inspecting a nail. "Is there a problem, Byrne?"

Another inhale. Another exhale. His fingers twitched. "Attacking the princess wasn't part of the plan."

"I got a better offer to amend the plan."

"An offer? From who?"

Thalassa's gaze was steely. "I don't share client information."

He stepped closer, glaring down at Thalassa. "And I don't take kindly to being undermined."

"Intimidation doesn't work for me, Byrne. My loyalty is to the highest bidder, so make a better offer, or get out of my business."

The side of his lip lifted into a wry smile. Fast as a sniper, his hand shot out, fingers wrapping around Thalassa's neck. She gasped as her feet left the ground.

Callan brought her face close to his. "How's this offer?" His voice was soft and sharp. A sheathed sword. "Stick to the plan I paid you for, and you can leave here with your life."

Thalassa's lips were tinged with blue.

He squeezed harder. "I don't tolerate traitors. Double-cross me again, and there will be nowhere for you to hide."

Callan dropped her. Thalassa stumbled against the wall and slid to the floor, hand at her neck. She coughed, gasping.

He stood over her, watching the bruises form on her neck. "Who paid you to kill the princess?"

Thalassa shook her head, still taking in great gulps of air. "Whatever you would do to me," she croaked, "he'd do worse."

"What else did he pay you for?"

"Nothing. Now that she's slipped away, my job for him is done."

Callan's blood simmered with rage. His carefully laid plans had just been obliterated. Worse was the thought of Catarina bleeding out on the floor.

He glared down at Thalassa. "And the rest of the plan?"

"Already in motion, just as we agreed."

Callan gave a curt nod, still seething. He told himself to walk away, started the motion. Then let his leg kicked out with an audible thump. He pulled his foot out of Thalassa's stomach and turned away.

Her retching echoed down the hall as he left.

Callan reached the fringes of the busy parts of the castle when a large shadow tickled his peripheries. His back pressed against the wall as a deep voice growled in his face.

"What the *hell* was that?"

His shoulders relaxed. He pushed his brother back, boldly meeting his glare. "What are you on about?"

Nolan glanced down the hallway. Ten years Callan's senior, and the spitting image of their father, Nolan looked as much like Callan as Callan looked like a sprite. Nolan was broader and darker, with eyes the color of freshly turned soil. Fine lines edged his eyes and mouth, while hints of gray peppered the slicked-back hair at his temples.

Nolan edged closer, still looming over Callan. "I thought this was supposed to be a *diplomatic* mission, Cal. You were supposed to use my intel to form an alliance, not put a match to this whole tinderbox."

"I made the best choice in the moment." Callan leashed his irritation. "This is the way forward."

Nolan shook his head. "I just don't understand why you're rushing this."

"Really, you don't?" he asked sharply. "You, who are supposed to be my eyes and ears in Liskow, can't see? Think about it, Nolan. Who is the real power here? Who is the one pulling all of the strings?"

Nolan's lips pressed into a line. Callan plowed on.

"We agreed my best option was to befriend Catarina. And now, without her mother dominating everything, she'll be free to make an alliance with us."

He made to move away, but Nolan's soft voice stilled him. "Is that really it?"

Calla glanced back at his brother.

Nolan's eyes practically burned into his. "I've seen the way you look at her, Cal. If she ever finds out…"

"She won't."

Nolan heaved a deep sigh but didn't protest. His arms crossed over a broad chest.

Callan frowned, his neck heating. It was an expression Callan had seen many times in his life. He still hated it.

"The king has asked to see you." Nolan said.

"Then let's not keep him waiting."

He followed Nolan through the palace, skirting servants and no less than five patrols. He leaned close to his brother after the last set of guards passed.

"You've certainly increased security."

Nolan glared down at him. "I do still have a cover to maintain."

They stopped outside the same carved doors as Callan's first audience. Nolan rapped a quick knock, then opened the door and motioned for him to enter.

Callan stepped into Adalric's study and was immediately struck by a slight chill. No fire burned in the hearth. The sun had moved away from the windows, and no lights shone in the room, casting long shadows.

Adalric sat in front of his desk, forehead pressed into his clasped hands. "Leave us."

Nolan frowned. "Your Majesty?"

"I wish to speak to Chancellor Byrne alone."

Nolan opened his mouth to protest, then thought better of it. He motioned for the two guards stationed in the room, and they left without another word.

Adalric dropped his hands, revealing swollen, bloodshot eyes. "You were the last person to see my children. Do you have any idea where they are?"

"I'm sorry, Your Majesty. I have no idea."

Adalric glanced away, swallowing hard. He avoided Callan's eyes as he spoke.

"I would not ask this of a foreign official, especially given our past with Galta." Adalric paused, swallowing again. "I've known for some time that my children weren't safe in their own home, but this... Please, Callan. I can't trust my own kin. Please, bring them home."

"I will do everything I can."

Adalric nodded, still looking away. The wrinkles around the king's eyes were deep as trenches in the dim light. "Nearly forty years she was by my side. I held her after every loss, through years of grief and wishing. And when our babies were finally born, I swore that I would protect them. And here I am, an utter failure. I wasn't even by her side at the end. My dear Eira."

Adalric's voice broke. His shoulders heaved with silent sobs.

Callan rounded the desk and laid a hand on the king's arm. Adalric's wet face gleamed up at him.

"Queen Eira's death will not be in vain," Callan murmured. "I'll bring your children home, I swear it."

12

Cora barely slept. The tiniest noises startled her awake and set her heart racing. When she did manage to fall asleep, she dreamed of her mother soaked in blood. Over and over again. She finally gave up when the sky began to lighten.

She shivered as she untangled herself from her blanket cocoon. She crept past Gray and Theo, into the kitchen. The pantry was pitch-black in the morning gloom. She rummaged blindly until she found a handful of energy bars. Warmth like a finger tapped against her shoulder.

Cora froze, ears straining. She tucked the bars into her pocket, then crept towards the front of the house. She peered through the front windows, stomach dropping.

Three black cars were driving through the main gate. She ran back to the den to shake Theo awake.

"Get up! We need to leave."

Theo sat up groggily, rubbing at his eyes. She moved to wake up Gray, but he was already sitting up.

"What's wrong?"

"Three cars driving up to the cabin. We need to go."

Theo sprang to his feet, all trace of sleepiness gone. He grimaced at the mess of blankets and pillows. "They'll know someone was here."

"We don't have time to clean up."

Gray shoved his feet into his boots, then slung his bag over his shoulder. Cora snatched her own boots off the floor as Theo laced his. She heard the lock click as they raced into the kitchen. They closed the door as quietly as they could, backing toward the exterior door.

"What do we do?" she whispered.

"Hope they didn't send anyone around the back and run like hell," Gray muttered.

Theo eased the back door open, and they filed through. Cora stared toward the trees where Gray's car was hidden. The expanse between the cabin and the woods stretched to eternity.

"It's now or never." Gray was staring at her. "Just don't look back."

She nodded.

Without another word, they sprinted.

A shout sounded behind them, but Cora kept her eyes trained forward. Then a large blast made her ears ring. The dirt next to her puffed, and she nearly stumbled. Another blast sounded before they reached the tree cover.

They pushed into the shadows until they couldn't see the cabin anymore. Cora's lungs were screaming. She staggered to a stop, leaning against a tree as she took in great gasps of air.

Theo was there in an instant, eyes wide. "Are you hurt?"

She shook her head, unable to speak yet. Gray scanned around them, completely rigid.

She noticed it then. The forest was utterly still. No birds, no rustling of small mammals.

A deep growl vibrated through her entire body. A primal instinct took over, urging her to run as fast as she could.

The shadows in front of her shifted, and a pair of gleaming amber eyes shone over their heads. A red glow grew beneath the eyes, and Cora realized that it was a mouth. Without thinking, she shoved Theo as hard as she could.

A jet of flame washed over Cora. All she felt was warmth passing by her. She closed her eyes against the brightness, counting the passing seconds. The fire died, leaving her standing next to a smoldering tree.

The dragon stared at her. It snarled, as if enraged that she was still standing there.

It moved faster than Cora could track, slamming her to the ground and knocking the air from her lungs. Leathery skin scraped against her, and pain sliced through her head.

The dragon shrieked as if she'd stabbed it. The weight disappeared from her chest as the dragon shot into the trees.

"Cora!"

Theo put an arm under her shoulders, easing her to a sitting position. She winced, a hand going to her head. She was in two places at once. Part of her saw Theo frowning at her, while another part of her flew through the brush. Another pain lanced through her head, then her vision settled.

Gray stared at her in shock. "What just happened?"

Approaching shouts jolted them back to reality. The tree next to Cora was still smoking, pointing to their exact position.

Gray and Theo each grabbed one of her hands and hauled her to her feet. They crashed through the underbrush, nearly colliding with Gray's car in their rush. He hardly waited for them to all get in before starting the car and slamming it into gear. He swung around the bungalow, following the same dirt track as the night before.

"Where does this road go?"

"It should cut across the property," Cora grunted. "But I have no idea how rough it is. Some of these trails weren't meant for cars."

"Looks like we're going off-roading then."

Gray tore down the road, taking the turns fast enough to upend Cora's stomach. She clutched the seat beneath her, knuckles white against the upholstery.

"How did anyone know we were up here?" Theo asked.

"Greta," Cora replied grimly. "I knew she recognized me last night. Someone must have paid her to let us go."

"Then how did they know we were here? There was no one behind us last night," Theo gripped the door as Gray pushed the car faster.

She shook her head. "I don't know."

"We can worry about that later. Right now, we have something more important to talk about." Gray wrenched the wheel, sending bits of gravel flying behind them.

She glanced at the mirror to find him staring intently at her. She

110

shrank back under his sharp blue stare.

"Something happened when you touched that dragon, didn't it?"

Theo twisted in his seat to frown at her. "It was like a...spark passed between you. I've never seen anything like it. And how did you avoid that fire blast?"

"I didn't avoid it."

Cora bit her lip, but she couldn't take the words back. Didn't want to take the words back. The weight of a centuries-old secret tumbled off her shoulders.

Theo gaped at her, Gray shaking his head with a chuckle.

"Drown me," Gray swore. "I owe my grandpa twenty credits."

Gravel crunched behind them, followed by a revving engine.

Cora whipped around in her seat. A black car fishtailed into position behind them, headlights flashing. Gray pushed the car faster. Her stomach lurched as they swung around another bend in the road. A fork loomed ahead of them.

"Any idea which way we need to go?"

"Left."

Gray wrenched the steering wheel, and they careened left, branches whipping against the car.

Theo braced one hand against the dashboard, looking pale. "Do we really want them following us out of here? We could try to lose them."

"Or get trapped," Gray grunted. "Or get lost on the trails."

The car behind them surged after, close enough that Cora could see the faces of the driver and passenger. She watched as the passenger window slid down and the slim barrel of a pistol pointed at her.

"Get down!"

She braced herself for the crack of breaking glass, but none came. Gray swung down another branching path, nearly taking out a tree. The car behind them couldn't correct in time. Their rear tire crunched into a log, bringing them to an abrupt halt. Cora sat back up, heart hammering in her chest.

"They were aiming at the tires," Gray said grimly. "I don't think we want to find out what happens if they catch us."

They drove for a few minutes in tense silence, eyes and ears alert for more pursuit.

Theo pointed out his window. "I can see the wall. We're at the edge of the property."

The road was little more than the impression of tire tracks between the trees. Gray rolled over small shrubs and fallen branches. Every crack and scrape against the bottom of the car made Cora sure they would pop a tire.

She swore she saw a large shape darting between the thinning trees, keeping pace with them. She gasped as pain sliced through her skull again. An image of a black car blocking the gate crystallized in her mind, then was gone.

"Stop!"

Gray slammed on the brakes, and they slid around the last bend. They came to a stop a few yards from the car blocking the gate. A few second later, the last car thundered up another trail to their left.

They stared at each other, eyes darting between the figures emerging from the vehicles.

"What do we do?" Cora breathed

"I'm still thinking." Gray said.

His hands clenched the wheel. She followed his gaze to the now empty car in front of them.

Theo came to the same realization. He shook his head forcefully. "No. You can't be considering driving into that car."

"I'm open to suggestions."

Cora groaned as her head reverberated. She stared out the window next to her as a pair of massive wings shadowed them.

The dragon landed with a tremendous beat of her wings, the car in front of them rocking from the force of the wind. The men outside the car hit the ground. A roar shook the trees around them, revealing a mouth full of teeth long and sharp as knives. Fear shone on every face across from them.

The dragon leaped forward, spines running down her back bristling. Her tail swept out, knocking men off their feet with a sickening crunch. One powerful back leg kicked out, sliding the car blocking them into the trees like a child's toy.

The gate!

The thought sailed from Cora. As if listening, the dragon swiped a clawed forelimb down, crushing the gate and flinging the twisted metal into the forest behind them.

The remaining car revved its engine. The dragon's head whipped in its direction. She snarled, lips pulling back from curved teeth. The edges of her mouth glowed red before fire poured out over the car.

Gray shook himself, slamming his foot on the gas and propelling them through the open gate. Cora twisted to watch as the dragon launched herself into the air, following them further into the mountains.

Callan walked around the massive Bjorn cabin with a frown. There was a soft clink against the toe of his boot. He bent down to retrieve an empty brass casing. He turned it over in his fingers, his frown deepening. He barely heard as Nolan came up beside him.

"Someone stayed the night here." Nolan's voice was cool, professional. "It seems like they left in a hurry."

Callan wordlessly passed the casing to Nolan.

Soon Nolan was frowning too. "I'll have my team sweep the property. If there's any trace of Princess Catarina, we'll find it."

Callan nodded, taking the casing back from Nolan. He stared out across the trees, a thin line of smoke puffing over the leaves. Worry gnawed at his gut. He hadn't had a chance to comfort her, to promise her everything would work out. And it would work out, just as he planned.

Nolan moved off to coordinate his team. Callan started toward the garden, picking up a few more casings. Daen intercepted him before he reached the first flower bed.

"Sir, Senator Hyrax wants to speak with you."

Callan followed Daen back to the cars. A small communicator sat in the trunk, an image of Senator Hyrax already projecting. The middle-aged man smiled at Callan. His gravelly voice boomed over the speakers.

"Chancellor Byrne! I've seen the holos out of Narous. Very nicely done there."

113

"Thank you, Senator." Callan folded his hands behind his back. "Things are progressing as we hoped."

"Good, good. How is King Adalric?"

"Grieving. The loss of his wife and disappearance of his children has left him a shell of his former self."

Senator Hyrax let out a wicked laugh. His dark eyes twinkled with unsuppressed glee. "Excellent. And what good fortune to have you at his side during this difficult time. Have you found the prince and princess?"

"No." Callan pushed down a flash of irritation. "It's only been a few hours, though."

"Ah, well, I have full confidence in you, Chancellor. After all, you aren't called the Hero of Galta for nothing. And how heroic it will be when you rescue the prince and princess of Liskow. Did I hear correctly that they were kidnapped by the People's Employment League?"

Callan nodded. "We can't be sure just yet, but that does seem to be the case."

"Good man. I'll update the senate on your progress later today. You're doing brilliantly, Callan. By the time you're finished with Liskow, it'll be ours for the taking."

"Thank you, Senator Hyrax. I'll update you again in a few days."

The feed cut off, leaving Callan staring into the trunk of an empty car. Daen came to his side, quiet as a fox. He lifted one dark eyebrow.

"What are you thinking, Lieutenant?"

"My honest opinion, sir?"

"Always."

Daen grunted, squinting out at the expanse of forest in front of them. "Someone is trying to take advantage of the chaos we've stirred up. We need to get a hold of the princess to stay ahead of them."

"I agree." Callan glanced out to where his brother stood instructing his team. "We'll let Nolan handle the official operation. I want you to quietly do your own search for the twins. I'll get you whatever resources you need. Just find me Catarina first."

114

Daen nodded, then slipped away to organize their own men.

Callan's eyes were drawn again to that wisp of smoke above the trees. One way or another, he'd find Catarina.

Gray rocked, then slipped away to examine their overturn
Clutching a crossbow drawn against that wisp of smoke above
the trees. But was it another, he'd find nothing.

13

They drove for an hour before anyone spoke. And even then, it was just for Theo to grumble that he was hungry. Cora pulled the energy bars from her pocket and passed them forward. She forced herself to eat one, chewing mechanically. Shortly after, Gray found a clearing just off the road to pull into. He cut the engine and twisted in his seat so he could face both Theo and Cora.

"It's time to talk about what happened."

"Yes, Professor Moore," Theo quipped. "Will there be a quiz after?"

Gray shot him a withering glare. Cora managed a smile.

"Do either of you realize what we just saw?" Gray pressed.

"Yeah, a dragon showed up and demolished those guys. I'm pretty glad it wasn't us."

Gray took a deep breath and turned from Theo to Cora. His gray eyes burned into hers. "Cora, do you know why that dragon protected us?"

"No," she whispered.

Liar. She knew the stories. The ones the Bjorns refused to acknowledge. The few remaining tales they'd tried and failed to erase. Her heart thundered inside her chest, because deep within, she *knew* what he was going to say next.

"She protected us because you bonded with her. You're a Dragon Rider now."

Theo glanced between them, shaking his head. She would have laughed at the disbelief all over his face if she hadn't been too occupied with her own denial.

"No *drowning* way."

116

"Where's your dragon, Cora?" Gray asked.

Something shifted in the back of her mind. She reached for it, wincing as it brushed against her consciousness. It was still forming, like a tender wound, but it was there. An image flashed into her mind, then was gone.

"She's watching us." Cora murmured.

"Then let's go out and meet her."

"No way," Theo interrupted. "You saw what she did back there, right? I say we leave her be and get the blazes out of here."

Gray ignored him, still fixated on Cora. She glanced out the window, suddenly unsure.

"It's your call, Cora. Only you can decide how this goes."

She inhaled, held it, then exhaled. Her hand grasped the door handle. "You two, stay in the car."

She shut the car door, cutting off their protests. She walked into the open clearing, straight toward the hiding dragon.

The dragoness eased out of the trees cautiously, amber eyes fixed on Cora. She prowled into the growing sunlight, allowing Cora to get her first good look. The dragoness was a tawny red, her belly white. Brown rosettes speckled her from nose to tail. A pair of ivory horns curved back, away from her ears, which flicked nervously. Her tail swished, the flat spade at the end fringed with short feathers. Her muscles rippled as she adjusted her wings, the tips leaving faint lines in the dirt.

The dragon snuffled the air, easing closer to Cora. Cora stayed still, sensing her unease. Awareness brushed against her mind, light as a feather. Curious.

The dragoness stopped an arm's length from Cora, eyes fixed on her face. They stared at each other for several heartbeats.

Slowly, Cora reached out her hand. Hot breath blew across her fingers as the dragon sniffed. Gingerly, she reached forward until her fingertips brushed scaly skin. The dragoness allowed Cora to stroke her nose. Warmth flooded her, and she smiled.

"Are we friends already?"

Movement flickered in the corner of Cora's vision. What felt like a thick rope whipped into her legs and knocked her onto her backside.

117

Stunned, Cora watched as the dragon's tail flicked back the other direction, leaving a light trail in the underbrush. The dragon studiously ignored her, stretching languidly.

Cora sat upright, glaring at the beast. "So much for that. What a pain in the—"

"She's testing you."

She glanced over her shoulder to see Gray rounding the car, transfixed by the dragon.

The dragon snorted in Gray's direction, then very deliberately began sniffing at the ground in front of her.

Gray eased forward, crouching next to Cora. "Dragons are typically solitary, but they come together to mate, and occasionally you see small groups living together. Every time dragons come together, they do this social dance. You have to earn her respect, prove to her that you're worth her time."

"But what about the bond? I thought neither of us had a choice."

Gray shrugged, still watching the dragon. "A dragon is still a dragon. From what I understand, the bond doesn't function properly unless Rider and dragon are working together."

Cora raised an eyebrow. "I don't think she likes me."

"Trust me, you'll know if she doesn't like you." At her questioning look, he continued. "She'd try to kill you."

"Great."

The dragoness's ears flicked back, as if listening.

"Why does she have spots? I've never seen a picture of a spotted dragon."

"That's because most depictions of dragons are the dragons that were bred by the Riders." Gray's eyes roved over the dragon.

"The Riders *bred* dragons?"

Gray nodded. "Much how humans have bred dogs. This dragoness is a wild phenotype."

She stared at the dragoness with new appreciation. "She's smaller than I expected. Is she full-grown?"

"Yes. Still a young dragon, but definitely an adult. If I had to guess, she's probably only five or six years old."

"I'm guessing the Riders bred them bigger?"

118

"And flashier. They had many feuds over breeding lines back in the day."

The dragon sniffed closer to them, lifting her head lazily until she was eye level with Gray. She snuffed loudly, sulfurous breath washing over them. After a long moment, she stretched out on the grass a few feet from them, completely at ease.

"Well, that's a good sign." Gray observed

Cora watched the dragon warily, waiting for her to swing her tail again. She kept one eye on the dragon as she turned back toward Gray. "Tell me about where we're going."

"It's called Stony Hollow, and it's part of a small sovereign state nestled in these mountains."

"And how come I don't know about it?"

"We make a point to fly under the radar." Gray shrugged. "We made a deal with Brand Bjorn, when he was nearly on his deathbed and exhausted from fighting the last supporters of the Dragon Riders. We got this sanctuary in the mountains, with freedom to govern ourselves and trade as we saw fit."

"In exchange for what?"

"Peace." Gray stared at the dragon wistfully. "A more powerful tool than you might think."

"How long until we get there?"

"Long enough for you to start thinking of names."

"Names?"

Gray nodded at the dragoness lounging before them. She frowned.

I don't suppose you'll tell *me what name you like?*

The dragoness gave no indication that she heard or cared. She rested her head over her large front feet. Her eyes were half closed, but Cora knew she was watching their every move. Those eyes followed her as she climbed back into the car.

Theo convinced Gray to let him drive once the sun had crested the tops of the trees. Gray and Cora dozed in their seats, but Theo was wide awake. He glanced up periodically, catching glimpses of the dragon trailing along above them. When Cora pushed him out of the way, it took him a few seconds to understand what was

119

going on. Then he'd seen the dragon looming over her and he'd just…frozen.

He swallowed the hard lump of guilt down. It settled down into his gut, right beside the other. The one he'd carried since the night Lane died.

Theo glanced in the mirror at Cora. He wished he was close enough to brush the hair out of her face. She shifted in her seat, eyes flying open. She breathed rapidly, shooting upright. Her fingers grasped at the ends of her hair.

"Hey, you okay?"

Cora found Theo's eyes in the mirror. He watched as the fear slowly left her face, his own body relaxing in time with hers. She dropped her hands to her lap, clutching them together. They were shaking.

"Every time I close my eyes, I see it happen. I see her lying there…"

Theo's heart squeezed. He knew exactly what she meant. He took them around a switchback, not really seeing the road.

"It took months after my brother died to sleep through the night."

"Did you…see it happen?"

"Yes." Theo had to swallow before he could continue. "He died in my arms as I was trying to get help. Sometimes I still dream about that night."

"How do you handle this?"

Theo offered her a grim smile. "Good friends make all the difference."

They fell back into silence. Gray stirred a few minutes later, sitting up in his seat. Theo had the impression he'd been awake for a while. Soon, the road ended in a wide gravel lot ringed by trees. Across from them, a set of thick wooden posts guarded a deep gorge. Theo parked the car in the lot as Gray frowned at the posts.

"There should be a bridge there."

"What happened to it?"

Gray shook his head, eyes troubled. "I have no idea."

Cora leaned forward, her head coming level with the front seat. Her breath caressed Theo's cheek as she gazed out the windshield.

Theo's pulse thudded through his body. He stared deliberately at Gray. "What do we do now?"

"I have an idea."

Theo and Cora followed his gaze up through the windshield. To the dragon circling above.

"You're sure this is the only way?" Cora fought to keep her voice steady.

"Unless you're a goat." Gray was annoyingly calm. "Move with confidence. She'll pick up on your nerves."

They stared across the gravel at the dragon. She licked her claws, pretending they weren't there. Her ears gave her away. They were alert, one of them pivoting back every few seconds to monitor Cora and Gray.

"There's no way I'm getting near that thing," Theo grumbled behind them.

Gray answered without taking his eyes off the dragon, "Feel free to take your chances with the mountain cats, then."

"A dragon is *way* worse than a cat."

"Not helping, Theo."

Cora took a steadying breath. She knew she was only delaying the inevitable. She began crossing the distance, gravel crunching beneath her boots.

The dragon's ears snapped in her direction. She still faced away from Cora, but Cora could see the muscles in her shoulders were taut.

Movement flickered in Cora's periphery. She barely had enough time to jump out of the way as the dragon swung her long tail. The jump brought her right next to the dragon's side.

She spun around, eyes locking with the dragon's. Amber eyes stared straight into her soul. Cora felt a tickling warmth in the back of her mind, just out of reach. Heat radiated from the dragon's chest, smoke coiling daintily from the edges of her mouth.

Cora stared right back into those slitted pupils, her voice low, soothing. "You know that won't work."

The dragon snorted in response, smoke rising from her nostrils too.

"Look, no matter how we both feel, we're stuck with each other now. So let's just try to get along, alright?"

Several long seconds passed before the dragon cooled, smoke no longer curling from her mouth and nose. Ever so slowly, the wing closest to Cora unfurled, exposing a spot just in front of her shoulder blades.

Cora held the dragon's gaze as she laid a hand on the spot. The dragon shivered. A flurry of images rushed through Cora's mind, too fast for her to comprehend. Before she could lose her courage, she pulled herself onto the dragon's back.

"Great work," Gray said softly.

Cora hadn't noticed him approach. The dragon eyed him warily.

Gray glanced at the dragon, then faced her. "You've done the first step, but she's going to test you. Just make sure you *don't let go.*"

The dragon straightened, rising to her full height.

Cora's heartbeat quickened, and she scrambled to hold on to the dragon. "Test me how?"

Gray stepped back to give the dragon room, his face grim. "She'll try to throw you off."

"What?"

The dragon's wings snapped open. Cora flung her arms around the animal's neck as she tensed. The dragon ran forward, her great wings beating down. Then they were airborne.

They climbed quickly, air rushing over Cora and raising goosebumps on her arms. She squeezed her eyes shut, bouncing in time to the dragon's wing beats. Long seconds passed before they leveled out, the dragon's wings stilling as they coasted.

Cora raised her head from the dragon's neck. Her breath caught as she looked around. Sunlight drenched the mountain peaks, sparkling as it hit a distant lake. She expected to be afraid, but instead, she was exhilarated. She laughed, spreading her arms to the sides and basking in the sunshine.

They glided on air currents for a short time. Then something shifted in the back of her mind. The dragon glanced back at her for only a second. Cora's heart skipped a beat. She threw herself forward, clinging to the dragon's neck again. The dragon tucked in her wings and dove.

Cora had to curl her chin down in order to breathe. She scrunched her eyes shut against the cutting wind as they hurtled down at an impossible speed. She opened her eyes a slit, green foliage rushing towards them.

The dragon's wings snapped open, jolting Cora. They skimmed over the trees, sending leaves flying in their wake. The dragon twisted her head to look back at Cora.

Cora met her gaze. *You won't get rid of me that easy.*

The dragon's head faced forward again, wings pumping faster. They ascended. Higher than before. The cold made Cora's fingers numb. She shivered, holding on as tightly as she could. They were high enough to see the horizon beyond the mountains.

Just when Cora thought they couldn't climb any higher, the dragon's wing beats slowed. Then stopped. She let herself fall, twisting slowly. It was all Cora could do to hold on, fingers, arms, knees clenched tightly to the scaly hide.

Then the dragon extended her wings, no longer falling. She wove herself in loops and curves, and still, Cora held on. She caught the dragon's eye again, and a sudden heat rushed through her.

It raced into every limb, to every finger and toe. Instinctively, Cora shifted until she had a firmer seat.

And in her mind, an iron link was forged. A rush of images played across her vision, still too fast to fully absorb. Then, a thought, almost like a roar.

My Rider.

Cora's body sang with the declaration. It thrummed through every fiber of her body until she thought she might burst. They landed with a bone-shaking thump, stirring up gravel dust. The dragon flared her great wings and shot a jet of flame into the sky. She fired until she was spent, then settled onto her belly so Cora could slide down.

Cora's legs wobbled as she touched the ground. She recovered, coming around to the dragon's face. She pressed her forehead to her dragon's, feeling her presence in her mind, purring steadily.

123

The world around them stilled, sensing the intimacy of the moment.

Their breaths mingled, moving in and out in sync. Cora trailed her fingers along her dragon's scaly hide, feeling the muscle corded beneath. It took her a moment to realize the pounding beat in the back of her mind was her dragon's heart. It pulsed through Cora's veins, just underneath her own heartbeat.

I feel you, Cora thought.

Her dragon grumbled in response, a contented sound that vibrated under Cora's fingers. An impression flitted through her mind, formless and incoherent. It was going to take a while to figure this out.

Cora didn't know how long they stayed like that. When she finally pulled back, Theo and Gray's eyes were on her. She ignored them for now, focusing on her dragon.

Can you carry all of us?

Her dragon snorted, hardly glancing at the men. She sat up straighter, wings snapping open and closed, then showed Cora an image of the sky.

Cora took that as a yes. She finally faced away from her dragon.

Both Gray and Theo watched her in awe. She swore Gray had tears in his eyes.

"She can take us across the gorge." Cora said.

Whatever spell held the clearing broke. Gray shouldered his bag, tightening the straps to keep it close to his body. Theo edged closer, watching Cora's dragon warily. He stopped just behind her.

"How was flying?" he asked.

"It was incredible. I've never experienced anything like it before."

"Do you know what you're going to call her?"

Cora looked over her dragon. Her spots rippled over taut muscles, every inch of her built for power, for speed. A memory surfaced in her mind. Her dragon tilted her head, watching the memory with her. She purred in approval.

"Do you remember the tournament a couple years back?" Cora said.

124

"The one that ended in fourteen hospitalizations?"

"No, the one before that. The guy who blasted through the rankings, won the whole thing, and retired the next day." Cora saw recognition dawn across Theo's face. "What was his name?"

"Makari Zarvas."

"She reminds me of him." Cora idly stroked her dragon's nose. "Makari."

Her dragon purred louder, nuzzling into her hand.

Cora laughed, and Theo cracked a smile.

"Makari it is, then."

14

Gray's cheeks were sore from grinning. He was flying. He stared at the trees rushing by below and whooped for joy. In front of him, Theo cringed closer to Cora. Gray laughed, holding his arms out to the side. Makari glided low, wings straining from carrying all three of them. His heart swelled as Stony Hollow came into view.

Houses clustered around a main square, a handful of larger buildings coming into focus as they neared. Gray scanned over them all: the dining hall, city hall, Rhetta's market, Brand's forge, the infirmary, and some new businesses. He also made out a whole swath of new houses under construction.

His grandpa's house was still easy to spot. It sat on a small rise at the edge of Stony Hollow, Grandpa's raised garden beds stretching over the entire two-acre plot. He pointed it out to Cora, and almost immediately, Makari was sweeping toward it. The wind brought the smell of the garden to them as they dipped lower. Lavender, mint, and oregano washed over him as Makari landed with a bone-rattling thump.

Gray was on the ground within a heartbeat. Theo and Cora slid to the ground slowly, stretching sore limbs. Gray ducked under Makari's wings as the dragon shook herself. He was across the front yard in three strides. He rapped on the door, bouncing on his toes. The blue-painted wood swung open to reveal a lanky elf. His brow was lowered, deepening the lines etched into his tan skin. Silver hair hung down his back in a tidy braid, while keen brown eyes focused on Gray's face.

"Grayson? What are you doing…" He trailed off as he noticed the dragon, eyes widening.

"Hey, Grandpa. I brought some friends for a visit."

He'd never seen Grandpa Reluraun speechless before. The old elf's eyes darted between him and the dragon.

The grin slid off of Gray's face. He cleared his throat, gesturing behind himself. "I want to introduce you to Cora and Makari."

Grandpa's gaze snapped back to Gray. His frown returned, deeper this time. He followed Gray the short distance to Theo and Cora. He held out his hand, introducing himself tersely, then stepped back to fully inspect Makari. The dragon straightened, watching Grandpa Reluraun intently.

"It's been a while since I've seen a wild dragon," he rumbled.

Cora glanced at Gray, who smiled reassuringly at her. It was as close to a compliment as she'd get from Grandpa right now. His attention shifted from Makari to Cora, his scrutiny sweeping her from head to toe. He shot Gray a glance that told him his grandpa knew exactly who she was. Grandpa shot a cursory look at Theo, then *hmphed*.

"No use standing around in the yard. I'll make lunch."

With that, Grandpa Reluraun turned and strode back into his house. Gray motioned for Cora and Theo to follow. Cora glanced at Makari. Some silent communication passed between them before Makari stretched out in the yard, head on her front claws.

"She'll be fine." Gray assured her.

Cora nodded, following him up the porch steps.

His grandpa's house was just as he remembered it. Sunlight drenched the living room in golden light, casting a glow over the green floral couches and frayed rug. A hall to the left led to three bedrooms and a tiny bathroom, while the rough wooden dining table stretched under the front windows. A wall separated the living room and kitchen, the scent of fresh herbs wafting from it.

Gray pulled off his boots and dropped them on the porch, motioning for Theo and Cora to do the same. He led them to the bedrooms, only staying long enough to drop his bag and check on the egg. He left Cora and Theo to settle as he made his way to the kitchen.

Grandpa didn't look up from his cutting board as Gray took a seat at the counter. "Well, are you going to start talking?"

127

Gray gave Grandpa the short version. Grandpa quietly continued chopping, letting him talk without interruption. He set down the knife once he finished.

"This isn't going to go over well," Grandpa warned. "You shouldn't have brought her here."

"She's a Dragon Rider. She has every right to be here."

Grandpa put up a placating hand. "I agree with you, but the others won't."

"She doesn't want anyone knowing who she is. She's asked me and Theo to keep it quiet."

Grandpa snorted derisively, dumping his ingredients into a sizzling pan. He meticulously pulled parsley leaves from their stems. "They're going to figure it out. Of all people to become a Rider, it had to be a Bjorn." Grandpa glanced up sharply. "It should have been you."

Gray suppressed a sigh. There it was. He shook his head, smothering a tiny spark of annoyance. "She's the Rider we need. I can feel it."

Grandpa Reluraun set down his herbs to stare at him. Gray fought the urge to squirm.

"If you really believe in her, then I'll train the girl."

"Thank you, Grandpa."

He opened him mouth to tell him about the egg. The words sat there, right at the tip of his tongue. He swallowed them instead.

Grandpa went back to his pan, spoon scraping softly against cast iron. "Although I don't know exactly what kind of training I can give her. I don't have years to teach her, not if she's planning on going back."

"I have to go back."

Gray twisted in his seat to see Cora lingering in the doorway.

Grandpa spared her a glance, spoon scraping against the pan. "Then anything I can teach you will be incomplete. However," he said quickly, cutting off her protest, "I will teach you what I can."

Gray caught the calculating look that crossed her face. Then, like a curtain drawn across her eyes, Cora's expression smoothed into unreadable politeness.

"Thank you," she said, sliding into the seat next to Gray.

128

Grandpa nodded, opening the fridge.

Gray leaned towards Cora. "You need to stop doing that."

"Doing what?"

"Pulling out the princess face. People will pick up on it."

"I don't have a—"

"I hope that tastes as good as it smells," Theo said, leaning on the back of her chair.

Gray caught a whiff of Theo's citrus soap as he leaned forward. Cora's soft inhale told him she caught it too. Gray resisted the urge to shake his head at the two of them.

Grandpa Reluraun regarded her sharply. "What sort of physical activity are you used to? I need to know what I'm dealing with before we start training."

Cora froze as all eyes turned on her.

Grandpa saw her hesitation and shot Gray an irritated glare. "I can't train her if she can't even lift a sword. I knew we'd have to cover the basics, but this? She'll be lucky to learn anything."

Cora's eyes dropped to the counter in front of her. Gray's heart squeezed at the way her shoulders curved in.

He rotated in his seat to face Theo. "If only we had a professional athlete to help with her training."

She gazed hopefully at Theo.

Theo glanced between them, eyes widening. He lifted his hands, head already shaking. "I'm no trainer. Besides, I haven't trained consistently in years."

"Please, Theo," Cora said softly.

He stared at her, hands lowering. Her eyes widened in silent pleading. Gray lifted a hand to cover his smile as Theo melted under her gaze.

"Alright, I can help you get stronger. Just don't expect me to take it easy on you."

"Wouldn't have it any other way."

Grandpa's eyes flicked between them. He frowned but didn't object. Gruffly, he set out steaming plates of vegetables and eggs. "We start tomorrow, then."

After lunch, Reluraun announced they would head into town to

129

get Theo and Cora some clothes. And more groceries. They followed the silver-haired elf down the dirt path toward town.

Eyes had always followed Cora wherever she went, yet she was completely unprepared for walking through Stony Hollow. Here, she had no title to hide behind. She shrank into Theo's shadow as they walked the dirt road into town. Every person stopped to stare as they passed. Most watched with curiosity, often offering smiles or warm greetings. Others watched with open suspicion.

Pointed ears in varying hues laid against hair just as varied. Some of the elves wore clothes nearly a century out of fashion. Most carried weapons. Cora had never seen such an assortment of weaponry out in the open before. Swords, daggers, bows, firearms. She even caught sight of a mace and a double-headed battle axe.

She leaned toward Gray as a pair of glowering elves watched from across the street. "What kind of town is this?"

Gray followed her gaze, waving to the elves. They nodded back tersely, still watching warily.

"It's a sanctuary, of sorts. At least half of the elves here served in the wars against Njal Bjorn."

Cora glanced away quickly.

Reluraun called impatiently for them to hurry up. Her head swiveled as she struggled to keep up, scanning the main road. They passed shops and houses, and more people. She saw some humans, several sprites with jewel-toned wings, a few mer with large eyes and scales shimmering along their cheekbones, and elves. More elves than she'd ever seen in one place.

Her chin came up a fraction. She refused to slump under their scrutiny.

Finally, Reluraun held open a shop door for them. Cora stepped over the threshold, blinking at the sudden change in lighting. Racks of clothes stretched along each wall and in neat rows across the floor. She skirted a handful of mannequins as she looked around. The clothes closest to the door were similar to the styles in Narous—bright colors and a variety of fabrics in the most popular silhouettes. As she wandered further into the store, the clothes seemed to shift through time. Long tunics, fitted pants, cloaks and long coats with shiny buttons. Cora ran a finger over a dark green tunic. It was softer than she expected.

"You have good taste. That wool came from the best flock of goats in Stony Hollow."

Cora started at the chipper voice. She spun to see a lanky elf half-hidden in a rack of clothes. Dark blue eyes peered at her behind thick, round glasses. With his arms full of clothes and his short, dark hair pointing in every direction, he reminded Cora of a mantis.

"It's beautiful," she said. "But a little old-fashioned for me."

He ran a calculating eye over her. "Well, I might not have a whole lot in stock for you, depending on what you're looking for. You're a lot smaller than most of my customers."

Cora smiled wryly.

Before she could reply, his eyes slid over her shoulder. "Ah, good to see you, Reluraun."

"And you, Tallyn. I see you've met Cora. She's a friend of Grayson's, along with Theo back there." Reluraun nodded to the far wall of the store. "They didn't pack enough for their visit, so they need a few things."

"Very good." Tallyn lifted a single finger to push his glasses up his nose. "Although it will take me a few minutes to get them put into our payment system. Siraye has to keep sending technicians up here to process credits."

Cora's heart dropped. She didn't have her holo- bracelet, which meant she had no credits. She took a step away from the clothes rack.

Gray and Theo materialized from the labyrinth of fabric behind Tallyn.

"You can just put them on my account today," Gray said.

"Well, that saves me a call down to the Hub. Good to see you again, Grayson."

Cora shot him a grateful smile. They broke off again to scour the rows. She picked a handful of things, keeping her pile small. Every time her path crossed Gray's, he added more.

"Are you planning on doing laundry every day? Because you'll have to if that's all you get."

"You're already being too generous, Gray. I'll make do."

"Don't worry about it. Besides, I know you can reimburse me later," Gray said with a wink.

She chuckled, relaxing. She caught up to Theo at the back of the store, an impressive pile of clothes on the counter.

Theo glanced over her choices, raising an eyebrow at the green tunic. "I didn't realize you were picking out costumes."

Cora shoved his arm. She plucked a lavender shirt from his pile. "And what's this? I didn't realize purple was your color."

Theo's face flushed as he snatched the shirt back. "There were only so many choices."

"At least mine matches my eyes."

"You're right. It does."

Her breath caught at the intensity of his gaze. Heat crept across her face and pooled in her belly.

Theo glanced back at the clothes as Gray and Tallyn approached, Reluruan trailing behind. "I can't wait to see you wear it."

Cora didn't get a chance to reply as Tallyn began tallying up their purchases. They left with bulging paper bags, following Reluraun's steady clip once again.

As they emerged into the blinding sunlight, Theo silently took her bag. His fingers lingered over hers, leaving trails of warmth across her skin. Cora rubbed her fingers together, heat crackling beneath her fingers like a living flame. She'd never felt this sensation before, not even when Callan had touched her.

Cora swallowed down a lump of guilt. One more thing she'd have to face when she returned.

Reluraun gave a thorough tour of Stony Hollow. By the afternoon, Cora knew where most everything was. Passing through the shops and houses reminded her of her nightly wanderings back in Narous. It gave her a sense of familiarity, even with the quieter, slower pace of Stony Hollow.

Reluraun led them away from the center of town, toward two larger buildings off by themselves. He pointed to the one on the left, a canvas bag of groceries swinging from his shoulder.

"That's the infirmary. Gods willing, you won't spend much

132

time there."

It was the largest building Cora had seen so far. Shaped like a long rectangle with neat rows of windows, it watched over the rest of Stony Hollow. Squat bushes flanked the double doors while tiny tufts of grass poked through the cracks in the pavement.

Reluraun veered toward the building on the right. It looked like the infirmary's younger cousin, but with long strands of wires snaking between windows and around doors. A slight humming came from the building, pressing on Cora's eardrums like a swarm of bees.

"I'll meet you later," Gray said from behind her. "I have an errand to run."

Reluraun twisted to watch Gray head over to the infirmary door, a knowing twinkle in his eye. Cora raised an eyebrow, but Reluraun said nothing. Instead, he yanked open the door in front of them, stepping over thick cables running across the threshold. Cora and Theo followed, the door swinging closed behind them with a soft click.

Inside, the building was a labyrinth of desks. The edges of the room were dim and cluttered with spare cables and papers, while the center of the room glowed from the light of active holo-screens. Each screen was set to a different stream, most of them muted or kept at a low volume. And connecting everything was a web of wires and cables. They snaked along the floor and ceiling and clumped under desks.

There were only one or two elves sitting in front of the screens, mixed into a collection of sprites and humans. None of them looked a day over twenty-five. They barely acknowledged Cora as she followed Reluraun toward the back of the room. She had to duck a few times to avoid bumping into bundles of cables.

Reluraun led them up a short flight of stairs to an upper story. The cables continued up as well, winding around the banister and edging the ceiling. The constant humming was starting to wear on Cora, her skull vibrating at the same frequency. Theo and Reluraun didn't seem to notice. Reluraun paused at the top of the stairs and twisted toward them.

"I know you want to keep your identity quiet," he murmured.

"But if anyone would benefit from knowing who you are, it's Siraye. No information comes in or out of Stony Hollow without her knowledge."

A sense of trepidation stole over Cora as they opened the door at the top of the stairs. The room on the other side was even more cluttered than the one below. Stacks of boxes reached to the ceiling, neatly labeled in a language Cora didn't recognize. Bundles of cables thick as ropes snaked every direction, disappearing behind one stack of boxes and reappearing a few stacks down the line. A handful of desks sat scattered across the floor, their work surfaces covered with bits of tech in varying states of assembly.

Her foot snagged on a roll of wires, sending her off-balance. A warm hand cupped her arm, pulling her upright. Cora sent Theo a grateful smile before moving away. Her flush was absolutely from embarrassment, nothing else.

Reluraun led them to the back wall of the room. She rounded a stack of boxes, squinting against the brightness. While the rest of the room was dim and packed, the back third had been cleared for a massive desk facing a bank of screens spanning the entire wall. A different stream played on each screen in the grid. Most were news casts, one or two were weather prediction channels, and the bottom right-hand corner was streaming some sort of soap opera.

Sitting in front of the desk, an open package of chips in her lap, was a willowy elf with white-blonde hair.

Cora was struck by how young she seemed. She usually had a hard time placing any given elf's age, but Siraye had a youthful roundness to her cheeks and a playful glimmer in her blue eyes. Her hair fell down her back in a loose braid, the tops of her pointed ears peeking through. Earrings studded the length of her ears and dangled from her lobes, making a faint tinkling sound as she turned her head.

She spun her chair away from the desk to greet them. Cora didn't recognize the band on her shirt, but she made a mental note to ask Siraye where she got her stretchy pants from.

"Hello, Reluraun. Who do you have with you?"

"Grayson's friends, Theo and Cora. They'll be staying with us

134

for a while."

Siraye bounced to her feet and extended a long-fingered hand to Theo. Her eyes scanned up and down in a way that made Cora take a step closer. Theo released her hand quickly. Siraye rotated to shake Cora's hand.

A flash of recognition lit her eyes. "Cora, was it?"

"Yes, my name is Cora."

Siraye nodded, giving her hand a little squeeze in understanding. Cora smiled, forgiving the feral look she had given Theo.

Siraye sank back into her desk chair and threw her arms wide. "Welcome to the Hub! The technological and informational center of Stony Hollow."

"Did your cable management guy quit?" Theo nodded to the nest of wires on the ceiling.

Siraye chuckled. "We don't have the infrastructure of some of Liskow's big cities, so it's taken some creativity on my end. It got out of hand pretty quickly."

"Maybe I can help you streamline at some point."

"You good with tech?"

Cora forced her face to remain neutral at the eagerness in Siraye's tone. Her eyes met Cora's for a split second, and another understanding passed between them. Siraye scooted away from the edge of her chair, putting more space between her and Theo.

"I graduated from tech school last year," Theo said, completely oblivious to their exchange. "I could help you optimize what you've got here."

"I'll take you up on that. I've trained everyone here, but I'm mostly self-taught. I might have to get you to teach some trainings for my whole team."

"What exactly do you do here?" Cora interjected.

Siraye shifted to give her full attention to Cora. She swept her arm over the massive bank of screens on the wall. "Monitoring, surveillance, security." She leaned back in her chair, hands behind her head. "I'm basically Stony Hollow's spymaster."

Reluraun rolled his eyes, breath huffing out in a soft snort.

Siraye shot him a half-hearted glare. "Don't pretend I'm not,

135

, Reluraun. How else would I know that Gray and his friends flew in on a dragon?"

"By looking up at the sky when they arrived."

"Or it could be my new monitors that alert when anything larger than an eagle flies over Stony Hollow."

"What's with all the holo- streams?" Theo cut in, drawing Siraye's attention from the scowling Reluraun.

"Stony Hollow maintains a certain level of, let's just call it 'anonymity.' There's an entire section of our population with active warrants out for their arrest. Among other things, I have scripts combing the holo- streams for mentions of our most wanted citizens."

"How are you able to shelter them here?" Cora asked, brows lowering. "Aren't you legally required to turn them in?"

"We're a sovereign state inside the borders of Liskow. It is up to our discretion how we handle anyone here with warrants in other countries. If they leave, however, it's out of our hands."

"Don't you need to trade? There's no way you're manufacturing everything you need," Cora mused.

"We have a select few trade partners," Reluraun cut in, shooting Siraye a sharp glare. "With contracts to maintain our privacy."

"So you hide out here in the mountains and Liskow ignores you?"

"Pretty much," Siraye agreed. "We stay in the background, live our lives in peace. I scan the holo- networks for whispers of Stony Hollow or its citizens, or for potential threats to our safety. My team covers the lighter topics: weather predictions, celebrity gossip, entertainment, etc."

"It's an impressive setup, that's for sure," Theo said appreciatively, taking in the bank of screens.

"Thank you! It's taken me the better part of a decade to get it here."

"Whatever did we do before," Reluraun drawled.

It was Siraye's turn to roll her eyes. "Rely on patchy gossip gathered every few weeks from our contacts in Liskow. What a brilliant system."

136

"Well, we'd best be going," he said, already heading toward the door. "We don't want to take you from your work."

"Before you go." Siraye pulled open a desk drawer and produced two holo-bracelets. "These are already connected to the local network. Everyone in town has one of my holos, preprogrammed with everyone's contact code, and a few of my personal upgrades."

"Thank you," Cora murmured.

"Nice to meet you Cora, Theo! I'll see you around!"

Cora barely had time to call out a goodbye before Reluraun shepherded them back onto the staircase. Siraye had already turned to her screens before the door closed behind them.

15

Gray kept a hand on his bag as he entered the infirmary. He didn't bother checking the battery on the portable incubator; he knew it was at two percent. He followed the only hallway to the very end, steeling himself. He couldn't put this off any longer.

He stopped in front of the heavy door and peered through the window. Of course she was still here.

Gray knocked loudly. Swift footsteps sounded on the other side, then the door swung open.

Dr. Isolde Waylen beamed at him. Long auburn hair fell over her shoulder in its customary braid. Freckles splashed across a straight nose and framed hazel eyes. She pulled him into a hug, the tip of her pointed ear brushing his jaw.

"Gray, you're home!"

He let his arms wrap around her. Her usual scent was masked by sharp antiseptic and hand sanitizer, but he caught just a hint of it as she pulled away. Lavender and mint tickled his nose, tightening his stomach.

Gray's hands dropped to his sides. "How are you, Isolde?"

"Oh, you know." Isolde waved her hand in a broad gesture. "Same as always. But you! With that scruff and satchel, you look straight out of an adventure novel."

Gray chuckled and rubbed the back of his neck. "I'll take that as a compliment."

"Oh, you should."

He was silent for a beat, unsure.

Isolde grabbed his arm, pulling him over the threshold. "What brings you to the lab? Surely it isn't little old me?"

138

Gray sighed and leaned back against a steel table. He reached into his bag and pulled out the portable incubator and egg.

Isolde trailed a finger down the glass. "Well, it's been a very long time since I've seen one of those."

"I know your incubators aren't calibrated for dragon eggs, but I was hoping—"

"Absolutely," the cut him off. "I think we can make it work."

She moved to the back corner of the room, Gray trailing behind. She tapped the screen on the lab's incubator and carefully adjusted the settings. He watched with a growing tightness in his chest. Isolde changed the last input just as the portable incubator died.

Gray removed the egg and placed it into the lab incubator. His fingers lingered, tracing the top of the egg. Isolde made a point not to stare, uncharacteristically silent. Finally, he pulled back, and the chamber sealed with a soft hiss.

"I was hoping we could keep this between us." Gray's voice was husky.

Isolde laid a hand on his arm. "Of course."

Gray glanced down at her long fingers. Isolde eased closer, her eyes jade in the bright light. She reached her other hand up to brush the top of his ears. Not quite pointed, but not round. Gray gently grasped her wrist, pulling her hand away from his face.

"Why do you push me away?" she whispered. "You know I don't care that you're only half-elf."

"I care, Izzy."

Isolde's lips quirked into a sad smile. "You haven't called me that since you were a boy."

Gray gave her a flat look. "Yes, when you used to babysit me."

He pulled back, heading for the door. Her voice rang in the empty lab.

"Do you know how many elves have *hundreds* of years in age gaps?"

"You know that isn't the issue."

"Then what is?"

Gray paused with his hand on the door handle. He saw her reflection in the window of the door. The longing on her face made his stomach clench.

Gray swung back around. "I want someone to grow old alongside me, Isolde. To be with me until the end. I won't ask you to watch me die, only to keep living for centuries after."

Isolde crossed the room as he spoke, eyes glistening. She clasped his hand with both of hers. "I would cherish any amount of time with you, Gray. It doesn't matter how long that is."

"It matters to me."

Gray pulled his hand from hers and left without looking back.

Theo couldn't stop thinking about his conversation with Cora in the shop. He'd never been so bold with her before. But seeing her holding the tunic that made her eyes shimmer like a freshwater pond, he'd let down the wall between them, just a little.

He knew why the wall existed. It was their silent agreement, their mutual understanding that they were friends, nothing more. That they *couldn't* be more. Even if Cora weren't the crown princess, Theo would keep her at arm's length away. If the past few years had taught him anything, it was that he always lost the people he loved the most. And after his reunion with Rolph, he refused to give the Red Gryphons any chance at harming Cora.

Theo walked into the room he shared with Gray to find it empty. Gray hadn't returned from his errand yet. Theo dropped his bag of clothes at the end of the pull-out cot. It looked like Gray had found some sheets and a pillow for him, after Theo practically forced him to take the bed.

Theo quickly arranged the sheets, then sank onto the soft blanket. He glanced over at the windowsill where he'd left his holo. It was blinking. He opened the waiting message, his heart rate picking up.

Did you get to Gray's grandpa's house? You're starting to worry me. Your nieces say hello.

Yes, we got here fine. I'm sorry I didn't check in already. How was the train?

Theo didn't expect his mother to respond right away, but within seconds his holo lit up again.

Long and uncomfortable. But the views! You've got to come visit, Theo.

How are Isla and the girls?

Your sister is so busy! Her fabric store supplies half of the fashion designers here, and the girls are so big. You should call them sometime.

Theo frowned at the message. Isla had never forgiven him for what happened. He remembered vividly what she'd said. How he should have stopped Lane, talked him out of it, or forced him not to go. That if Lane would've listened to anyone, it was Theo. Then Lane would still be alive.

Mentally, he knew there was no stopping Lane. That if Lane hadn't gone, much worse would've happened to their family. But in his heart, Theo agreed with her. He knew Mom meant well, but he couldn't face Isla again. Not yet.

I'm glad you're enjoying yourself. Tell them I say hello.

I will. How's Cora doing?

She's fine. She's been through a lot.

Give her a hug for me. Talk to you soon. Love you.

Love you, too.

Theo set his holo back on the windowsill and lay on top of his cot. He stared up at the ceiling, finding a bit less tension in his body. His mom was safe, happy.

His mind caught on her request to hug Cora for her. He pictured folding Cora into his arms, close to his body. Something stirred within him, and his imagination progressed, picturing her arms around him, her lips pressing against his.

Theo sat up, passing a hand over his face. He definitely would *not* be doing that.

Yet when he fell asleep that night, he dreamed of kissing Cora, again and again.

Cora slept fitfully that night. She'd startle awake in the night, unable to remember where she was. Then she'd roll back over and toss and turn. When the sun began to drench the walls of her room, she sat up and rubbed her eyes. She swore she'd felt Makari in her mind a few times, but she couldn't piece together what was reality and what was the misty remnants of broken dreams. She swung her face toward the window, drinking in the warm morning light.

The room was the smallest she could ever remember sleeping in. If she lay down on the worn rug, she could likely touch both the bed and the wardrobe across from it. Hanging plants trailed from the curtain rod down to the narrow dresser under the window, casting shadows across the floor.

Cora pushed herself off the bed and crossed to the freshly filled wardrobe. She'd barely finished dressing when a soft knock echoed against her door.

"Cora, are you up?"

Theo's voice held a sleepy edge that made her ears burn. She shoved off the sudden embarrassment.

Don't be silly.

"Yes, I'm awake."

"Reluraun said he has one last thing to show us. We're meeting him out in the yard right now."

Cora's stomach let out a soft grumble, her lips pulling down into a pout. Hopefully whatever Reluraun wanted to show them wouldn't take long.

Theo was still there when she opened the door. A laugh bubbled up as she took in his outfit.

He glanced down at the purple shirt. "Well, now I feel self-conscious."

"No, you look great! Really, no jokes."

"I've heard that before."

"I mean it this time." Cora laid a hand over her heart, arranging her face into a serious expression. "I promise."

A slice of sunlight fell across his eyes, turning them into molten pools of honey. She hadn't realized she'd stepped closer to him. Something flickered in the depths of his eyes that set her heart pounding. She sensed that she was standing on a cliff, flirting with

142

the edge. If she stepped too far, she'd fall. And she wasn't sure she'd ever get back up again.

"Well, good," he murmured. "I'd hate to disappoint you."

"Right," she muttered, stepping around him. "Do you think Reluraun has food out there?"

He chuckled, following her out the front door. Reluraun and Gray stood in the yard, tossing food to Makari. A contented hum filled the back of her mind. Makari easily snapped bits of meat from the air, eyes half-closed as she soaked in the sunshine.

Reluraun turned as they approached. He reached into a basket at his feet, tossing two round objects over his shoulder at them.

Cora reached up, but it sailed over her head. Theo caught them both, handing one back to her. It was a roll, perfectly golden and warm. The scent of butter and yeast filled her nose as she leaned in for a bite. She was pleasantly surprised to find the middle bursting with eggs and sausage. She finished it before they reached Gray and Reluraun. Wordlessly, Theo reached into the basket and handed her another one.

"Did you sleep alright?" Gray asked her.

She heard what he didn't say. Her room was right next to the one he shared with Theo, and her bed creaked when she moved.

She forced a thin smile. "Well enough."

Gray nodded, tossing Makari another scrap of meat. Reluraun waited until they finished eating before gesturing for everyone to follow. Makari sprawled in the sun as he led them away from Stony Hollow, toward the mountain slope.

They followed a narrow dirt trail up steep switchbacks. They took frequent breaks for Cora and Theo to avoid getting lightheaded. Even Gray struggled to maintain Reluraun's steady pace. They hiked for about a half-mile before reaching a flat stretch of stone sheltered by a small overhang. Lichen grew along the stone, following the path of bumps and divots.

As they drew closer, Cora realized that there were carvings under the little plants, worn down by time. Reluraun trailed his fingers over them until he found what he was looking for. A loud grinding grated against her eardrums as he pulled back a latch, then the rock face split down the middle and swung inward. .

143

Reluraun stood in the doorway, his eyes shining. "I haven't been here in many, many years," he whispered. "I think it's finally time."

Gray reached into the bag slung across his shoulders to produce three flashlights. Cora and Theo each took one, sending beams of light slicing into the darkness beyond the doors. Reluraun stepped over the threshold, his footsteps echoing on the smooth stone floor.

They walked down a short hallway into a huge cavern. Sunlight shone in narrow beams through the wall across from them. Three tiers of carved stone doorways jutted into the cavern, open to the air. To their right was another short hallway identical to the one they'd entered from, while to their left were four hallways leading deeper into the mountains.

Cora spun slowly, taking in the room. Her toe connected with a small stone, sending it skittering across the open space. She looked down, sweeping the beam of her flashlight across the floor. Beneath a thick layer of dust was a tile mosaic of a dozen dragons in flight, each bearing a Rider.

"What is this place?"

"This is Aurestyn." Reluraun's rich voice echoed through the still cavern. "An ancient Dragon Rider city. One of the first."

She spotted dull paintings against the walls. They were little more than impressions of color under the dust and dark.

"There were many Rider cities, once. They were beacons of learning, of trade, of peace. Many disputes were settled in their halls." Reluraun's gaze swept over the mural at their feet. "Then the Nine Guards seized control of the Riders and centralized their power in Liskow. The Rider cities were reduced to outposts and watchtowers, with only a single squadron of Riders left in them. Until the Bjorns took power." He didn't look at her, but Cora felt the sting of his pain. "They destroyed any Rider city they could find, slaughtering anyone they could get their hands on. Our sanctuaries turned into tombs within a matter of months."

Reluraun finally looked up at her. His eyes held an anguish that squeezed her heart until she couldn't breathe.

"I was there when Njal attacked. I watched my city fall, watched my friends bleed and die defending it. My own dragon

144

refused to leave his mate, even after she fell. He held off the attackers so that I could escape with the wounded. I spent years in hiding, until I came here. I helped found Stony Hollow to protect Aurestyn, to give us a sanctuary again."

Tears rolled down her cheeks as he spoke. Reluraun's own face was wet. He didn't bother wiping it.

"I've made peace with my past," he continued gruffly. "But I want to make something very clear. When you enter these halls, you leave your past behind. You are no longer a Bjorn, no longer a princess. You are a Rider. You are a symbol of strength, of peace, of hope. Are you ready to begin?"

Cora looked around the cavern again with fresh eyes. She looked at the face of each Rider in the mosaic on the floor.

A soft scraping echoed from the balconies above them. Cora looked up to see Makari watching her. A powerful thrum resonated down the bond, filling her mind.

She turned back to look directly at Reluraun. "I'm ready."

Theo *felt* something when Cora looked back at Reluraun. Power emanated from her in that moment, singing in his blood like an insistent hum. It was infectious. He fought the urge to bounce on his feet as Reluraun led them around Aurestyn.

Reluraun showed them the ancient library, which was vandalized some time before he discovered the Rider city. They briefly visited the living quarters and the baths, then they explored the training rooms. There were several sparring rings, rows of practice dummies along the walls, and an armory full of ancient weapons and leather pads of every shape and size. Before they left, Reluraun began Cora's first lesson, making her practice her stance and a few movements with empty hands again and again. To Theo and Gray's chagrin, he'd made them participate as well.

Afterwards, they went up to the aerie to prepare a nest for Makari. It took them nearly the rest of the day to get it ready, after the dragon finally deemed one of the cave-like rooms worthy. They had to scrub centuries of dirt and grime off the walls and remove the dessicated carcasses of some unfortunate animals. Then they had to haul fresh straw all the way up from Stony Hollow for

Makari to bed down in. By late afternoon, Theo was sweaty, tired, and itchy.

They all basically collapsed after dinner, not saying a word to each other. Now, the enormity of what they'd undertaken loomed before him. Cora was determined, yes, but inexperienced. Theo would be starting her training from the absolute beginning.

A thought tickled the depths of Theo's mind, one that he refused to let rise to the surface. The training rooms reminded him vividly of the boxing gym he'd once gone to with Lane. And thoughts of his brother inevitably led to memories of the one night he wished he could forget. He shoved those thoughts down, let them be drowned out by a different one.

This is a bad idea.

The thought was on a constant loop in Theo's mind. He bounced on his toes in Reluraun's front yard the next morning, waiting for Cora to emerge. Reluraun managed to find an assortment of workout equipment. They had weights from five to fifty pounds, jump ropes, even boxing gloves and pads.

Theo gave the boxing equipment a wide berth. Just brushing his fingers against the hand wraps brought him back to long nights in the ring. He still felt the impact of hitting an opponent's face reverberate up his arm. The rush of adrenaline as he drove another fighter across the ring. The surge of satisfaction as an opponent dropped to the floor. Theo shared that insatiable need for victory with Lane. It was the reason his brother was gone.

The front porch creaked, bringing Theo back to the present. Cora stumbled down the steps, rubbing her eyes. Her steps were heavy with sleep, the planes of her face soft and open. Her hair was ruffled, short strands sticking at odd angles. Theo realized he'd never seen her first thing in the morning. A quiet voice in his mind whispered that he wouldn't mind seeing her first thing *every* morning. Theo smothered that voice.

"Not a morning person, huh?" He asked.

Cora shot him a groggy glare. He laughed, earning him a smack on the arm.

"Let's just get started before I change my mind."

Theo showed Cora how to warm up, his own muscles

146

protesting. He recovered quickly, his body responding to the movements. She groaned and muttered as she moved, only able to stretch half as far as he could. This was going to be more work than he thought.

Theo adjusted tack. He kept their workout simple, taking time to show her proper form. Slowly, the sleep drained from her eyes. Her face flushed, sweat glistening at her hairline. She copied his movements precisely, pausing only when she needed to wipe sweat from her face. Her chest heaved as she fought to keep pace with him, but she never complained.

Theo called it before they hit an hour. He folded his body into a stretch. Cora struggled to copy him, sweat dripping into her eyes.

"No, like this."

Without thinking, Theo straightened towards her. His fingers glided over her, adjusting her posture. He pulled his fingers back and looked up to find her eyes only a hand's breadth from him.

Cora stared at him, her flush deepening. Her eyes dipped down to his lips, just for a split second. His pulse pounded in his ears.

They stayed there for a beat too long, unwilling to move.

Theo cleared his throat, forced himself to move back. "That should be enough for today." His voice was hoarse. "Don't want to wear you out too much."

Cora's eyes followed him as he headed back into the house. He went straight into the bathroom to take a cold shower.

Cora spent the next few days in a blur. She woke early each morning to train with Theo, then met with Gray to work on bonding with Makari. After lunch was training with Reluraun, and in between was a constant stream of work.

Everyone was expected to work in Stony Hollow. She weeded gardens, picked produce, fed livestock, counted inventory. Anywhere an extra set of hands was needed, she was there, often alongside Theo and Gray. She'd already learned so many people's names.

Cora welcomed the work. She was so sore and tired at the end of each day that she was asleep as soon as her head touched her pillow. It kept the nightmares at bay and distracted her from thoughts of Arik. For a while. Soon, she'd have to face the hard knot of emotions curled in her gut.

When her mind wasn't full of training, she found her thoughts drifting back to Narous. Arik was still missing. Siraye and her team gave daily highlights from the holo- networks, and the trending stories were still theories on what had happened to him and Cora.

Occasionally she caught snippets of Callan on the holo-streams while she bustled around town. In quiet moments she remembered those intense blue eyes staring into her soul. A hazy sense of guilt curdled her stomach, mixed with gratitude for how he'd stepped up in her absence. If the holo- streams were to be believed, Father was leaning on Callan to keep things running.

At the end of her fifth day in Stony Hollow, Cora found herself alone in Reluraun's house. She powered on his holo- screen and browsed the networks. She paused as a story flashed across the screen. Several arrests were just made of suspected PEL members. The Watchers claimed they were there the night of the gala, both in the palace and on the streets. Their families claimed they were innocent. A few had tried to run from the Watchers. One was in the hospital.

Cora shut off the network, her hands shaking. The walls seemed to press inward, cutting off her air. She shot to her feet and fled to the bathroom. Maybe a shower would help. She cranked the hot water until the bathroom mirror was coated in steam. She stood under the stream, willing the water to drown out her thoughts.

She stayed just long enough to stop trembling. Water droplets followed behind as she padded to her room and dressed. Cora pulled on the green tunic, the soft fibers gliding under her fingers. The scent of clean wool grounded her in the present. She would get to the bottom of the mess back home when she returned. For now, she could only focus on fixing the gnawing in her belly.

Cora walked through the too quiet house, stopping in the kitchen doorway. So far, Reluraun had cooked for them every night. But tonight he'd been called away to a meeting of some sort. He'd been vague about the details, but Gray revealed it was a long-standing dice game with some of the other town elders. She wasn't sure where Gray or Theo were.

She twisted the hem of her tunic between her fingers. She knew the kitchen was full of ingredients. The problem was, she'd never cooked anything in her life.

Her stomach growled loudly. There was one other place she could go.

Cora abandoned the kitchen to pull on her boots. The sun was sinking below the tops of the mountains, casting long shadows. She didn't mind the dim lighting. Her eyes adjusted quickly, sharp enough for her to avoid the growing pothole in the road. She wove between houses and stores, following the strengthening smell of food. She didn't recognize the spices in the air, but she recognized the tangy smell of yeast. She followed her nose to the dining hall, a large rectangular building near the center of town.

A few others trailed in front of her, letting a slice of bright light out as they opened the door. Cora slipped in behind them, salivating at the aroma wafting through the building. Most of the open space was filled with rows of tables and benches. A line of people snaked along the edges of the room toward the back, where a long counter stretched, covered in steaming dishes. She joined the back of the line, impatiently shuffling along behind those in front of her.

She craned her neck to peer at the dishes, scowling at the back of the tall elf in front of her. She snatched a plate and silverware from a waiting table. She resisted the urge to tap her fingers against the ceramic bottom. Finally, it was her turn. She gazed down the row of serving dishes. She saw red sauces studded with pieces of meat and tomato, yellow stews teeming with fresh herbs, a nearly endless array of cooked vegetables, and several pans of white, fluffy rice.

"You're Cora, right?"

She started, tearing her eyes away from the feast. A young sprite stood on the other side of the counter. His bright red hair stuck up at the ends, while his green eyes nearly matched his translucent wings. They shifted with a slight buzzing sound.

"I'm Reed," he said, releasing his large serving spoon to extend a hand.

Cora shook it quickly. Her eyes fell back down to the food in front of her. "What smells so good?"

"Have you never had curry?"

Cora shook her head.

Reed's eyes lit up, and he eagerly wielded his spoon. He took her plate and began filling it, chatting away as he did. At the end of the bar, he grabbed two pieces of soft flatbread and added them to her nearly overflowing plate. Cora thanked him, making sure to hold the plate with both hands. She spun toward the half-full tables, intending to take the closest seat and wolf down her food.

A shock of black curls on top of a tall head caught her eye first. Theo. She wove through the maze of benches to slide into the spot next to him.

"This must be the famous Cora." A gruff voice said.

Three elves sat around Theo, nearly as tall and broad as he was. Next to Theo sat a male elf nursing a mug of ale, by the smell. His straight, dark hair flopped into his eyes. A long, pale scar ran down the side of his neck, disappearing into his shirt. It stood out starkly against tan skin. He watched her with eyes glimmering with mischief.

Across from Theo sat a female was idly pushing grains of rice around her empty plate with one umber finger, an amused expression on her face. Tight curls were contained to a bun at the crown of her head. Her dark eyes slid across Theo's face, a smile tugging the corners of her lips to reveal a flash of bright white teeth.

Next to her was a male almost unrecognizable as an elf besides his pointed ears. He held none of the carefully crafted grace that Cora had come to associate with elves. Scruff covered his jaw and cheeks, broken in a few places by pale scars. Unkempt waves of brown hair were tied into a short knot behind his head. His clothes were sturdy but frayed around the edges. And nearly every bit of exposed skin was scarred. Cora fought the urge to stare at his hands where they wrapped around his mug. She'd never seen so many scars on so little skin before.

"I didn't realize that I was famous." Cora replied.

"Word spreads fast in a small town," the scarred elf said. "That and just about everyone has seen your dragon by now."

She nodded, mouth full. The elf next to Theo leaned forward and caught the attention of the she-elf.

"That reminds me, Daethie." His eyes sparkled. "It looks like we're getting married."

She choked on her drink, droplets splattering the table in front of her. "Excuse me?"

"The last time I asked when you were going to marry me, you said when the Dragon Riders returned. So…"

"You're an idiot."

The last elf shook his head, facing Cora. His low voice was like boulders scraping against each other. "Don't mind them. Daethie will never admit it, but she's got a soft spot for Orym here."

"I do not!"

"Then why have you been putting up with him for the last century and a half, eh? I'm Phaendar, by the way."

Cora nodded again, mouth still full. She was only a quarter of the way through what Reed gave her, but her mouth was burning. She swallowed and reached over to steal Theo's water. She chugged it as the elves started chuckling.

"I guess I'll get us more water," Theo laughed, snatching both empty glasses off the table.

"First time having curry?" Orym shuckled. "You must be from the valley, then."

Cora tracked Theo as he left, swiping at her running nose. "It's delicious, but I'm going to need more water."

That earned her another chuckle. She pulled off another piece of flatbread as the elves nursed their drinks.

"I'm glad to finally be across from another Dragon Rider," Daethie commented. "Maybe we'll see the end of those blasted Northerners. And their blazing monarchy."

"That would be the day," Phaendar agreed. "Maybe I'll actually set foot in Narous again."

Cora had to swallow hard around her suddenly tight throat. "Why can't you set foot in it now?"

"Because we're war criminals," Orym answered, taking a long swig from his mug. "And we're still wanted."

"I thought everyone was pardoned."

151

Daethie's eyes glinted wickedly. "Most were. But we gave those barbarians hell. I heard Njal had nightmares of us until he died."

"It wouldn't matter if we had been pardoned," Phaendar growled. "Those drowning mudwalkers have no respect for anyone but themselves. I hope their precious prince and princess are never found."

Cora had never been more relieved to see Theo. He set two large glasses of water on the table and began talking animatedly. She didn't hear what he said, timidly scooping up more curry. Her appetite had all but vanished. She forced herself to clear most of her plate before excusing herself.

Gray trudged away from the gates of Aurestyn, rubbing bleary eyes. He had hoped to find breeding records in the ancient library, but so far all he'd accomplished was clearing out enough debris to move around the space. It had taken hours to sort through the rubble. Several bookcases had collapsed, covering their books in layers of wood and dust. He'd had to keep stopping to pluck splinters out of his hands. He was fairly certain there were still a few stuck in his skin, but he was too tired to care.

Gray paused on the path outside Grandpa Reluraun's house. No lights pierced the gathering shadows. The only sound was the swaying of herbs in the soft breeze. He knew he should go in and wash the dust out of his hair. Instead, he headed into town. Gray stepped to the side as a petite silhouette emerged from the dark.

"Hey, Gray." Cora paused on the road. "Where have you been?"

"Cleaning out Aurestyn's library. Do you want dinner?"

A shadow fell over her face. She shifted on her feet, moving away from Stony Hollow. "I just had some. Thanks though. Good night."

She hustled away before Gray finished his own "good night." Cora didn't often share her emotions, but something was clearly troubling her. He frowned, foreboding settling in his chest. Maybe he'd be able to tease it out of her during training tomorrow.

Gray continued on his way, cutting through back streets and a few manicured yards to reach the dining hall. He smelled it before the door even opened. He took the worn wooden steps two at a time, exchanging greetings with people leaving as he slipped in. He nodded to Theo as he stepped into the line.

Within a few moments his plate was heaped with food. Orym waved him over to take the place Theo had just vacated. Gray settled onto the creaky bench, spoon in hand before his plate was fully on the table.

"You look awful," Daethie said over the rim of her mug.

"Yeah." Orym pinched Gray's sleeve between his thumb and forefinger. "Did you get a job at the mill or something?"

Gray swallowed before pulling his sleeve away from Orym. "I've been cleaning the library in Aurestyn."

Orym let out a low whistle. "So the old man finally let you in, eh?"

"Show a little respect," Phaendar rumbled from across the table. "That 'old man' is still a Dragon Rider."

"Yeah, and he used to assign me the worst jobs."

"You're just still mad that he caught you in the barn with Glassinda," Daethie said.

"Can we please not?" Gray said, louder than he intended.

"Sorry, Gray," Orym muttered apologetically. "But if it makes you feel any better, your mom was a great—ow!"

Daethie glared, ready to kick him again. Gray shot her a grateful look.

Phaendar leaned forward, studying Gray's face. "What do you think of the new Rider?"

"Cora's got something special about her. I felt it when we first met."

"Do you think she has what it takes?"

"Do you? You've been around more Riders than me."

Phaendar rubbed a hand over his beard, considering. He glanced at Orym and Daethie. "Things were…messy, at the end. It was getting harder to separate the good Riders from the bad, even before the invasion. What do you two think?"

"Well, I only saw female Riders in certain contexts," Orym said. "I'd have to take her out to the old barn to compare… *Would you stop kicking me?"*

Daethie took another pull from her mug, blatantly ignoring him. She looked between Phaendar and Gray as she thought. "She seems quiet. Not a bad thing, in my opinion." She shot a sidelong look at Orym. "Girl's a workhorse, though. From what I hear she's going from sunup to sundown, training and working around Stony Hollow."

Phaendar frowned, hand in his beard again. "She's got work ethic, I'll give you that. I don't know, there's just something about her that's bothering me."

"Are you bothered, or are you just not ready to serve the Riders again?" Daethie asked shrewdly. "It's been a long time since anyone's expected anything from you."

"I, for one, am ready to serve again," Orym said, eyes glinting wickedly. "She can tell me exactly what to do—"

Orym snapped his mouth shut at Daethie's warning glance. Gray pushed aside his empty plate. He was just about ready to stand when Phaendar's eyes swung back to him.

"You're handling this well, kid."

"What do you mean by that?"

"You don't have to play dumb, Gray. Everyone here knows how much you've always wanted to be a Rider."

Gray breathed slowly through his nose. There it was again. He was tempted to just outright tell the elf that he wasn't so sure anymore. It wasn't worth the effort.

He leaned forward, his finger tapping the table as he spoke. "I'm fine. Cora is going to make a great Rider, and I'm *happy* for her. Besides, with the return of the Riders, it's more likely I'll find a dragon of my own."

Like the one currently in the infirmary's incubator.

Gray read the skepticism on Phaendar's face, but the grizzled elf didn't push it. Gray stood and bid them all a good night. As he walked out the dining hall doors, he didn't go home. He made his way across the dark town to the infirmary.

He circled around to the back door, entering the access code Isolde had given him. He wove between the cold metal tables of the lab, eager to check on the egg. The heat and humidity levels

154

were still good, at least.

He watched the tiny dragon shift inside the shell long into the night.

Gray was up early the next morning. He waved to Theo and Cora in the front yard on his way to Aurestyn. He passed through the front doors, over the mosaic floor, and down into the mountain. His footsteps were the only sound as he followed the rightmost hallway to an intersection. He turned right down a short hallway and into the library.

The stone chamber stretched out like a long rectangle in front of Gray. The right side of the room was full of windows looking down the mountain into a green valley below. He had managed to clear the single remaining table in the room. A small stack of books sat on one corner—the ones he had salvaged from his cleanup efforts the day before. He'd scrounged up two usable chairs and set them next to the table.

To his left, the library stretched into darkness. Toppled bookcases blocked the way deeper into the library, while books lay scattered every which way, many trapped under rotting planks of wood.

Gray stared at the debris. Just looking at it made his fingers sting from all the splinters he'd removed. It could wait until tomorrow, when he actually remembered to bring gloves with him. He faced away from the mess and settled into one of the chairs at the table. It creaked ominously as he sat. He eased his weight down slowly, afraid it might collapse under him. It held.

Gray released a breath before taking the top book off the pile. Clouds of dust danced in the sunlight pouring through the windows. He eased open the first book, wincing at the sharp crack of old leather. A glance told him this book was an inventory of the city's pantry. He set that one aside. The next book was a clothing catalog, complete with sketches of available designs. Gray flipped through a few pages before setting that one aside as well.

The third book grabbed his attention immediately.

Rider bonds vary in strength and connection. Our scholars

155

scholars have been unable to determine a predictable cause of this variation. We only know that some Riders are able to connect so intimately with their dragons that they are essentially one creature. When observed, dragon and Rider's movements are perfect accents to one another. They flow like water, synchronous and majestic. Riders who have experienced this phenomenon have described it as an otherworldly state. It is as if they are at once in their own body and in their dragon's body. We must conclude this can only stem from divinity. And so we call them gods-blessed.

Gray flipped the page, frowning at the faded words. Half of the text was unreadable. He could make out a list of gods-blessed Riders, and what he could only assume were records of their feats. He paused to read another legible passage, tilting the book to better catch the light. He leaned back in his chair, looking out to the valley far below.

Grandpa Reluraun told him stories of gods-blessed Riders when he was younger. According to him, the very first Riders were all gods-blessed. It became increasingly rare as the Riders grew, until by the very end, it was virtually unheard of.

The soft scuff of a shoe just outside the library brought Gray's attention to the doorway. Cora peered in, a distinct slouch to her shoulders.

"Are you ready?"

His eyes skated over her, lingering on her posture. She'd been gaining confidence over the few days they'd been in Stony Hollow. Her Rider training was paying off as her edges lost their roundness, already showing signs of tightening into corded muscle. But whatever had rattled her last night was still evident in the way she carried herself today.

Gray shook himself, realizing he was staring. "Yeah, let me just put some of this away."

Cora came over to the table. She fingered the edge of the clothing catalog, taking in the sketches. "What are you reading about?"

Gray gently took the catalog from her, spinning the book he'd been reading so she could see it. He stacked the rest of his pile

156

while she read.

"Some Riders were so attuned to their dragons that they became one with them. Their pupils would turn slitted like a dragon's, and they would move in perfect sync with their dragons." He caught Cora's skeptical expression. "*Perfect* sync. Like watching one creature. They called them gods-blessed. According to that book, it was a sign that they had a true bond. That Elidi herself had orchestrated their bond. The most powerful Riders in history were gods-blessed."

"Do you believe in the gods, Gray?"

"Yes. Don't you?"

She looked away, out through the windows. Gray stayed quiet. If he'd learned anything from fieldwork, it was that patience was usually rewarded.

"I think they sound like a convenient way to justify anything you do."

"That's pretty cynical."

"Maybe."

Gray waited for her to say more, but this time his patience earned him nothing. Eventually, he shrugged and gestured to the doorway. "Let's find Makari, then."

Gray stayed at the edges of the training ring, observing Cora and Makari. They were in the caverns directly below the aerie. These rooms were large enough for multiple dragons to train in at once. Packed sand covered the cave floor, while obstacles were arranged on the ground and suspended in the air. Cora sat on Makari's back, a pouch of meat scraps clipped to her belt. She urged her over, around, and through obstacles, tossing her rewards when she obeyed.

Gray sat on a ledge carved from the stone wall, likely for observations like this. He watched as Makari resisted direction, often needing three or four attempts before doing what Cora asked. They completed the entire course before Makari returned to a clear section of ground in front of Gray. She flopped onto her belly, nearly throwing Cora off.

Cora scowled. "Obstinate reptile."

157

Makari snorted, her long tongue flicking out once before disappearing back into her mouth.

"You've got to be patient," he said. "You've been training for less than a week."

"And the more we train, the less motivated she is," Cora said, shaking her pouch for emphasis. "She doesn't even want the meat anymore."

"Maybe she wants something else as a reward."

"Like what?"

"I'm not sure." He leaned closer to Makari's spotted face. "You could try *asking* her."

Cora folded her arms, but her eyes unfocused. In response, Makari rolled onto her side. Cora leaped off before her leg could get pinned beneath the scaly side. The dragon stretched lazily, head faced away. Cora muttered a curse.

"I guess that means she wants a break." Gray said.

Cora glared at him, then sat down on the ledge with an exasperated huff.

Gray passed her a water bottle. "So, what's bothering you?"

"Besides the stubborn mass of lizard sh—"

"You know what I mean."

She took a long drink, avoiding his gaze. Gray half-expected her to change the subject or put on her diplomatic smile and shut him down. Instead, she leaned back against the cavern wall and met his stare.

"Everyone here is kind and welcoming. They always say hello or offer to help."

"But?"

"But if they knew who I was, they'd hate me."

He didn't contradict her.

Cora nodded, smiling wryly. "They would expect me to be just like the ancestors they fought centuries ago, even if I'm nothing like them. As is, they expect me to be and to act like the old Riders. I don't even know how to do that. Or if I want to."

"The return of the Riders *means* something to them, Cora. Those were their heroes."

"What were the Riders really like?"

158

Gray spread his hands. "I'm not the one to ask. Grandpa was a Rider. You should ask him."

She was already shaking her head. "I've already heard plenty from Reluraun. He likes to tell stories while he teaches," she added dryly. "He was in Narous, with the Nine Guards. Not exactly a good representation of what the Riders were."

"Then ask Phaendar, or Daethie, or Orym. Or any number of elves here."

"They all served the Nine Guards, Gray. Other than Reluraun, most of them weren't even *born* before they took power. And the ones that were weren't Riders, or close to them. According to everyone in Stony Hollow, *you* are the resident Rider expert."

Gray passed a hand over his face. He'd spent so many years reading every scrap of paper about the Riders, jotting down every story he was told about them. He knew Grandpa still had every single notebook he'd filled growing up. Even the ones he'd tried to get rid of. The sentimental old elf had them all stored in his attic.

"I can't tell you all that much about the early Riders." Gray sighed. "So little has survived from their founding. All I know is that they were formed by the goddess Elidi to defend the world from a great evil. They drove the evil back and brought peace and safety to the world. The goddess charged them to maintain that peace and safety. And then the gods went silent, and the Riders were left on their own.

"They couldn't all agree *how* they were meant to maintain peace and safety. Several factions formed among the Riders. Some became scholars, using their dragons as a way to travel the world and then recording what they learned. Some became advisors, often residing long-term in certain countries' courts. Some became nomads, traveling the world and offering help to whoever needed it. And some became mercenaries, some honorably, and others not."

"So what happened to them?" Cora pressed. She pointed a stern finger at Gray. "And don't give me that whole 'they angered the gods' line. What did they *do*?"

"From what I know, new Riders joined a faction based on their own personal philosophy. They existed like that for centuries. But, as time went on and some factions grew larger, they started fighting among themselves. The fighting grew progressively worse, and nine Riders saw an opportunity. They formed an alliance; they would work together to consolidate all the Riders into one group, with themselves as the leadership. And they were highly effective. Within ten years, the majority of the Riders were under their control.

"And that's where things started going downhill," Gray said, a familiar eagerness blooming like a fire lily in his chest. "The Nine Guards shared power decently well for the first three to five years. But as is to be expected, everyone wanted more power for themselves. They began jealously guarding breeding lines of dragons, and carefully monitoring new Riders. Only those who had been approved by the Nine Guards could even attempt a bond, and only with a Rider-bred dragon. Bonds with wild dragons were outlawed. Any unauthorized bonds were subject to execution."

A horrified expression settled across Cora's face.

He nodded grimly. "Both Rider and dragon were killed. The number of 'unauthorized' bonds I found was…unsettling, to say the least. Things devolved the longer the Nine Guards were in power. Assassinations were common, infighting was expected, and propaganda was plentiful," Gray said, then paused.

His own religious beliefs were tenuous at best, but Cora's? She didn't seem the devoted type.

"Look, you're not going to like hearing this, but here it is. Elidi was angry at what her Riders had become. They went from a force to protect the world from evil, to a handful of power-mad despots. The final nail in the coffin came when it was revealed that the breeding nests in Narous were taking entire clutches of eggs and turning them into powdered eggshell."

"Like you told us about that night at the duel?"

He nodded. "I don't know exactly what eggshells are supposed to do, but the claim is that they hold tiny traces of the gods' power. Consuming them is supposed to give you that power, whatever it means."

"So Elidi set out to destroy the thing she created?"

"I think you probably know that part of the story better than I

160

do."

Cora was quiet for a beat. She looked out at Makari, fingers twisting the ends of her hair. "The story I was told growing up is that a woman with fiery hair appeared to Njal Bjorn in a dream. She told him of a land across the sea, ready for him to conquer. She promised that if he journeyed with his bravest warriors, she would protect him."

"Protect him how?"

"You're really going to make me say it?" She faced him, eyes filled with pain, and guilt.

"I'm not going to make you do anything, Cora."

She barked out a wry laugh. "Why not? I've already betrayed my family by becoming the thing they set out to destroy. I might as well reveal a three-hundred-year-old family secret as well."

Gray's heart panged at the bitterness in her tone. What burdens had been laid on those young shoulders? Likely the same ones he'd felt himself. The legacies of their ancestors.

"Your family carries Elidi's Blessing."

"Yes, the direct descendants of Njal Bjorn are impervious to fire and heat."

"But no one else?"

"Not that I know of."

"Wow." Gray leaned back, mind reeling.

"What?"

"Just that, of all the people in the world, the one that is able to get close enough to bond a wild dragon is a Bjorn. That's gotta mean something."

"That the gods have a cruel sense of humor."

"Why are you so hard on yourself?"

She folded her arms, watching Makari shake sand off of her wings. Gray sensed that whatever door she'd opened for him was beginning to shut again. Just when he thought it was about to lock him out, Cora left it cracked.

"Because I can't afford to screw up, Gray. Too many people will get hurt if I do."

Cora left their ledge to climb onto Makari's back. Gray watched as they launched into the air, leaving him behind.

16

Callan rolled onto his side, blankets tangling in his legs.

A gentle hand skimmed along his forehead, pushing his hair back. He smiled, eyelashes fluttering open to a pair of pale green eyes staring at him. Catarina's long golden hair splayed on the pillow like a cape. He reached forward to tangle his fingers in the strands. Warmth pooled in his abdomen as their faces drifted closer.

Callan woke with a start. A tablet lay on the bed next to him where he'd dreamed of Catarina. The tiny wires that once nestled inside a princess's ceramic phoenix were plugged into the display port. The recording had paused on an image of Catarina curled in her own bed. She was so peaceful in sleep, like a maiden waiting for a kiss to wake her. He traced one finger over the curve of her lip. He wished he could feel her warm skin under his touch.

Reluctantly, he unplugged the wires and climbed out of bed. He was showered and dressed when a knock echoed against his bedroom door.

"Come in."

Daen gave him a crisp nod as he entered. He gave the rumpled bed a cursory glance, eyes catching on the wires still resting on top of the blankets. "Did something happen to the phoenix in the king's office?"

Callan followed his gaze, expression neutral. "It broke before I could make the swap," he said smoothly. "I was checking if there was any footage."

"Anything interesting?"

"No."

Daen had been at his side during the entire blood-soaked week before they'd taken Pyrus. He'd saved Callan's life multiple times. And yet, Callan refused to admit what he'd done. That he hadn't given Catarina the phoenix because he thought he'd learn something, but just because he wanted to know the true princess. What he'd recorded with the phoenix was just for him.

"Shame," Daen said, head swiveling away from the bed. "It's time to leave, unless you're trying to be late."

"Then let's not keep them waiting."

Callan followed Daen out to a waiting vehicle. He nodded to his men as he passed, replying to greetings called his way. The energy in the air was palpable. With the plan in motion, his men were eager to do their parts. All of the waiting in the guest wing had them chomping at the bit.

Daen opened the door for Callan, and he slipped into the sleek black car. The interior smelled of new leather. He settled back as Daen took the seat next to him. They sat in comfortable silence as the car rolled past the castle gate and into Narous. They navigated winding roads, past mansions and shops, until they were surrounded by towering skyscrapers. The glass panels reflected their car as they passed, as if a giant mirror trailed alongside them. They pulled up to a slightly shorter building with a scrolling holo-stream at the top.

Callan frowned at the video. He found most holo- streams to be nothing but inane gossip. Frivolous, but useful. He arranged his face into a polite smile as the car turned into a parking garage under the building. A small crowd of employees in crisp suits was waiting for him.

"You ready for this?" Daen asked quietly.

"Of course I am."

"Your brother asked me to remind you to avoid anymore... 'improvisation' is how he put it."

A flash of irritation shot through Callan. Nolan had a lot of opinions for someone who had spent the entirety of Galta's latest conflict miles away. "His concern is touching."

Daen chuckled darkly. "I'm just the messenger, sir. You know where I stand."

With that, Daen slipped out of the car. He circled around to open Callan's door.

Callan took a beat to school his expression before gliding out of the open door. He was quickly surrounded by the waiting crowd of employees. They whisked him into an elevator, which deposited them several floors up.

Callan followed their brisk pace onto a small sound stage. Several cameras and lights were trained on a set of cushioned chairs.

A short woman rose to greet him. She wore a white pantsuit and emerald-green blouse, the same shade as her translucent wings. She held out one ebony hand, gold bracelets tinkling as Callan shook it.

"Chancellor Byrne, it's a pleasure." Her rich voice resonated through the small space. "I'm Tara Brandlen."

"Thank you for having me." Callan pulled out his most charming smile.

Tara returned the smile, the slightest flush coloring her cheeks. She motioned for him to sit. Callan settled into the chair and was swarmed by a flurry of activity. A fluffy makeup brush swiped across his face while a microphone was clipped to his shirt. He blinked as a blinding light shone directly in his eyes.

"My assistant said she sent you the interview questions?" Tara asked.

"Yes, I've gone through them."

"Perfect! I may ask a follow-up here or there, but generally, I'll stick to those questions." Tara shuffled through a stack of note cards in her lap. "Have you ever been interviewed before?"

"Not like this."

Tara shot him a dazzling smile. Perfect white teeth flashed against deep red lips. She leaned forward, voice dropping. "Just pretend there's only you and me. And if you forget what you were going to say, just move on."

Callan returned her smile, casually crossing one leg over the other. The thrumming energy in his veins came from anticipation rather than nerves. Here was where months of planning started to pay off.

164

Everyone left the stage except for Callan and Tara. Blinking red lights appeared on the cameras, and all but the blazing spotlights dimmed.

Tara twisted to flash the camera her brilliant smile. "Hello and welcome to the *Brandlen Report*! I'm Tara Brandlen, here with Galta's new Chancellor, Callan Byrne." She gestured to him with one long-fingered hand. "Thank you for joining me today, Chancellor."

"Thank you for having me."

Tara's features dimmed into carefully arranged solemnity. "I just wanted to say thank you for keeping our interview, given the circumstances. How shocking was it, during the attack at the anniversary gala? Here you were, hoping for a break from conflict, and then you were just thrown right back in."

Callan matched her serious tone, a small frown creasing his forehead. "It was shocking, to say the least. It took me right back to the streets of Bilae. And just like in Bilae, I feel like I lost my comrades." He paused, allowing emotion to bleed into his words. "Maybe I could have saved Queen Eira, or prevented Princess Catarina and Prince Arik from disappearing."

"Is there any word on the prince and princess' whereabouts?"

"All I can say is that we're optimistic that both of them are safe, and we're doing everything in our power to bring them home."

"We?" Tara leaned forward, a gleam in her eyes. "So it's true that you are helping search for our missing royals?"

Callan nodded. "The Galtan Senate, my delegation, and I are helping in whatever ways we can here in Liskow."

"And is it true that you have…personal reasons for searching for Princess Catarina?"

"Well…" Callan inhaled deeply, letting the word linger as Tara waited with a ravenous expression. "Yes. I won't be able to rest until I see her again, safe and sound."

The words charged the air like a brewing thunderstorm. Tara looked into the camera with barely concealed glee. They both knew that within hours, this interview would be on every holo-stream.

165

Tara moved along into the rest of the questions they had prepared. Callan gave his answers, only half paying attention. He hoped Catarina would see, wherever she was, that she heard what he'd said. He meant every word.

Callan was sitting in the back of the car about an hour later. He waited until the door closed before letting his polite smile collapse. Daen slid in next to him, a mobile communicator in hand. He nodded to the young soldiers driving them, and the car rolled into motion. Daen faced Callan, a familiar gleam in his eye.

"Did you find something, Lieutenant?"

"Yes, sir," Daen replied eagerly.

He tapped his holo- bracelet, and an image appeared above his arm. A man in his early twenties. He was clean shaven, the sides of his hair cropped close, while the top was a nest of unruly curls tumbling into light brown eyes. Callan could only see his head and torso, but he didn't miss the broad shoulders or curve of muscles under his shirt. He had an immediate dislike of the man.

"Who's this?"

"Theodore Sturn, twenty-four years old," Daen said. "He was a semi-pro boxer from ages fifteen to eighteen. About a year later went to tech school, currently holds a job at Townsend Repairs."

"And why do we care about Theodore Sturn?"

"Because"—Daen smiled triumphantly—"this is who Princess Catarina spends her nights with."

Callan glanced at his lieutenant sharply. Daen simply nodded, that smug smile still in place. Callan looked back at the image of Sturn, distaste curling his lip back. He resisted the urge to swipe a hand through the image.

"One of the palace guards on her rotation got chatty," Daen continued. "Any time the princess goes out into the city, she meets up with him. According to our friendly guard, she always knows where he is. He thinks they have some sort of private holo- chat, but they haven't been able to trace it."

"What's their relationship?" It came out through his teeth.

Daen raised an eyebrow at the tone. "Friendly." He shook his head at Callan's expression. "That's what he said: just friends.

166

Usually they meet at a pub called the Dragon Slayer. Sometimes they go to the night market. Occasionally they'll get dinner."

"Maybe we should pay Sturn a visit, then," Callan ground out.

"Already did. The house is empty." Daen tapped his holo again, swiping through a series of images. "He lives at this address with his mother, but neither of them are there."

Callan leaned forward to scroll through the images. Daen had managed to get inside the house and look around as well. It was shabby, but neat. And utterly empty.

"Any other family?" Callan asked.

"A sister in Campray . Brother and father are both deceased."

"You set up a watch on the house?"

"Yes, sir. Anyone comes back, we'll know."

Callan nodded, leaning back in his seat. Daen dismissed the images and began booting up the mobile communicator. It beeped softly as he worked.

"Senator Hyrax requested a call," Daen said. "I assumed you'd want my report first, sir."

"Good work, Lieutenant."

Callan flexed his fingers as the signal booted. He glanced sidelong at Daen, keeping his tone casual. "Any update on my package?"

"Your powder finished processing yesterday. It should be here tonight." Daen set the communicator on the seat next to Callan, not looking at his commanding officer. "I noticed yours was already gone."

"It takes time to reach full potency. I won't be caught off-guard this time around."

"All I'm asking is for you to be cautious with your supply. It's going to be a lot harder to get now that our source has been discovered."

"We'll make sure to fix that once we control Liskow."

The communicator lit up before Daen could reply. Senator Hyrax's upper body appeared next to Callan. As usual, he wore spotless robes over a three-piece suit. The colors were muted over the transmission, but Callan could clearly see the black phoenix embroidered on the breast of his red senatorial robes.

167

Senator Hyrax smoothed back his graying hair, exposing a prominent forehead and straight smile. "Ah, Chancellor Byrne, the man of the hour!"

"Senator. How are you today, sir?"

"Excellent, excellent! I just saw your interview on the holostream. Fantastic job, son, truly. You'll have them eating out of the palm of your hand by the end of the day."

Callan sat up straighter, swelling with pride. He tipped his head graciously to Senator Hyrax. "Thank you, sir. Your enthusiasm is much appreciated."

"You deserve all the praise, boy." Senator Hyrax's eyes gleamed across the transmission. "I will admit, I was concerned when I heard you had started growing ah, close to the princess. But now, I'd say you've given us a prime opportunity. We can take Liskow without spilling a single drop of Galtan blood."

"Speaking of, we have a new lead on Princess Catarina. I'm optimistic that we'll find her soon."

"I'm glad to hear it. You're doing a great service to your country, Callan. Out of the ashes…"

"We rise."

The transmission ended, and Daen began putting away the mobile communicator. Callan looked out the car window, surprised to find they were almost to their destination. The palace walls rose high above the street to their left, while to their right sprawling lawns surrounded mansions of varying styles. No two were exactly alike, other than their need to outdo their neighbors.

Daen leaned forward to stare out Callan's window. "I used to want to live in a house like that one day."

Callan clapped him on the shoulder. "And now you'll live in a palace."

Their car rolled up the long driveway of a mansion constructed from pale gray stone. Flower beds overflowed with bunches of pink and purple blooms all around the house. The heady floral scent invaded his senses as the door swung open. He followed Daen up the sweeping front steps, resisting the urge to cover his nose.

"I still don't know why you took this meeting," Daen

168

grumbled.

"Do you have somewhere better to be?"

His lieutenant didn't respond.

The front door—painted a soft lavender—swung open, revealing an aging butler. Callan exchanged a glance with Daen before stepping over the threshold.

The inside of Lady Stellana's manor was just as grand as the outside. Callan's boots clicked across white marble floors, up a curved staircase carpeted in plush white. The gray and white color scheme continued through the parts of the house he could see, with splashes of purple and pink mixed in. They followed the butler down a wide hall into a sitting room overlooking the back gardens.

The room was smaller than Callan expected, given the tall ceilings and open layout of the main areas they walked through. Here, it was just big enough for two couches and three chairs arranged in a rough circle. There was a fireplace against one wall, a pair of end tables, and a window that took up the entirety of the back wall.

Lady Stellana perched casually on one of the chairs, her face to the window. She turned as they entered, flashing them a perfectly white smile. "There you are. Please, sit."

Callan settled on the middle of the couch closest to Stellana. He was near enough not to appear rude, but his position on the couch left no room for another person, unless they sat in his lap. He wouldn't put it past Stellana to try. He made a point not to stare at the plunging neckline of her silk dress. His eyes drifted past the red lipstick she wore and the black liner around her eyes.

Stellana brushed her loose hair off her shoulder and rested her head on her hand. "You're looking well today," she purred. "I hope you aren't losing too much sleep over our dear, lost princess."

Callan smiled tightly. "It's hard to relax knowing she is likely in danger."

"How is your search going?"

"I'm afraid I can't share that information."

"Like the tip to check the Bjorns' hunting cabin?"

He stilled. Stellana smiled triumphantly at him.

"How did you hear about that?" he asked, an edge to his voice.

169

"Really, it's so simple to put a tracking device into someone's belongings." Stellana leaned closer. "Particularly when you have friends in the palace. A shame that it fell out when the bag was set down. Especially considering she slipped away."

Callan's mind whirled. No one on his or Nolan's team had found any sort of tracking device. Which meant it had already been retrieved. Callan remembered the shiny brass casing he'd picked out of the dirt.

Anger surged through him. "Am I understanding that *you* sent someone up there to kill Princess Catarina?"

"If you'd like to get technical, then yes."

Heat built in Callan's veins, threatening to burst out of him. He shot to his feet, fingertips burning. "Then *technically*, I'll be bringing you to the palace for questioning."

"You haven't even heard my offer yet." Stellana stared up at him from under her lashes.

Despite himself, Callan's temper cooled. "What offer?"

"I am part of an organization. One that has been here longer than you can imagine. We've had a special interest in the throne of Liskow and have been looking for opportunities to, shall we say, *change* the succession. However…" Her voice rose slightly, cutting Callan off. "Given the circumstances *you've* created, we have prepared you an offer."

She paused, her deep brown eyes holding Callan's captive. Her voice took on a fervor he had yet to hear from her.

"Join our organization. Let us help you take Liskow, then help us achieve our own goals."

"And what, exactly, would I gain from this arrangement?"

"Besides the throne you're so desperate for? Access to our intelligence, a wealth of knowledge lost to history, and your precious Princess Catarina, safe and sound."

Callan stood to face the window, hands sliding into his pockets. He stared at the garden without really seeing it, processing Stellana's words. "Why is your organization so interested in me?"

"We've been keeping an eye on you since the Galtan revolution. That, combined with how you're handling the situation here…" There was a slight pause. "It's impressive. We think you

170

here…" There was a slight pause. "It's impressive. We think you could be a great asset to our cause."

Callan pivoted, strolling closer to Stellana. His lips lifted in a tight smile. "Or is it that you see how close I am to taking Liskow, and you want a piece now?"

Stellana stared up at him in amusement. "You've no idea what you're playing at, Callan. You're here because of a vendetta between a few senators and the king. If you *truly* want to take Liskow, you'll need to play your hand very carefully. We can ensure your success."

Callan's hands slipped out of his pockets to grip the arms of Stellana's chair. He leaned over her, fingertips white where they dug into the fabric.

"See, I don't believe that our purposes are truly aligned. And I don't appreciate others getting in my way." He kept his voice low, the first warning of a coiled viper, ready to strike.

"We have more connections than you could ever imagine." Stellana matched his tone, a dangerous gleam in her eyes. "Perhaps *you* should be worried about getting in *our* way."

Callan's fingertips once again began to heat. A wisp of smoke wafted from the arms of Stellana's chair, the scent of singed fabric stinging his nose. Rage poured through his veins, stoking the fire coursing through him.

Stellana glanced at his hands, now faintly glowing red. "I wouldn't have guessed you were one to ingest dragon eggshells," she said, eyes coming back to find his. "You should be careful. I've heard their power is quite addictive."

"If your *organization* so much as harms a hair on Catarina's head," Callan growled, "I will find every last one of you and end you, slowly. And I'll start with you."

He straightened, leashing his anger before he set the entire house ablaze.

Stellana glanced down at the black handprints now seared into her furniture. "I'll take that as a no, then?"

Callan jerked his head at Daen, who rose to his feet. Together they left Stellana in her smoking armchair.

Callan was looking forward to a quiet evening. His temples pounded after all of the meetings and conversations. He closed the distance to his rooms, ready to sink into a plush chair and relax.

The door was cracked. Of course his day wasn't over yet.

He knew who was waiting before he crossed the threshold. Nolan slouched in an armchair, a short glass in his hand. He'd dropped the tight-laced security guard persona, instead looking like the brooding brother Callan remembered. He looked as tired as Callan.

His dark hair was mussed, like he'd been running his hands through it. Rough stubble shadowed his jaw, nearly matching the dark look in his eyes. Callan knew his brother rarely drank. It had been a vice of their father's, one that Callan hadn't seen, being so young when he died. But Nolan had seen it. Seen enough of it to swear off drinking entirely. Almost entirely, by the looks of the brown liquid coating the bottom of his glass.

"I thought you'd given that up."

"I had," Nolan rumbled. "Until I started undercover work."

Callan strolled past him to the drink cart. He sniffed the still open bottle, wincing as his nostrils burned. "More stressful than you anticipated, then?"

"You have no idea," Nolan muttered darkly. "The sacrifices I've made these last few years."

The cart rattled as Nolan dropped the bottle back down. He worked to keep his hands steady, knocking back the brown liquid before he could lay into his brother. Nolan wanted to lecture him about *sacrifice*? As if he didn't know what that word meant. Intimately.

Nolan didn't seem to notice his mood. "I saw your interview this morning. You did well."

Callan swallowed, taking a long moment to steady his voice. "Thank you. Senator Hyrax was also pleased with my performance."

He rounded Nolan's armchair, settling into the seat across the rug.

Nolan's face soured. "You need to be careful with Hyrax. He's been waiting a long time for his shot at power, and he only acts in

172

his own interest."

"*Senator* Hyrax was instrumental in my election as Chancellor."

"Exactly." Nolan leaned forward, finger tapping his glass for emphasis. "Why you? Yes, you made a name for yourself during the revolution, but there were other notable generals, most of them more experienced than you. Why pick the youngest and least experienced?"

"Did you only come here to belittle me?" Callan's voice shook. A prickle of heat danced along his fingers. He was nearly spent, but he had enough to incinerate his brother where he sat.

"I'm trying to help you, Cal! Hyrax is a snake."

Callan shot to his feet, voice rising. "The *senator* is a great man! He supported me when no one else would!"

"You mean when I wasn't there." Nolan's face was unreadable, his voice soft.

Callan glowered at him, hot anger burning through his veins. "While you were off doing gods knew what and I was left behind. While I watched Mother deteriorate, listened to her cry for you, for Father. For the baby she lost. Senator Hyrax pulled us out of that stinking slum and made sure that I got an education and a place in the world."

Nolan slammed his glass down on the low table, rising to his own feet. Callan's rage flared as he looked up to meet his brother's red-rimmed eyes.

"And Hyrax promised *me* that my salary would go back to you and Mother! I slaved for the rebellion for *years* before you joined! I worked myself ragged to make sure you were safe, had a roof over your head, that Mother had her medicine. I did everything I could to take care of you both!"

"Mother's medicine," Callan scoffed. "That quack doctor was afraid of her gift. He prescribed that poison to smother it."

Nolan passed a hand over his face. "It was for her hallucinations, Cal. It was the only thing that calmed her down."

"It suppressed her visions!"

"She never *had* visions!" Nolan roared, his alcohol-scented breath washing over Callan. "I know you don't want to hear it, but it's the truth. Mother never recovered from Father's death. Or the baby's."

"You might not believe in her visions, but I still do. She saw things only the gods could have shown her."

"Believe what you want, Callan. It doesn't matter now, anyway."

"It will when I fulfill her visions of me," Callan growled. "I *am* the hero she prophesied, just wait and see."

The anger in Nolan's eyes dimmed. His shoulders fell, and a shadow passed over his face.

Callan met his stare, his rage simmering beneath the surface. He didn't shrink under the disappointment in his brother's eyes. He'd stopped caring what Nolan thought a long time ago.

"Sorry, Cal. I didn't come here to fight. I just wanted to congratulate you on your interview." Nolan let out a soft sigh. "I'll let you get back to your evening."

Callan watched as his brother slicked his hair back with a hand, then buttoned the top of his uniform into place. His shoulders drew back, and his expression cooled into bland indifference. The head of security once more, he left with a crisp "good night."

Callan stared at the door for a long moment after it closed. The heat in his veins slowly dissipated, pooling deep in his belly as a faint warmth. Nolan's lack of faith had bothered him as a child, but he'd grown in his own convictions. One day, when he brought peace and order to the continent, Nolan would see. They'd all see.

17

Cora followed the now familiar path through Aurestyn to the training rooms. The stone of the corridor gave way to packed sand. She wrinkled her nose at the stale smell of sweat that never truly left the caverns.

Reluraun was already waiting at the furthest training ring. She passed by the other four on her way, ducking around practice dummies. She was careful to step over the cables from the lights they had brought in, bathing everything in a warm yellow glow. He leaned against the table in front of the weapons rack, nodding to her in greeting.

Cora returned the nod, setting her water bottle on the table before retrieving her practice sword. She practiced her stances, squeezing the dull sword. Her feet and arms moved together as she continued from one form to the next.

"Relax! You look like an android."

A flicker of annoyance nearly broke her concentration. She shook out her limbs, willing them to relax. A whisper of Reluraun's voice tickled her ear from one of their first sessions.

"You are water flowing around a boulder. The sword is part of you, part of that flow."

Cora reset, repeating his words in her mind. She gripped the practice sword with both hands, the dull blade singing as she danced between forms.

"Good! Faster!"

She obliged, her feet kicking up little puffs of sand. Her arms swung, her feet flying across the ground. All she could hear was the air entering and leaving her lungs. She stepped through her final stance, coming back to the room.

Reluraun nodded approvingly. "Very good."

Cora gave him a sweaty smile. She retrieved her water bottle and emptied it, laying down her practice sword.

Reluraun watched her thoughtfully, fingers drumming against the table. He rounded the table, stopping in front of the weapons rack. He reached up and pulled something down. She approached cautiously, water bottle forgotten on the ledge of the stone bench.

"You've been doing well, better than I expected, actually," Reluraun said. "But the longsword is ill-suited to you. I think these would be a better match."

He gestured to a pair of gleaming swords laid out on the bench. She lifted one of them, surprised by how light it was. The blade was thin and sharp, shorter than her practice sword. She moved through her first set of forms, the blade ringing as it sailed through the air.

"Learning to wield two swords takes a great deal of coordination," he warned. "Not many choose to do so."

"I'll do it. I want to learn."

Reluraun nodded, carefully taking the blade from Cora and placing it next to its mate. He pulled two short practice swords off the wall and handed them to her. She took them to her normal spot and assumed her first stance. He took up a position next to her, holding his own pair of practice swords.

"Your hands complement and support each other." He spoke as he moved through his forms. "Otherwise they will get in your way."

Cora copied his movements, moving slowly and deliberately. She swept her right hand out, then her left. And promptly smacked her leg. She inhaled sharply, rubbing the spot.

"Again."

She obeyed, managing to avoid hitting herself again. Reluraun made her repeat the form five times before moving on to the next. Her muscles were already aching, but she ignored them, copying him exactly.

He led her through three forms before lowering his swords. "Good. That's enough for today."

"I can keep going."

"Knowing when to rest is just as important as mastering your forms," Reluraun said curtly. "Even Riders with enhanced recovery, need to avoid overworking their bodies."

Cora knew better than to argue. She placed her swords back in their spot on the rack, gaze lingering on the gleaming double swords Reluraun had shown her. Soon, she'd be able to use them. She grabbed her water bottle, ready to head back to Stony Hollow, when an unfamiliar voice echoed through the training rooms. She looked up to see an elf with shaggy light brown hair striding over.

"Uncle Reluraun!"

"Finnelas," Reluraun grunted. "What are you doing here?"

"Baeros is back. He's asking for you." Finnelas faced Cora, extending a hand with a wink. "Hey, I'm Finn."

"Nice to meet you." Cora whirled back toward Reluraun. "You don't mean Lord Baeros?"

"Yes. He's one of a select few that Stony Hollow trades with. He's not due back for another week."

Finn shrugged. "All I know is he's here, and he wants to speak to you. Are you teaching Cora swordplay?"

Finn stepped up to the weapons rack next to Cora. As he came closer, she realized he was just barely taller than her. Most elves towered over her, but she came up to Finn's chin.

"She's a Rider, isn't she?" Reluraun snipped.

Finn was unfazed by his annoyance. "When are you going to teach her about firearms?"

"You know how I feel about those."

"You need to enter this century, Uncle Reluraun. Regardless of how you feel, everyone she fights is going to have a firearm."

"If you think it's so important, *you* teach her."

"Okay."

Reluraun muttered something under his breath and stalked out of the training room.

Finn shot her a cheeky grin. "He's too easy to rile up. What do you say?"

"Say to what?"

"Shooting. Looks like you've got some free time, and I was

about to go myself. A few of us are going to test out some new toys Baeros brought up."

"Sure, why not?"

Cora spared one last glance at the double swords hanging on the rack before following the still grinning elf out of the practice rooms.

Cora blinked in the sudden sunshine, half-blinded after the dim halls of Aurestyn. Finn led her to an open field where a handful of elves and sprites were busy setting up paper targets. A folding table was already assembled, a line of firearms spread across it. Boxes of ammunition lay stacked at one end, ready to be loaded into magazines.

"Have you ever handled a firearm before?" Finn asked.

"No."

Finn handed her an empty magazine and opened a box of ammo. He showed her how to load the bullets in, speaking as his fingers pushed the rounds in one at a time.

"There are four basic safety rules you should know. Number one." Finn set down his now full magazine and grabbed another. "Treat every firearm as if it's loaded. Number two: keep your finger off the trigger until you're ready to shoot. Number three: only point your firearm at something you're willing to destroy. And number four: know what's behind your target before taking your shot."

Finn set aside another full magazine, glancing up to check her progress. She'd managed to load all but the last round. He took it from her, shoving the spring down and sliding it in.

"Alright, repeat the rules back to me."

Cora did, earning her a satisfied nod from Finn. They loaded a few more magazines as the rest of the group came back to the table. He introduced them all, quickly enough that she had a hard time keeping everyone's names straight. A set of earplugs was pressed into her hands, and she stuffed them into her ears.

Finn stayed next to her as the others grabbed firearms off the table. "Anything you want to shoot?"

"How about that one?"

178

Cora pointed to a random firearm, and Finn picked it up. It was a large handgun, and it made her hands feel tiny. She did her best to wrap them around it the way Finn instructed her to. He made a few adjustments before nodding at her to squeeze the trigger. She did, nearly jumping out of her skin when her wrists snapped upward. Finn's shoulders shook with laughter. He adjusted her grip and motioned for her to try again.

Cora emptied the gun's magazine, shots going wide. Her last one managed to hit the paper, and she whooped in delight. Finn exchanged the handgun for one that was slightly smaller. She squeezed her hands around it, more confident this time. Although still outside of the printed target, each shot made a hole in the paper.

Finn had her keep shooting until she'd run a magazine through each firearm on the table. None of her shots made it close to the bullseye, but by the time she was finished, she felt comfortable holding each firearm. Even the long, heavy rifles, although she preferred the handguns. She helped the group take down the shredded targets and pack up the firearms.

"We're all headed to the dining hall," Finn said. "Want to come with?"

"Yeah, that sounds great."

She walked alongside them to the dining hall, laughing and joking. A warm feeling settled over her, and she realized that she was *happy*. In the last several years, she'd only truly felt this light when she was out with Theo. And even then, she'd only ever been an observer. She'd never allowed herself to truly be a part of the city, knowing that each time, she'd have to return to the palace. But here, in Stony Hollow, she was just like everyone else.

A pang pricked her chest as she realized that she wouldn't be able to stay here, either. She considered, for a moment, staying. Leaving behind her old self, her old world. It could be easy, to disappear, even fake her death.

But the price was high. If she were ever found out, the rest of the Bjorns would hunt her down, if only to make an example of her. And what about Arik? She still didn't know where he was, or if he was alright. She couldn't abandon her family, her people.

179

Cora shoved her thoughts down as they filed through the dining hall's doors. She expected to see the long line of people waiting, but instead, everyone was crowded around the corner farthest from the food. A holo-screen in the corner displayed a familiar face.

She sat in an empty seat as close to the screen as she could. Her world narrowed to the set of blazing blue eyes staring through the screen. The scar on Callan's face stood out starkly under studio lights, his mahogany hair gleaming. A beautiful woman interviewed him.

"And is it true that you have *personal* reasons for finding Princess Catarina?"

"Yes. I won't be able to rest until I see her again, safe and sound."

Callan gazed into the camera, and it was as if he were looking directly at her. Her heart raced, even as his gaze moved away. And then the implications of what he'd said sank in, and her heart twisted.

A warm presence settled onto the bench next to her. She glanced up at Theo. His face settled into a neutral expression, but for just a moment, she was sure of what she'd seen there. Jealousy.

What have I gotten myself into?

Gray pushed open the lab door, passing a hand over his face. He didn't bother flipping on the lights. They would probably make his headache worse, anyway. He followed the same path he always did, weaving between steel tables to reach the far corner of the room. He checked the temperature and humidity of the incubator before finally glancing at the egg. The shell was cracked.

He stared in disbelief. The egg wiggled, the web of cracks along the shell pulsing. He dropped into a rolling chair, watching the cracks expand again.

Time stilled as his focus narrowed to the wiggling oval in front of him. A seam slowly opened around the shell, until he could see the tip of a leathery nose poke out. He laughed, his heart nearly bursting with joy.

The hatchling took only a moment to breathe in the air outside before attacking its shell. Bit by bit, the pieces collapsed around it, leaving a panting, wet dragon in their wake.

Gray carefully lifted the lid of the incubator. He leaned down, mesmerized by the tiny dragon. He blinked tears out of his eyes.

The dragon cocked its head, staring back with amber eyes. The hatchling was too wet to discern its color, but spots dappled it from nose to tail, stark in the dim light.

"Hello, little one."

Gray lifted his hand, reaching out to the hatchling. It watched him curiously, nostrils flaring. His fingers drifted closer. Inches separated them. His heart clenched tightly, and his fingers stopped.

He stared at the tiny dragon. He willed his fingers forward, to try to form a bond. They refused. The hatchling staggered forward, sniffing.

A warmth spread through the back of his mind, urging him forward. Gray yanked his hand back.

The warmth retreated, leaving a sense of… disappointment in its wake. The tiny dragon glared at him, flaring its wings in annoyance.

Gray sat back, arms crossing over his chest. He couldn't leave the dragon in the lab. He needed to move it, get it food, water. How would he get it out without touching it?

That warmth flared at the base of his skull. *Touch it.*

Gray swallowed, glancing around the room. Anywhere but at the dragon.

He spotted an empty box tossed into the corner. He left his chair to grab it, only fairly certain it would fit the hatchling. He laid the box on its side inside the incubator, the flaps facing the baby dragon.

Gray was patient. He watched as the hatchling edged forward, investigating the strange opening. He stayed perfectly still, waiting until the dragon was completely inside the box before closing the flaps.

Not so much as a single scale brushed his finger. Gray checked that the box was secure, ignoring the enraged hiss emanating from it. He gathered the rest of his things and silently left the lab behind.

18

Cora shot straight up in bed, chest heaving. Her back was slicked with sweat, the sheets tangled around her legs. She glanced around as the dream faded to incoherent wisps. Her room looked strange in the dark. She reached for her holo, instinctively opening her schedule. It was blank. Cora rubbed her eyes, taking in the room again. She wasn't at home. Right. She chuckled wryly. What would Mother say—

She cut off the thought before it finished. Mother wouldn't say anything to her anymore.

A cold hollowness filled her, driving away any lingering drowsiness. The threads of her thoughts tangled around her, threatening to drag her down.

Cora threw off the covers and dressed. She scraped her hair into a messy tail and jammed her feet into her shoes. She needed to *move*.

She was running as soon as her feet left the porch. She didn't have a plan for where she was going. She just moved one foot in front of the other until a familiar presence stirred across the bond.

Cora faced Aurestyn, legs pounding a rhythm with her breath. She only slowed once she entered the ancient stone halls.

Makari was waiting on the ledge of her nest when Cora skidded to a stop. She climbed up without hesitation. She had barely settled onto Makari's back before the dragon leapt into the frigid sky.

Cora didn't think she'd ever get tired of flying. The cold air whipped past her face, turning her cheeks and ears pink. Makari's powerful downbeats set them bobbing in a soothing rhythm. Cora leaned close to her neck, feeling her body relax even as her legs

182

squeezed her tight. They soared over trees so dark they looked black in the pre-dawn light, circling slowly.

Cora knew the moment Makari spotted her prey. Her head snapped to the side, muscles taut. Cora had a split second to tighten her grip before they fell into a steep dive. She leveled out only a handful of feet above the ground, shooting like an arrow toward the fleeing deer. It didn't stand a chance. Cora clung to her as she shook her head, teeth clamped around its neck.

She slid down as Makari feasted. She stretched her limbs, taking in the gradually lightening forest. The stillness pressed against her eardrums. It combined with the hollowness inside until it threatened to swallow her.

She dropped to the ground and started her pushups. She lowered and raised herself until sweat dripped onto the ground and her muscles screamed in protest. She switched to sit-ups, each movement punctuated by the cracking of bones as Makari devoured her prey.

Once she was aching throughout her core, she began to lunge. One leg, then the other. She had switched to squats by the time Makari licked her last claw clean. She watched through half-lidded eyes as Cora stretched again.

She cocked an eyebrow at the dragon. "Are you finally finished?"

Makari languidly stretched each limb. She shook, her long tail snapping into Cora's leg and knocking her over.

She glowered at Makari. "That was rude."

Makari snorted, lowering one shoulder pointedly. Cora climbed onto her back, wincing as her muscles protested. She was going to regret her choices when it came time to train with Theo. Just his name sent a tiny spark alight in her belly, driving her grief back a fraction. She found herself counting down the hours until their training sessions. She couldn't remember the last time they'd spent so much time together. Yet another thing her mother would disapprove of.

Makari took them back to Aurestyn. Cora slid down her back, feet rustling the straw strewn across her nest. She yawned, then spun in a circle and curled up against the far wall.

Cora shook her head at the dragon. "Worn out already, huh?"

She was prepared for the swinging tail this time. She hopped over it, then scurried out of the aerie before Makari could whack her again. She jogged back to Reluraun's house, already regretting her early morning workout.

Theo showed no sympathy to her soreness, making her run through even more reps before she collapsed onto her back, chest heaving.

"I can't believe how far you've come already."

Cora twisted her head toward Theo. He was panting just as hard as her, cheeks flushed beneath his warm brown skin.

"Far from what, exactly?" she grumbled. "Because I feel like I'm dying."

"Have you seen yourself lately? I feel like I'm dying, and I've only done one workout this morning."

Cora sat up, looking down at herself. Cords of muscle ran up and down her arms. She placed a hand to her abdomen, feeling the hardening muscles there as well. She stretched her legs out in front of her, watching her muscles tighten and flex.

Her eyes trailed upward to find Theo watching her. His gaze sent a warm shiver skittering across her body. Her eyes caught on the empty water bottle clenched tightly in his fist, then trailed over to his now drenched shirt. It clung to him, contouring around muscles she wasn't even aware a man could have. Her cheeks flamed, and she tore her gaze away.

Really? Everything you have going on, and this *is what you're thinking about?*

The thought was like a bucket of ice water washing over her. Cora shoved herself onto her feet, pointedly looking away from Theo's wet clothing.

"I should find Gray. Don't want to keep him waiting."

She swore she felt Theo's eyes on her back as she walked away. Another set of eyes came to her mind unbidden. Intense blue, staring straight into her soul.

"I won't be able to rest until I see her again ..."

Cora's gut twisted with guilt. Her emotions snarled around each other once again, twisting and pulling until she didn't know

184

where one ended and another began. Irritation rose to the top of the mess, overshadowing the rest as she made her way into the dragon training caverns.

Gray was already waiting for her, a book open on the ledge next to him and a notebook in his lap. He twisted his pen between his fingers, lost in thought. It took him a few seconds to realize she was there.

"Oh, there you are, Cora. Where's Makari?"

Cora called for Makari down the bond. There was silence on the other end. Frowning, Cora tried again, louder. There was a vague stirring in her mind.

MAKARI.

Irritation, matching her own, pounded into Cora's skull. She ignored it, calling the dragon once again.

Makari retreated from the bond, and a few moments later she sailed down one of the air shafts connecting the cavern to the aerie. She circled lazily before landing in front of them with a giant puff of dust.

Gray and Cora coughed, fanning the air to disperse some of the particles. Makari glared at them as she settled back onto her haunches.

"Someone's moody today." Gray observed.

A tiny cloud of smoke puffed out of Makari's nostrils in reply.

Gray motioned for them to get started. Cora dropped down from the ledge to the floor, intending to climb on Makari's back. Before she got within three feet, Makari rolled onto her back.

"What has gotten into you?" Cora asked, exasperated.

Makari swiped her tail, stirring up a scent that Cora could just barely detect. She wrinkled her nose at the musky smell. Makari rolled back onto her stomach and stuck her rump in the air. When Cora still didn't understand, she pushed an image into Cora's mind. It was of another dragon, but somehow, Cora knew this one was male.

"You've got to be kidding me."

"Is something wrong?"

She faced Gray with an exasperated expression. It took her a moment to figure out how to explain it to him.

"I think Makari's in heat."

The dragoness tossed her head, wriggling her back end again before rolling onto her back.

Gray began writing in his notebook, glancing up at Makari to see what she was doing.

"You're *writing this down?*"

"I'm a researcher, Cora," he said flatly. "And there are currently *no* studies published on dragon mating behavior. Of course I'm writing this down!"

She lifted an eyebrow as he scribbled furiously. Makari continued to pose and preen, her tail waving like a feathery flag. Cora clamped down on a rising wave of irritation. It wasn't worth the energy to fight with the frisky dragoness.

"I don't think Makari is going to train today."

"Yeah, probably not. We can call it until her heat cycle is over."

"How long will that be?"

Gray tapped his notebook with the back of his pen. "I guess we'll just have to wait and find out."

Great.

Cora was still irritated when she joined Reluraun later that day. It didn't fade as they warmed up with her basic forms. Afterward, he tossed her what looked like a leather harness.

She caught it reflexively, wincing as a strap smacked across her cheek. "What is this?"

"A back sheath. Today we will be practicing your draw."

Cora fumbled with the buckles for a few minutes before finally getting the sheath in place. Reluraun helped guide her practice swords into place. They settled across her back, the hilts just above her shoulders.

"I have found that the most comfortable place for your sword while riding is on your back. It takes practice to get accustomed to."

She nodded. She reached up and grasped the hilts of her swords. She pulled up and out...and hit the back of her head.

Reluraun straightened his face, but not before she caught his smile. "Again."

186

Cora lost count of how many times she went through the motions. She successfully drew the swords about a third of the time. The other times she managed to knock them into her skull. Her head was pounding by the time Reluraun called for her to move on.

Cora swept one hand out and knocked it into her other blade. She tried the other hand and did it again. She groaned in frustration.

"Slow down. Breathe."

Cora obeyed, her sore muscles screaming from the effort. Her hands trembled with fatigue, but she managed to practice her forms without knocking her blades together again.

Reluraun's face was unreadable as he called an end to practice. He waited until she'd put away her practice swords before speaking again.

"Siraye informed me this morning that your mother's funeral will be tomorrow morning."

She froze. Her back sheath hung off her body, only half unbuckled.

"She's offered to set up the broadcast on the screen in my home. I already have an errand to run tomorrow, so you can have the house to yourself if you wish."

Cora forced herself to swallow. "Thank you. I'd like that."

Reluraun nodded, then left without another word.

Cora finished removing her back sheath and set it on the table in front of the weapons rack. She no longer felt her irritation, or the heaving mass of emotions from earlier. Instead, she felt utterly numb.

The sun had no right to shine so brightly. The birdsong in Reluraun's garden grated against Cora's ears. Neither Siraye nor Theo commented as she slammed the window shut, startling the offending birds. No one else had stayed in Reluraun's house. Gray told her it was to keep her identity secret, but she knew it was to give her privacy.

Siraye stepped back from the glowing holo- screen. Footage of Narous scrolled past, sending a punch of homesickness into her

her gut. Flowers hung from windows, streetlights, balconies. Petals floated down to the street every time the wind blew, dusting the stones. Cora settled onto the couch across from the screen, fingers tangling in the hem of her black shirt.

Wordlessly, Siraye and Theo sat on either side of her. Their warmth did nothing to thaw the ice in her veins. She was distantly aware that someone was speaking over the video feed .

Her world narrowed as six palace guards appeared carrying a deep brown casket. Piled high on the lid were boughs dripping with white flowers, tendrils reaching nearly to the ground. And in the center, an explosion of fire lilies.

The sight of the crimson flowers cracked Cora's resolve. Tears streamed down her face as Father took his place just behind the casket. Siraye slipped an arm around her shoulders. Cora hardly noticed.

The procession began at the palace gate. People lining the streets threw flowers down in front of the pallbearers. Behind her father, a violinist began a slow tune. She recognized it as Mother's favorite lullaby. Her own mother had sung it to her, and she had sung it to Cora and Arik.

Hot tears flowed faster down Cora's face as she watched the trailing procession toward Narous' eastern gate. Warmth enveloped her hand as Theo's long fingers twined with hers, squeezing gently.

Mother's casket was carried past the outermost city wall, to a small hill covered in purple flowers. Headstones and statues emerged from the swaying grass like sentinels. The pallbearers lowered the casket next to an open grave, where the lid was opened one last time. Cora stared at her mother's still face, so peaceful, and so…empty.

I hope you're at peace. Goodbye, Mother.

A stillness settled over Cora. Her tears slowed, and a weight lifted off her chest.

Father brushed a hand across Mother's cheek, his own face wet. He stepped back, nodding.

The casket closed with a resounding thump. Father collapsed across the smooth wood, a wail tearing from his trembling lips.

The lightness, the growing feeling Cora didn't dare name,

vanished. Fresh tears spilled off her chin.

Someone in the crowd started the mourning song. She couldn't find the voice to sing, but she hummed along.

Siraye and Theo stayed silent next to her. His thumb stroked her finger. Cora clung to his hand as her heart cracked in two.

Cora perched on the edge of her bed. The image of her father collapsing on top of her mother's casket was burned into her brain. She would never forget the anguish on his face. She desperately wanted to comfort him, to hold him as he broke. She hadn't dared contact anyone, convincing herself it was too dangerous for all of them. But now, as her grief threatened to swallow her, she found she didn't care.

Siraye's voice echoed in her mind. *"Messages sent from within Stony Hollow are untraceable."*

Cora shook her holo awake, fingers poised to type out her message. Would Father even be ready to talk to her? There was a good chance he'd already found the bottom of one of the bottles in his office.

Her fingers were moving before she finished the thought. She hadn't realized that she'd memorized his contact code. The response was almost immediate.

Catarina! Are you alright? Where are you?

Cora took a breath, fingers flying as she fired back. She was prepared for the questions.

I'm fine. I'm safe. How is my father?

She could practically hear Callan considering how to respond to her. She didn't realize she was holding her breath until his next message finally came through.

He's devastated, Catarina. I've never met a man more in love with his wife. He's also worried sick about you and your brother.

Do you know where Arik is?

No. My men are working round the clock to find him, but our resources are limited. Where are you? Can you leave?

189

She stared at those two letters. What happened to Arik? It wasn't like him to disappear. Her mind filled with visions of her twin, each one worse than the last.

I can leave whenever I want. I'm with someone I trust. Please, tell my father that I'm safe and I'll be back soon.

Catarina, please don't go. Let me bring you home.

Home. The word rang in her mind. She glanced around Reluraun's tiny guest room, taking in the narrow dresser, the trailing potted plants hanging from the curtain rod, the worn rug beneath her toes. This wasn't her home. Neither was the lavish room she'd spent the last twenty years of her life in. She didn't know where home was anymore.

Keep looking for Arik. You'll hear from me again.

The overbearing sunshine had turned into charcoal-colored clouds by dinner time. Thunder vibrated through the walls, shaking the bed. Rain pounded against the roof like an army marching across the shingles, and lightning flashed bright enough to illuminate every detail of her room. Each time Cora began to drift, another violent boom rattled the house, startling her awake. She lay back on the bed, giving up on sleep.

Instead, her mind turned over and over. Why hadn't Arik returned to the palace by now? It wasn't like him to stay away from home, to stay away from Father. The possibilities were endless and horrifying. Cora's mind spun itself until she was physically dizzy.

She sat up and planted her feet onto solid ground. The rain outside had slowed to a gentle cascade, the sudden quiet jarring.

She grabbed her boots and snatched a jacket from her wardrobe. She tiptoed to the front door, easing it open just wide enough to fit through. She shoved her feet into her boots on the front porch and tied them. Then she walked out into the rain.

Cora vaguely knew where she was going. She had to backtrack a few times, disoriented by the rain sliding down her face. Out of the darkness rose Stony Hollow's only apartment complex. Most of the town's single residents lived in the four-story building. Cora spotted a directory just inside the tiny lobby. She found the number she was searching for, then jogged up to the third floor, leaving a trail of water behind her. She counted down the doors, knocking quietly on the last one in the hall.

It cracked open to reveal a slightly disheveled Siraye.

"Cora? What are you doing here? It's late."

"I'm sorry, did I wake you up?"

"Kind of." Siraye yawned. "I dozed off reading my book. I was just dragging myself to bed. What's up?"

"I need you to find someone for me."

19

Faster," Theo urged. "Twist your whole body into it."

Cora punched again, twisting from her hip. Her wrapped fist connected with Theo's glove with a soft thud.

"Come on, Cora. You've got more than that."

She fell out of her stance, glaring at Theo. Sweat slid down her spine in a steady flow. Her fingers ached from curling them close to her palm for so long. "I need a break."

Theo wasn't fazed by her sharp tone. He didn't move from his stance, gloved hands held out for her. "You need to master your form. You're so close."

Frustration flared inside her.

Across the yard, Makari's ears pricked in her direction. She lifted her head, nostrils flaring.

Cora sensed the dragon's attention in her mind. The mental brush sent her bristling. Her teeth ground together, hot anger flashing through her.

"I've had enough." She snapped.

"You can't walk away in the middle of a fight," Theo replied. "You have to keep going, no matter what."

His calm demeanor was like nails dragging across her skin.

Makari rose onto her feet, fixated on Cora. Her lip curled back as a soft growl rumbled from her. It was a sound of approval.

Theo cut his eyes to Makari, holding his ground. Cora found it infuriating.

Makari pressed against her mind, stoking her rage. Faster than she'd ever moved before, Cora's body twisted. Her fist collided with his hand with a resonant smack.

Theo stumbled back a step, eyes going wide. He stared at her, mouth slack.

Then he let out a loud whoop, startling Makari. The dragon snorted smoke at him and sank back down to the ground. Her eyes swept over Cora before she settled, tail wrapped loosely around herself.

"That's what I'm talking about!"

Theo's praise swept over her, sending a different kind of warmth through her body. He motioned for her to do it again.

Cora obliged, her body sailing through the movement. One fist, then the other barreled into Theo's padded palms.

Makari's attention settled on her like a physical weight. Heat blazed in her belly, flaring as Makari purred in approval. Cora straightened out of her stance, panting.

"Come on, I know you've got more in you," he pressed.

She did. It pulsed in her veins—her body longed to move. She shook her head. "I don't want to hurt you."

Theo sobered, hands faltering. His honey eyes met hers. The fire in her core leapt under his gaze.

"Don't worry about me, Cora. Right now is about you. I can be your punching bag for as long as you need."

She heard what he didn't say. That he knew. Knew that she needed to let out all that she kept shoving away before she exploded. He'd felt the energy charging her muscles, urging her to move, move, *move*. Cora settled back into her fighting stance.

The world narrowed down to Theo's raised hands. Cora breathed deep, releasing her stranglehold on her impulses. Like a cobra, she struck. Her body pulsed, her fists going forward and back faster than her brain could register. She quieted her mind, focusing on the targets in front of her. Twist, smack, twist, smack.

Theo backed away from her onslaught. He grunted as her fists connected again, and again. The crackling fire in her veins built to an inferno. Every inch of her skin burned as she pressed forward.

Makari stalked behind her, keeping pace as Cora drove Theo back further. The dragon purred and huffed, approval singing across the bond. Theo panted, fighting to keep his hands up. Sweat shone on his face and arms. Cora struck again, watching his muscles flex and strain to absorb the impact of her blows. She continued her momentum, leg flying into Theo's stomach. He crashed onto his backside with a surprised gasp.

Slowly, Cora became aware of her surroundings again. Her posture relaxed, and a dull soreness settled over her limbs. But the pulsing energy remained.

Theo winced as he climbed to his feet. He pulled the pads off his hands and flexed his fingers. "There's the Cora I've been waiting for."

Cora stepped closer, heat still skittering across her skin. Her eyes flicked over his bare arms, corded with muscle. They lingered at the neck of his shirt, and she found herself wondering what he'd look like without it.

She dragged her eyes past his sharp jaw and straight nose, back to those warm eyes. "And what, exactly, have you been waiting for?"

Theo's quiet voice rolled over her like distant thunder. "For you to stop holding back."

She was close enough to touch him. The heat from their exerted bodies mingled, carrying a musky scent with it.

Cora leaned forward, head tilted up to meet his eyes. "I'm not the only one who's been holding back."

Theo stared down at her. His eyes fell to her lips, then back up. Her pulse pounded in her ears. Theo took a deep breath through his nose, then stepped back. Her face flushed for an entirely different reason.

"We should talk...first."

The words were like a gust of cold air across her face. The raging heat filling her belly snuffed out, replaced with gut-wrenching shame. She had nearly crossed a threshold she swore she *never* could.

"Actually, it's fine," she insisted. "We don't have to do this right now."

"Come on, Cora. We have to talk eventually."

"Talk about what, Theo?"

The words snapped out of her before she could stop them. The immediate hurt clouding his eyes made her wish she could pull them back.

Theo crossed his arms over his chest, expression guarded. "What's going to happen when we go home?"

"What do you mean?"

"You're going to be queen, Cora."

There it was. The conversation looming over them for years. Secretly, she'd hoped they would never have it.

She heaved a sigh and sank onto the ground. After a breath, he joined her. The mere inches of space between their bodies yawned like a chasm.

"What happens is that I won't see you anymore," she whispered.

"It doesn't have to be that way."

"Yes, it does."

Theo bristled. His face darkened as he faced her. "Why does it?"

"Because they'll eat you alive!" she snapped. "The court will tear you apart and leave nothing left."

"I can handle myself," he replied stubbornly. "I'm not afraid of some haughty rich people."

"That's the problem, Theo. You won't play their games. And if you don't play, you don't survive."

Cora met his guarded stare. As she spoke, his eyes flashed blue in her mind. Guilt twisted her gut as she remembered the last man she'd almost kissed.

Her eyes fell to her lap as her cheeks flushed red. She couldn't bring herself to look at him as she continued.

"I won't bring you into that world."

"Thanks for the honesty." Theo pushed to his feet and began walking away.

Cora shot after him, jogging to catch up with his retreating form. "Theo, don't do this, please."

He stopped, and Cora had to circle around to face him. The pain etched across his face was like a knife in her gut.

"What's the point, Cora?" His hands punctuated his words. "You and I both knew this day was coming. It's the reason we've never had this conversation. Isn't it?" He nodded at her confirming silence. "Well then, there's no need to continue. I'm here, as your friend. I just don't think we should be alone together anymore."

She nodded slowly, stomach sinking clear to her toes. "If that's what you want."

"It is." Theo paused, as if considering whether he should continue. "Because I don't trust myself not to do something we'll both regret."

"I'm sorry."

The words hung lamely between them. Cora was sorry. She was sorry for the life she led, sorry for the world she lived in, sorry for the danger that hung over everyone around her. But most of all, she was sorry for the hurt shining in Theo's eyes. She wanted to cross the distance between them and smooth the crease between his brows with her fingers. She remained rooted to the spot instead.

"Don't be." Theo's sad smile threatened to crack her heart into a thousand pieces. "You don't owe me anything, Cora. I'll see you later."

She watched him leave, sensing more than seeing Makari come up next to her. Emotions washed through Cora. Guilt, longing, and grief had their say. But as Theo vanished into town, they were all replaced with that burning anger. She let out a guttural yell and kicked at a clump of grass.

Makari sat on her haunches, tracking the movement. Cora rounded on the dragon.

"You stay out of my love life," she growled. "Don't think I didn't notice you egging me on earlier."

Makari snorted as if to say, *And?*

Cora's body calmed, but the anger still sang in her blood. Makari watched her with keen eyes. The dragoness brushed up against the bond. Cora knew the anger was there to stay. And Makari knew it too.

Gray bounced on the balls of his feet in the dim morning light. The sun hadn't crested the horizon yet, the crisp air raising goosebumps on his bare arms. Theo stood next to him, arms crossed. They stared at the door of Reluraun's house.

"Does she always take this long?" Gray asked.

196

"She's not much of a morning person."

Cora stumbled out the front door towards them. She rubbed at her eyes, a deep scowl on her face. Gray tried and failed to suppress a smile.

She shot him a withering glare. "Don't say a word. You're far too happy to be up at this blazing hour."

"Careful, Cora, your princess is showing."

Cora snorted, pulling her hair back.

Theo rolled his eyes at the both of them. "Just start warming up, or I'll make you both do extra pushups."

"You're sadistic," she retorted.

"Noted."

Gray glanced between the two of them. They refused to look directly at each other, their banter lacking its usual flirtation. He frowned, trying to decide if he should say something. The opportunity passed as Theo began leading them through the warmup.

For a while, Gray felt good. They stretched, then jogged. Theo told Gray to go at whatever pace he wanted. Theo hung back, jogging backward to urge Cora to keep going. Gray spun around as well. Cora didn't bother glaring at them. Her face was flushed, and her stride much shorter than theirs, but she kept going.

They had a brief rest after jogging. Then Theo brought the weights out. Cora selected the lightest ones, while Gray chose a set from the middle of the pack. He quickly regretted that decision. The weights grew heavier with every exercise Theo prescribed.

The sun had risen enough to kiss the horizon, sending shafts of light to glisten in the beaded sweat on Gray's forehead. The air no longer felt crisp to him. Every breeze was a welcome reprieve from the drops of sweat rolling down his back.

Theo called for another break. Cora let her weights thud to the ground, shoulders slumping. Gray nearly did the same. He forced himself to carry the weights back to their place in line. He tried not to drag his feet as he retrieved his water bottle from the front porch. Theo followed him, tossing Cora her water along the way. She caught it from where she lay on the ground.

"How are you feeling, Gray?" Theo asked.

He swallowed, setting down his now half-empty water bottle. "Like I'm not as fit as I thought I was."

"You can't be that out of shape." He chuckled. "Don't you do a ton of hiking for your job?"

"Hiking isn't the same as this."

"But you've trained before, right?" Cora sat up, fixing Gray with a thoughtful stare. "Reluraun made it sound like you were experienced."

"Yes, Grandpa trained me years ago. He always thought the Riders would return."

Cora glanced away. She tossed her water bottle to the side and got to her feet. "Alright, Theo, what torture do you have planned next?"

Gray was sore all over. His muscles protested at the slightest move, reminding him just how long it'd been since he trained. Showering helped a little. The hot water eased some of the pain, but it sapped his motivation.

He stared at the untouched paperwork next to his bed. He'd sent one message to Dr. Lander since they arrived, then hadn't even checked for a response. He'd been too occupied with the library cleanup. Or maybe he'd been avoiding the paperwork. But now his muscles spasmed at the *thought* of moving more ancient debris.

I have to do it eventually.

Gray forced himself into the creaky desk chair, banging his knees as he settled. He took a few minutes to organize his notes, frowning at a few papers smeared with mud. They were almost unreadable. Hopefully they were backed up on the tablet.

He dug it out of his bag, tracing the webs of cracks across the screen. Unbidden, a heart-shaped face framed by light pink hair rose to the surface of his mind. He hoped Ophelia was doing alright. She was resilient, more than him, but he'd seen the pain behind her smile.

Maybe he should message her… No. He needed to work. Besides, he'd been bold enough going to see her. He'd probably scared her off, especially since she hadn't tried to message him.

Was she waiting for him to reach out first? It had already been a couple of weeks. Was it too late…?

The tablet chimed, now fully booted up. The sound jarred Gray out of his thoughts. He was being ridiculous. And procrastinating.

He swiped through the sheets of scanned data, letting out a relieved breath that the smeared paper was already in the dataset. He cleared his mind and dug in, compiling data for the interns to graph. He typed as he went, outlining their research paper. He finished his outline and paused. Dr. Lander had probably already started on the paper.

I should see how far she is.

A few taps on the table screen had his messages pulled up. There was indeed a brief response from Dr. Lander dated two weeks earlier. And five separate messages from the university department head. Gray's stomach sank. Fall term was only two weeks away. He should be done with his research for the summer and well into lesson planning. Instead, he was here, playing librarian and avoiding his work.

And the baby dragon.

Gray stifled that nagging voice. He still didn't know what to do with the hatchling. He checked on it every day, giving it food, water, new bedding. But he still didn't know what to do next. Could it survive on its own? Did mother dragons teach their young to hunt, or could they survive on their own from hatch? Knowledge the Riders had, lost with them.

He shook his head, bringing his wandering mind back again. No matter what, he'd have to be back before term started, or he might not have a job to come back to. He typed a quick message to Dr. Lander, then faced his work. His tablet chimed only a minute or two later.

Gray! Dr. Lander is out of town right now, so I'm managing her inbox. How are you? Where are you? This is Ophelia, by the way.

Gray tried to ignore the way his heart skipped when he saw her name. It quickly sank. Would she be mad at him?

Hey, Ophelia. I've been visiting my grandpa, and the signal up here is patchy.

Hopefully she wouldn't catch the fib. Siraye, however, would flay him for lying about her network.

> Where's Dr. Lander? She doesn't let just anyone read her messages.

> Family emergency. And would you trust the other interns with your inbox? She said she'll be back tomorrow. What did you need?

> I just wanted to see how much of our paper she's written already. And I have some data sets for the other interns to graph.

> She hasn't had much time to work on the paper. She's been swarmed by the university filling out reports and stuck in meetings. They pulled me in, too. Mostly to make sure I wasn't going to sue them for our, uh, incident in the field. They keep asking where you are, too. Apparently someone isn't responding to their messages.

Gray's hand rubbed the back of his neck. He was going to have a lot to sort through when he got back to Narous. Another message pinged across his screen.

> How's that package I gave you? Still intact?

It took him a minute to understand what she was getting at. Unease bubbled in his chest at her need to veil her question.

> I opened it a few days ago. I'm still trying to decide if it can come in the field with me, or if I should leave it here.

> Take good care of it for me. I want to hear all about it when you come home.

No other messages came through. Ophelia must've stepped away or gotten busy. Still, he stared at the message for a long time, a smile spreading across his face. She wanted to see him when he came back.

"No."

It came out sharper than Theo had intended, but he didn't bother to rein it in.

Cora glared up at him, fists on hips. He returned the look.

He loomed over her, arms crossed stubbornly across his chest. His fingers itched to make contact with her. He clamped them down on his biceps instead. He'd meant it when he said he was still her friend. He loved her, even if he couldn't love her as something more. Whatever had sparked between them had to be tamped down, even if Cora had cornered him in the training rooms. He let the simmering tension between them fuel his irritation instead.

"I need *real* experience, Theo."

He tried not to focus on the tiny crease between her brows, or the way her lips parted when she was angry.

He eased around her, careful not to touch her as he passed. "Not from me, you don't."

He heard the soft patter of her footsteps as she jogged to keep up with his quick strides. A prick of guilt twisted his insides, and he slowed.

"You're my trainer!"

Theo whirled around to face her. She pulled up short less than a hand's breadth from his chest. Her breath breezed across his throat as she regained her balance, struggling to keep from bumping into him. Without thinking, his hand shot out to steady her. It was gentler than his tone.

"Which *you* roped me into." He ignored Cora's cringe at his words. "To help you *work out*. And yet here I am, teaching you boxing after I told you that I wouldn't. If you're so desperate for a sparring partner, then *find someone else*."

"I've seen you spar with some of the others. Why won't you spar with me?"

"It's different."

"What, because I'm a woman?"

Theo shot her a withering glare. "You know that's not why."

"Then what is it?"

The determination on her face nearly broke his resolve. Skies, Cora had no idea how powerful that expression was. She also had no idea how powerful Theo's hands could be. He'd sent many opponents to the medics. A handful had never dueled again. He remembered all of their names.

Theo drew his hand away from her, suddenly aware he was still touching her arm. An image of Cora, bloodied and broken, forced its way into his mind.

He swallowed, taking a step away from her. "Don't put me in a position to hurt you, Cora. Because I can't do it."

"I know you won't hurt me, Theo. I trust you."

He would've preferred it if she'd slapped him. If she'd yelled or stormed off. Anything but those words. His voice was low and rough when he spoke again.

"You don't know anything about sparring. And frankly, you're not ready."

He watched the hopeful light in her eyes go out, then come back as a searing blaze of anger. She stepped closer, head tilting back to glare up at him.

"We'll see about that," she growled.

Cora shoved past him to stalk out the front doors. He stood in the dim stone hallway, breathing deep to settle his nerves.

As his mind calmed, the implications of her words sank in. Theo's stomach dropped, and he raced down the hall after her. He knew where she was going.

Several people trained together a few times a week just outside Stony Hollow. Somehow, he knew who she'd be talking to before he saw them.

She stood in front of Orym, Daethie, and Phaendar, one hand on her hip.

Shit.

Theo hustled down the slope away from Aurestyn, sliding to a stop next to Cora.

Phaendar passed a keen eye over them, a frown settling over his face.

"I'm always up for a spar," Daethie said, grinning wolfishly.

Deep shit.

Theo grabbed Cora's arm, spinning her to face him. She pulled out of his grasp like a garden snake.

"This is a bad idea." Theo fought to keep his voice steady. "Let's just think about this for a second."

"I'm done sitting around and *thinking* about things," she snapped. "You said to find another sparring partner. I found one."

Theo felt eyes on them. His attention flicked over the group, who had all but stopped training. Orym was shooing people back, creating a loose circle of space for Cora and Daethie. Tension sang through the air, the anticipation right before a fight. Theo's muscles tensed by reflex.

Cora didn't notice or didn't care. She pulled a set of wraps out of her pocket and wound them around her hands. Someone had found a set of wraps for Daethie as well. Orym came back over and whispered something in her ear. Daethie laughed, her teeth a flash of white against her deep brown skin. Theo watched as coins slipped between them, then Orym and Phaendar backed up to join the circle of onlookers.

"Is this really what you want?" Theo murmured.

Cora didn't look at him. "You don't have to watch."

Theo's hands curled into fists. He had the urge to shake her, to try and snap her out of this mood that had settled between them. Or better yet, to throw her over his shoulder and carry her away from here.

Instead, he folded his arms across his chest. "Someone has to be here to take you to the infirmary afterward."

She didn't respond, but he saw a muscle tick in her jaw. Across the circle, Daethie finished adjusting the mass of dark curls on top of her head. She gestured for Cora to join her.

Cora entered the circle without another word to him. She took her stance across from Daethie. At least her form was good. Daethie settled into her own stance. Her form wasn't perfect, but she moved with practiced ease. Theo caught the hungry gleam in her eyes, his stomach clenching into a tight ball.

Cora let Daethie make the first move. Daethie was nearly a head taller, her reach longer, but Cora moved quickly. He was struck by how graceful she was. She danced away from Daethie on light feet, ducking away from the elf's blows. He spotted it the moment Cora dropped her guard.

Daethie's fist was there instantly, connecting with her stomach with an audible thud. Her other fist connected with her head. Theo's bones rattled in sympathy as the blow landed. Cora stumbled to the side, eyes unfocused.

This was no coordinated match. There was no long game, no holding back until the third round. It was quick and brutal.

Daethie's leg snapped out, sending Cora to the ground.

Theo couldn't contain himself any longer. He rushed forward and shoved Daethie back before she could land another blow.

A strong hand landed on his arm, and he faced down Phaendar.

"Take it easy there."

"This match is over."

Theo's voice held a calm he didn't feel inside. He didn't dare look at Cora, afraid he'd launch himself at Daethie. He glared down Phaendar, who slowly lifted the hand off his arm.

"She asked to spar," Phaendar said quietly. "There's no need to get in the middle."

"No need? This is nowhere close to a fair fight, and you know it. I'm putting an end to this before it goes any further."

"She's a Rider. She'll recover."

"She's not ready."

"*She* is right here," Cora grumbled, staggering to her feet.

"See, she's fine," Phaendar said, gesturing to Cora. "Let the girl finish."

Theo opened his mouth to respond. Cora cut him off before he could.

"Back off, Theo. Now."

Her tone stopped him cold. In that moment, she wasn't his best friend reining him in. She wasn't even the angry woman who'd demanded a sparring partner. She was a queen, a commander, and she expected to be obeyed.

Theo knew from the way Phaendar shifted that he felt it, too. The air stilled around them.

Slowly, Theo backed away. Cora settled into her stance, determined. Phaendar leaned toward him as Cora and Daethie reengaged.

"You're doing a good job with her." Phaendar kept his voice low. "I've seen enough of Reluraun's work to know it isn't thanks to him she's gotten this far already. But you've got to let her test her strength. You've got to let her *fail*. Because like it or not, she's a Rider now. And it's better for her to fail here than freeze when it counts."

"Everyone keeps assuming she'll go into some sort of combat. What if she never does? What's the point of putting her through this?"

"An optimist, huh?" Phaendar chuckled darkly. "I've met plenty of Riders in my life, kid. Even the most peaceful ended up fighting at some point. Riders have a power unlike anyone else. She's going to have a target on her back for the rest of her life. In my experience, it's best to get used to that sooner than later."

Theo wanted to tell him that Cora already knew what that felt like. More so than he'd ever realized before they left Narous. He wanted to tell Phaendar that she was already strong, that she didn't need to be put through more pain to prove that.

He could only watch as Daethie continued her assault. She found every opening in Cora's guard, blows landing with thumps that set his teeth on edge. Cora slowed, not even trying to land a hit anymore. When Daethie knocked her to the ground again, she stayed there.

Sensing that it was over, the crowd dispersed. Phaendar glanced once at Theo before joining Daethie and Orym, who were exchanging more coin.

Theo approached Cora slowly. She was on her back, breathing deeply, one hand over her face. Angry words bubbled to the surface as he lowered into a squat next to her. They evaporated as he took in her swollen, bloody lip and dazed eyes.

"Let's get you out of here," he said gently.

He slid an arm under her shoulders and slowly lifted her into a sitting position. She inhaled sharply, eyes closing.

He frowned. "You probably have a concussion."

"Is that your professional opinion?"

"Yeah," Theo grunted, pulling her to her feet. "I've had enough of them to know."

He kept a steady arm around her as they made their way to the infirmary. He stopped outside the front doors, unable to make himself get any closer.

Cora pulled away, a knowing glint in her eyes. "I can take it from here. Thank you, Theo."

He nodded, heart pounding as the sharp smell of disinfectant wafted from the building. Cora opened the door without another word, leaving him standing outside, alone.

20

Every part of Cora hurt. She went straight from the infirmary to her room in Reluraun's quiet house. Luckily, she only had a mild concussion. And several bruises across her body. Thanks to the Rider bond, the swelling in her lip had already gone down.

Every muscle ached. Every little movement made her wince. But it was nothing compared to the swelling shame invading her body.

Theo was right; she hadn't been ready. She couldn't shake the feeling of helplessness as Daethie's fists pummeled her body. She'd been unable to even attempt to fight back. It was harder than she'd imagined it would be. But worse than that—she'd lost control. She'd let the simmering, insistent need to do something take over. Even now, she could feel it burning her shame to ashes, consuming her senses until all she wanted was to move.

She growled in frustration, tamping it back down. She could examine those feelings later. Right now, there was something else she needed to do.

Cora left the empty house again, threading her way across Stony Hollow. She passed Gray in the street, who told her where she needed to go. It was only a few minutes before she was standing in front of the Hub.

Cora nodded to Siraye as she passed. She followed the faint scent of citrus to the back of the communications station. Theo's legs poked out from under a desk.

She knelt down next to him, squinting to see through all of the wires. "Siraye roped you into helping out, huh?"

He shrugged, not looking at her. "I offered."

207

She bit the inside of her cheek. The silence stretched between them as she watched him work.

"I'm sorry, Theo. I should have listened to you."

His hands froze. He took a deep inhale before coming out from under the desk. He rested one arm on his knee, a twist tie spinning between his fingers.

"No, I should have listened to you." Theo's honey eyes flicked to hers, cutting off her protest. "I wanted to keep you from getting hurt. I still want to, but I realized I can't prevent that from happening. All I can do is prepare you for it."

"So…does that mean you're going to spar with me?"

"Cora." He sighed. The twist tie stopped spinning as he leaned forward. "There are reasons why I stopped fighting in the first place. And seeing you like that… It brought up bad memories."

"You know you can talk to me about it, right?"

She leaned forward too, her hand coming to rest on his. They were close enough to feel each other's breath. The hand beneath hers turned, fingers interlacing with hers. Theo's eyes shone with a light that knocked the breath out of her lungs. Her eyes fell to his lips, and she started wondering why she hadn't kissed him already.

"I've never really told anyone about what happened," he murmured.

"Then maybe that's a sign you need to."

"Any what if it changes what you think of me?"

Cora dragged her eyes back up to his. The dark curls on the top of his head were falling into his eyes again. She'd always loved that he left the top long, that he let the coils brush up against his eyebrows. It was a stark contrast to the close-trimmed sides. He usually kept his face just as neat, always shaved smooth. But under the lights of all the holo-screens of the Hub, she saw dark stubble dusting the lower half of his face. It combined with the shadow over his eyes, making him seem older, lonelier than he ever had before.

She reached up to brush a stray curl away from his eyes. "Nothing could change what I think of you."

Theo gave her hand a squeeze. The shadow lifted from his face, and he drifted closer. The tips of their noses brushed, sending a spark into her veins. He released her hand, pulling back.

Cora's face flushed. She jammed her hands into her lap, nodding behind Theo. "What are you working on?"

"Looks like a rodent chewed on one of the cables," Theo threw a thumb over his shoulder. A touch of redness had crept across his face. "Siraye doesn't have a replacement, so I did my best to get it working again."

"So, you were hot-wiring a computer?"

"That's not what that means."

Cora rolled her eyes, the tension dissipating. Her fingers found her hair, winding through the short strands. "Clearly I don't really know anything about tech."

"Why would you? You're a princess, not an engineer."

"I know, it's just…" She shrugged. "It's what Liskow is known for, and it's become my family's legacy. It's by far the biggest positive change since…"

Theo frowned as she trailed off. He nudged her leg with his toe, bringing her eyes back into focus. "Cora, what's wrong?"

"I just remembered a project my father took me to check in on," she murmured. "Greta was on my security team that day."

"And?"

"And she's the guard that let us go a few nights ago." Cora paused, waiting for a light of understanding to shine in Theo's eyes. "I'm confident she's the reason we were ambushed at the cabin. If she was willing to betray me so easily, I don't even want to consider who might know about this project."

"How bad are we talking?"

"We could be the next Galta."

Theo stared at her for a long minute. She couldn't track all of the emotions playing across his face. Finally, his eyes cleared, and he sat up straight.

"What do you want to do?"

"What do you mean?"

"I mean, what do you want to do about it, princess?"

She sat in shock for a beat, Theo watching her patiently. Cora waited for panic to set in, waited for her brain to scramble for a response. Instead, she was filled with resolve. She knew exactly what she wanted to do.

"Let's talk to Gray. I think he'll want to help."

Theo took her outstretched hand. He rose to his full height, gazing down at her in a way that made her heart skip. "Let's go."

"What exactly are we looking for?"

Gray had several maps on the library table. Most of the surviving maps were centuries old and crumpling at the edges. He had quickly—and carefully—rolled those up and moved them out of the way. He managed to dig up a couple of maps from his grandpa's house that were only twenty years old. He laid them end to end, covering an area that spanned the entire northern quarter of Liskow.

Cora frowned over the maps. "From what I remember, most of the research facility is underground," she said, leaning closer to the table. "All that can be seen above ground is a small building and a fence."

Gray scanned the maps, but nothing jumped out at him. The area Cora was searching was virtually empty of any kind of settlement. His fingers tapped against the table.

Theo leaned over her shoulder to stare at the maps. "Maybe you and Makari should fly over the area, see what you can find."

"We could," Cora hedged. "Although we would be exposing ourselves to anyone we fly over."

"We might have to, if we can't pinpoint it on one of these maps."

"Maybe not," Gray interrupted, powering up his tablet. "One of my colleagues is studying deer populations in this region. Maybe there's something useful from his latest research."

Theo and Cora pored over the maps as Gray went searching for the data. They stood close, but not quite touching, constantly aware of where the other was.

Gray shook his head, smiling. Let them figure it out on their own.

He found what he was searching for a couple of minutes later. He sent the images to his holo, then projected them over the paper. Topographical lines appeared over the maps. Gray shifted them until they aligned. A rectangular shape appeared about thirty miles east of Stony Hollow.

"That's it," Cora said, pointing.

"You're sure?"

She nodded, eyes locked on the spot. "I can feel it."

Gray glanced at Theo. Theo took a moment before nodding once.

Gray marked the spot on the paper map, then dismissed the overlay. "What's the plan, then?"

"When I went to this facility before, the project was largely conceptual," she explained. "There were prototypes of a few pieces and sketches of the rest of it. I need to see how far it's gotten."

"Are you going to tell us what this mystery project is? Or is that below our pay grade?"

She spared Theo a withering glance. The levity was short-lived as her brows lowered. Gray's stomach tightened at her expression.

"It's a flying vehicle," she kept her voice low. "Only big enough for one person, meant to be fast and maneuverable. They called it a Shrike."

"Shrike?" Theo asked. "What is that supposed to mean?"

"A shrike is a bird," Gray murmured, stomach twisting tighter. "Also called a butcher bird."

"So it's a weapon." Theo's voice carried a sharp edge. "A single-person flying weapon. Well, haven't we come full circle. They've created a man-made Dragon Rider."

Cora winced. Gray recognized the expression crossing her face. Makari wasn't happy, and she was expressing it down the bond. He rubbed the back of his neck, frowning down at the map again.

Gray knew how Stony Hollow would react to the news. Most would see it as a perversion of the Riders; the religious would see it as blasphemy, and those who lived through the worst oppression—the ones who waited for fire to rain down on their heads at the slightest wrong move—they would see it as a return to dark times. If the news made its way into Narous…

"The PEL could use this to start a full-scale civil war."

"Which is why it would be a disaster if this project leaked," she agreed. "It's a grenade with no pin, just waiting to go off in our

211

hands."

"My access code should get us into the facility, and into any database we might need. We need to steal the plans for the Shrike." Cora glanceded up from the map, eyes hard. "I can't trust this information with anyone. We sneak in, we steal the plans, and we figure out what to do with them afterward."

Theo crossed his arms, frowning down at her. "It might not be that simple. The plans won't just be available for the taking. And even if they are, there will be backups, and backups of the backups."

"Siraye might be able to help," Gray said softly. "She could create a virus that would corrupt the entire database, make everything unusable. The only problem is nothing would survive. Are you willing to sacrifice whatever data is stored on those computers?"

Cora stared straight at Gray, straightening to her full height. There was no hesitation in her clear green eyes.

"If it means avoiding a bloodbath? Absolutely."

"Alright then. If I know Siraye, she already has something ready to go. When are you going to leave?"

Theo slung an arm around Gray's shoulders. "Don't you mean 'we'?"

Gray froze. He blinked at Theo a few times, slowly processing. "You want me to come too?"

"Why wouldn't we?"

"You're part of the team," Cora said simply.

She leaned into his other side as Theo steered them toward the door.

A slow smile crept across Gray's face. He cleared his throat, suddenly hoarse. "Let's go talk to Siraye, then."

21

Theo kept glancing up as Gray drove. The flash drive Siraye had given them sat heavy in his pocket, along with her precise instructions. Their conversation had tapered off nearly fifteen minutes earlier, and now Gray sat stiff in the driver's seat. Theo glanced up again. It was too dark to see Cora and Makari anymore.

"She's fine, Theo."

"She's hundreds of feet up in the air on top of a flying, fire-breathing murder lizard."

"A 'lizard' that's more likely to murder you than her."

"Well, *that* makes me feel better."

"She can handle herself. You don't need to hover."

"I don't know what you mean."

"Yeah, you do." Gray glanced over at him, one eyebrow lifted.

Theo slouched in his seat, fingers picking at a loose thread on his pants.

"You should say something to her."

"It's not that simple, Gray."

"It could be."

"No, it couldn't. Cora doesn't want it."

Gray shot him another glance. "Are you sure about that?"

"Positive," he muttered. "But even if she did, there are things Cora doesn't know about me. Things that I'm not sure I *want* her to ever know."

There was a long moment of silence as Gray pulled off the road. He turned the car off, facing Theo.

"I'll just say this." Gray waited until Theo gave him his full attention. "Life is too short to waste. And if you want any chance at a relationship with Cora, you need to trust her."

Gray gave him one last, piercing stare before reaching into the back seat for the bag Siraye packed them. He dug out their earpieces, handing Theo one while he pushed the other into his ear.

Theo took the tiny electronic and jammed it in. It couldn't block out Gray's words. They tumbled through his mind as their earpieces crackled on.

"Cora, can you hear us?"

"Loud and clear. Skies, you drive slow! Makari and I have been circling for at least twenty minutes."

Gray rolled his eyes toward Theo. He managed a smile, shoving his thoughts away to deal with later.

They climbed out of the car as quietly as possible, Gray slinging the bag over his shoulders as they crept through the thinning brush. They kept to the side of the road, crouching behind a large bush as the gate came into view.

It was open. And there were no guards in sight.

Theo exchanged a glance with Gray. "Cora, can you see anything?"

"We're too high up. We might be seen if we get closer."

"It's worth the risk. Something isn't right."

She didn't respond. Theo watched as a dark shape glided over the facility in front of them. It made a sweeping pass before rising out of sight.

"The PEL is here."

"Are you sure?"

"I saw Thalassa Mellis walk into the facility."

Gray shot Theo a questioning look.

Theo stared at the open gate, fingers closing into fists. A rush of jitters swept through him. "Your call, Cora. Are we doing this?"

There was a beat of silence between the three of them. When her voice crackled in his ear, it was icy.

"Yes."

Wordlessly, Gray reached into their bag and pulled out two black cylinders. They were about as long and thick as Theo's forearm, with a hard plastic grip at the bottom. Siraye had called them shock batons when she'd showed them how to power them on. She'd also warned Theo not to touch them when they were on, unless he wanted to get knocked out. He twisted the grip with both hands.

The end of the shock baton exploded with blue light, pulsing beneath black mesh. A soft humming sounded, like a beehive buzzing in his hands. Theo checked the power level before twisting it back off. Gray checked his own shock baton, then settled the bag more securely across his back. They left the cover of their bush and approached the gate.

"What's the plan?" Gray asked softly.

"I see six people hanging around in front of the door. We'll have to get past them to get inside."

Theo and Gray crept along the road into the facility. There were a handful of scrawny trees and bushes lining the gravel, then yards of grass and dirt. The back of Theo's neck prickled, and his head swiveled back and forth.

He spotted two lumps under a scraggly bush. He noticed a dark streak leading from the road to the lumps as he got closer. He stopped once he could make out two sets of boots.

"I think we just found the facility guards."

Gray muttered a low curse. Theo's hand tightened around his shock baton. They skirted the bodies, continuing on to the end of the tree cover.

Just as Cora said, there were six people under the building lights. Rifles rested casually on shoulders or hung from slings. Theo and Gray stared as the group burst into laughter, shattering the quiet around them.

"Let me handle this."

A shadow shot down in front of the building, sending out a great gust of air. The ground shook as Makari landed and let loose a bone-shaking roar.

Several of the PEL guards fell backwards as they scrambled away from the dragon, weapons forgotten. One guard raised his rifle and was met with slashing claws. Makari backhanded two others into the wall. Her tail whipped around, tripping another as he tried to flee.

Theo twisted his shock baton on, jogging forward to catch a

guard that slipped under Makari's wing. In a matter of moments, all six were on the ground.

Makari growled low, sniffing at the unconscious guards before lowering onto her belly. Cora slid down from her back, stumbling a bit as she hit the ground.

Theo took a step forward, hand coming up to help her. Gray cleared his throat loudly, and Theo's hand went to his hair instead.

Cora glowered at the facility doors. "We've got to get those plans before the PEL does." She twisted to look at them. "Are you ready?"

"Ready as I'll ever be," Gray replied.

Both sets of eyes turned to Theo. His heart squeezed, instincts telling him to grab Cora and run far away. He stared down into her green-flecked eyes and squeezed his baton.

"Lead the way, princess."

Cora tried to convince Makari she was too big to fit inside. The dragoness responded by bashing in the front door and strolling through.

Makari kept shifting her wings, flinching every time they brushed against the walls. Cora sent an *I told you so* down their bond. Makari growled at her.

"Could you stop antagonizing your dragon?" Gray muttered.

Cora swore Makari looked smug.

The four of them crept deeper into the facility, passing a handful of dead guards as they went. Twice, they had to stop for her to use her access code on a door. Each time, Makari had to twist her body to fit her wings through the opening. The second time, she left long claw marks on the walls as she squirmed through. They walked down sloped hallways, their footsteps echoing in the stillness.

Cora slowed as they approached one last door. It was ajar, its access panel hanging by a few wires. She motioned for them to be quiet as she eased forward. The door opened onto a catwalk at least twenty feet above the floor. She peeked through the crack to see a huge room beyond. Dozens of tables in neat rows covered the floor below. Papers were scattered all over, while half-finished prototypes spilled wires everywhere.

She pushed the door open slowly. It swung inward soundlessly.

"I can't see anyone." She kept her voice low. "Stay quiet, just in case."

Cora slipped through the door, grateful for her years sneaking around the palace. Theo came behind her, followed by Gray. They were both passably quiet as the three crept further onto the catwalk. She winced as Makari's claws clacked against the metal beneath their feet. Her head whipped around to glare at the dragon. Makari's ears flattened against her head, teeth flashing.

Just stay there, Cora growled through the bond.

Makari huffed, pressing against her mind. Cora's nose filled with what Makari had already sensed.

Five unfamiliar scents wafted through the space. They were only traces; the individuals they belonged to already moved on. She gave Makari a grudging glance.

Gray watched them with barely concealed amusement. Theo's face stayed carefully neutral.

"Come on." She sighed. "We better move faster if we want to catch them."

They found a set of stairs and jogged down it. Makari ignored the stairs, leaping over the railing and onto the floor in a graceful arc. Cora continued her brisk pace at the bottom of the stairs, leaping over an overturned container with hardly a thought. Theo and Gray kept pace, weaving through the tables to either side of her as they went. She slowed as they approached the back wall.

Directly across from her rose a beast of curved metal glimmering in the dim light. The front was half curved glass, with a sharp nose jutting forward. To either side was a set of propellers framed by short wings. A pointed tail shot out behind the body, a miniature propeller attached to the back. Makari stalked next to Cora, hackles raised.

"I'm going to take a wild guess that's the Shrike," Theo said.

"It's a lot bigger than the last time I saw it," Cora replied.

Makari stared at the aircraft, her pupils dilating. Heat wafted from her sides, her leg muscles coiling beneath her. Cora stroked the bond, hoping to soothe her. She was met with a primal fury that nearly knocked her over. Makari growled, deep and menacing. Cora felt the rage of a goddess in that sound.

Gray laid a hand on her arm. Sweat gleamed on his forehead, and she realized that Makari must be giving off more heat than she realized.

"You need to calm her down." Gray kept his own voice calm, but fear gleamed in his eyes. "If she flames in here, we'll be trapped in an oven."

"There's gotta be some sort of fire suppression system," Theo said, swiping sweat out of his eyes.

"Not one built for dragon fire."

Makari, Cora tried. *Hey, girl, it's okay.*

Makari snarled in response.

Before Cora could reach out again, Makari's tail swung, shoving all three of them back. She leapt, slamming into the Shrike with a boom. Metal screeched as her claws dug in and ripped. Cora stumbled back as a large sheet of metal crashed to the floor at her feet. The frame of the Shrike warped and bent as Makari's hot breath turned it red. One wing clanged to the floor while the other crashed into a table thirty feet away.

Makari exhaled the last of her heat and prowled back from the heap of mangled parts where the Shrike once stood. Her satisfied grunt echoed in the now silent room.

"Well, they know we're here *now*," Theo grumbled.

Cora tore her eyes away from the wrecked Shrike. To their right was a door and another hallway. They moved down it at a fast clip, Makari once again taking up the rear.

Cora slowed as they passed a room filled with rows of humming black stacks. Wires snaked between them, and lights flashed and blinked.

Theo leaned over her shoulder to peer inside. "Looks like a server room. How much data are they storing down here?"

Gray leaned over her other shoulder as they stopped in the doorway. He shot her a sidelong glance. "Do you still want to unleash the virus here? There's no telling what information is on all of those servers."

"What choice do we have?" she asked grimly. "It's better

218

erased than in the hands of someone like Thalassa Mellis."

Cora ran back down the hall without waiting for the men to catch up to her.

Voices drifted down the hallway. She exchanged a glance with Theo and Gray. One by one, they powered on their shock batons. Makari snorted, picking up on the tension.

Easy. Cora brushed a light hand against her neck. *We don't want them to hear us.*

Makari lowered into a stalking crouch that made Cora glad she wasn't the dragon's prey. They eased forward, Theo and Gray close enough for their breath to rustle her hair. The voices grew louder.

Cora peeked around the side of the third door. Inside, Thalassa leaned over the shoulder of a lanky young man. They stared at a glowing screen as the man tapped at a keyboard. Two others sat at their own keyboards, while one man leaned against the wall.

Cora pulled back, motioning for Theo and Gray to follow her.

"How much time do you need to launch the virus?" she whispered.

"Shouldn't take more than a couple of minutes," Theo murmured back. "But I need to get to one of those computers to plug in the drive."

Makari nudged her arm, pressing an image into her mind.

Cora glared at the dragon. *We need the computers to* work. *You can't just incinerate them.*

Makari let out an irritated snort. They glared at each other before the dragon finally sat back on her haunches. She bared her teeth in annoyance.

"We still have the element of surprise," Gray said, one eye on Makari. "Cora and I can get their attention while you handle the virus."

"Think you can keep up with me, Gray?"

Gray smiled grimly, adjusting his grip on the humming shock baton in his hand. "Absolutely."

Time slowed around Gray as he entered the room. His shock baton crackled as it swung towards the man leaning against the wall. He barely had time to stand up straight before it crashed into him. Gray was already turning as he slumped to the floor.

He snatched the chair out from under the woman at the closest computer, dumping her onto the ground. She stood, knife flashing in her hand. He pushed the chair towards Theo, eyes locked on the woman before him.

She darted forward, light glinting off the edge of her blade. Gray brought up his shock baton. The knife screeched against the metal cage of the baton, sending a shower of sparks across their boots. She dropped the knife with a gasp, hand shaking from the jolt of electricity.

Gray lunged, and she dove out of the way. He pulled back, bouncing on the balls of his feet. He heard his grandpa's instructions in his mind, drilling fighting instincts into him.

The woman dodged him again, missing his shock baton by a hair. She was good, but she hadn't been trained by a Rider. Gray watched her muscles coil. He knew exactly what she was planning.

He caught her foot as it came up and shoved her off balance. He pounced, touching the electrified end of his baton to her skin. She dropped to the floor.

Gray spun, and the rest of the room came into focus. Theo sat in front of a keyboard as lines of text scrolled past him. Two other PEL members lay on the floor, leaving Cora and Thalassa facing each other.

Thalassa held a firearm pointed directly at Cora. "You can go ahead and put down your little fly swatter."

Gray dropped his shock baton to the floor with a thunk. He glowered at the merwoman. Thalassa didn't bother glancing at him.

"Nice haircut, princess. Oh, don't look so surprised," she purred. "I've studied your face enough to know it without your usual pound of makeup."

"What are you doing here?" Cora's voice was icy.

"I could ask you the same thing, *Your Highness*. Felt the sudden need to stroll through a secret government facility?"

"You didn't answer my question."

"And you know exactly why I'm here, so let's move on, shall we? Hold out your hands."

220

Cora cocked an eyebrow but otherwise refused to move.

Thalassa dropped the taunting smirk. "I don't have all night, princess. I know people who will pay good money for you, and many more who would pay for your body on ice. Either way, you're leaving with me. Or"—Thalassa's arm swung smoothly to point her gun at Theo—"things are about to get very messy."

Gray knew Cora was fighting to keep the panic out of her eyes. She failed miserably. He nearly jumped as the first man he shocked started to stir. He glanced over at Theo. Theo stared at Thalassa with unmasked hatred. His fingers were poised over the keys, a command blinking on the screen in front of him.

A deep growl reverberated through the floor. Thalassa's eyes turned to the doorway, then widened in shock.

Makari's head and neck glided into the room. The opening was too narrow for the dragon to fit anything else. She stood there filling up the only exit as the temperature began to rise. Thalassa stumbled backward until she hit the computer desk behind her.

It was Cora's turn to smirk. "I'm sorry, you were saying?"

Cora couldn't keep the smug smile off her face. She delighted in Thalassa's terror.

Makari growled again, shaking Thalassa's crew to full consciousness. One of them screamed, backing as far away from Makari as she could get.

Thalassa shook herself, training her gun on Cora again. "Pull yourselves together," she snarled at her crew. "Get your beast out of the way, Catarina."

Cora glared at Thalassa, hatred burning through her veins. Makari snarled, the air around her snout shimmering with heat. Cora spotted motion behind Gray. She twisted her head to watch as the man behind him darted forward. He snatched the shock baton off the floor and swung it at Makari.

Her ivory teeth flashed as they clamped around his arm. She lifted him off the ground and shook. His scream was cut off as his body slammed into the far wall.

Thalassa's face paled. She gaped at the dragon, the barrel of her gun dipping.

Cora's body moved without thinking. Her foot snapped forward, connecting hard with Thalassa's side. The woman's breath rushed out in a gasp as her firearm clattered to the ground.

As if some spell had broken, the room erupted into chaos. Cora was vaguely aware of Theo and Gray entangled with Thalassa's crew as the merwoman sprang at her.

Cora grunted as a sharp elbow dug into her gut. She got her hands up into her fighting stance, but she couldn't keep up with Thalassa's blows. She moved like a hurricane, faster than Cora could anticipate. Cora backed away, unable to do more than fend off Thalassa.

She saw the fist coming for her head too late. Pain exploded in her temple, and she staggered. Thalassa's lip curled back from her teeth in a sneer. She opened her mouth to speak but was cut off by a sharp screech.

Makari's claws raked across the metal floor as she strained against the doorway. Frustration roiled from her and into Cora. Cora couldn't feel the heat coming off her in shimmering waves, but she knew the dragon wanted to flame. She wanted to release the building pressure in her throat and turn the room into ash.

Cora scrambled to send soothing thoughts to Makari. *Easy, Makari. Gray and Theo are still in here.*

Makari's eyes darted over to where Theo and Gray struggled with the remaining PEL crew. She swallowed, tendrils of smoke puffing out of her nostrils. Her eyes focused back on Thalassa, one curved claw reaching toward her.

Thalassa backed up to the desk, an eye on Makari. She snatched a drive out of the computer port and shoved it in a pocket. When her hand emerged, she was clutching a shiny black ball. She clicked a button Cora couldn't see, and it started clicking.

"Until next time, princess."

Thalassa tossed the ball across the room as it clicked faster. It rolled up against the wall, the clicks nearly on top of one another. The clicking stopped.

There was a split second of silence before a loud boom shook the floor. Cora dropped to the floor as shards of debris flew through the room, followed by a cloud of dust.

Theo dropped down in front of Cora, startling her. His eyes raked her face. "Are you alright?"

"I'm fine." Cora pushed to her feet with a groan. "Just bruised."

Gray stared out into the hall next to Theo, brow pulled low. She didn't like his expression.

"We need to catch up with Makari before she barbecues them all," Gray said warily.

Cora felt her dragon's simmering rage. She pushed into Makari's mind as they jogged down the hallway after her. Thalassa and her crew were keeping ahead of the dragon—barely. A hot, seething part of herself thought it might enjoy watching Makari rip apart her mother's killer. Makari responded to her train of thought, surging forward and leaving deep gouges across the walls as she passed.

Cora pushed herself faster, legs pumping double for each stride from Theo and Gray. Makari's snarls and growls echoed down the halls, growing louder the farther they went. They burst into the main chamber with the rows of tables.

It was on fire.

Makari pounced onto a table, knocking it into the next row. She narrowly missed Thalassa's crew. She bellowed in rage, then shot a jet of flame so bright it nearly blinded Cora. Alarms blared overhead, echoing against Makari's wrath.

Thalassa raced up the stairs at the far end of the room, only two crew members behind her. Cora watched as Makari turned her flames toward them. The stairs glowed red hot as Thalassa threw herself onto the catwalk. Makari tensed, ready to launch herself forward.

Gray grabbed Cora's arm to get her attention. He was practically shouting in her face to be heard. "You need to calm Makari down! If she flames again, she'll make herself pass out. There's no way we could get her out of here!"

Her heart squeezed in panic. Her mind surged forward, bumping clumsily into Makari's presence. Cora mentally rebounded as if she'd hit a brick wall. Her hands began to shake. She couldn't feel the growing heat in the room, but her body reacted anyway. Sweat slicked her palms and shone on Theo and Gray's faces. She closed her eyes, pushing harder into Makari's mind. Makari growled and lashed her tail.

Come on, let me in.

Makari swung her head around, baring teeth as long and sharp as daggers.

Cora shoved with all her might. Her senses were immediately overwhelmed. Her nose filled with the scent of blood. All she wanted, all she *needed* was to move. To tear, to rip, to *shred*. She could practically taste it. Could feel the crunch of bones between her jaws. And beneath it all was a blistering, burning fury.

Cora slammed back into her own mind with a gasp. She trembled from crown to sole. For a moment, she felt those claws piercing her body, rending her. She took a step back, eyes wide with horror. The sheer power of the dragon before her rammed into her mind. Cora was afraid she would wet herself.

"Cora." Gray's calm voice grounded her. "Look at me."

She obeyed, eyes still wide.

He put his hands on her shoulders and leaned down until they were at eye level. "You are not helpless here. You are a *Rider*. She will listen to you. Just don't back down."

Cora drank in the trust filling Gray's eyes. She guzzled it down until she felt steady enough to nod.

Gray released her shoulders and stepped back.

She took one step forward. Then another. She had Makari's full attention now. The wall of fury was still up in Makari's mind. Even without it, she saw how the dragoness sized her up. She swallowed down another wave of terror. Bond or no bond, Makari could kill her in an instant.

Cora closed her eyes as she once again approached Makari's mental wall. She didn't shove or force her way through. She made herself as unyielding as that wall, a solid mass of calm energy. She passed through into Makari's mind and again met the inferno.

Makari.

The thought resonated through their bond like a thunderclap. Makari stood erect before her, wings flared. Her mind roiled, shying back from Cora.

224

Peace, Makari. The words flowed from Cora on their own. *You are safe. We are safe. Easy now.*

Cora opened her eyes. She kept a foot in Makari's mind to prevent getting kicked out again.

Slowly, Makari relaxed. Cora retreated as Makari settled back into herself. The dragon exhaled in a deep gust, exhaustion replacing the rage in her eyes. She seemed smaller as she settled her wings close to her body again.

Cora waited until Makari was fully back to herself before pivoting to check on Theo and Gray. Gray grinned at her as Theo fiddled with a panel on the wall.

"The fire sprinkler system is shot." He swiped at his face, pausing mid-motion to hack out a cough. "It doesn't even register that there's a fire. Whoever installed it is an idiot."

Theo slammed the panel shut. Cora glanced at the room as one of the walls groaned. Flames licked across workstations and climbed walls. She glanced back to see Theo and Gray wiping at their faces again. Her heart dropped when she saw how unfocused their eyes were. She grabbed their arms and started shoving them toward the nearest staircase.

"Too late for that now," she huffed. "Let's get you out of here."

Cora refused to shy away from their sweaty shirts as she pulled them along the catwalk. Twice Gray stumbled, nearly dragging them all down. Theo swayed, his eyes staring sightlessly ahead.

Makari leaped up on the landing behind them. She looked worse for wear herself. Her wings tucked limply against her sides, head drooping.

"Go ahead of us. You'll be faster, anyway."

Makari soundlessly obeyed. Cora's heart squeezed. She could worry about her dragon later.

She pulled Theo and Gray's arms around her shoulders. She tried not to stagger under their weight. She blinked smoke out of her eyes, urging the men to keep moving their feet. Before the end of the first hallway, she had to save her breath. The smoke scratched her lungs, and clouded her gaze.

By the end of the second turn, they had slowed to a shuffle. She winced as they banged into a corner, nearly invisible through the haze. Gray coughed on her left, swaying and nearly taking all of them down.

Cora longed to reach out to Makari and borrow some of her strength. She didn't dare, not when her dragon already seemed so spent.

Cora's legs trembled. She kept putting one foot in front of the other. Kept forcing smoky air into her lungs. So slowly, the front door came into view. She surged forward, pulling Theo and Gray out into cool night air. She made it a few feet away from the building before collapsing to the ground, Theo and Gray falling with her.

She pressed her cheek into the short blades of grass. She took great gulps of air, savoring the rich scent of wet earth next to her nose.

She didn't know how long she stayed there. She could've stared there all night; she was so exhausted. Instead, she pushed up onto her knees to check on Theo and Gray.

Their skin was hot to the touch, and no longer sweaty. Their eyes were open, but unfocused, and they responded with little more than weak coughs when she spoke to them.

Makari slunk over to nuzzle their cheeks, a warning singing across the bond.

"What do I do?" Cora whispered.

Makari whimpered, nudging Gray with her nose. He didn't so much as blink at her.

Panic rose in Cora's chest, chasing away the heavy exhaustion. She didn't know how to help them. Her hands rose to tangle in her hair, holo- bracelet glinting under the facility's exterior lights. Cora tapped the surface with trembling hands. It only rang once before a high voice pierced the night.

"Hey, Cora, how's the mission?"

"Siraye! I'll tell you about it when we get back, but right now I need help."

The elf's voice sobered. *"What's wrong?"*

Cora described the fire and Theo and Gray's condition. She heard the faint sound of tapping as she spoke.

"You need to lower their body temperature. Do you have any

226

water with you?"

"I think there's some in Gray's car. Hang on."

Cora jogged up the gravel path, legs screaming in protest. She skidded to a stop next to Gray's car, yanking open the trunk to find a small stash of water bottles.

"I found some water. I hope it's enough."

"Great! Knowing Gray, you should have plenty. It'll be faster if you drive it down to them."

"Um." She blinked slowly. "I don't know how to drive."

"Well, Cora, you're about to get a crash course."

22

With Siraye's help, Cora managed to drive the car over to Theo and Gray. Makari stood guard over them, pausing her vigil to nuzzle their hands. Cora didn't bother counting the water bottles. She snatched three and raced over to her friends.

"Pour water under their armpits," Siraye's voice instructed from Cora's holo. *"Other good places are their heads and necks."*

Cora drenched Theo and Gray as best she could. They were already looking a bit better in the cool night air.

"Thanks for your help, Siraye," she said. "I'm going to drive us home. Don't wait up. It'll take me a while."

"Don't take too long. It looks like someone finally heard the alarms you set off."

"How on earth do you know these things?" Cora grunted as she helped Theo into a sitting position.

"It's a gift. Maybe I'll teach you when you get back."

She hung up before Cora could respond. Cora shook her head and leaned down to help Gray. Makari edged closer, lowering her neck so he could hold onto her. Together, they were able to help Gray, then Theo into the car.

Cora closed the door and found Makari a hand's breath away from her. Makari brought her head low, nearly shoving Cora over as she rubbed against her. She scratched her dragon's ear and reached out with her mind. Makari's thoughts were lined with remorse. Cora stroked her nose, sending soothing thoughts.

"I would have done the same thing," she murmured. "At least we made it out."

Cora would never forget the rage she'd felt from Makari.

Mostly because she'd felt a spark of it inside herself.

A deep purr interrupted her thoughts. She smiled at Makari, giving her one last scratch before pulling away.

"You'll have to fly without me."

Makari shook out her wings, letting them reach their full size with a soft snap. Her claws curled into the ground, then uncurled, leaving behind deep gouges. She gave Cora a hard stare before launching herself upward. Cora watched the night swallow her up before climbing into the driver's seat.

The car crawled out of the facility gate. She gripped the wheel tightly, afraid to go any faster. Makari pressed an image into her mind of cars driving toward the facility. Gritting her teeth, Cora pushed the gas pedal harder. The car lurched forward, trees starting to whip past as they hurtled down the road.

Relax. You can ride a dragon; you can drive a car.

Cora repeated that to herself as the road twisted and turned into the mountains. Gradually, her arms and shoulders relaxed. She even released the wheel to blast cold air through the car. By the time Theo and Gray were coming back to themselves, she was shivering.

"I didn't know you could drive," Theo grumbled from the back seat.

"I can now. Mostly."

"Cora." Gray's soft voice was laced with awe. "That was… The fact that you got us out by yourself —"

"Let's not do this," she cut in, sharper than she'd intended. "You wouldn't have even been in there if it wasn't for me."

"No one forced us to go."

"And it probably won't be the last time something like that happens," Gray pointed out.

Cora pursed her lips. She didn't voice the nagging thought on her mind. The thought that once she returned to the palace, to her old life, that whatever she accomplished out here would disappear. She would have to go back to being little more than a political prop for others to use.

And after tonight, after having to step up to save her friends' lives, another, quieter thought kept whispering to her. That she wasn't sure she *could* go back. More importantly, that she didn't want to.

It took the three of them twice as long to get back. Cora insisted on driving the whole way, only stopping once to retrieve the leftover bottles of water for Theo and Gray to drink. She grudgingly drank half of Theo's after he threatened to sit on the side of the road until she did. Makari was waiting at the base of the bridge. Cora hated climbing onto the exhausted dragon's back, but there was no other way.

It was after midnight when Makari thumped onto the gravel driveway of Reluraun's house. The lights were all on inside.

They had barely climbed down when the front door flew open. Reluraun stomped onto the porch and crossed his arms. His face was unreadable in the dark, but Cora felt his eyes boring into her.

Siraye stepped around Reluraun, racing down the driveway like a hare. She threw her arms around Cora.

"Sorry," she whispered meekly. "It sounded like you were in trouble, so I told him what happened."

"It's okay. Thank you for your help tonight."

Siraye gave her a squeeze before giving the same treatment to Gray and Theo. She gave them one last stare before tossing her silver braid over a shoulder and escaping into the night.

Gray squared his shoulders and pushed to the front of their group. He kept his tone casual as they approached the porch. "You're up late, Grandpa."

"Kitchen. *Now*."

Reluraun waited for them to file in before slamming the door shut behind them. He strode to the head of the table and crossed him arms again as they each took a seat in the cold wooden chairs.

"Is something wrong, Grandpa?"

Cora had never seen this calculated coolness from Gray. He had the practiced air of someone who had been yelled at by Reluraun many times.

Reluraun shot him a glance dripping with ire. "Don't play games with me, boy. You know *very well* what's wrong."

Gray shot to his feet, the legs of his chair scraping loudly. He leaned forward, stabbing a finger into the table as he spoke. "Don't bring that up now. I'm not a child anymore. I understood what I was getting myself into. We all did."

"You're only twenty-eight years old. By elven standards, you *are* a child. Now *sit down.*"

Reluraun didn't wait to see if Gray obeyed before rounding on Cora. He didn't yell, yet every word echoed through the room like a thunderclap.

"And you. It's not enough for you to disrespect Rider training practices. You have to completely dismantle Rider protocol as well! There is a proper order, and a proper way to handle missions, and you are *not* ready. I haven't seen this level of entitled, insubordinate behavior in centuries!"

She sat up straight. Indignation boiled through her veins, but she kept her voice calm. "And how, exactly, was I insubordinate? The last time I checked, there was no one to be insubordinate to."

Reluraun's face reddened. She ignored how Gray's eyes darted between them, focusing on Reluraun.

"You put everyone you took with you in danger, including your dragon," Reluraun pointed one long finger at her. "All to protect your family's *reputation.*"

"Yes, I did it to protect my family." Cora couldn't stop the scalding anger from pouring off of her tongue. "Do you know what happens to a monarchy during a revolt? Just look at what they did in Galta. I'm not going to just sit back and watch as my family's corpses are nailed to the city gates."

"Riders are *supposed* to put the greater good above all else." Reluraun's fist thumped against the table in emphasis. "You can't just abandon your oaths whenever you feel like it!"

"*What* oaths?" Cora roared. She shot to her feet, glaring across the table at Reluraun. "I haven't sworn any oaths, mostly because you still don't trust me with any Rider traditions. So much for being an unbiased trainer."

"I took you on, didn't I? Against my better judgment. I warned you to abandon your Bjorn ways to be a Rider."

"You mean the Riders whose entire culture collapsed? The ones who were conquered by a bunch of 'backwater barbarians'? With the help of the Riders' own patron goddess, according to some."

She barely stopped to take a breath, plowing on before Reluraun could form a response. "Even if I wanted to abandon my heritage, I can't just stop being a Bjorn. Mostly because I already have a duty to my country, my family, my people. My bond with Makari doesn't change that. So no, I won't sit back and watch when I can do something about it."

Silence pressed against Cora's ears as she and Reluraun glowered at each other. His anger hung about him like a thundercloud, charging the air.

"Then I want no part in your training."

Reluraun left without another word.

Callan was getting tired of meeting in dim back rooms. The musty scent of disuse reminded him of his childhood home. He thought he had rid himself of that smell for good.

His footsteps echoed against the stone floor, breaking a silence as thick as honey. He still found the quiet of the old palace jarring. The thick stone walls blocked any sound from the bustle just a few halls away. Callan pushed open one elaborate wood door and faced a familiar set of thrones.

Thalassa already leaned against the stone chair at the head of the room. He walked through the Riders' chamber, unable to escape the feeling that they were watching him. She wordlessly held out her hand as he approached, a sleek drive laying across her palm.

He turned the drive over in calloused fingers. "I take it you didn't have any trouble?"

"Nothing I couldn't handle. I can't go back for the prototype, though."

"Why not?"

"Because the facility is nothing but ash now."

Callan glared at Thalassa. He worked to keep his anger at a low simmer. "That wasn't part of the plan."

Thalassa looked as if she'd bitten a lemon. She crossed her arms and glared back. "It wasn't my doing," she hissed. "A Dragon Rider showed up."

Every one of his muscles froze. He blinked once, twice,

232

struggling to comprehend what she'd just told him. Then her words hit him with full force, heating his rage to a roiling boil. His next words came out as a low growl.

"That's not possible."

Thalassa was unfazed by his temper. Insufferable woman. His fingers itched to curl around her neck again.

"Believe what you want. I, however, have no intention to be nearly flame-broiled again. If she brings that dragon around, I'm out. No matter how much you offer me."

His fingers flexed around the drive still in his hand. It was like an anchor, allowing him to focus. The red at the edges of his vision slowly faded, but his jaw remained clenched.

"Did you recognize this 'Rider'?"

"No."

An unexpected wrinkle. Callan slipped the drive into his pocket, not trusting himself to hold it any longer.

"Your plan will fall apart if this gets out," she said flatly.

"Will it now? You say that as if you know anything about my plan."

He threw her a withering glare that she met with sharp eyes. She straightened from her casual lean against the stone chair. She prowled forward, her low voice carrying in the still chamber.

"Don't I? You're making the same plays you did in Galta. Stir up the peasants, create unrest, and use the ensuing chaos to eject the monarchy and set yourself up as the new head of government." Thalassa's voice dropped even lower as she neared. "Liskow is a fat, juicy plum just ripe for the picking. It has resources Galta desperately needs, and an organic discontent that just needs a little fertilizer to grow into full-scale civil unrest. It's brilliant."

"But?"

"But Liskow hasn't gotten over its hero worship of the Dragon Riders," Thalassa said flatly. "Enough people would see a return of the Riders as some sort of sign from the gods. They'll drop you like yesterday's trash. Then all of that planning will be for nothing."

Thalassa was less than an arm's length away. She watched him warily, tensed and ready to spring at his slightest move.

233

He slid his hands into his pockets. "Let me guess, this is the part where you offer to take care of my problem for a fee?"

She let out a mirthless laugh. "Absolutely not. I wouldn't touch that dragon with a ten-foot pole."

"Then why bother telling me this?"

"Whatever you're going to do, I'd do it quick." Her shoes clicked crisply as she stalked past him. She paused at the door, twisting to glance over a shoulder. "You can send the rest of my payment the same way as last time. I'm finishing my last part of the bargain, then I'm getting the hell out of here."

The door closed quietly behind her, leaving Callan to sink down onto the nearest stone chair. The significance of meeting in this room finally sunk in. He glowered at the empty thrones. He wished he had something to smash them all to rubble.

The Dragon Riders had failed. They didn't deserve redemption. And the senate was counting on him. He needed to gain control of the situation.

Callan's holo chirped softly, interrupting his thoughts. He opened the message, and a ghost of a smile touched his lips.

We found the prince.

Gray hadn't slept well. The silence emanating from his grandpa's room hung over the entire house. He'd struggled to hang on to sleep until the sun painted the garden in shades of gold. He finally gave up and threw on fresh clothes. He eased by Theo's still sleeping frame into the hall. He passed Grandpa and Cora's empty rooms.

Gray's mouth twisted into a frown. Grandpa's words still stung against his skin like paper cuts. He hadn't seen that expression on Grandpa's face since the night his parents died. Gray had been reckless that night, too. The only difference was that this time he knew the dangers. The thought set his stomach churning.

He stopped outside Aurestyn, realizing where his feet had taken him. He considered turning back. He didn't have anything for it. There was that spark in his mind again, urging him forward.

Gray listened, his steps echoing against the smooth stone floor. He veered away from the hall that led to the aerie, following

234

the path down to the hatchery. Warm air engulfed him, carrying a whiff of sulfur. He'd never been down to the hot spring that heated the hatchery, but he could guess how pungent it was.

He followed the narrow stone hall up to a waist-high wooden gate. Scratches marred the smooth surface and criss-crossed both sides of it. Gray leaned over the gate and scanned the cavern beyond. It was roughly circular, with a dirt floor and several rock shelves along the wall. He'd left piles of straw on several of the shelves for the hatchling, but they were all empty. His eyes roved over the space until he spotted the baby dragon. It was curled up on the leftover straw, nose tucked under its tail.

Gray hadn't had a chance to study the hatchling's anatomy, but staring at it sleeping peacefully in the straw, he had the distinct impression it was female. She lifted her head as he eased through the wooden gate. He lowered himself to the dirt floor, keeping his distance as she stretched dainty wings. A yawn split her mouth, revealing tiny white teeth framing a pink tongue. Her spots gleamed ebony in the lights strung around the cavern. Her skin had darkened to a jet black, the first black dragon he'd ever seen. Grandpa had once told him they were exceptionally rare.

"You are full of surprises, aren't you?"

The tiny dragon sneezed, then glared at him as if it were his fault. He chuckled, holding out a hand for her to sniff. Her nostrils flared just inches from his fingertips. Her ears flicked toward something Gray couldn't hear. She whipped around, dropping into a crouch.

He watched as she skulked to a shadowy section of the cavern. Her muscles bunched, then she leaped. There was a high-pitched squeal, then silence. The hatchling returned to her straw with a rat hanging limp in her mouth. Gray listened to her dig into it, his mood darkening with every passing minute.

Part of him whispered that he should be recording her behavior. He couldn't summon the energy to do it. He kept replaying memories from the night before. Remembering how scared he felt as Makari flamed. He'd kept his calm in front of Cora, but he'd been on the verge of panic. He could still feel heat pressing on him, shoving away any rational thought. Even with all of his study and

235

fieldwork, even with all his grandpa's stories, he'd never truly felt the power of a dragon. Until last night.

As the hatchling made quick work of her prey, Gray's certainty grew. He couldn't handle a dragon. He didn't want to try. This baby needed to go back into the wild. The thought made him cold, as if a warm presence withdrew at the idea.

"What are you doing down here?"

His head whipped toward the wooden gate. He hadn't heard Cora approach. He'd been too deep in his own thoughts.

"Why are you here?" he asked.

Cora leaned her arms on the top of the gate. Where the wood was about waist height on Gray, it came up nearly to her chest.

"Makari's been sniffing at this tunnel like crazy." Cora's eyes landed on the hatchling. "I think I know why."

Gray rubbed the back of his neck sheepishly. She lifted one eyebrow, waiting for him to speak.

"I brought her back from my research trip. I wasn't sure she would even hatch," he rambled. "I didn't want to get anyone's hopes up."

"Relax, Gray. You don't have to explain to me why you wanted to keep her to yourself."

"Don't I? This would be part of your job, as our only Rider."

Cora crinkled her nose at the idea. "I think what constitutes my 'job' is up to me to decide. And I'm deciding to stay out of your business."

"I appreciate it."

There was a beat of silence. He felt her eyes searching his face, but he kept his own trained on the hatchling.

"Have you tried to bond her?"

"No."

There was a soft clicking as Cora unlatched the gate and slipped through. She settled on the ground next to him, hardly making a sound. She watched him with the same quiet intensity as the baby dragon in front of them.

"Why not?" she asked.

Gray blew his breath out through his lips, debating how much to share. As he considered, an overwhelming need to speak swept

236

over him. He rotated to face Cora fully.

"I was born in Stony Hollow, spent the first few years of my life here. My parents loved these mountains. But Stony Hollow is tiny. When I started school, there were three of us in class together. So my parents and I moved to Narous. I loved it there, and I loved coming back here every summer. Everything was great."

"But?"

"All my life, I heard the whole town going on about how I would bring the Riders back. They were all so *certain* that I could do it. Then in Narous, I was top of my class. I thrived at school, and the teachers noticed it. It made me into one cocky son of a kraken."

Cora chuckled appreciatively. She watched him with those keen eyes while Gray continued.

"My parents were investigators for the city Watchers. They often worked odd hours, so I'd hang out with my school friends. I was fourteen, and they were working late. My friend's dad was a customs officer. He told us about some of the shipments he inspected, told us he was suspicious that someone was trafficking dragons, but he couldn't prove it. Naturally, we decided to check it out. I was destined to be a Dragon Rider, right? This is what Riders do. So we snuck out to the receiving yard. And we found a juvenile dragon in a shipping crate. Ever the heroes, we got to work setting it free. What I didn't know is that my parents were with the city Watchers to bust the dragon traffickers."

"What happened?"

"The details aren't important." He swallowed, voice suddenly thick. "We set the dragon free, and it wisely flew away as fast as it could. But the traffickers were members of the Red Gryphons. They didn't go down without a fight. My friend and I got caught in the chaos, and my parents died protecting us."

Hot tears slipped down his face. They caught in the stubble he still hadn't bothered to shave.

Cora laid a gentle hand on his shoulder. "It's not your fault, Gray. Your parents still would've been there if you hadn't gone."

"But they might have made it back alive."

Her lips pressed into a line. After a moment, she shook her

head, eyes bright. "You don't know that. You can't keep carrying the burden of what *might* have happened. Personally, I think what you did was brave. Not many people would risk themselves like that."

"With good reason," Gray muttered. He sighed, a weight lifting from his shoulders. "Thank you, Cora. The same is true for you, too."

"What is?"

"I've seen the look on your face. It's the same one I've had for years." He waited a beat before continuing. "Your mom's death isn't your fault, either."

It was Cora's turn to glance away. She pulled her knees up to her chest, withdrawing. "Doesn't make it hurt any less though, does it?" She breathed deep, blinking back tears. "At least you were *doing* something. I just stood there and watched."

He waited for her to say more. She pursed her lips, as if swallowing anything else she might want to tell him.

"Is that why you work so hard?" Gray asked. "You don't have to prove anything, Cora."

"I need to prove it to myself," she murmured.

Gray closed the distance between them, pulling her into a one-armed hug. She loosened, letting her head rest against his shoulder.

"I might not have the experience of my grandpa, but if you want, I'll train you."

"Only if you train *with* me."

Gray stared at the hatchling, curled up once more and watching him with half-lidded eyes. A soft purring emanated from her nest of straw. He felt it as if she were curled against his chest.

"Deal."

238

23

Cora left Gray at the entrance to the hatchery. She checked on Makari one last time, triple-checking that she had clean water. Makari huffed at her, annoyance flickering over their bond at her mothering. Cora ignored her, spreading out some clean straw for good measure. Makari shot her a glare before launching herself into the open air.

Cora dragged herself toward Aurestyn's entrance. She'd been up since dawn, unable to sleep any longer. Not that she'd gotten much sleep to begin with. She'd run for an hour, leaving her legs aching. Or maybe they ached from the workout she'd done after. She rubbed her eyes.

Her holo lit up, reminding her of the unanswered message from Siraye. She swallowed a sigh. She hadn't showered the night before, and the grime clung to her like a second skin.

Cora paused just outside the great hall. She hadn't used Aurestyn's baths before, but the hallway was just to her right. Siraye could wait long enough for her to wash.

She followed the gently sloping hall, the air heating as she descended. The same hot springs that warmed the hatchery filled deep pools carved into the stone. She stopped next to the first pool. There were several halls branching off to other pools beyond, but Cora didn't feel like venturing further. She unlaced her boots, noting that someone had left a scrub brush and bar of soap on a tray next to the edge.

Her clothes dropped to the floor, and she slid into the warm water. Steam wafted around her as she sank up to her neck. Her toes just barely reached the bottom of the pool. She let the water soothe the knots out of her muscles.

Cora allowed herself a few minutes before drifting over to the soap. She'd just started scrubbing when wet feet slapped the floor in one of the halls to her left. Her head whipped around to see Theo emerge from one of the other bathrooms.

Wearing only a towel.

Theo's eyes locked with hers, and he froze. His face turned a fiery shade of red, and Cora realized just how much of her was above the water. His eyes stayed trained on her face as she dipped lower. She couldn't keep her own eyes from flicking across his torso.

She'd seen his arms plenty of times, their thick cords of muscle familiar to her. Her gaze trailed across his pectorals, following the water beading along the planes of his skin. She certainly didn't count his visible abdominal muscles—six—or linger on the sculpted line of his shoulders. No, she dragged her eyes back up to his, trying and failing to let them linger.

Cora swallowed, certain her face matched his. "I didn't know anyone else was down here."

"Sometimes I come down here after a workout." Theo's voice came out hoarse. He had to clear his throat before he could continue. "Don't have to worry about hogging the bathroom."

"Well, I guess I figured out who brought the soap."

No wonder she'd liked how it smelled so much. The sharp citrus and mint filled her nose, wafting through the air as if drawn to Theo.

Silence stretched thick between them.

Finally, he tore his gaze away from her face to glance at a room off to the side. "Well, um, I should change. I'll be out of here in a minute."

Cora pressed up against the edge of the pool, water up to her chin. She definitely did not think about what his bare chest looked like as she waited. And she definitely was not disappointed when he emerged a minute later, fully dressed.

He gave her a tiny wave before scurrying away from the baths. She counted to ten before peeling herself away from the wall.

Her holo pinged from her pile of clothes. Cora rinsed the soap

240

out of her hair, then it pinged again. She pulled herself out of the bath as it pinged for a third time. She snatched a towel from a rack in the far corner as yet another ping sounded. Exasperated, she opened the messages.

Cora.

Cora, read my messages.

CORA!

I FOUND YOUR BROTHER!!!

She'd never dressed so fast in her life. She wrenched her clothes over her still-damp skin, then raced toward the Hub. Her muscles protested as her legs pumped. She burst through the front doors and across the lower floor. She raced up the stairs, each footfall landing with a metallic clang.

Siraye swiveled in her chair as Cora skidded to a stop in front of her desk. "Finally! I've been trying to get a hold of you all morning!"

"Did you really find him?"

Siraye tapped a few keys, and the center of her display played a short loop of footage. It appeared to be a security camera outside of a factory. And slipping inside the building was Arik.

Cora blinked back tears. She threw her arms around Siraye and squeezed. "You're brilliant! Thank you, Siraye!"

Siraye wrapped her long arms around Cora and squeezed back. When they parted, her own eyes were misty. "Happy to help. I'm pretty certain I located this building. Do you want the coordinates?"

"Yes!"

Siraye brought up a message window and began typing. Cora swiped at her eyes, feeling a presence at her elbow.

Siraye glanced over her shoulder. "Oh, hey, Phaendar."

Cora spun. She hadn't heard his footsteps over the whirring of the fans.

Phaendar's eyes were locked on Arik's face. "Who is that?"

"That's Cora's brother."

Phaendar's head turned slowly to stare at Cora, and her

stomach dropped.

He stared at her, fists curling at his side. "You certainly look different in person. Nice haircut."

Siraye whirled around, eyes flicking between the two of them. Cora met Phaendar's eyes steadily while her heart thudded in her chest.

"Is something wrong, Phaendar?" Siraye asked carefully.

"Yes, something is wrong," Phaendar growled. "The gods have given up on us. Elidi chose a damn *Bjorn* to be a Dragon Rider!"

The air sucked out of the room. Siraye kept glancing between them, a glimmer of panic in her eyes. Cora straightened to her full height, tilting her head back to stare Phaendar down.

"And now you probably want *our people* to go rescue the little prince. Well, guess what, princess." Phaendar leaned forward, hot breath blowing into her face. "I won't be helping."

He bumped into her as he stomped out the door. His fist curled around something in his hand, crunching it. Cora stumbled a step, resisting the urge to rub her shoulder.

Siraye stared at her in horror. "I'm so sorry, Cora. I wasn't thinking!"

"It's okay. They were going to find out eventually."

Siraye's shoulders slumped. She finished typing and wrung her long fingers. "The coordinates are sent. If there's any way I can help, *please* tell me."

Cora gave her shoulder a squeeze. "I will. Thank you, Siraye. Really."

Siraye nodded, sitting up a little straighter in her chair.

Satisfied, Cora followed the path Phaendar had stormed down. She waited until she left the Hub behind before letting the worry show on her face.

"They've called a *town meeting*?" Gray asked. "I thought those happened once a decade."

Cora glanced between Gray and Reluraun. It had only been a few hours since Siraye gave her the coordinates to Arik's location. Theo and Gray talked her out of leaving immediately, instead offering to help her research where he was. It was a tiny town about an hour south of Narous, with nothing of significance other than a single factory. They were nearly ready to broach the topic of another house guest with Reluraun when he'd entered the house, stone-faced. He still refused to look directly at her.

"They do," His tone was clipped. "And when something pressing comes up."

She could guess what had come up. She didn't care if Phaendar could break her in half; she was ready to punch him.

"No use dallying," Reluraun said. "Let's go."

He left the door open behind him, expecting them to follow. Theo shot her a wary glance. She stalked after Reluraun, not waiting to see if Gray and Theo were coming. They caught up to her, their long legs taking half as many steps as hers.

Anger simmered in Cora's veins. Her fingers curled and uncurled as she approached city hall. Makari prodded curiously at the bond, sensing her agitation. Cora didn't respond, letting her leaking anger be answer enough. A few people trickled into the hall ahead of them. Gray reached out to open the door, and she stepped inside.

Nearly every seat was full. She spotted three empty seats—in the very front row. Theo nudged her, leading the way up the aisle. The low drone of conversation grated against Cora's ears as she followed him to the empty seats. Reluraun had already settled himself on a small raised platform with the other town elders. She felt many eyes on her and caught a few wisps of conversations with her name. She ignored them all. Instead, she stared at the town elders, one hand gripping the edge of her seat like a vise.

Across the aisle sat Orym, Daethie, and Phaendar. Orym stared at her with open hostility. She caught his gaze burning into her face from the corner of her eye. Daethie and Phaendar watched the town elders with the same intensity that she did.

Makari brushed up against the bond, and Cora let her into her mind. Her dragon had taken up a watch outside city hall. Next to her, Theo brushed his knuckles against the hand gripping her seat. Her grip loosened, and he twined his fingers with hers. Cora knew that whatever happened, she had them both at her side.

Reluraun stood and walked over to a small podium at the center

243

of the platform. He tapped the microphone, gathering everyone's attention. He glared across the room, silencing the last lingering conversations.

"Thank you for coming tonight. An issue has been brought to our attention—"

Phaendar shot out of his seat, cutting Reluraun off. "We all know what's happened, Reluraun. We've been lied to!"

A grumble of assent rolled through the crowd. Cora didn't need to see the glares levelled at the back of her head.

Reluraun's lips curved down in distaste. "Who has lied to you?"

"You, Grayson, Siraye. You promised us a Dragon Rider, but instead you brought a Bjorn into our home!"

The cry that followed made Cora's ears ring. Her stomach tightened, but Makari pressed more firmly against her mind, steady and strong.

Reluraun banged his hand against the podium. "None of us lied to you. You never asked about Cora's ancestry."

"Withholding information is the same as lying!"

She clenched Theo's hand. The simmering anger bubbled up, threatening to boil over.

A voice in the back of her mind was screaming at her to stay put, to stay quiet. Instead, her eyes locked with Phaendar's. She glared at him, shooting to her feet.

The room quieted, attention pinned on Cora.

"So what?" she snapped. "Why does it matter who my family is?"

"The Bjorns invaded our land!"

"*And?*" She turned her glare on the crowd. "That was *three hundred years ago!*"

"Some of us were there," Daethie growled, earning an appreciative murmur from the crowd. "We remember."

"Congratulations! Would you like an award?"

Makari hummed in approval, feeding her anger. Gray rose next to Theo, spreading his hands in a placating gesture.

"Let's all take a breath here," he said soothingly. "This whole thing has been blown out of proportion. Cora is here to learn, not

244

invade."

"Know thy enemies better than thy friends," Daethie hissed. "Haven't the Nine Guards drilled that into us since we were babes?"

"Cora isn't your enemy!" Theo shouted.

Cora laid a hand on his arm. "What *exactly* are you afraid I'll do?"

"We've seen what dragons can do," a voice called across the room. "You could turn yours on us!"

"Why would I? You've taken me in, and I've gladly worked all across this town for you!"

Phaendar faced her, scanning her up and down with a sneer. "The precious princess had to get her hands dirty."

"Cora," Reluraun warned. "Sit down. You aren't helping anything."

"No," she growled. "I'm not just going to sit here and listen to this. You want me to leave, then fine, I can leave."

"Who said anything about leaving?" an elderly elf grumbled behind Reluraun. "She should be grounded until further notice."

"There's no need for that," Gray protested.

Rage flared. She straightened to her full height, a deathly calm settling over her. "I won't be separated from my dragon."

"Who says you have a choice?" Phaendar said quietly.

He edged forward until he stood over her. All conversation in the room died. The air felt thick around her as every eye in the room watched them. Theo tensed next to her, perched at the very edge of his seat.

Phaendar gave him the barest of glances. "I think I can take a little girl and her over-eager watchdog."

"I don't care what you think," she replied coldly, before Theo could intervene. "And I don't care what you decide, either. The rest of you can sit around and debate, but I'm going to get my brother."

Cora twisted away from Phaendar with a final glare, her shoulder bumping against his arm as she walked away. Theo shot up behind her. She felt the passing air as his fingers just missed her arm.

"Cora, wait!" he called.

She darted down the aisle, angry people rising in her wake. The room filled with a cacophony of voices all fighting to be heard. The sound deadened as the door banged shut behind her.

She didn't wait to see if anyone followed. She couldn't see Makari in the dark, but she knew her dragon was trailing behind. Cora thought about returning to Reluraun's first. But why give anyone time to catch up to her?

She cut down a narrow opening between two houses. Beyond the shadows was the outskirts of town, a clearing large enough for Makari to take off in. She was nearly to the end of the alley when two dark figures appeared, cutting her off.

"Oaths are a funny thing." Daethie's soft voice carried down the narrow space. "Simple in theory, but what do you do when oaths contradict each other?"

Cora took a step backward, further into the shadows. Grass shushed behind her. She didn't need to turn to know she was trapped.

"All of us swore to serve the Riders," Daethie continued in that soft voice. "Then, when their very existence was threatened, we swore to kill any Bjorn who crossed our path."

"Quite the dilemma," Orym said next to her. "It begs the question, why would the gods allow such an abomination in the first place?"

"And yet we stand in the perfect position to correct it," Phaendar's voice rumbled behind Cora.

They were nearly in striking distance. Cora froze, panic clawing its way up her throat. There was a shrill scraping sound, then the alley was bathed in an orange glow.

She dared to look back as Makari's mouth cracked open, curved white teeth flashing like knives in the darkness.

Phaendar froze, frowning up at Makari. "You wouldn't risk your Rider. You'd barbecue her too from that position."

"Are you willing to bet your life on it?" Cora surprised herself with how steady her voice was. "Even if she doesn't flame, she'll still rip you apart if you harm me."

"I can think of worse ways to go," Daethie said stubbornly.

"I can't," Orym grumbled. He took a step back. "I've seen how dragons treat their prey."

"Coward."

Phaendar backed away, hand falling from the blade at his side.

Makari eased closer to Cora, ambers eyes fixed on Daethie.

Reluctantly, the elf sheathed a long, black dagger. Cora hadn't seen it in the dark.

Daethie bared her teeth. "Keep your drowning Northern face out of my sight. Or I'll gut you, dragon or no dragon."

"Is that what they decided at the town meeting, to send you three?"

"They haven't decided anything yet," Phaendar said. "We slipped out while they were still yelling at your boys."

"So you took matters into your own hands."

Silence met her.

Cora nodded once, edging forward, to the clearing. Orym took another step away, clearing a path. A growl from Makari sent Daethie back a single step. The elf's eyes shone with murderous rage as Cora strode past her.

Makari squeezed her lithe body through the alley, tail whacking into Daethie as she passed. Daethie fell onto her backside, grunting. Cora swore her dragon sniggered in delight as she climbed on.

Makari's wings snapped open, then sent them into the air with a powerful thrust.

Cora didn't look back as they left elves standing in the darkness once more.

24

"Is the team ready?"

"Yes, sir."

Daen kept a measured gait next to Callan, hands clasped behind his back. Callan reviewed the data on the tablet in his hands. Retrieving Prince Arik should be simple. He was in a small town just south of Narous, barely more than a factory and a few homes. The factory was owned by a minor noble, his girlfriend's uncle.

Callan handed the tablet to Daen. "I want to leave within the hour."

"Yes, sir. I'll inform the team."

Daen backed away, letting him finish the short walk to his rooms.

Callan paused as his door came into view. Nolan was waiting for him. His brother jerked his head toward the closed door.

"Senator Hyrax wants to speak with us. He's already waiting."

Callan opened the door, not bothering to wait for Nolan.

Senator Hyrax's head and shoulders were hovering above the mobile communicator on the low table in the sitting room. He smiled broadly, throwing his arms out as Callan came into view.

"Callan, our brilliant Chancellor! I knew you'd come through, son."

Callan's chest swelled a bit. He allowed a modest smile, bowing his head in acknowledgment. "Thank you, sir. I can't take all the credit, though. My team has been working nonstop."

"Callan, my boy." Senator Hyrax chuckled, shaking his head. "When you're in charge, you *always* take the credit. Good to see

248

too, Nolan."

"Senator." Nolan bowed his head politely.

"What is your plan now that the prince has been located?"

"I'm assembling a team to retrieve him now."

"And what of the princess? Any news on her whereabouts?"

"Still nothing. Although…" Callan shifted on his feet. "I've had some contact with Princess Catarina."

Nolan's eyes drilled into the side of his face. Callan refused to acknowledge him.

"Interesting." Senator Hyrax looked him over sharply. "Is there a reason you kept that to yourself, Chancellor?"

"There isn't much to share, Senator. She contacted me asking about her father."

"Did she give you any indication of where she is?"

"No." He spared Nolan the briefest glance. "I don't believe she's been kidnapped, either. She made it very clear that she feels safe."

"So, she's free to leave? Then I wonder if your plan to retrieve the prince is enough."

"Sir?"

Senator Hyrax paced slowly, coming in and out of frame. "We have a unique opportunity in front of us. What if, instead of your men going to retrieve Prince Arik, we send in Mellis and her people? We can have her lay a trap for the princess, draw her out. And then"—Senator Hyrax gestured to Callan—"Chancellor Byrne can ride in and save them both. I wonder what emotions such bravery would stir in the princess?"

"Princess Catarina would likely come if she felt her brother was in danger," Nolan agreed.

Callan took a moment to consider, his finger tapping against his leg. The thought of having Catarina back quickened his pulse. And to think, how quickly the rest of their plans would fall into place.

"I'll give the order immediately. Thank you, Senator."

"Thank *you*, Callan," Senator Hyrax replied. "You've nearly won this fight for Galta. I look forward to hearing from you when the prince and princess return home."

The feed cut out, leaving them in silence.

Nolan clicked off the communicator, his fingers lingering to drum the top of the device. "I'll have my people start circulating rumors about this plan. They can plant intelligence for us to find and trace back to Mellis."

"I'll meet with her," Callan said, already typing a message into his holo. "Although I have a feeling we're nearing the end of her cooperation."

"What makes you say that?"

Callan told him about their last meeting. Nolan's eyes widened with every word. He sank down onto a plush chair, staring at his brother.

"And you're just *now* telling me she met a Dragon Rider? This changes everything."

"It changes *nothing*," Callan snarled. "Even *if* there is a Rider out there, they clearly have no plans for Liskow. Or else why wouldn't they be out in the open?"

"And yet they just happened to be in a secret government facility. I need to monitor this situation. Do whatever you have to for Mellis' cooperation."

Nolan left swiftly, brows knit together. Callan sent his message to Mellis, then immediately began typing another.

Cora's holo was dinging before they'd gotten an hour into their flight. One was another apology from Siraye. Cora skimmed the paragraph before dismissing the message with a swipe of her finger. Another was a message from Gray. It was also laced with apologies, and a request to come back and talk. The last message was from Theo. She knew what she'd find before she opened it.

Where are you??

Siraye found Arik. I'm flying to his coordinates.

She told us about that. Gray and I will drive and meet you there. Don't do anything stupid without us.

Irritation flashed through her. She scowled, her fingers
250

punching the keys as she replied.

I'll be back before you could even drive there. Just wait at Relu-raun's. I'll be fine.

Daethie, Orym, and Phaendar disappeared at the meeting. Did something happen?

She took a long time to reply. She could practically see Theo stewing on the other end. She wasn't sure what he'd do if she told him the truth. Better to be vague.

We exchanged some words. I think it's safe to say we won't be having dinner with them anymore.

Did they try to hurt you?

No.

Technically, she wasn't lying. They hadn't had a chance to do more than intimidate her.

Stay out of trouble until I get back, okay? I'll let you know when I'm flying home.

Cora set her hands on Makari's neck, enjoying the rush of wind against her face. Makari's wings spread out to either side of them, tilting with tiny adjustments as they soared along the updrafts. Every few minutes, a powerful wing beat would send them bobbing higher, before they settled into a coast again. She was starting to doze when her holo chimed again. What now?

Catarina! I know where your brother is!

She straightened, all sense of drowsiness gone. The town she was flying to wasn't far from Narous. If Callan went to get him, he'd be there before her. Would that be so bad? At least she knew Arik would be safe with him. But if they got there at the same time, they'd expect her to come back, too. She wasn't ready to face that choice.

Where is he?

In Rydon. It's a small town just south of here.

251

Are you going after him?

Yes, we're going now. But Catarina...we think the PEL is looking for him, too. They might already be there. I promise, I will do everything I can to bring him home.

Her heart stuttered. She managed to send Callan a thank you before gripping Makari again with trembling fingers. Makari's ears flicked back to her, worry traveling down the bond. Cora couldn't breathe. She saw her mother fall, over and over again.

Makari pushed into her mind, harder this time, breaking the spell. Cora leaned over her neck, one thought pounding through her mind.

Faster.

Cora kept telling herself it was a cloud. She wanted it to be a cloud. But if her nose hadn't given it away already, the flecks of ash floating by did. Makari swept below the billowing smoke, not bothering to hide. There were no sounds of fighting, no gathered vehicles. All she saw was a small stream of people throwing buckets of water at the burning factory. It was like using an eye dropper against a bonfire.

Makari landed with a ground-shaking thump, smoke billowing around her.

Someone screamed, but most gawked at the spotted dragon. A few kept dumping their buckets of water.

Cora slid off Makari's back, grabbing the nearest person's arm. "What happened?"

The middle-aged woman blinked at her, still stunned. It took her a moment to reply. "A bunch of people in masks showed up and raided the factory. They pulled some people out." The words tumbled out of her like she couldn't say them fast enough. "They shot the foreman, and the owner. They took someone, then they set the whole place on fire."

Cora ran a hand through her hair, fighting the urge to cry. Arik was already gone.

A scream shot from the building, along with shattering glass.

"Are there still people in there?" Cora asked.

"A few." The woman appeared on the verge of tears, too. "The door is too hot. We can't get to them."

Cora didn't hesitate. She sent a thought to Makari, and her dragon moved into position. She yelled at the people to move out of her way.

Makari's tail smashed into the nearest door, revealing a raging inferno. Cora dashed through the opening. The heat was nothing to her, but the light was nearly blinding. She darted into the ruined factory, dodging sparking wires and overturned workstations. In the farthest corner, a half-dozen people huddled as far from the flames as they could manage.

She skidded to a stop as smoldering debris tumbled from the ceiling in front of her. The building was nearly ready to collapse.

Cora hurried over to the survivors. "Come on, we need to move."

They stirred groggily, barely conscious. She searched for a closer exit, squinting against the brilliant flames. There was another door just a couple of feet away, blocked by debris. She called for Makari.

Less than a minute later, her tail smashed through that door as well. Cool air rushed in, reviving Cora's terrified charges. She ushered them through the doorway, half-carrying the last one. Makari covered them with one long wing as the roof caved in behind them.

The other townspeople gaped at them for a heartbeat. Even the most diligent in the bucket brigade stopped to stare. A cheer cracked through the stillness, and a few people rushed forward to help the coughing survivors.

Hands clapped Cora's back while a few brave people tentatively extended fingers toward Makari. She allowed them to stroke her neck and side, preening under the attention.

Cora accepted their thanks for a few minutes before making her excuses. She climbed onto Makari, waving to them before they launched into the air. Makari made one low circle before climbing into the sky.

The town shrank below them as they left. Cora spotted a line of black cars speeding toward Rydon. Callan and his team. She tore her eyes away as the dark swallowed them.

Her pulse returned to normal, soothed by Makari's wing beats. The night settled around them, the only sound the rushing wind in her ears. She ducked her head against Makari's neck and let the tears fall.

Cora remembered to send a message to Theo halfway through the flight back. She hoped he was asleep at this hour, but it was just as likely he was still awake, waiting for her. Makari kept up a low, soothing purr as they flew. Cora sank lower onto her neck, eyes drifting closed.

She startled awake as Makari's feet hit the ground outside Reluraun's house. She dug her fingers into Makari's scaly skin to keep from falling off. She lowered fully onto her belly for Cora to slide down.

She walked around to face her dragon, pressing her forehead into Makari's. Makari nuzzled closer, her rumbling purr shaking Cora's bones. She kissed Makari's nose before creeping into Reluraun's house.

The only light came from the moon, slicing through the windows in long beams. Cora tiptoed to her room, virtually silent. She eased the door closed behind her with a soft click. She glanced out the window, checking that Makari was heading back to the aerie.

Instead, she found her dragon curled up beneath her window. Cora's heart swelled. She sent a rush of warmth down the bond and was rewarded with another purr. She smiled as she faced away from the window. She collapsed onto her bed, falling asleep to the sound of her dragon.

Cora's bedroom door burst open, startling her awake. Weak sunlight filtered through her curtains and into her eyes. She sat up blearily as a tall shape rushed to her bed.

Before she could process what was happening, Theo swept her into a bone-crushing hug, his cheek pressing into her hair. Slowly, her arms wrapped around him. His warmth enveloped her, and when he spoke, she felt it rumbling through his chest.

254

"What happened?"

"I was too late." Her voice cracked. "Arik's gone."

Tears leaked out onto Theo's shirt. One hand slid to the back of her head, his thumb brushing against her cheek. Cora squeezed him tighter, the tears falling freely now.

Time stilled as he held her. The wall between them crumbled with every passing second. Held in Theo's arms, a feeling settled over her, filling her up, easing her pain. *Home.* This was home.

"You need to see this," Gray's voice said from the doorway.

Cora pulled back, swiping at her face. One of Theo's hands stayed on her waist.

"We'll be right there," he said, eyes never leaving her face.

He waited until she was done composing herself before his hand slid into hers, fingers twining. Gray had already disappeared into the living room. They followed after, hands joined.

When they rounded the corner into the living room, the holo-screen was on. And filled by Thalassa Mellis' face.

"We tried to be peaceful, but our message was not received. So we made our voices louder, and yet they've still fallen on deaf ears. Our dear monarchy continues to produce and employ androids. The People's Employment League destroyed one of those android factories last night, where we found a new model designed to replace city Watchers. Machines will not only take those jobs but will also be used to enforce so-called 'justice' with no oversight." Thalassa's eyes were filled with cold hatred. "We found something else in that factory, as well. Our previous efforts at reaching our monarchy have failed, so we're trying one last time. Since our king is too drunk to do anything these days, we turn to Crown Princess Catarina. My contact code is on the screen. Meet with me, alone, or we will make an example of your brother. The people will not be ignored."

Cora pulled her hand out of Theo's. Her fingers were typing before Thalassa finished speaking.

Theo put warm hands on her shoulders, spinning her to face him. "What are you doing? This is a trap."

"Of course it is." She tapped in the final digit of Thalassa's code. "I'm going anyway."

"Like the *depths* you are."

Cora glared up at him. "If I don't, they'll kill him. They've already killed my mother, Theo. I'm not losing Arik, too."

Gray twisted around from his spot on the couch, dismissing the holo- feed on the screen. "We'll go with you."

"No. She said to go alone. I'm going alone."

She shrugged off Theo's arms and turned back to her room. She typed as she walked.

Where do you want to meet?

Cora changed into a fresh shirt and socks, then pulled a spare pair of boots from her wardrobe. She heard Theo's footsteps as she finished lacing them. She pulled a thin knife from the top drawer of her dresser, then slipped it into a special sheath inside her right boot.

"That's your great plan, a boot knife?" Theo's voice was laced with sarcasm.

"At least I won't be going in unarmed. Do you have a better plan?"

"Yeah, I do, actually. Stay here."

"I can't do that."

She moved to push past him, but he blocked her way. She placed her hands on her hips, glaring up at him.

"Cora, this plan is stupid."

"I know."

"Then let us help you."

"Theo, you know what it's like to lose family," she hated the glimmer of grief shining in Theo's eyes at that. "If this was Isla, or your mom, would you really risk their safety?"

Theo pressed his lips together. He had to look away from her intent gaze. "No, I wouldn't. But I also wouldn't go alone."

She lifted an eyebrow, and he loosed an exasperated sigh.

"All right, fine, I would!" Theo leaned down to better meet her eyes, his breath tickling her hair. "But I don't matter, not the way you do. Please, Cora, don't go alone."

Her breath hitched. She'd never heard his voice so close to breaking before.

She laid a soft hand against his face, her thumb tracing the

256

curve of his cheekbone. His hand rose to cover hers, gentle, but steady.

"But what if they hurt you, too?" she whispered. "Or Gray, or Makari?"

"They can try," Theo said darkly. "Trust me, Cora. We're better together."

She stared into his honey-brown eyes. Cora's heart slowed as a sense of calm stole over her.

She nodded. "Together."

Gray's footsteps clomped down the hall, louder than usual. Cora dropped her hand, and they both turned as he approached.

"I just got a message from Siraye," Gray said grimly. "The second town meeting just wrapped up. They've decided to ground Cora, forcibly if necessary. If we're leaving, we need to go now."

Gray and Theo walked into their room to grab supplies. Cora's holo chimed while she was waiting.

Good to hear from you, princess. I'm told your family has a private cabin. We'll meet there.

Her heart squeezed with trepidation. Gray and Theo emerged, and together they left Reluraun's house. Cora told them where they were going as she climbed onto Makari's waiting back. They climbed on behind her, Gray clutching a gas can for his car. Makari pushed off, straining against the weight of all of them.

Cora took one last look around Stony Hollow as Makari soared away. There was no going back now.

25

They landed next to Gray's car, still half-hidden under the trees. Gray slid down to fill the tank, but Theo lingered, his arms around Cora's waist. She leaned back against his chest, just for a moment. He gave her a tiny squeeze before following Gray into the car. Makari watched him walk away, a low purr rumbling through her. They waited until Gray's car roared to life before taking to the skies again.

A chill swept through Cora that had nothing to do with the screaming wind in her hair. It chased away the lingering warmth from Theo's touch, leaving her fingers numb. Every passing minute twisted her muscles tighter until she thought she would burst.

Finally, the sweeping cabin property came into view below. Makari banked, making slow circles as Gray and Theo caught up to them. Makari landed in front of the gate she'd destroyed the last time. There was still an upside-down car in the brush outside the mangled metal.

Gray's window slid down, his head poking out to speak to Cora. "What now?"

"Flying in will draw too much attention. Makari can sneak through the trees, while the rest of us drive down to the staff bungalow again. At least from there we can see the cabin."

Gray nodded, and Cora climbed off Makari's back. She stopped to lay a hand on Makari's forehead. She leaned into the touch, ears flicking back and forth nervously.

It'll be alright. Just stay near.

Makari snorted in acknowledgment, then veered into the trees and disappeared. Cora felt odd riding in the back seat instead of on

Makari's back. Funny how quickly that had changed.

Gray drove down a dirt path, following the trail of chaos they'd left behind. They parked behind the bungalow, out of view of anyone who might walk down from the cabin. They crept through the underbrush as close as they dared.

The property was deserted.

"I don't see a single guard," Gray muttered.

Theo glowered at the cabin. "Something isn't right."

Cora agreed. Her heart hammered in her chest, and she had to clench her hands to keep them from shaking. Makari kept feeding her strange scents, also on high alert.

Cora took a deep, steadying breath. "I don't have much of a choice though. I'll plan on leaving through the kitchen to meet up here. Be ready to leave in a hurry."

Gray passed out the comms they'd used at the facility. Cora pushed it into her ear, shifting her hair to make sure it was covered. Theo reached over and squeezed her hand. She gave him a thin smile before circling toward the front of the cabin.

She met no one on her way, saw no one around the property. She stuck to the tree line until she reached the end of the main drive. She took a moment to pull a few burs out of her clothes before trekking back up the gravel road to the cabin. There was a single guard outside the front door, dressed in black. He was vaguely familiar, but she couldn't place him. Wordlessly, he opened the door for her.

She heard muffled voices from somewhere in the cabin as he led her away from the door. There were signs of a struggle throughout the house. Pictures askew, furniture knocked sideways. Muddy boot prints marred the floor beneath her feet, some little more than brown streaks.

The guard opened the door into the den, gesturing for her to enter. She took another steadying breath, expecting to be surrounded as soon as she entered. Instead, a familiar figure stood in front of the fireplace, staring at the curling horns above it.

"Callan? What are you doing here?"

Callan's face broke into a wide smile. He crossed the room in three long strides, sweeping Cora into a hug. His arms curled around her, pulling her in close as his scent filled her nostrils. She was bombarded with an overwhelming sense of wrongness. She laid her hands against his back lightly before pulling away.

"We traced Thalassa here," Callan fingered the ends of her hair. "We thought we'd only find Arik, but then we saw her message to you and decided to wait."

"Arik's okay?" she whispered.

"He's fine. He's just in the kitchen."

Cora glanced at the door, ready to sprint through it. Yet something nagged at the back of her mind. Makari brushed up against the bond, sensing her unease.

"You cut your hair."

"Yes," she replied absently. "I'm going to check on Arik…"

She moved one foot toward the kitchen when his voice stopped her.

"Where have you been, Catarina?" Callan's tone held a tinge of hurt.

Her head cocked to one side. "I've been staying with a friend."

Worry lined his eyes, still studying her hair. A thought kept tickling the back of her mind. An equation that didn't add up.

"How did you get here so quickly?" she asked.

"I told you, we traced Thalassa here."

"I heard that. But I know how long the drive from Narous is. I should have gotten here before you."

Callan spread his hands. "I don't know what else to tell you, Catarina. Maybe you misremembered the distance."

Cora pursed her lips. She knew exactly how long the drive from Narous was.

"Should we go see Arik?" Callan gestured toward the kitchen.

He turned away without waiting for an answer. A part of Cora was yelling at her to leave it alone, but that nagging thought was growing more persistent. She snagged Callan's arm, intending to get his attention. Instead, she froze.

Her fingers pressed against cool metal beneath his shirt. Callan glanced down at her hand, then at her face, his blue eyes unreadable. Cora pushed up the fabric of his sleeve, revealing a slim dagger in an armband. She stared at the blade, a memory

260

flashing before her eyes.

A crowded party, her mother pressed to her side. A flash as Thalassa lunged, so brief, but so close. Callan stumbling into them. Her mother's gasp, then red everywhere.

Cora dropped Callan's arm like she'd been burned. She stared into those soul-searching eyes. Her voice was steady, even as the rest of her shook.

"It was you, wasn't it?"

"What are you talking about?"

"You, with this knife. You killed her."

"What are you talking about? Are you alright?"

Callan reached out to touch her face, but she stepped back.

Without thinking, her stance adjusted. Her right foot moved back, and she shifted to the balls of her feet. And then she was twisting, her arm moving faster than she could process. Her fist slammed into Callan's jaw.

His head snapped to the side, eyes wide with shock.

Her chest heaved. She wanted to rage, to scream, to hit him again. Instead, she spoke with deadly calm.

"Why am I here, Callan?"

"What do you mean?"

"I *mean*, what do you want, Callan?"

Callan straightened, working his jaw a couple of times. His eyes were guarded when he replied, "What I've wanted for a while now. You, by my side. Think of what Galta and Liskow could do *together*."

"What did he just say?" Theo's voice was practically a growl in her ear.

"That explains a few things..."

"Think of all the good we could accomplish together. Catarina, come back to Narous with me. I can fix everything."

Silence stretched between them. He took a step forward, gazing down intently at her.

Cora returned the gaze, searching Callan's eyes. "Were you dropped on your head as a child?"

He blinked a few times, his brow furrowing. "Excuse me?"

"It's the only explanation I can think of for how deluded you

261

are."

Callan's lips parted in shock. Before he could reply, his earpiece crackled, catching Cora's attention.

"Sir, one of the men thinks he spotted a dragon. Should we engage?"

Cora paled.

Callan gaped at her, shaking his head slowly. "No, *no*. It can't... How did you get here?"

"Cora," Gray's voice warned in her ear. *"You need to get out of there."*

Callan's jaw clenched. He turned hardened eyes on her. Cora took a stumbling step backward, ice creeping through her veins.

"It's you," he growled.

She swallowed, mouth suddenly dry. "What do you mean?"

"You're the Dragon Rider."

Callan stepped forward, and Cora stepped back. The back of her knees hit the chair, and she fell into the seat. He loomed over her, hands on the armrests to either side of her. His earpiece crackled again, and he removed one hand to touch it.

"Sir, orders?"

"Keep an eye on the dragon. Norris, secure the prince."

Cora glanced toward the kitchen, gut twisting. Her eyes snapped back to Callan as his hand thumped back onto the armrest.

"I'm giving you one last chance, princess. You can come with me willingly. Or..."

Her head whirled around again as a plate crashed in the kitchen. Arik's voice came soon after.

"What are you doing? Get your hands off me!"

Cora glared at Callan, temperature spiking again. "What happened to protecting my family?"

"Our situation has changed."

Another crash from the kitchen. She heard the undeniable thwack of skin hitting skin. Cora's head and shoulders fell. She scanned in front of her, heart thudding.

"You"—her eyes flicked up to meet Callan's—"can drown in the depths."

Cora brought her leg up, directly between Callan's. He curled

262

into himself with a whimper, face red.

She darted past him and shoved the kitchen door open. Arik was grappling with one of Callan's men, his back pressed into the counter. Cora snatched the knife from her boot, gripping it with white knuckles. She slid across the kitchen floor, slashing the man's leg as she passed. He cried out, dropping to his knee.

She pushed herself to her feet and grabbed Arik. He gaped at her, then at the knife in her hand. His head whipped back to the groaning man on the floor as she urged him on.

"What are you doing?"

"I'll explain later. For now, we need to run."

"Are you insane?"

"It's up for debate."

Boots clomped towards them. Cora swore, shoving him towards the back door. Arik opened it a crack, and she peered out. Their path was clear, for now. Makari pressed into her mind, images flowing past.

"Three vehicles full of Callan's men just pulled up," Cora said. "It's now or never."

Arik laid a hand on her arm, stopping her. "How do you plan on getting us out of here?"

"There's a car waiting behind the bungalow. Please, Arik, I need you to trust me."

He nodded, pulling the door fully open. The twins raced for the tree line. Cora called Theo and Gray, letting them know where they would be. Their heads popped around trees, staring beyond the twins to the cabin.

"We're already in position," Theo responded. *"Just keep running. We'll cover you."*

A bang sounded behind Cora. She ducked instinctively. Arik swore next to her as bullets whizzed past. Cora put a hand up to help protect her eyes from the puffs of dirt exploding around her.

"Why are they shooting at us!" Arik cried.

She slowed, letting Arik get ahead of her. They were within a hundred yards. Pain seared across her leg. She stumbled, crying out. Her hands shook as she examined the wound. Only a graze, luckily. There wasn't much blood, but her thigh burned.

263

"Cora!"

A shriek pierced the air behind her. She twisted back to see Makari clutching a man in her talons. He flailed and screamed, his gun abandoned on the roof.

Makari growled, dropping him into a pair of shooters, knocking them all down.

Cora climbed to her feet, teeth gritted. She forced her legs into motion. She didn't get far before a rush of warmth flashed past her other side.

Cora whipped around to see Callan holding a ball of fire in his hand. He threw again, setting the grass behind her on fire. Cora retrieved her knife, holding it tightly.

"What are you *doing?*" Arik cried, only a few feet from the trees.

Gray edged out of the tree cover, reaching toward her brother . Theo had already made it as far as the blazing grass would allow, his form shimmering through the waves of heat.

"Don't do something stupid," Theo rumbled in her ear.

"Get my brother out of here."

"Cora." Gray's voice was tense. *"You don't know what he's capable of. Get out of there while you have the chance."*

She glanced up at the cabin. The shots had stopped, silenced by Makari's rampage. Her dragoness continued to harry Callan's men. The ones still standing.

"Get Arik out of here. Makari and I can catch up."

"We're not leaving without you."

The fire growing in Callan's hand did nothing to warm the ice in his eyes. He took in Arik, Theo, and Gray, free hand reaching to his ear.

"Anyone still holding a firearm, shoot them."

"No!"

Callan threw before Cora slammed into him. Arik barely flinched, ducking into the trees as bullets rained down. She didn't have time to see if Gray and Theo were alright before she tumbled.

Cora and Callan rolled. When she popped back up, her knife was gone. A shadow passed overhead as Callan got to his feet.

Makari soared over the cabin, grabbing men as she passed and dropping them. Callan's men were forced to split their attention between her and the others.

Cora and Callan remained focused on each other. His face hardened, both hands smoking. Cora settled into a fighting stance, forgetting about her knife. It was useless to her now. Her mind flicked to her last sparring match. Callan was at least a head taller than her. His reach was longer, muscles rippling along his limbs. She couldn't take many hits from him.

Callan lunged. She silently swore, barely dodging. Callan assumed his fire was an advantage in this fight. He came in again, hands aflame. She stepped inside his reach, grabbing his wrist as it slid past her. She used his momentum, flipping him over her shoulder. Callan grunted, expression darkening.

Cora only had a moment of confidence. Then she was in the dirt too. She rolled, letting Callan's fist slam into the ground.

Next thing she knew, Callan was on top of her.

"You lost," he snarled. "Better to give up now."

"You underestimate my stubbornness."

Cora swung, but Callan caught her wrists, pinning them. She shoved down a wave of fear. She had to be able to get out of this. Callan motioned for one of his men to come help while Cora scrambled.

Makari, she thought desperately.

Makari swept toward them, her powerful downbeat kicking up a breeze. She shot over and swung her leg, sending Callan flying. Cora scrambled to her feet. Makari banked, coming back for her. Callan's remaining men fired at Makari, driving her back.

"Come on, Cora!" Theo's voice echoed in her earpiece as he yelled from the edge of the trees.

She nodded, legs already moving. She had to trust Makari to keep from getting shot.

Theo stepped towards her, hand outstretched. He spun back behind a tree as more bullets flew.

Cora pushed her legs faster. She couldn't hear anything over the bursts of gunfire. She could almost feel the shade of the tree cover.

A shadow slammed into her, sending her to the ground again.

"I'm losing patience, Princess. This is your final chance to come with me."

Cora staggered to her feet. With effort, she pulled herself up to her full height. "I've already made it clear, Callan. There's no possibility of that."

Callan's mouth set into a grim line. "Then you're only in my way."

Callan rushed in, swinging. She reached up to block it, gasping. Sharp pain sliced across her arm, warm blood dribbling onto her hand.

Callan came again, light glinting off a sharp blade. She swore, backing away. His attacks came faster, his movements precise. Cora barely registered someone calling her name as she frantically danced away from Callan. Another slice landed on her leg, then her cheek.

Cora panted. She heard Makari roaring nearby, but it was nearly drowned out by the shooting. She had to stay focused. Focus…

Callan stopped. Cora glanced down, confused by the handle sticking out of her abdomen. Had she even felt that? Warmth flowed around her as he pulled back. She looked back up and had to squint. Where had the fire come from?

Makari landed next to her, hot flames spilling from her mouth, driving back Callan and his men.

Cora swayed, her head in a fog. An arm wrapped around her, catching her before she could fall. Theo. She had never seen him so panicked before. Her vision darkened around the edges, Makari's head swimming out of focus as she guarded them.

A wave of pain washed over her, carrying the last of her adrenaline with it. The darkness claimed her.

Theo cradled Cora to him. He wouldn't—couldn't—think about the sticky feeling between his fingers, pressed tightly against her stomach. She would tease him to no end if she found out how clumsily he mounted Makari. When. *When* she found out. There had to be a when. Was she always this pale? He leaned as close to Makari as he could, struggling to block Cora from the raging wind.

266

Makari sensed the urgency. Her great wings pumped with fury, sending her far ahead of the car. She slammed down in front of the infirmary, nearly sending Theo flying. He didn't care. He scrambled off her back on shaking legs, doing his best not to jostle Cora.

He burst through the doors. Within seconds he was surrounded by voices shouting out orders. They brought a stretcher, and he laid Cora down gently. Clean hands replaced his, pressing down at the wound that was too red, too wet.

Just as quickly, Theo was left alone. He glanced around the small waiting room. There was no shortage of empty chairs, but the sudden quiet and the stinging scent of antiseptic reminded him of a truly awful night he had spent in a waiting room not unlike this one. He shuddered.

He burst through the doors again, his heart pounding. Makari was lying just outside the doors, tail whipping. Theo collapsed on the grass next to her and waited.

Six years ago

"I don't think this is a good idea, Lane." Theo kept his voice low. "If he just wanted to talk, why aren't we doing it at the club?"

Lane's eyes kept sweeping the dark street. This side of the city barely had any streetlights, and of those, half of them were broken. Most of the buildings were crumbling stone, the cobbles beneath their feet choked with scraggly weeds.

"Because he doesn't just want to talk," Lane replied gruffly. "Or else we wouldn't be meeting in Red Gryphon territory."

Theo swallowed, glancing behind them. He felt countless eyes watching him from shattered windows.

He grabbed his brother's arm, stopping him. "You don't have to do this. We can turn around right now."

Lane pressed his lips into a thin smile. "You don't have to come with me."

Theo considered. He would hate himself for it afterwards, but right then, he truly considered going home. Every part of him screamed they should leave. Instead, he shook his head.

267

"If we don't win, we don't get paid. And you know how much Mom counts on us." Lane started walking again. "Besides, I needed an excuse to bash his face in after what he did to Isla."

Theo couldn't argue with that. They strode deeper into the ruined streets. They slowed as they found the only building with lights on in every window. A handful of people loitered on the streets around the building, music and voices pouring out of the windows. Lane's face set with determination as he pushed open the door.

Theo's chest rattled in time to the music, the bass shaking the walls around them. It had once been an office building, judging by the desks and rolling chairs pushed into the corners of the room. Shabby couches were scattered through the space, most of them occupied. He didn't let his eyes linger on the gangsters lounging across the couches. A few women lay across laps, drinks in hand.

Lane strode through the middle of the room to a reception desk-turned-bar. The bartender jerked his head toward the stairwell without a word.

Theo's anxiety grew with every stair. They stopped a handful of times as gangsters clanged down. Lane ignored the hostile looks thrown their way. They stopped at each floor, and each time they were ordered upward. They climbed all the way to the top floor.

Theo spoke before Lane could pull open the door. "Are you sure about this? We can still leave."

Lane shook his head. "*You* can leave. I have to go through with this."

"And if you don't?"

"They want to make an example of me," Lane murmured, glancing at the door. It was the first sign of nerves he'd let show. "If I go back now, they'll come after all of us. Better to get it over with now."

Theo let his hand drop. "Let's go, then."

The corner of Lane's lip lifted in a smile. He squeezed Theo's shoulder before leaving the stairwell, Theo right behind. They walked down a short hallway and into what was once a large conference room. Windows stretched across the far wall, lights from the city shining like neon stars through the glass. The middle of the room was clear, while more couches lined the edges, newer than the ones downstairs. Theo counted a dozen gangsters, all wearing red masks over their faces. A few women wandered the room, serving trays in hand.

At the head of the room sat three men Theo didn't recognize. He did recognize the burly man standing next to their leather couch.

"I'm surprised you showed up," Gregor sneered.

"I'm surprised you're still standing," Lane said coolly.

Gregor scowled. One eye was swollen shut, his lip split. Theo spotted a few other bruises on his face and neck. He knew there were more under his shirt. Lane was taller and leaner than Gregor, but Theo knew exactly how powerful his punches were. It was like taking a bullet to the gut when Lane let himself loose. Gregor had once been a competent fighter, but he'd come to rely on his opponents letting him win. Theo hadn't seen Lane knock someone out so fast in his life.

"How long have you been boxing, Sturn?" one of the men on the couch asked.

He didn't look like much to Theo. Average height and build, pale skin and hair. He wore a crisp suit with no tie. His cold brown eyes swept over both of them, leaving Theo feeling exposed. He had the irresistible urge to run.

"Three years, sir." Lane added the last word reluctantly.

"Long enough to know how this works," the man continued, his voice dangerously soft. "Gregor never loses."

"Everyone loses at some point."

"Including you? From what I understand, you have quite a lot to lose." His eyes flicked to Theo. "Seems like a lot to risk."

"Then Gregor should have left our sister alone."

A wicked smile curved Gregor's mouth. Theo's fists curled at his side, his fear burning away in an instant. Lane clearly hadn't hit him hard enough.

"Ah, so this is personal." The man in the suit leaned further back into his seat. "I feel for you, truly I do. But unfortunately, I can't let this matter go. Too many people already question us, and your little stunt has stirred up unrest."

269

He snapped his fingers, and Theo was gripped by two masked gangsters. They pinned his arms back, straining as he fought against their hold. Gregor stepped toward Lane, hands already curled into fists.

"It's a good thing your brother's here," Gregor said. "It saves us the trouble of dumping your body into the sewer."

Lane brought his hands up, grim-faced. Gregor came in swinging, toying with him. Lane avoided him easily. Theo could only watch Gregor's fist connect with Lane's head. His brother recovered quickly, striking Gregor's gut with a grunt. Lane pressed forward, pummeling Gregor again and again. The man on the couch watched quietly, tracking every movement.

Just when Theo thought the fight was over, that Lane had won again, the man nodded.

Gangsters descended on him.

"Lane!" Theo's voice ripped from his chest.

He rushed forward, nearly breaking free of the hands holding him back. Two others stepped up to contain him, but he kept straining toward his brother. He couldn't see Lane through the people surrounding him. Fists and feet flew, connecting with solid thumps. Then, a sharp crack, followed by Lane's scream. Theo swore he heard his own heart crack.

He thought the beating would never end. There were more snaps and more screams before the man on the couch finally called off his gangsters. The hands holding Theo back disappeared, and he sagged to the floor. He shoved himself to his feet and raced to Lane's side.

He didn't recognize the strangled sound that escaped him. He could hardly look at Lane. No one stopped him as he slung Lane's limp form over his shoulders.

He barely remembered leaving, Lane's weight like a boulder against his back. All he could think was that he needed to get him help. Eyes followed him as he left Red Gryphon territory, but still no one stopped him.

He flagged down a pair of city Watchers, and moments later was climbing into the back of an ambulance with Lane. Lane reached toward Theo with a weak hand. Theo grabbed it, squeezing as if he could hold onto Lane's life.

"Theo," Lane croaked.

"It's going to be fine," he said, tears streaming freely down his face. "We're getting you to the hospital."

Theo didn't register the guarded glances the paramedics shared. He could only stare at Lane's ruined face, nearly unrecognizable as the brother he loved.

"Mom, Isla..." Lane took a ragged breath. "It's your job...to take care of them...now."

Theo squeezed Lane's hand tighter, shaking his head. Lane's chest didn't rise again. Theo shook his arm, yelling at the paramedics to do something. They shoved Theo out of the way, hands flying as they tried to revive him.

It was too late.

Lane was already gone.

26

Callan could only stare over the wall of flames as Catarina's dragon flew off. The heat singed his skin, but he didn't back away. It fueled the fury raging inside him.

A hand landed on his shoulder, trying to pull him away from the spreading fire. He spun, hand lashing out to wrap around the man's neck. He shoved, throwing him onto the ground, gasping and spluttering.

Callan stepped over him as he turned away from the empty sky. Daen was already giving out orders, overseeing first aid for the injured. The handful who hadn't survived had already been moved to the side.

Daen finished his orders before coming to Callan's side. "I've already sent word for a team to come through and clean up after us."

"Did you see what she is?" Callan's voice shook with unrestrained fury.

"Yes, sir. I know how you feel about dragons."

"How could she betray her country like that? How could she betray me? She's not who I thought she was."

"Do you think she's been a Rider this whole time?"

"I don't know." Callan shook his head, hands warming again. "But we need to accelerate the plan. We need to take Narous before she tries to bring that thing back."

"The Senate will want to hear about this before the plan changes."

"The plan isn't changing," he spat through clenched teeth. "The timing has always been under my discretion, and I'm telling you our timetable is moving forward."

Daen nodded, face unreadable. If he disagreed, he chose not to say so. He folded his hands behind his back, the picture of military discipline. "I'll see that the next phase of the plan begins as soon as we return."

"Good. Have you gotten more eggshell powder for me yet?"

"Yes, sir. It's waiting in your room at the palace. Although I wasn't able to get much."

"Then I need you to find me some other options as well."

Daen faced him with concern in his eyes. "Are you sure, sir? There's a reason you aren't supposed to mix them."

"The gods have blessed me with the ability to unlock the eggshells' power. I will use every ounce of that to wipe the last trace of the Riders from the earth. I'll show everyone who has the gods' favor now."

His fingers sparked, tendrils of smoke curling around his hands.

Daen stared at him. He opened his mouth to speak, then closed it again. He tapped a fist to his chest in a salute before excusing himself.

Callan let the heat die from his fingers. His reserve of power cooled to little more than a single ember in his chest. He glowered at the sky once again. He had been touched by the gods. He had been given access to power. No one could change that.

Callan stalked into the cabin, waving away a soldier with a med droid. He snatched a bottle of water from another soldier as he passed, draining it before he hit the driveway. A car was already waiting to take him back to Narous. He climbed in without a word, sure of what he had to do next.

He arranged the meeting on the drive back. He lit and extinguished his fire in a steady rhythm as they drove. The car veered away from the palace, driving along the neatly paved streets of the upper city. They pulled into the drive of a familiar manor. The pink and purple flowers were just as fragrant as last time, and they still gave Callan a headache. He swiftly climbed the wide steps, passing underneath the white marble pillars framing the door.

He tapped his foot impatiently as he waited for the door to

He didn't wait for the butler to greet him before sweeping into the house. The middle-aged man's lips puckered in distaste. He led Callan through the gray and white manor, to the same room he'd met Stellana in before.

She perched on a light purple armchair, a silky house robe falling off one shoulder.

"Callan," Stellana purred. "It had been so long since our last meeting. I was beginning to think you weren't coming."

He took a seat across from her without bothering to be asked. He sat forward, eyeing the throw pillows distrustfully. "I've been considering your offer. And I've decided to accept."

"Have you now? Well, I'm afraid the offer has expired."

"What?"

Stellana set aside the book she had been reading, carefully avoiding Callan's gaze. "We don't appreciate being left waiting, Callan. It was assumed that you had declined our offer."

He took a breath, hands clasping in front of him. He smiled, forcing himself to be civil. "Well, I'm here now. Surely, we can come to some sort of agreement."

Stellana met his eyes, her usual warmth gone. She dropped the flirtatiousness from her tone. "I'm afraid our situation has changed."

"What exactly could have changed it so quickly?"

"The return of the Dragon Riders."

Callan's jaw clenched. His fingers began to warm as he fought to keep his voice steady. "How does that change anything?"

"My dear, it changes everything. Including what we thought of you. It seems you aren't who we hoped you were after all."

Callan shot to his feet, hands blazing.

Stellana rose in tandem, her hand glinting. He glanced down to see a stiletto knife pressed against his ribs.

She regarded him icily. "Don't make the situation worse, Callan. You want to be careful who you make enemies of."

His blaze disintegrated. He held his hands up, and Stellana lowered her knife. She didn't put away her blade.

"It's time for you to leave."

"Why? Why would you go from trying to kill her to choosing

274

her over me?"

Stellana gave him a sympathetic pout. "Because the Riders are a symbol, Callan. Even more so than you've become. And their return means that the gods are coming out of the shadows once again."

"The gods *rejected* the Riders!" he shouted.

He knew he'd lost his grip on his temper. He didn't care. All he wanted was to watch every inch of this house reduced to ash.

"Not anymore." Stellana watched him with a steady eye. She brandished her knife at him, tone as sharp as her blade. "I see the gleam in your eye. Harm me, and your end will be anything but swift or painless. Now get out."

Callan flexed his fingers. He debated for one delicious moment letting the last of his fire take this room. Instead, he rallied his self-control and gave her a stiff nod before veering away. He pushed the door open with one hand, then twisted to look at Stellana over his shoulder.

"The gods have chosen me. Soon, you'll see the mistake you're making."

He let a bit of heat into his palm, pressing it deeper into the wood. He let the door snap shut behind him, his handprint still smoking as he left the manor behind.

Callan worked quickly, fueled by his lingering rage. The last pieces he needed fell into line, and he sent out his final messages. Within hours, Galtan troops would be in Narous to help keep the peace.

Daen was waiting in his sitting room when he arrived, a tantalizing array of objects before him on the table. Callan knew his lieutenant well. Well enough to see the anxiety most people would miss. He caught it in the tense angle of Daen's shoulders and the way he stood completely still.

Callan didn't acknowledge it, simply sat on the edge of the chair nearest the table. He also didn't acknowledge the tension in Daen's voice.

"I've managed to find a few things for you locally," Daen said stiffly. "I have a few more on their way."

275

Callan fingered the glass vials in front of him. One contained an iridescent powder that seemed to change colors depending on how the light hit it. Another contained a pale lump suspended in liquid. The last was a massive black beak.

Daen's lips curved down as he watched Callan handle the objects. "Powdered unicorn horn, pickled gryphon gall bladder, and a kraken beak. All of them claim to lend magical powers to anyone who consumes them."

Callan unstopped the vial with powdered unicorn horn. He dipped a finger in, then sucked off the powder. It left a bitter taste on his tongue. The other two would have to be prepared before he could try them.

"Well done, Daen. Are there any updates on the prototype?"

"We were fortunate to find a facility that was already creating another one. Thanks to the schematics from Mellis and a quiet seizure of the facility, the newest model is nearly finished."

"Excellent."

His fingers curled around the vial of unicorn horn until his knuckles were white.

If Catarina survived, she'd come here. If not for Callan, then to reunite with her father. And he'd be ready for her.

27

The first thing Cora noticed was a soft beeping next to her. Her fingers curled over stiff sheets, and there was a warm weight on top of one of her hands.

She pulled her eyelids open with effort, blinking against the sudden brightness. A large, brown hand covered hers. Her eyes slid up the muscled arm to find a head of dark curls resting against the edge of her mattress.

"That can't be comfortable." Her voice was thick and raspy.

Theo's head shot up. Relief flooded his face as his fingers laced through hers. His eyelashes were wet. He laid his other hand against her cheek, thumb sweeping slowly across her skin.

"Where are we?" she croaked.

"The infirmary," Theo said. "Reluraun wasn't too pleased to hear about our trip."

Memories came flooding back, sweeping away her lingering drowsiness. Cora made to sit up straighter, wincing at the tugging sensation across her gut.

Theo's hands were on her shoulders, gently pushing her back down. "Hey, not so fast. The last thing you need is to rip out your stitches."

"Where's Arik?" She couldn't keep the edge of panic from her voice.

"He's safe," Theo said quickly. "He's just down the hall. A little banged up, but no serious injuries."

Cora's body relaxed. She shifted her torn shirt to investigate the bandages circling her torso. "How bad was it?"

"If you weren't a Rider, you'd be dead," a crisp voice said from

277

the doorway.

Cora looked up to see an elf with a long auburn braid tapping impatient fingers against a clipboard. Her white coat had the name *Dr. Waylen* embroidered across the chest.

She leveled a stern glare at Theo. "I told you to get me as soon as she woke up."

Theo returned the glare. "You got here before I could."

Dr. Waylen leaned out into the hall, calling to someone Cora couldn't see. She then marched to a monitor next to Cora, barely giving her or Theo another glance. She scribbled a few notes on her clipboard.

"Your vitals look good, and as long as you don't do anything stupid"—she shot a dark glance at Cora—"you should be fully healed in a few days. Which is not nearly long enough, in my opinion, but that's the way it goes with reckless Riders."

The fingers still locked with Cora's clenched.

She frowned at Dr. Waylen. "Did I do something to you?"

"Maybe next time you act without thinking, you'll consider the other lives you put in danger." Dr. Waylen glared at both of them before folding her hands over her clipboard. "As far as I'm concerned, you are free to recover at home. You'll need to be back in four days to have your stitches taken out. Where you go after that is in the hands of the town council. Good day."

She spun on her heel and left, braid swinging behind her.

Cora and Theo exchanged a glance. Maybe Gray could explain what that was all about. She barely had time to process the interaction before Arik barreled into the room. He pulled her tight against his chest before practically shoving her back into the bed.

"What in the *blazing depths* was that?"

All the warmth bled from Theo's eyes. He sat up straighter, subtly leaning over Cora. His voice was naked steel.

"That was Cora saving your life."

Arik's head swung over to Theo. His eyes flicked up and down, lingering on their joined hands. Cora stifled the instinct to pull her hand away.

"Do I know you?" Arik asked coolly.

Theo didn't get a chance to respond. Gray hurried into the

278

room, relief filling his face. Reluraun followed much slower, along with several town elders, and Phaendar. Cora shifted herself upright, sitting as tall as she could manage. On instinct, she reached out to Makari. The bond was faint, as if her dragon was far away.

"Dr. Waylen says you'll make a full recovery." Reluraun kept his tone neutral. "You'll stay here until then."

"What exactly is this?"

"It's a hostage situation." Arik glared at Reluraun and the town elders.

They gathered at the foot of Cora's bed, the space between them and her like a yawning pit. Gray stood next to Theo, watching his grandfather with trepidation. Phaendar hovered to the side, one hand on the hilt of his dagger. Cora shifted to put herself between him and her brother.

"You're not hostages," Reluraun growled.

"Then are we free to leave?" she asked pointedly.

The silence was answer enough. Cora reached out to Makari again, her unease growing at her dragon's faint response.

"Where is Makari?"

"We don't know," Reluraun admitted. The rest of the elders seemed content to let him do the talking. "We went to secure her and found her already gone."

"She does have good instincts."

"You are hereby grounded until further notice."

"And what's stopping me from calling Makari here and leaving whenever I please?"

"You aren't the first Rider we've had to contain, girl," Reluraun said icily. "We have plenty of methods for securing dragons, some more pleasant than others. Considering your dragon's temperament, I don't think you'd be fond of the methods we would use."

Cora's lips pressed into a line. The thought of Makari contained, or hurt, sent a spike of rage burning through her blood. Her next words were sharp as claws. "Do you really think it's wise, keeping the heirs of Liskow prisoner? You will be crushed, and then everything you've worked so hard for will be in ruins."

279

"I think Liskow has their hands full with Galta at the moment."

"What does that mean?" Cora tried to contain her rising alarm. "What happened?"

"There was a riot last night," Gray said quietly. "More violent than the others. Several buildings were bombed. Callan has called in the Galtan military to help reinstate order in Narous."

"According to *who*? The Galtan delegation is in Narous to discuss an alliance, not invade the capitol," Arik snapped.

"Tell that to the *friend* who threatened you and stabbed your sister," Theo snarled.

"Enough." Reluraun's voice cut through the room. "No one in Liskow knows you're here, and they are now too preoccupied to send anyone to retrieve you if they did."

"So, what do you want?" Cora asked. "That's what this is about, isn't it? You want something from us, and we're stuck here until you get it."

Reluraun turned to the gathered elders behind him. A sheet of papers passed into his hand, which he tossed onto the bed at her feet.

"The town council has drawn up a treaty. You will swear your oaths as a Dragon Rider, which include loyalty to Stony Hollow and its people. You will provide seats on your council for Stony Hollow residents of our choosing. And you will sign into law that any future Dragon Riders will be trained in Aurestyn."

"How many council seats?" Arik asked warily.

"Half the council."

Cora's rage burned, mingling with a growing sense of disgust. She glared at each of the town elders in turn. "You don't want a return of the Riders. You want a return of the Nine Guards. You don't care about what the Riders stand for. You just want power."

"You don't know what you're talking about, child," Reluraun retorted. "You have no idea what we lost when we came here."

"I know where I stand," she said. "My answer is no."

"Don't make any rash decisions." Reluraun started moving toward the door, the other elders already filing out. "We'll give you time to think it over. In the meantime, Phaendar will be out in the hallway to keep an eye on you. Orym and Daethie are also

280

watching the infirmary, as well as some of their friends. Their conflicting oaths prohibit them from harming you, but they've been instructed to keep you here by whatever means necessary."

Phaendar gave her a crooked smile before staring pointedly at Arik.

She swallowed, then nodded once. She understood perfectly.

Reluraun stopped in the doorway, surveying Cora and her friends. His gaze lingered on Gray, expression unreadable. He turned and disappeared down the hall.

Phaendar sauntered after him, the door closing with a final click.

Theo lay down on Cora's bed. Gray hadn't commented when he went into her room. He hadn't said much of anything since they'd gotten back. Theo knew Gray well enough now to know that he didn't agree with the town elders. The silence between Gray and Reluraun lay thick over the house, like a summer night that refused to cool off.

Theo told himself that was why he went into Cora's room instead of the one he shared with Gray. To give Gray some time to himself.

The honest part of him knew he just wanted to breathe in her scent, free of the sharp smell of the infirmary. He'd refused to leave her side until she woke, shooting dark looks at anyone trying to shoo him away until they'd finally left him alone. It had taken all his self-control not to shred that ridiculous treaty into a thousand pieces. He'd nearly lost her, and all they could think about was how to use her. After everything, she was just a pawn to them. Like they didn't even know her.

A soft chime from his holo interrupted his thoughts. For just a second, he thought it might be Cora. But her holo sat on the dresser next to him. Theo could only think of one other person it could be.

Are you alright? The news from home has me worried about you.

I'm fine, Mom, still away from Narous. What have you heard?

My friend from the hospital, Gina? She told me about the increase in patients. People getting attacked on the streets, factories looted and

increase in patients. People getting attacked on the streets, factories looted and destroyed, Galtan soldiers patrolling the streets. She said there's
more soldiers than Watchers now.

Theo passed a hand over his face. Gina was always trying to
coax Mom back into nursing. All it ever did was make her moody
and distant.

I haven't heard much about home, just what's on the holo-streams. You're still staying with Isla for a while, right?

It took a long time for Mom to respond. Dread curdled in his
gut with each passing second.

I think Isla is ready to get back to her routine with the girls. She's
built quite a life here. Gina told me the hospital is looking for someone to
join Labor and Delivery. I think I'm finally ready to work again.

That's great, Mom, really. Just stay with Isla for a little longer,
please. Wait until things calm down back home.

I will. When are you coming home?

It was his turn to pause. He glanced around Cora's room, her
absence like a hole in his chest. No one had said he was a prisoner
here alongside her, but even so, he wouldn't leave without her.

Soon. Enjoy your time with Isla. Love you.

Love you, too.

Theo took his holo off and left it next to Cora's. Exhaustion
washed over him as he settled onto her pillow. She'd been in
surgery for hours, then he'd been unwilling to fall asleep in case
she woke up.

He slept for a few hours, his dreams shifting and changing
faster than he could track. He sat up, disoriented for a moment. He
glanced down at his shirt, stiff and stained. He'd cleaned his hands,
but he hadn't been willing to leave her long enough to shower.

He left her room, still groggy and tired, but unable to sleep any
more. He showered and changed before throwing his stained shirt
in the garbage. Even if he could get the stain out, he'd never be
able to look at it again.

He was out the door within a half hour of waking. The sun warmed his neck, drying his curls into tight coils as he walked. He made one stop on his way to the infirmary, picking up breakfast for him and Cora.

He ignored most of the people he passed, although he felt their eyes on him. Some glared with open hostility. He met them with cool indifference. Theo refused to glance at Orym on his way into the infirmary. He hadn't forgotten their confrontation with Cora, even if she wouldn't talk about it.

Theo was careful not to drop crumbs on the pristine hall of the infirmary. His fingers, consequently, were now smeared with powdered sugar.

Voices cut through the cracked door of Cora's room. Theo paused outside the door, catching a glimpse of her frown.

"This isn't up for debate, Arik."

"This is not the time to get all high and mighty, Cat. We are completely at their mercy here."

"So you want me to just give in?"

"I want to live long enough to go home, to see Father and Liana again."

Theo peered into Cora's room. The twins faced each other next to her solitary window.

"I won't let them hurt you," Cora said, eyes flashing.

"How can you promise that? What are *you* going to do about it?"

"What is that supposed to mean?"

Arik's arms waved as he punctuated his words. Theo couldn't see his face from this angle, but he saw the tips of his ears grow red. "I don't know what you *think* you're doing here, but this isn't the time to half-ass something, Cat. You're not some ancient warrior hero. You're a politician, and it's time you start acting like it."

"The last time I checked, politics wasn't about just giving in to demands."

"Then negotiate! Or is that too difficult for you?"

"You have no idea what that word even means," Cora snarled. "The golden boy who's had everything handed to him on a silver tray. It must be *so hard* to have nothing expected of you."

"This again?" Arik snapped, pacing away from Cora. "I carry plenty of expectations, like keeping your head attached to your shoulders. Meanwhile you have to quit moping and talk to people. What a burden."

Cora stepped closer, glaring up at her brother. Her hands clenched into tight fists at her sides. "We both know they'd rather it was you," she said, almost too softly for Theo to hear. "That they wish you'd been born first and been heir, but instead, we're all stuck with me."

"And yet, instead of doing something useful about it, you just ran away."

"What are you talking about?"

"I'm talking about the fact that my sister has spent years skulking around alone at night, and I was the *only one* on your security team who didn't know about it. What were you thinking, Cat?"

Tears glistened in Cora's eyes. Theo glanced away, shame flooding him at his intrusion.

"I was thinking that I was suffocating, and I needed some space to breathe."

Arik's voice hardened. "Don't you ever get tired of playing the victim, Catarina? So many people would kill to be in your position, but you can't be bothered to put in a real effort so that you can do what, exactly? If you just tried—"

"Cora."

The sharpness of the word cut Arik short. "What?"

"I have *always* preferred Cora."

"I don't see how that is relevant right now."

"And that's the whole problem."

Cora's clipped footsteps drowned out any response from Arik. She threw open the door, coming face to face with Theo, his fists still white-knuckled around the napkin that had once held her pastry. He gazed down at her, guilt twisting his gut at the look on her face.

Another tear slipped down her cheek as she faced away from him to glare at a figure a few feet down the hall. Phaendar glanced

284

up at her, picking dirt out of his nails with a knife.

"Take all the time you need, Princess," he replied with mock sweetness.

Cora didn't glance at Theo again as she disappeared down the hall. He rotated to watch her go, gut twisting.

"Do you make a habit of eavesdropping?"

Theo's head whipped back around at the disdain in Arik's voice. His lip was curled in a sneer.

"Does it count as eavesdropping when the entire building can hear you?" Theo retorted.

Arik crossed his arms, glaring. Theo found a growing sense of satisfaction that the prince had to look up at him.

"I suppose you're the reason my sister has been sneaking out for years."

"Cora makes her own choices."

"But you were there?"

"Yes, I was." Theo's blood heated, and he found himself itching for a fight. "She's my friend."

Arik stepped closer, his eyes blazing. "A friend who could grant you untold wealth and power."

"I have Cora's best interests at heart," Theo growled. "Which is more than you can say."

"I'm her brother." Arik's face was red. "I know her better than anyone."

"Apparently not."

They stared at each other, Arik's teeth grinding.

Theo stood his ground. He watched the debate in the prince's eyes. Theo was ready.

Then Arik stepped back, eyes hateful. "She can waste her time for now. But don't think for a second that I'll let you anywhere near her once we get home."

Arik stalked off, leaving Theo with nothing but the crumbs in front of his boots.

Cora kept replaying Arik's words as she locked the bathroom door behind her. They cycled over and over in her mind, sometimes joined by Devita. Father. Mother. They crackled and popped and hissed like flames slowly devouring her.

"You can't be bothered to put in a real effort."

The realization burned through her, crumbling her last defenses. No matter what she did, she wouldn't be good enough. No amount of effort would ever be enough.

Cora released her last bit of composure. She sank to the cool bathroom floor, the door a solid weight behind her as she let go. The tears flowed freely. They drenched her face and dripped onto her shirt.

Cora didn't know how long she sat there. A light pressure in her mind told her that Makari was trying to get her attention. She felt along the bond, and concern washed through her mind. It was stronger than the last time she'd felt Makari. Her dragon was coming closer, checking on her.

I'm fine, she sent. *Just sad.*

A soothing purr echoed through her head. Cora's lips twitched up in a tiny smile. She let her dragon's comfort wrap around her as she wiped her face.

When her tears were spent, Makari was there, waiting. Cora felt a nudging in her mind. She opened herself to Makari, sensing a question in the dragon's mental presence.

We'll have to go home soon.

Makari showed her a valley cupped by snow-capped mountains. Cora's heart twisted at the sight.

She shook her head. *No, my home.*

Cora showed her Narous, taking her down some of its twisting streets. Makari drew back. She frowned, showing her images from around the city. Her dragon drew back further, silence ringing in Cora's skull. She clenched her fists, forcing herself to show Makari the palace. A growl vibrated down the bond. Makari shoved into Cora's mind, the image of the valley back.

Cora winced, a stab of pain lancing through her head with the force of that mental image. *I have to go back to Narous, Makari.*

Makari growled again, the bond weakening as she retreated.

Fresh tears rolled down her chin. How could Cora explain? Makari wouldn't understand the laws, the chains shackling Cora to her throne. The word that haunted her, now pounding through her

286

skull.

Treason.

Cora shoved herself to her feet and turned the cold water on full blast. She splashed at her face, washing the tears down the drain.

She opened the door to find Phaendar waiting at the end of the hall. He certainly took his job seriously. Part of her wanted to rush at him, to let all of her pent-up frustration out. Her better judgment warned her that was a stupid idea.

Instead, she veered away from him back to her room. She knew he was following, keeping between her and the exit.

Arik didn't come back. Cora spent the next three days mostly alone. Theo came as often as Phaendar allowed him in. The visits became less frequent as the days went on. On the morning of day three, she heard him yelling at Phaendar.

"You can see her after the council's met with her," was all Phaendar would say.

It had been hours since then. She'd tried to open her door and catch a glimpse of Theo, but it was locked. The quiet pressed against her skin like a physical force. As far as she knew, he hadn't tried to see her again. Gray hadn't tried at all. She could only imagine what he thought of the situation.

Dr. Waylen returned in the afternoon to remove her stitches. The tall elf woman barely said a word as she worked. She removed the bandages to reveal a pink scar nearly eight inches across. She efficiently snipped the stitches and pulled them out. Cora winced as it tugged at her tender skin. Dr. Waylen didn't notice or care. She pulled her gloves off with a snap and nodded at a pile of clothes on the edge of the bed.

"I was instructed to bring those in for you." She shot an irritated glare toward the hall. "Next they'll have me bring your food in, too."

Dr. Waylen stomped out of the room without another word.

Cora had barely finished changing when a sharp knock echoed against the door. She turned around to see Reluraun enter with Phaendar.

"No council this time?" she asked icily.

"I offered to come alone." Reluraun settled onto the edge of a chair across the room. "I hoped I could talk some sense into you."

"What do you expect me to do, Reluraun? Give in? Erase everything my family has fought for?"

"Can you blame the council? Many of us remember a time before *your family* sent us into hiding. You've given them a chance to have their old lives back."

"And I'm supposed to believe you aren't one of 'them'?" She fought to keep her voice steady. "I know we have our differences, Reluraun, but I never expected you to use me."

"You act like we're stripping away your power."

"Aren't you? I read the papers." Cora snatched them from the bedside table. She waved them towards Reluraun. "If I sign this, I'll be at the town council's beck and call. I won't be able to do anything without their approval."

"Only as a Dragon Rider. We made certain it wouldn't violate any laws regarding your status."

She barked out a bitter laugh. "And yet you also assume to hold my dragon hostage in Aurestyn."

"There is no aerie in Narous anymore," Reluraun replied coolly. "It only makes sense she would nest here."

"This is a hostile takeover," Cora snapped, dropping the papers to the bed. "You're no better than Callan and his soldiers."

"Because your ilk were so much more *civilized* when they invaded," Phaendar growled from her left.

He'd crept within a few feet of her while she argued. She glowered at him, refusing to shrink from his slow advance.

"How many times do I have to hear this argument? Those were my ancestors *three hundred years ago*. I am not them." Cora swung her head back to Reluraun, even as her instincts screamed not to let Phaendar out of her sight. "What happens if I don't sign?"

Reluraun leaned back in his chair, hands folded over his stomach. The wrinkles around his eyes cast deep shadows across his skin. "Stony Hollow has no prison, so you'll be kept in an empty house. You will be under constant guard. Any attempt to leave or summon your dragon will result in bodily harm to her or you."

"And Arik? Theo?"

"Arik will be confined with you. As for Theo." Reluraun let out a long exhale. "He must stay in Stony Hollow. What he does with his time here is up to him, however." His voice dropped to a low rumble. "If he attempts to release you, his life is forfeit."

Cora turned away from Reluraun. She gazed out the window, scanning for the dragon she knew rode the winds high above. Silence stretched between them as she took a moment to compose herself. She refused to cry in front of Reluraun.

"We only need one of them." Phaendar's low voice was just behind her shoulder. "And her brother seems more willing to listen to reason. Let's just be done with this already."

Cora caught the flash of a blade in the window reflection. She didn't dare move.

"Back away, Phaendar." Reluraun's voice was calm. "The brother isn't a Dragon Rider. And despite your hatred for the Bjorns, you still owe the Riders your loyalty. And your respect."

She heard the soft scraping of Phaendar's knife returning to its sheath. Slowly, she spun around to face them.

Phaendar backed to the nearest corner, his mouth set in a grim line.

She folded her arms to keep her hands from shaking. "I need some guarantees."

"Such as?" Reluraun prompted.

"I need you to guarantee Arik and Theo's safety. And that Makari can safely land in Aurestyn and Stony Hollow."

"How do I know you won't let your dragon raze the entire village to the ground?"

"How do I know you won't kill Arik or Theo as soon as you get what you want?"

"Point taken," he grumbled.

She breathed in, then out. She'd known where this was going. The slow separation from Theo had been a warning, a taste of what would come if she refused. It was the first time in weeks she'd felt truly powerless. She was trapped, as surely as if they'd wrapped

289

her in chains and thrown her into a cell. There was no way out. At least, not one without unacceptable losses.

"I'll sign."

Reluraun nodded, rising from his chair. His expression was utterly unreadable, no hint of triumph or surprise. "I'll let the council know. They'll want to assemble, have you sign during an official meeting. In the meantime, you are free to roam Stony Hollow, with a guard. You are not allowed into Aurestyn without the town council's consent."

"What about my training?"

"You can resume training tomorrow." Reluraun lifted a shrewd eyebrow. "Practice weapons and hand-to-hand combat only."

Cora didn't argue. She had no use for a real weapon, anyway. She'd lost.

Reluraun gave her a final nod before sweeping out of the room, Phaendar close behind.

She stared out her window for a while. Long enough to watch the guards outside the building rotate. She waited until the sun had fully sunk behind the mountains before leaving her room. An elf she didn't recognize leaned against the opposite wall. He said nothing as she left, merely fell into step a few feet behind her.

Cora breathed deeply, savoring her first taste of fresh mountain air since she'd entered the infirmary. It eased some of the lingering tension in her body. She followed the now familiar path through town, passing almost no one on the way.

No one paid her any attention as she slipped into the dining hall. Most of the town had already gotten dinner. A handful of people were scattered among the long tables, their plates clean or almost clean. Across the room a small group clustered around a single table. Cora made her way toward the food line, passing by the crowded table.

Daethie, Orym, and Phaendar sat with three other elves, tall mugs of ale in front of them. The others pressed around the table exchanged coins, betting on the drinkers. Cora started as she recognized the elf nearest to her.

Lord Baeros.

"So you *are* here, Princess Catarina." Baeros smirked.

"I prefer Cora." She hated how hoarse she sounded.

"Hmm, I suppose it helps you pretend to be one of the common folk."

Cora glared at him as his companions snickered. Her hands curled into fists at her side. He fingered the rim of his mug, shooting her a sideways glance. Cora fought the urge to punch him.

"Although it seems you've been pretending for quite some time," Baeros continued. "If my sources are to be believed. Such a dangerous game, given the succession laws, don't you think?"

Cora's jaw tensed. She was considering the best angle to swing from when Phaendar grunted across the table, drawing her attention. He leaned back in his chair, fixing her with a hard stare.

"The old Riders used to join us. Care to continue the tradition?"

Cora sensed them leering at her, hoping for an excuse to humble her. Her eyes never wavered from Phaendar as she sat at the table across from him.

"I'm in."

Theo fumed for most of the day. If anyone but Phaendar had told him he couldn't see Cora, he would have gone anyway, consequences be burned. But he was smart enough to know when he couldn't win a fight. So he'd left, and stewed. He passed the infirmary at regular intervals, waiting to see Cora emerge. He was nearly ready to go by again when Gray stopped him.

"I need to do something," Gray said roughly. "Train with me?"

Theo took one look at his expression and nodded. It wasn't long until they were both slick with sweat. They only spoke when Theo corrected Gray's form or called encouragement. Gray moved with focus, his movements growing in power over time. Theo finally had to call it as dusk settled over Reluraun's yard.

Gray stilled, chest heaving. "Grandpa went to talk to Cora a couple of hours ago. The council sent him to convince her to sign the treaty."

"Did he?"

Gray shook his head. "I don't know."

Theo stared out towards Stony Hollow. He was done waiting,

Phaendar or not.

"Of course."

"Then keep a bag packed. One for Cora, too."

Theo turned back toward Gray. With the lights from the house hitting his face, he looked like a burning hero.

A tiny flicker of hope sprang to life in Theo's chest. "What are you planning?"

Gray's eyes flicked toward Aurestyn. "Just be ready."

With that, Gray left. Theo watched him for a minute before heading inside the house. He packed two bags with some extra clothes and food. He glanced around Cora's room, searching for anything else important. If she had something she cherished, he didn't know about it.

He intended to go straight to the infirmary. He wove through Stony Hollow, cursing himself for not bringing a light. He nearly knocked Reed down in the dark

"Sorry."

The lanky sprite waved him off. "No worries, Theo. Are you coming to the dining hall?"

"Is something happening?"

"Cora is drinking with Phaendar and Daethie. Apparently, she and Baeros are the only ones still in it with them. I'm betting she outlasts Daethie."

Burn me. "Let's go."

Theo's heart squeezed as he and Reed headed for the dining hall. A handful of others streamed into the building with them, all headed for the crowded table across the hall. He stepped out of the way as an unconscious elf was dragged out by his companions. A cheer vibrated through the floorboards, bringing his attention back.

Music blared from someone's holo as he drew closer. He stretched up, his head higher than most of those gathered. Even with his height, he couldn't see the table through all the bodies pressed together.

Another cheer pulsed in his chest. He inhaled deeply to steady himself, then pushed his way forward. He earned himself a few curses, but Theo didn't bother acknowledging the people whose toes he stepped on.

He made it to the front of the crowd, and his stomach dropped. Cora swayed next to the table, cheeks flushed bright red. She had stripped down to a tank top and leggings, even managing to kick off her boots. She pushed the hair out of her face, wobbling as she lifted her mug toward the crowd and downed it. The crowd roared again.

Across from Cora, Daethie slumped forward, eyes closing as her cheek hit the table. Metal gleamed to Theo's sides as money passed hands. Baeros leaned back in his seat, an amused smirk on his face. He had apparently forfeited the drinking game, his mug still full in front of his seat. Phaendar glared at Cora, his cheeks almost as red as hers. He knocked back another mug, gaining another cheer from the crowd.

Theo had seen enough. He laid his hand over Cora's, keeping her drink on the table. "I think it's time to go home."

Cora blinked up at him, eyes glazed. Her brow furrowed slowly. "But." A small burp interrupted her. "But I'm win... winning."

One glance at Phaendar confirmed her claim. The hatred churning in his gaze made Theo's fingers clamp tighter over Cora. He straightened to his full height, staring straight at Phaendar.

"We're done here."

"Rules are rules, boy," Baeros drawled. "Last man standing wins. Leaving now would be an insult to dear Phaendar."

"*Drown* your rules," Theo growled. "I'm taking Cora home."

Cora took a step forward, looking like she would protest. Then she stumbled into the table, knocking over the drinks. Phaendar stood, swearing down at his soaked pants. Theo wrapped an arm around Cora, his hand firmly on her waist.

"Look at the little princess," Phaendar sneered. "Can't even handle her ale without someone swooping in to save her."

Theo's knuckles went white. He turned an icy glare on Phaendar, stilling the room.

"Maybe you should show your Dragon Rider a little respect. And since you've made absolutely sure that she can't fight back herself, anyone who has a problem can deal with me." Theo jerked his chin toward Phaendar's arm. "Now drop the knife in your sleeve before I break your wrist."

Theo kept staring at Phaendar. If the elf refused, he could push Cora back with one hand while jabbing with the other. He didn't doubt his odds with Phaendar so drunk.

The old warrior stared back, fingers twitching at his side. No doubt running the odds himself. The blade slipped from his sleeve into long fingers. Slowly, Phaendar set it on the sticky table.

Theo raised his eyebrow ever so slightly. Phaendar's lip pulled back from his teeth. But he backed away from the table, and the knife.

Theo waited until Phaendar was a healthy distance away before glancing down at Cora. She had passed out against his side. Theo scooped her into his arms, glaring once more at Baeros and Phaendar. With his heart still pounding in his chest, he carried her back home.

28

Gray knew what he had to do. He'd known for a long time, but now he was finally ready. He hiked up to Aurestyn in the gathering dusk, grateful for his half-elf genes that allowed him to see in the dark. His heart thudded within his chest in anticipation. A warm wind practically pushed him towards the stone doors of the Rider city. He crested the final rise, then came up short.

"I knew you'd come up here eventually," Siraye said from her perch on a boulder just outside Aurestyn.

She wasn't alone. Gray saw Finn and a few other cousins, as well as sprites and elves he'd known his entire life. Nearly a dozen people waited for him.

Gray opened his mouth to speak, but Siraye held up a hand to cut him off.

"What the town council is doing is wrong," she said. "We know you feel it, too. We want to help you break Cora out."

"How did you know I was going to break Cora out?"

"I know everything, remember? Like how Reluraun went to talk to her this afternoon. And that she agreed to sign the treaty."

"That's news to me."

"The town council called a meeting for noon tomorrow," Finn added. "They're going to have her sign in front of the whole town."

"That doesn't give us much time," Gray muttered. He surveyed his friends and relatives. Their determination steeled his resolve. "If you're sure about this, then gather anything you think we need. Meet me back here in fifteen minutes."

"Where are you going?" Siraye asked as the group began to

dissolve.

"There's something I've been putting off. I'll be back soon."

Gray crossed the threshold into Aurestyn. He'd come to love the musty smell of the old city. His gaze swept over the atrium, lingering on the mosaic floor. He had a feeling this would be the last time he saw this place. Even if he returned to Stony Hollow, Grandpa Reluraun would likely never let him enter this hall again.

Gray walked down the dark hallway into the mountain. The air warmed as he neared the hatchery, carrying the scent of sulfur with it. The little black dragon was waiting for him, alert in her nest of straw. Gray knelt in front of her and reached out his hand.

She eased closer, nostrils flaring. She seemed to sense what he wanted. Her head butted into his hand, and pain lanced through his skull. She hissed, shying away. She was only gone for a moment before she came back to push up against him.

Images flashed through Gray's mind. New scents and sounds overloaded his senses as he adjusted to the presence in his head.

His dragon butted up against him, nearly sending him sprawling. She'd already grown to the size of a small dog, her wings almost comically large for her body. She scrambled up his arm to nestle across his shoulders, her claws putting holes in his shirt where she clung to him.

Gray laughed as her purr reverberated through his body. "Don't get used to that," he murmured. "You're already almost too big to ride on my shoulders."

She only nestled in further, her head coming to rest across his chest. Gray climbed to his feet, careful not to jostle her. She stayed firmly rooted to his shoulders as he began his climb back out of Aurestyn.

"How do you like the name Nova?"

Nova purred louder than Gray had ever heard in his life. She was still purring as he brought her out into the night.

Cora woke with a splitting headache. Her eyes had barely opened before she found herself hurtling for the toilet. She heaved for an agonizingly long time, then lay on the cool floor.

It was several minutes before she realized that she wasn't in the infirmary. She was back at Reluraun's.

She pushed herself upright, groaning as the room spun. It took an age before she was able to get up, and even longer before she was dressed. She stumbled down the hall into the living room. Theo was waiting for her on the couch.

"Where are Gray and Reluraun?" she asked groggily.

"Neither of them came home last night." Theo's words were clipped and tight.

She fought back a groan. It was too early to deal with his anger. "Whatever you want to say, just say it. I don't have the energy for subtlety."

"What were you thinking last night?"

"That I needed a drink."

Theo stood up from the couch, coming around to tower over her. He kept his arms folded tightly over his chest. She met him glare for glare.

"What are you trying to prove, Cora?"

"What are you talking about?"

"You know what I'm talking about."

She glanced away, hands shaking. "I'm signing the treaty today."

"Is this about what Arik said to you?"

Her lips pressed together.

Theo leaned down until they were at eye level. When she didn't meet his gaze, he turned her head with one finger. "Cora, if I've learned anything about your brother since meeting him, it's that he is a giant ass."

She huffed out a short laugh. "He's right, though."

"Your brother doesn't know the first thing about you."

"How are you so sure?"

"Because I know you."

"Do you? I mean, really?" Cora swallowed, eyes suddenly wet. "All I've ever done is disappoint people."

Theo leaned closer. "That's *dragon shit*, and you know it."

She had to look away from those intense eyes. She shook her head, forcing herself not to cry.

"Is that how your family talks to you?"

297

Her eyes snapped back to him. She'd never heard such rage in his voice before. A thousand excuses sprang to mind, a thousand reasons why. She opened her mouth to say one, but it wouldn't come out.

"Yes."

Theo's eyes smoldered. His hand dropped from her face as he paced away from her. His fingers curled and uncurled, then smacked into his palm as he worked to calm himself. "Why do you put up with this? You never said it, but I've always known this isn't what you wanted. Why not give the throne to your brother?"

"Because I can't."

"You can do anything you want! You're a blazing *Dragon Rider!*"

Cora stepped forward, catching Theo's arm to stop his pacing. He stared down at her, chest heaving.

"I. Can't."

"Why. Not."

"Because some ancestor of mine was so *pissed off* that his only child didn't want the throne that he made abdicating an act of treason," she hissed. "And since then, every power-hungry Bjorn cousin has tried to use that law to their advantage. If I even tried to abolish that law before the council, my family would use every scrap of influence they have to keep it in place. Then try me for treason anyway."

Theo froze. A few tears escaped down Cora's cheeks as the fight went out of him. Her voice was softer as she continued.

"My mother has been cultivating my public image for years now, trying to make me into a media darling. Trying to make me so beloved, so non-threatening that the Bjorns wouldn't try to kill me again," she swallowed, refusing to look at him. "I tried to do something for myself, something that got me out of the palace, out of my room. Tried to claw out a life for myself outside of my duty. But Arik made me realize that no matter what I learn here, no matter what I become, I have to go back. And I'll be dragging Makari with me. I'll be locking us both in a cage."

Theo stepped closer and laid a gentle hand on her cheek. His fingers were warm against her skin. She leaned her head into his touch.

"You need to choose your own life, Cora," Theo murmured. "And whatever you decide, I'll be there. If you want to run away and never look back, I'll follow. You want to go back, I'll campaign to change the law. But I won't let you give up. Not now, not ever. You are a *force*, Cora. Don't let them take that from you."

His gaze warmed her from her scalp to her toes. She no longer cared that tears flowed freely down her face.

She stared at her best friend, heart swelling. Her hands moved on their own. They wrapped themselves in the front of Theo's shirt, pulling.

And then Cora's lips were on his.

Theo froze.

A heartbeat passed. Cora was sure she'd made a mistake.

Then his other hand moved to her back, pulling her closer. Her lips parted in a soft gasp. He deepened the kiss, his mouth moving in time with hers. Cora moved with him, unleashing a part of herself she had kept hidden for far too long. The part that was just for him.

Cora untangled her hands from his shirt. One hand traced its way around his abdomen, coming to rest against his lower back. The other tangled itself in those midnight curls. They were as silky as she imagined. They coiled around her fingers as she stretched onto her toes. She wanted him closer. Wanted to satisfy that burning need to touch him.

Theo reached his arms around her thighs and lifted. Cora laughed against his mouth, both arms circling his neck as her feet left the ground.

He broke the kiss, his chest heaving against hers.

Cora rested her forehead against his. "Tired of bending down?"

Theo chuckled, the sound reverberating through her bones. "It's fine. I already knew you were a pain in the neck."

Her offended squawk was cut off by another kiss. Then he reluctantly let her slide down to the floor. The gaze he set on her made Cora's toes curl in her socks.

"What now, princess?"

"Now we prove my brother wrong."

Gray hadn't functioned on so little sleep since he was an undergrad. They'd crammed into Siraye's apartment, staying up most of the night to form their plan. Nova darted around the room, soaking up pets and scratches from anyone willing to give them. Everyone watched her in awe. Siraye's eyes kept welling with tears. Gray might have been emotional himself, if not for his focus on the problem at hand.

"I'm worried about trying to get out of here in a rush," he said, well after midnight. "Makari can carry three people, but she has to fly low. That puts her in just as much danger as taking multiple trips."

"If we got a car up here, we could shove Theo and Arik into the backseat while Cora flies off," Finn said, absently stroking Nova, curled up in his lap.

"How would we get a car up here? The bridge still hasn't been fixed."

Siraye and Finn exchanged a glance. Several of Finn's friends shifted warily in their seats. Gray's eyebrows lifted, waiting for someone to explain.

"Several of us like to trek down to Narous for a weekend here or there," Finn revealed. "Years ago, we built our own bridge further down the mountain. The road's a little rough, but we could still get down there in a hurry."

"How does no one notice you're gone?"

"Because we've got the spymaster on our side." Finn cut a sly glance at Siraye.

"Even though you've never invited me along," she grumbled.

"Maybe if you actually took a day off now and then."

"Do you have cars down there?" Gray cut in, waving his hand to get their attention. "Because we need to get them up here now if we want to pull this off."

"We can go get them," Barden chimed from the couch. "We can get your car, too, Gray."

Gray fished his keys out of his pocket and tossed them to Barden. He and three others slipped out of Siraye's apartment.

Gray leaned over Siraye's kitchen table, fingers drumming the

300

surface. "Are we worried about anyone following us?"

"I don't think so." Siraye's earrings tinkled as she shook her head. "Going after Cora and Arik outside of Stony Hollow territory is risking war with Liskow. No one on the council is desperate enough for that."

"Are you sure about that? I would've said the same thing a few days ago."

No one responded. Gray met the eyes of each person in the room. His voice was low, but it carried through the quiet.

"Before any of you go through with this, I want you to understand what you might be giving up. There's a very good chance that none of us will ever be allowed back here."

"Even if Cora weren't a Rider, what the council is doing is wrong," Finn replied firmly. He leaned his arms on his knees, hands clasped into fists. "I couldn't live with myself if I just watched it happen. If it means never coming back, then that's that."

Gray saw his sentiment reflected in the eyes staring back at him. Slowly, Gray nodded. Nova leaped onto the table next to him, tail curling around herself as she sat.

"We'll need a distraction while we grab Theo and Arik," Siraye said.

"How much time will you need?" Gray asked.

"A few minutes, at least."

Nova leaned into Gray, sensing his growing unease. He knew what he needed to do, his resolve strengthening with every passing hour.

"The council can't sign the treaty without every member present," Gray said, idly stroking Nova's ear. "I can stall my grandpa while the rest of you grab Theo and Arik. If they're out of danger, Cora can get herself out."

"Are you sure, Gray?"

Siraye's large blue eyes were filled with concern. How many times had he come to his friend to vent about his grandpa? Too many to count. She knew how much Grandpa Reluraun expected from him. She also knew how much they loved each other.

Gray put on a smile, knowing it didn't fully reach his eyes. "It's time."

Siraye squeezed his shoulder. He patted her hand before facing the room again.

"We should all get some rest. Gods know we're going to need it."

A few people left to their own apartments, but most found a spot of furniture or floor to curl up on. Siraye handed out a seemingly endless stream of blankets and pillows. Gray took an empty spot of floor near the kitchen. Nova curled against him, her soft purring lulling him into a deep sleep.

29

Cora could've let the world burn around them as she kissed Theo. They spent several minutes wrapped in each other's arms, exploring thoroughly.

Theo pulled back first, just far enough to disconnect their lips from each other. His heart pounded against her, nearly in time with hers. "I've waited a long time to do that."

"Me, too."

Cora reluctantly slipped out of his arms. She smoothed down her mussed hair and rumpled shirt. Rich sunlight bathed the living room, turning his eyes into liquid gold.

She blinked, glancing around the room. "What time is it?"

"I don't know." Theo glanced down at his bare wrist. "Midmorning?"

"I got a message yesterday that I'm signing the treaty at noon."

The joy on his face evaporated. A shadow fell as his anger returned. "What did Reluraun say to you yesterday?"

"Hey, breathe," Cora said gently, laying a hand on his arm. "You know what he said. I can't let you or Arik, or Makari be used against me. At least if I sign the treaty, you'll all be safe."

"I'd rather spend my whole life here than let them manipulate you into this."

Her mouth ticked up into a sad smile. "And what about your mom? Don't you want to see her again?"

"My mom," he said slowly, frown deepening. "Burn me, I need to tell you something."

Cora listened as he relayed what his mother said. Any lightness she felt vanished.

"Let's get this signing over with then." She started toward the door. "I want to get down there before Callan does anything else."

"The town council won't just let you leave, even after you sign." Theo grabbed her arm, stopping her before she crossed the room. "Besides, Gray said he had a plan."

"What kind of plan?"

"All he said was to pack a bag for each of us."

"So what do we do? I can't just sit here."

Theo reached forward to tuck a strand of hair behind her ear. The tenderness of his touch stalled her breath.

"I'll follow you anywhere, princess. Just tell me where to go."

"Let's start by getting out of this house."

Theo's hand slipped into hers and squeezed. Together, they walked out into the blazing sunshine.

Phaendar lounged in Reluraun's yard, scowling at the house. Vague memories of the previous night surfaced in her mind. She got the impression that something happened between Theo and Phaendar, a suspicion that deepened as they threw dark looks at each other.

"I can't wait to be done following you around," Phaendar growled.

"You could start now. You already got what you want," Cora shot back.

"Not until the ink's on the paper."

Theo gave her hand a little tug, motioning toward Stony Hollow. She stayed rooted in place.

"Why do you hate me so much?" Cora asked.

"Besides the fact you're a bald-faced liar?" Phaendar retorted.

"And you would have been so welcoming if you knew who I was to begin with."

"You Bjorns are all the same," Phaendar spat in disgust. "Expecting everyone to fall at your feet like you're the gods' gift to the world."

Phaendar was on his feet now, face reddening. Her anger flared to match his. Theo took a subtle step between him and Cora.

"This grudge you're holding is *burning* ridiculous," she snarled. "When have I even—"

304

"I failed them!" Phaendar roared. "It was my job to protect the little ones. The hatchlings, the novice Riders. But your ancestors, *your kin,* slaughtered them all."

Cora took a step back under the force of his rage. She stared into his anguished eyes and let his words sink in. This was the heritage he feared. What they *all* feared she would do.

"You're right that I'm not the old Dragon Riders. But I'm also not those men. *I'm not them,* Phaendar. I can only imagine the depth of your pain." She swallowed. "The guilt. But you didn't fail them."

"What do you know about it?" he snapped.

"I held my mother as she bled out. I did nothing. I just stood there." Cora inhaled deeply, pushing down her swell of emotions. "I know for a fact you didn't just stand by and let it happen. You did everything you could."

Phaendar glared down at her. Every ridge and plane of his face was hard as stone. "You know nothing of what happened that night."

"So show me."

"What?"

"Yeah, what?" Theo echoed.

Cora ignored him, her eyes fixed on Phaendar. "Spar with me. Consider it a rematch for our drinking game."

Phaendar's expression slid from shocked disbelief to dangerously calculating. She didn't miss how his eyes flicked up and down, sizing her up. He shot one wary glance at Theo before coming back to her face.

"Are you sure about this, girl?"

"Absolutely."

Phaendar smirked. On anyone else, it might have been cocky. On the muscular elf, it was predatory.

"Alright. The outside sparring ring, one hour."

Phaendar strolled away, still smirking.

Theo stepped closer, his citrus and mint scent filling Cora's nose. "This is a bad idea."

"Trust me."

Cora twisted her head to gaze up at him.

305

Theo nodded once. It was enough.

Gray only slept for a few hours before the alarm on his holo went off. He was stiff and sore, still in the same position curled around Nova. Others were also stirring, some already gone.

Siraye came out of her room as Gray stood, a bag slung across her chest.

"The cars are waiting," she said, taking the blanket he'd been using and folding it.

Gray stretched, his back popping loudly. "Is anyone going to find four random cars suspicious?"

"Nah," she replied, tossing the folded blanket into a basket. "Baeros and his grunts are still here with their vehicles, so a few more won't be too strange."

"How did *he* get up here without the bridge?"

"Same way we're getting out of here."

Gray lifted an eyebrow and Siraye shrugged.

"Who do you think showed us this road in the first place?"

"Fair enough," Gray agreed. "Are you ready?"

"Ready as I'll ever be. This is my first trip to Narous."

Gray caught the sadness in her smile. Siraye loved the Hub, almost as much as she wanted to see the world. He'd been surprised when she took the position.

Gray bumped her shoulder with his. "You're going to love it."

He helped Siraye finish tidying her apartment as the last stragglers got up and moving.

A short knock sounded on the door before Finn burst in.

"Cora challenged Phaendar to a sparring match," he said breathlessly. "Now's our chance."

"They'll all be in one place," Siraye agreed. "Do you know when?"

"About an hour."

Siraye exchanged a glance with Gray. Nova sauntered over from her spot on the floor, tail whipping in anticipation.

Gray gave her a nod. "Get the cars into position, oh, and grab Cora and Theo's bags. I'll keep Reluraun busy."

306

Cora scraped her hair into a short tail, ignoring the gathering crowd. She picked Theo's tall head of curls out. They locked eyes, and he gave her a slight nod. She returned it, eyes sliding away again. They snagged on a head of blond hair at the very edge of the ring. Arik's eyes were dark as a storm cloud. Her lips pressed into a line. She'd deal with him later.

Cora busied herself with wrapping her hands. She didn't care to count those milling around the sparring ring. But she knew most of them had work they were supposed to be doing. She knew immediately when Makari showed up.

Their bond had remained silent since the fight. Makari shoved her way to the very edge of the sparring ring and lay down with her head on her front legs. She was the picture of boredom and ease. The only thing that gave her away was her flicking tail.

Cora locked eyes with her dragon. Makari didn't send anything down their bond, but Cora knew that she was waiting for something. Some sign that she could trust her.

Cora swallowed, breaking eye contact. Makari's presence hummed in the back of her mind.

She shoved down a surge of doubt as she and Phaendar entered the sparring ring. It was little more than a circle of dirt marked by a line of white paint. She had to either hold him to the ground for a count of ten or knock him out of the ring. There was always a chance that he would yield, but she didn't find that option very likely. She wouldn't put it past Phaendar to kill her and make it look like an accident, treaty or no.

Cora came in swinging, hoping to take Phaendar off guard. He let her come at him, smirking as he easily dodged her blows. She danced back, then darted forward again, searching for openings. He deflected the blows that actually made contact, her fists sliding across his arms harmlessly. He seemed content to let her wear herself out. She swallowed a frustrated growl that threatened to claw its way up her throat.

Phaendar's smirk deepened, then his fist flashed toward her.

Pain exploded across Cora's side. She struggled to catch her breath as she stumbled back. He pressed forward, forcing her back again. Her teeth ground together as she blocked blow after blow.

Her stance faltered, just for a moment, and her head rang, stars sparking across her vision.

Cora retreated another step, arms shaking. Her body screamed in protest, begging her to stop.

She set her stance again. She sensed Makari sit up, knew that her dragon's entire focus was on her. Cora slowed her breathing, continuing to track Phaendar's movements as she centered herself.

If Phaendar beat her, fine. But it wouldn't be because she gave up. Cora was tired of giving up, of giving in. She was tired of letting others make decisions for her. She had chosen this fight, and she was going to give everything she had left.

She felt the shift immediately. An alignment that traveled from her head to her toes, making her stand up straighter, pull her arms in tighter. Her mind focused, and everything else went quiet.

New strength surged through her. Her heart rate slowed, steadied, beating in time to a larger, deeper beat.

Phaendar's eyes went wide. His jaw fell open, and his stance slackened.

Cora didn't hesitate. She swept forward, her fist pounding into Phaendar's jaw. His head swung to the side, and he stumbled. He scrambled to reset his stance, but Cora was already there. Her knee buried itself in his stomach, while her other fist slammed against the side of his face.

Phaendar sprawled onto the ground, blood dribbling down his chin.

Her body yearned to keep going, but she held herself back. Phaendar held his hands up in surrender.

Cora forced herself to lower her arms. To take a step back.

Phaendar rose slowly, eyes still full of wonder. He stared at her, then put his fist over his heart and bowed.

"Well met, Dragon Rider."

Makari's head loomed over her shoulder. Cora hadn't noticed her approach. Her head swung around, taking in the silent crowd. She watched in stunned silence as they saluted her. Satisfaction thrummed through her.

She glanced up at Makari and swore the dragon grinned.

Gray knew where to find Reluraun. Mulch crunched beneath his feet as he walked between the neat garden beds in the yard. His grandfather sat on a stump outside the open shed, his water bottle already half gone. He'd hung his straw hat on the shed's door handle while he wiped his forehead with a handkerchief. He barely spared Gray a glance as he approached.

"Seems like you'll have plenty of squash this year," Gray said casually.

Gray sensed rather than saw Nova peeking around the corner of the house. She grumbled curiously, itching to join him. Gray firmly told her to wait until he called.

Grandpa eyed him warily. "Well, out with it."

"I'm going to Narous with Cora and Theo."

Grandpa grunted noncommittally. Gray glanced into the shed, eyes catching on two long objects leaning against the back wall.

"You don't have anything to say about that? I find that surprising."

"You've made your mind up. Not sure what there is to say."

He stepped into the shed and retrieved the objects. He laid them carefully on the ground, then began unwrapping the cloth covering them. The dull blades of two practice swords gleamed in the afternoon light.

"Then why don't you spar with me?"

Grandpa scowled at the old practice swords. The leather grips were worn, blades scratched from years of use. "I'm too old for that."

"You weren't too old when you taught me." Gray hefted his old sword. The grip that had once felt too large for his hands now sat comfortably in his palm. "Or are you just afraid to lose?"

Grandpa threw his damp handkerchief to the ground. He snatched his practice sword off the ground and marched a few feet from the garden beds to an open stretch of grass. Gray followed at a measured pace, swinging the blade a few times. It sang through the air, lighter than he remembered.

Grandpa only waited a breath for him to find his footing before going on the attack.

Gray retreated, barely managing to fend off Grandpa's swings

309

The old elf was surprisingly strong. His motions were precise, honed over centuries of practice.

Gray's own training returned to him, his practice over the last few weeks lending confidence to his defense. Grandpa's voice was the only sign of his strain, puffing out in irritated growls between swings.

"After all I've taught you, molding you into a Rider, one human girl shows up and undoes *everything*."

Hot anger pulsed in Gray's veins, lending his next block extra power. He pressed forward, sending Reluraun back a step.

His grandpa's eyes blazed with ire. "You let one *Bjorn* turn your head."

"And what if she has a point?"

Gray pressed forward again. Sweat slicked his hands and brow, but still he continued, driving Grandpa back another step.

Grandpa struck again, the force vibrating up Gray's arm and shoulder.

"So everything I worked for was meaningless?" he snarled. "Everything I did was wrong?"

"No." Gray forced his grandpa back again. He could sense the elf starting to tire. "But I know you, Grandpa. You really mean to tell me that you never once questioned if what you were doing was right?"

Sweat poured down Grandpa's face. He blinked it out of his eyes, barely defending against Gray's next slice. "It was the way things were."

Strain was painted across his face, Gray's next strike sending his sword tumbling to the ground.

Gray let his own sword fall to his side. "Don't you think the way things are should be better than they were before?" he put a hand on Grandpa's shoulder. "I believe you did your best, Grandpa. But I'm choosing the kind of Rider I want to be."

Grandpa Reluraun's head snapped up at the words. His eyes widened, and in them, Gray saw a glimmer of hope. A smile spread across his mouth.

"There's someone I'd like you to meet," Gray said.

He reached down the bond, and Nova came bounding over the

garden beds. Her wings snapped open, catching the breeze and letting her glide a foot off the ground. She landed next to Gray, then pounced on Grandpa's shoelaces. He watched in awe as she spun around him, sniffing his clothes.

"This is Nova."

Grandpa squatted, reaching a tentative hand to the hatchling. Nova bumped his hand eagerly, a deep purr vibrating her entire body. Gray grinned at them.

"A black dragon," Grandpa murmured. "Rare indeed. Fitting for you, Grayson."

Gray's heart swelled. Nova rolled in the grass, already bored.

Grandpa straightened to face him again. Gray realized with a start that he was now taller than his grandpa.

"You need to stay and train," Grandpa insisted, "With the treaty signed, this is where all Dragon Riders will gather for training. I need you here to help me."

"There won't be a treaty, Grandpa."

A cloud passed over Reluraun's face, his eyes flashing like lightning. He took a step toward Gray, every inch the Rider he once was.

"What have you done, Grayson?"

"I made a choice."

Grandpa Reluraun's face twisted with fury. He snatched the practice sword off the ground and attacked with renewed strength.

Gray scrambled to block the strike, grunting at the force of it. He breathed deeply, eyes tracking his grandpa's movements. All he had to do was keep him busy for a few more minutes.

The countdown had begun.

30

Theo stared at Cora in wonder. He'd forced himself to watch every agonizing minute of the match, every muscle clenched as Phaendar hit her again and again.

He'd seen the shift as soon as it happened. Cora stood straighter, and her eyes changed. Her pupils turned slitted, like a dragon's. Power radiated from her as she struck, Makari moving in time with her. They were one creature—every movement perfectly in sync, like a dance.

She'd stared out over the crowd with those slitted eyes. His awe echoed through the crowd as they saluted her. He saluted too.

Then she'd blinked, and her eyes returned to normal. But the shift was still there.

Phaendar couldn't stop staring in shock.

Theo hugged Cora, purposefully blocking her from Phaendar's view. "You were incredible."

"Thank you," she said, words muffled against his chest.

Her head cocked to the side just before Theo heard footsteps approaching.

Arik frowned at Cora, glancing between her and Makari. He opened his mouth to speak but never got the chance.

A loud roar overpowered the crowd, then people were jumping out of the way. Three cars skidded to a stop around them. Makari growled, the spines along her back bristling. The door nearest them opened, and a silvery head popped out.

"Siraye?"

"Theo, Arik, get in!" Siraye called. "We're busting you out of here!"

Theo's heart swelled, echoing the hope filling Cora's eyes. He swooped down to lay a kiss on her cheek.

"Go," he whispered against her skin.

He gave her a nudge toward Makari. She gave him a lingering look before scrambling onto her dragon's back.

Theo spun and grabbed Arik's arm, hauling him toward the car.

"What are you doing?" the prince snapped.

Theo shoved him into the car before climbing in after. Siraye didn't wait for the door to close before hitting the gas. He gripped the seat in front of him, craning his neck to see Makari and Cora shooting into the sky.

He cursed as Siraye swerved, and his head banged against the window. "Who let you drive?"

Siraye wrenched the wheel again, hard, sending him sliding into Arik. The prince grunted as he was shoved against the door frame.

"Maybe you should put your seat belts on then," Siraye warned.

Theo didn't have to be warned twice. It clicked into place just as the car rocketed down a bumpy gravel road. He stared out the window again, then wished he hadn't. To their left was a steep drop-off down to a thick forest below.

He swallowed, turning away from the window. "Where are we going?"

"We have a meet-up spot with the others," Siraye answered, knuckles white around the steering wheel. "Then we're headed to Narous."

"Did Gray do this?"

"With some help."

Siraye slowed as the road twisted sharply. Theo felt the shift from rough gravel to smooth pavement as they rolled onto a long bridge.

Siraye kept her eyes straight ahead. "I don't suggest looking out the windows." Her voice was shaky. "Especially if you're scared of heights."

Theo knew he should listen to her. His curiosity got the better of him. They were on a narrow bridge, the only thing separating them from a long drop a short guardrail. The canyon was only a few hundred yards wide. He counted every second it took to cross it.

The tires hit gravel again and he exhaled slowly. He hadn't realized he'd been holding his breath. He glanced across at Arik, satisfied to find him pale and tense as well.

Siraye drove for a few more minutes before pulling off in a small clearing. A shelter nestled between the trees, with just enough space to park three cars side by side.

It wasn't long before two more vehicles joined them. Theo waved to Finn where he sat behind the wheel of the car closest to them. He spotted a few more familiar faces as they waited.

A shadow passed overhead, then the car rocked back and forth as Makari landed in the clearing. There was just enough room in front of the cars for her wingspan.

Siraye rolled down the window, leaning her head out. "Did you see anyone following us?"

"No," Cora called back. "Are we waiting for anyone else?"

"Gray said he'd be here."

Theo twisted in his seat to check the road they'd turned off. They waited, engines idling. Five minutes passed, then ten. He was ready to hike back and look for Gray himself when a car pulled into the clearing in a cloud of dust.

Gray's window slid down, revealing a steadily bleeding gash across his cheek.

"Did everyone make it?" he asked.

Siraye nodded.

Gray jerked his head back toward Stony Hollow. "We should leave. They were getting a team ready to send after us when I left."

Windows rolled back up and they were on their way again, careening down the mountain. Theo kept a hand on the door, watching as the trees whipped past them. It wasn't the same path they'd taken to Stony Hollow, but at their current pace, he was sure they'd make it to Narous by nightfall. He pressed his head to the window, gazing up.

A smile spread across his face as he watched his Dragon Rider lead them home.

Cora stroked Makari's neck as they flew. Their bond thrummed between them, stronger than before. She knew that all it would take was half a thought, and they would snap together again, completely in sync. Contentedness flowed between them. A part of her she hadn't even known was missing settled into place in that sparring ring. Connected to both Makari and Theo, Cora had never felt more completely herself.

She hardly noticed the hours ticking by as they soared southeast. Makari's wings beat a steady rhythm that lulled her into a doze. Makari nudged the bond, rousing her before diving to the ground. They were at the very edge of the foothills, looking down on Narous. The last bits of sunlight were fading, casting deep shadows over the plains around the city. Lights shone like neon stars in the gathering dark.

The cars pulled up next to Cora and Makari, facing the side of a steep hill. Cora saw nothing remarkable about the scraggly brush covering it. She watched as Finn hopped out of his car and trotted into the bushes next to it. There was a loud creaking sound as part of the hill swung inward, raining dirt and leaves. Makari sat up straighter, chest expanding as she inhaled deeply. She made an eager sound deep in her throat at the scent wafting from the dark tunnel.

Dragons.

Cora sensed through their bond that the scents were old, but it didn't dampen Makari's eagerness. She wanted to launch straight into the void in front of them. Cora held her back, letting the cars cut the darkness with their headlights. Makari huffed indignantly.

You might be able to see in the dark, but I can't.

Makari took that as a challenge. Cora gasped as their minds snapped together again. Details crystallized around her as they stalked into the tunnel. It was wide enough for two cars to drive side by side, the ceiling soaring another fifteen feet above Makari's head. Cora's sense of direction slipped away as the tunnel twisted away from the opening. They stopped when it opened into a large cavern.

Cora couldn't tell if the cavern was natural or man-made. It

315

was large enough that Makari could have circled it in a few wing beats, the edges of the room too dark for her enhanced sight. A breeze blew through the space from another tunnel across the cavern.

The sound of closing car doors echoed as everyone climbed out and stretched. Her legs wobbled as they touched the ground, sore from clinging to Makari for hours.

Siraye nearly knocked her over again as she pulled her into a hug. A laugh bubbled up from within Cora. She let it grow, relief washing through her, until both she and Siraye were nearly in tears. She was still grinning as they pulled apart.

She could almost ignore the frown etched into Arik's face. She lifted one eyebrow in his direction. "Shouldn't you be celebrating, too? We're almost home."

"Yes, almost directly underneath in a smelly cave. I'm thrilled."

"You're welcome."

Cora faced away from him as Theo and Gray approached. Gray wrapped her in a tight hug, strands of her hair catching in the stubble on his chin. She cocked her head as he pulled back, a familiar scent lingering around him. Makari leaned down, snuffling eagerly.

"Am I missing something?" Theo asked, coming to slip his hand into hers.

Gray grinned. Cora knew who was coming around the side of his car before the little dragon came into sight. She was at least twice as large as the last time Cora had seen her. The baby ran up to Makari, purring loudly.

"I named her Nova," Gray said.

"Glad I'm not the only Rider anymore."

Theo stared at them, mouth parted. Cora laughed again, squeezing his hand.

They left the dragons to bond while they helped unload the cars. She was blown away by how thoroughly everyone had prepared. They pulled out bedrolls and tents, camp stoves and food.

She paused, finding the stash of weapons. Right on top were

316

the twin swords and back sheath. She ran her fingers over them, the weight of what she was about to do settling over her.

"Finn insisted we also bring a firearm for you," Gray said at her shoulder. "But I had a feeling you'd want these."

"What will Reluraun say when he sees they're gone?"

"It doesn't matter. They're yours," Gray replied firmly. "We also grabbed some armor we think will fit you."

Cora buckled on her sheath and drew her swords. Their weight settled into each hand like an extension of her arm. She moved through her forms, blades singing through the air. They slid back into their sheaths across her back with hardly a whisper. She glanced up to find everyone watching her. She swallowed, her voice carrying in the vast chamber.

"I can't even begin to thank you for what you did." She met everyone's eyes in turn as she spoke. "Whether you did it for me, or because of Gray, either way, I can never repay you. And now, I have to go back and stop Callan. I won't ask you to risk your lives to help me, and I understand if you want to leave now. But..." Cora paused as her eyes met Theo's. "I could use some help."

Siraye stepped forward. "I'm here to help."

"Me too," Finn said from where he was loading bullets into magazines.

"Riders need to stick together," Gray said.

Offers of help echoed around the cavern, even a grudging one from Arik. Her eyes once again found Theo. He stared at her with a warmth that made her legs wobble again.

"I'm not going anywhere, Princess," Theo said. "Better together, always."

31

Cora slept better than she had in weeks. Makari curled around her, creating a cocoon of warmth under one outstretched wing. Theo and Gray were in a tent nearby, everyone else scattered throughout the cavern. Her sleeping roll didn't provide much padding against the cold stone floor, but she didn't care.

The sound of sizzling eggs chased away the last fragments of dreams overflowing with dragons and phoenixes. There was a tentative hopefulness in the air at breakfast. It filled Cora up, even more than the food.

"So what exactly is the plan?" Arik asked, hardly waiting for the dishes to be put away.

Cora met the scowl on his face, like a gathering thunderhead on the horizon. There was trouble brewing in that expression.

She sat up straighter, projecting cool authority. "We need to get an idea of what's really going on in Narous. A few of us should go out into the city and scout around."

"I can go," Finn offered. "Barden and I know some people we can talk to."

Cora nodded as Gray also offered, along with three others. Theo was the last to offer to go into Narous.

"I'll go with you," Cora said.

"No," Theo and Arik said together.

They shot each other dark looks, as if offended that they agreed on something.

"Like it or not, I have contacts in the city, too," she replied.

"I can talk to them," Theo said before Arik could respond. "It isn't worth the risk."

318

Cora pushed herself to her feet. "I wasn't asking."

She watched a muscle in Theo's neck tighten as he clenched his jaw, but he didn't argue.

Arik shot to his feet, head already shaking. "That's not happening."

Theo swung around to face Arik, voice low and cold. "She's made up her mind. Besides, I'll be with her."

"How comforting," Arik drawled. He sidestepped Theo, stalking closer.

Cora didn't miss how Theo angled himself between her and Arik.

"I'm still your Protector, and I'm not going to sit here and let you risk your neck," Arik said, face flushing.

She met her brother's eyes, their dark blue depths as stormy as his expression. He stood over her, his bulk crowding her view. As she noticed the flush building under his skin, something in her snapped.

She stepped closer, tilting her chin to maintain eye contact. Her lips pulled back from her teeth as her words came out in a barely contained snarl.

"I think you're forgetting, *little brother*, that as heir and Rider, I outrank you twice. I'm going. You're staying. That's the end of it."

The cavern had gone eerily quiet as everyone watched them battle.

Arik blinked in surprise. He recovered, his face reddening. "Staying here? Like he—"

"Think about it," Cora said sharply, cutting him off. "You're extremely recognizable, and you have no contacts in the lower city. You're better off staying here."

"So this is how it's going to be now? I never took you for a tyrant."

"I'm not. I'm just sick of being pushed around."

She stepped away, leaving Arik to fume. She turned sharp eyes back to the group, raising her voice to carry across the cavern.

"We'll meet back up by noon. Then I want a viable plan by nightfall."

The stillness broke into a flurry of activity. Within a few

319

minutes, she was ready to leave for the city. She'd even managed to find a scarf to cover her hair. Makari huffed at her, claws scraping against the stone as she flexed and released them.

Cora stroked her face soothingly. "Soon, you'll be flying out of here," she murmured. "But for now, I need you to stay hidden. I need you to protect everyone staying behind."

Makari's chest swelled, and she tossed her head. Cora smiled, bidding her a quick goodbye before catching up with the others.

They drove two cars as far into the tunnels as they could. They parked in a smaller cavern, the tunnel on the other side too narrow for cars to pass. The floor sloped upward as they hiked to one last cave, just big enough for all of them to squeeze into. Several tunnels branched upward, their walls too smooth to be natural.

"Which one do we take?" Cora asked, glancing between the dim passages.

"The far left spits you out near the university," Finn said, pointing. "The middle left one take you to the south end of the night market. The middle right takes you to the arena. And the far right comes up in the storeroom of the Dragon Slayer."

Cora and Theo exchanged a glance.

She gave him a little nod. "We'll take that one."

"I'll take the one to the university," Gray said, already in motion.

An elf split peeled off to join him while the other four split between the remaining tunnels. Theo led the way into their passage, his hand finding hers in the dark. He had to duck a few times as they walked, allowing a little light to leak over his shoulder from the end of the passageway. She nearly ran into him when he stopped to look upward.

A wooden ladder led up to a square above them. Light leaked through the boards of the trap door, piercing the thick darkness of the tunnel.

The warmth of Theo's hand left hers as he ascended the ladder. He pushed against the trapdoor, grunting as it creaked open. Light flooded the tunnel around his silhouette. Cora threw her hand up, squinting against the brightness. She waited just long enough for her eyes to adjust before climbing up after him.

She was only halfway out of the trapdoor when heavy footsteps pounded down the stairs. She heaved herself out of the tunnel just as Sloan froze in the doorway, mouth falling open. They all stared at each other over the cases of bottles for a long moment. Then Sloan crossed the room in four long strides and swept them both into a hug.

"I've been worried about you two," he rumbled in his deep bass. "No one's seen you in weeks."

"It's good to see you," Theo said, pulling back with a smile. "We've been out of town."

Sloan glanced down at the trapdoor. "So it seems. I heard about the attack on the palace, and then there were rumors you were dead." He turned shining eyes on Cora. "Well, I'm just so glad to see you again."

Cora touched his arm, her own eyes growing damp. He put a hand on top of hers, giving a little squeeze before addressing both of them again.

"What are you doing back, though? It seems smarter to stay gone right now."

"What's been going on, Sloan?" Theo asked.

"Nothing good." He sighed, stroking his thick ginger beard. "The People's Employment League has been stirring up trouble left and right. And not just protests anymore. They've been looting and destroying just about anything they can get their hands on, particularly machines. I've got Watchers and Galtan soldiers in and out of my pub every day, sometimes drinking, sometimes arresting some poor sod. I had a few asking after you, Theo."

"What did they want?"

"Didn't say. Just that they were looking for you. I had one of your co-workers—Donald, I think—in asking if I'd seen you. Said he'd been to your house and there were soldiers watching it."

Cora glanced at Theo. A shadow fell over his eyes, darkening his features. She didn't have to ask to know where they were going next.

"Thanks, Sloan," he said, reaching out to shake his hand.

Sloan took his hand, clapping his other onto Theo's shoulder. He nodded to the back of the storeroom. "You better use the delivery entrance. I've got a few soldiers sitting at my bar right now. I'll leave it unlocked for you. Don't come back through the front."

Cora nodded gravely, unnerved by his serious tone. Sloan reached for a bottle, nodding at them one last time before disappearing into his pub. She followed Theo as they wove between the stacks of barrels and bottles to the back door. Theo cracked it and peered out before motioning for her to follow.

They'd only made it down a handful of streets before a familiar shadow darted into their path. Cora nearly stumbled as the small form launched into her, wrapping thin arms around her torso.

"Mila! What are you doing in this part of town?"

"I was running an errand for Mama," she replied, grinning up at her. "I lost two teeth!"

"I see that." Cora chuckled. "Please tell me you stopped putting up posters?"

Mila's grin disappeared. She shivered, goosebumps rising all along her arms. "Mama made me stop a couple of weeks ago. The soldiers keep taking people away."

"Taking who away?"

"The people who paid me for the posters. And some others, too. Where have you been? I missed you."

"I missed you, too." Cora gave her another squeeze. "You should get going, though. Don't want your mom to worry about you."

Mila dashed off with a wave. Cora faced Theo, their grim expressions reflections of each other. They continued their way to his house, keeping to shadowed side streets. They had to backtrack several times to avoid Galtan patrols. The streets were silent, like the entire city was holding its breath.

They finally stopped a few houses down from Theo's house. They peered around the corner at his yard. It only took a couple of minutes to spot Callan's men. They were dressed in plain clothes and trying to act casual.

Cora recognized one from the palace. "Your mom is still out of town, right?"

"Yes," Theo said tightly. "I don't like the thought of her

322

coming home to this."

"We'll get Callan and his men out of here. I promise."

They watched for another minute before slinking back into the shadows to return to the tunnels.

Cora listened intently to each report as everyone returned to the main cavern. It was the same as she and Theo heard—the people were on edge. They were turning on each other, reporting neighbors and co-workers for suspicious activity. Most of them returned after a few harrowing hours of questions. A few were still missing.

Siraye managed to connect a tablet to the local holo- network. It was a constant stream of reports of damage and violence, mixed with a group of nobles and ministers calling for military aid from Galta. Cora's anxiety hardened into anger. At least she knew who was in Callan's pocket.

Just when things couldn't get any worse, Gray returned with the last scouts. The look on his face made her stomach drop.

"Callan's men took my entire research team in for 'questioning,'" Gray said numbly. "They entered the palace a few days ago and haven't been seen since. They even took my injured intern from her physical therapist's office."

"Why would he want your research team?" Siraye asked, glancing up from her tablet.

"I don't know."

"Could it be he figured out you were with me?" Cora said quietly.

Gray shook his head, lips pressed into a line.

Cora paced around their camp, one hand in her hair. She spoke mostly to herself as she walked, the sound carrying across the camp. "We need to move quickly. This has already gone too far. But we can't remove a hundred Galtan soldiers alone. We need help."

"We should just go home," Arik said. He laid another log on the crackling fire. "The palace guard is loyal to us, then we can just call in the army."

"Callan controls the palace and has access to Father. Besides, if we call in the army, we'll be the aggressors. It'll mean full-scale war with Galta."

"What if we got the people on our side?" Theo asked, drumming his fingers against his leg. "We could unite them, get them to fight back against the Galtans."

"I don't know if I have enough political power for that." Cora stopped pacing. "They don't see me as a military leader."

"But there is a symbol they *would* recognize," Finn cut in from across the fire. "And there's two of you."

He stared pointedly at where Makari and Nova lounged. Makari lifted half-lidded amber eyes. Her tail swished back and forth as she sensed everyone's attention shifting to her.

Cora's heart rate picked up. Finn was right. It was time to embrace what she'd become.

She turned to Gray. "What do you say?"

"I'm ready if you are."

"How do we do this? We'll get shot if Makari and I just fly over the city."

Siraye tapped her fingers against her tablet thoughtfully. "I think I can tap into the network if I can get access to some better equipment. We could broadcast you to the city, let people know you're here."

"What kind of equipment do you need?"

"Anything with a bigger power source, or a direct connection to the network will do."

"I think I know where we can find equipment and give you an audience," Finn said.

"Where?" Cora asked

"Well, there just so happens to be a duel tonight…"

Theo breathed slowly, working to calm his nerves. Sloan was more than happy to give him access to the elevator. Everyone else had taken the longer route to the stadium, but Theo needed entry to the stands. He rolled his shoulders, willing them to relax. He hadn't heard anything in nearly an hour, which he chose to mean that everything had gone smoothly so far. He just needed to get into position.

His earpiece crackled, losing signal as the elevator descended. The doors slid open, and the crackling stopped. He could just barely hear Siraye's announcement that she was tapped into the network over the crowd.

He slid into a seat, shaking awake the holo- bracelet he'd been given. This section of stands was sparser than the others, spectators choosing seats closer to the tunnels duelists used to enter the arena. Theo knew from the maps he'd been shown that the dusty tunnel directly across from him was where Cora would emerge. He settled in to wait, finger hovering over the button to record.

"And here I was, thinking you'd disappeared for good this time," an oily voice said behind Theo.

The muscles in his shoulders tensed all over again. He made himself pivot, slowly, casually, to look at the seats behind.

Rolph leaned forward, his saggy jowls rough with stubble. Theo smelled alcohol on his breath. He didn't dare look as Rolph's cronies slipped into the seats to either side of him.

"You're looking particularly awful today," Theo drawled. "Did the strip club revoke your membership again?"

Rolph's lips pulled back from his teeth in a sneer. Theo drew back, casting the briefest glance at the men to either side of him. The sleeves of their shirts were rolled up, showcasing taut cords of muscle along their hands and arms. They matched Theo for height, each one alone outweighing him.

"I lost a lot of money when you didn't show up that night." Rolph's low voice cut across the noise of the arena like a knife. "I was nearly laughed out of Matteo's good graces." Theo cast Rolph a sharp glance, earning a dark chuckle from the stocky fighter. "You hadn't heard? I'm his third now."

Theo's hands curled into fists at his sides. Searing rage simmered in his veins.

Rolph's eyes lit up at the expression on his face. The men at his sides leaned closer, elbows taking over the armrests of Theo's chair.

"I was going to give you a shot," Rolph rumbled. "Let us settle this on even footing. But Matteo remembers your brother. Remembers you. He wants us to settle this privately. Back in Red

325

Gryphon territory."

In an instant, the burning rage turned to ice. Theo cast another glance to the men on either side, calculating his odds. If he left this arena with them, he wouldn't be coming back.

Rolph leaned in closer, a wicked smile curling his lips. He opened his mouth again, but whatever he was about to say was drowned out by a low growl. It echoed through the cave around the arena, raising the hairs all along Theo's body.

Then, directly across from him, a red glow lit the tunnel.

The stands fell silent as thick smoke billowed across the arena floor. Theo flicked his holo -bbracelet, setting it to record. Another growl vibrated around them, and the men next to him shrank back. He couldn't help the smile curling his lips as the smoke swirled, stirred by the beat of powerful wings.

Makari burst through the cloud, sweeping around the arena. Screams turned to gasps as the crowd spotted what Theo's eyes were already locked onto.

Cora sat between Makari's shoulders, spine straight even as her body shifted and swayed in perfect sync with Makari's movements. Her eyes were clear, focused, cutting across the arena as she met the stares of the gaping crowd.

A queen surveying her court.

Makari circled the arena twice before twisting in the air and landing with a powerful thump that sent the remnants of smoke blowing across the crowd.

Gray strode out of the tunnel, Nova perched across his shoulders.

Cora's voice echoed through the cave the arena sat in, utterly calm.

"The Dragon Riders have returned." Her eyes met Theo's across the arena. "And we're here to take this city back."

Her words rang through the arena, hanging in the air with the last traces of smoke.

Then the crowd erupted into cheers.

32

The Galtans came in the name of peace, and yet they patrol the streets like an occupying army. This is your only warning. Leave now, or you will be removed. The Riders will not tolerate you terrorizing the people of Narous any longer. It's time they had their city back."

Callan swiped a hand through the projection, dismissing the feed. Malice burned through him until he could no longer stand it. He overturned the table with smoking hands, sending the projector and his dinner skidding across the floor.

Daen entered the room with hardly a knock, casting a wary eye over the mess.

"Did you do as I asked?" Callan barked.

"Yes, he's waiting in the hall. Do you want this cleaned up first?"

"Leave it." Callan waved a dismissive hand. "Send him in."

Daen gave him a long stare before turning back to open the door.

A pale man with icy-blond hair and a well-tailored suit entered the room. His hands were in his pockets, calculating brown eyes sweeping the room with interest.

"You must be Matteo," Callan kept his tone polite.

"That is what my colleagues call me." His voice was polished, but cold.

"I was told you could help me with a particular thorn in my side."

Matteo sat in one of the sitting room armchairs, not waiting for an invitation. He crossed an ankle over his knee, one hand propped up against his chin.

Callan remained standing, folding his hands behind his back. "And what thorn is that?"

"A man name Theodore Sturn."

Matteo's lips curved down slightly.

Callan caught the slight tightening of his fingers and smiled slowly. "So you do know him."

"He and his brother were an annoyance to me several years ago. I haven't had to deal with him since." Matteo picked at a stray piece of lint. "What has he done to you?"

"It's less what he's done to me, and more what he means to someone else."

"Ah, you're looking to use him against someone. Why didn't you say so in the first place?" A cruel smiled stretched across Matteo's mouth. "What are you hoping to do to him?"

"I want him dead."

"I can arrange that."

"You'll have to get him alone," Callan warned. "If you try to kill him in front of his girlfriend, she'll kill you first."

"I'm hardly worried about a lovesick woman."

"It's her dragon you should be worried about."

Matteo's eyes widened, the only sign of surprise on his smooth face. Callan had the impression he wasn't easily surprised. He recovered quickly.

"Understood. Now we just need to discuss payment."

"I don't care how much it is. Just give me a number."

"Typically I would add a fee for increased risk, but seeing as this is a nuisance of my own as well, I'll only charge you half. My secretary will send the details in the morning."

Matteo rose, buttoning his suit coat. He extended a hand to Callan, who shook it. Matteo gripped tightly, leaning in until his breath blew across Callan's face.

"I look forward to working with you in the future, *closely.*"

"And I look forward to seeing your results."

Callan allowed a little heat into his hand.

Matteo's hand shot out of his with a gasp. He stared down at the reddening skin, his frown returning. He left without another

328

word.

Cora dreamed of flying Makari through the arena all night. Cheers had followed them when they eventually flew back through the caves and tunnels. She'd been in front of plenty of crowds in her life, but it was nothing compared to facing a crowd on the back of a dragon. She'd never felt a stronger sense of purpose in her entire life.

Siraye shook her awake, chasing away her dreams. Cora swatted at the slim elf's hands sleepily. She tried turning over and going back to sleep, but Siraye shook her again.

"Cora, get up! Come see!"

She sat up, eyes still closed. Long—and surprisingly strong—fingers wrapped around her arm, hauling her up and out of her blankets. Cora stumbled after Siraye, rubbing sleep from her eyes. She passed a hand through her tousled hair, no doubt making it worse.

Siraye pulled her over to the cars, then shoved a tablet into her hands. It took Cora a long moment to process the video feed in front of her.

"The people are fighting back," Siraye said eagerly, jabbing her finger at the tablet. "They've started pushing Callan's men toward the palace. The lower city is already completely free of Galtans."

All traces of sleep were gone. Cora shoved the tablet back into Siraye's hands. She strode back into the middle of camp, calling everyone to the campfire. A few sleepy heads popped out of tents as she yelled.

"This is our shot, before Callan's men get organized. Everyone, get up and gear up! We're taking the city. Now."

Movement exploded around her. Food was shoved into outstretched hands almost as quickly as weapons.

Siraye pulled her back to the cars again, shaking out a tight black suit and handing it to her. "Baeros always bring us samples to test out. I think this one will fit you."

Siraye stood in front of her, blocking any potential eyes as Cora stripped down to her underclothes and slid into the tight suit. She tugged at the high neck as Siraye pulled the zipper up.

329

"What exactly is this for?"

"The fabric can supposedly stop a knife," Siraye explained, digging in the trunk again. "And these should take a couple of bullets for you."

She emerged holding a set of thin black plates. She secured the largest two across Cora's chest and back, then a smaller set to the fronts of her thighs. Cora stretched, testing the armor. It took a few minutes to adjust, but she found the weight comforting.

"Armor can only do so much for you," Siraye warned, giving her a sharp stare. "So just try not to get hit."

Cora nodded as Siraye took a step back.

The willowy elf circled her, a smile stealing across her pink lips. "You look hot."

"Siraye!"

"What? You do!" She laughed. "And lethal."

Cora didn't respond. She'd learned exactly where to put her blades to end a life. Multiple places to put her blades, really. A part of her still hoped she'd never have to use that knowledge.

Makari brushed against her consciousness, bringing Cora's head around a moment before a shout rang through the camp. She was already moving to meet the disturbance. Theo fell into step next to her as she went to greet the two figures emerging from the shadowy tunnels.

Orym and Phaendar approached slowly, palms up in a gesture of peace. Makari stood guard at the edge of camp, glaring down with fierce amber eyes. The elves bowed to her, keeping their hands away from the weapons hanging from their belts.

"What are you two doing here?" Theo snarled.

They didn't react to the sharpness of his tone. They just straightened, hands still up.

"We're here to serve our Rider." Orym's voice rang across the distance between them.

"How do I know you're not going to try to take me back? Or kill me?" Cora demanded.

"The gods have spoken," Phaendar said. "And if a Bjorn is good enough for the gods, then she's good enough for me, too."

Her eyes pricked, and she found herself blinking rapidly. A

330

slow smile crept across her face.

Her eyes flicked to the tunnel behind Orym and Phaendar. "Daethie?"

Twin shadows fell across their faces. Orym stared down at his boots, as if just hearing her name was painful.

"She's even more stubborn than I am," Phaendar grunted. "Let's just say, I wouldn't wander into any dark alleys when she's nearby."

Cora crossed the short distance between them, holding out her hand. They each clasped her forearm, their hands easily circling her arm.

Phaendar glanced over her shoulder, chuckling softly. "Your boy doesn't look too happy to see us."

"You two better play nice with him. There might not be any hope for your faces, but I'd like to keep his free of scars."

"Really? Because the ladies always tell me how dashing mine are." Orym waggled his eyebrows, one finger tracing a scar on his chin.

"We'll stay out of trouble," Phaendar promised, tapping a fist to his chest in a salute.

"Hey, Gray!" Orym called. "Where's this dragon of yours?"

In a blink, they were gone, absorbed into the ranks like they'd always been there.

Cora finished checking her armor and weapons, tightening her bootlaces and sliding a sleek handgun into a holster strapped to her thigh. She surveyed the camp when she was done. The tents and bedrolls were stowed away, the fire put out, and the dishes stored. Their small company was outfitted similarly to her. She didn't see any other black suits, but she spotted many plates of body armor and a few helmets. Each person carried a mix of rifles, handguns, knives, and swords.

As the last people finished adjusting their straps and buckles, they formed a loose circle around her.

"Alright. We're going in fast but quiet." Cora spun as she spoke, checking in with each person. "Siraye, do you have everything you need to tap into the Watcher network?" A nod from the silver-haired elf. "Finn, how are those explosives?"

Finn held up a small black ball. "I've got about forty of these babies ready to go. Should be enough to send some Galtan soldiers into hiding. I've also got about three dozen smoke bombs."

"Great. Go ahead and pass those out." She turned away as the spheres passed hands. "We're targeting Galtans, not Watchers. Confuse them, corner them, do whatever you need to do to drive them to the palace and away from the city. We know there are civilians out there. Keep them safe. Organize them if you can, otherwise get them out of the crossfire." Heads nodded across the circle. "Makari and I will be your eyes in the sky. I'll be calling out their positions while we try to keep their attention. Gray, can you handle getting into the palace on your own?"

"I should be able to sneak in, especially if I use your old passage."

"Just be careful. It might be guarded now. I'll do my best to keep the Galtans focused on me." Cora paused to meet each person's eye again. "I know the risk each one of you is taking, and I just want to thank you. For me, and for my people. Now let's put an end to Callan's games."

She felt eyes on her as everyone made their final preparations. She knew who she'd find before he appeared at her elbow.

"Are you sure this is going to work?"

Cora glanced up at her twin. She heard the concern hidden just beneath the question, saw it in the lines between his brows.

"Yes. I am."

Arik's mouth ticked up in a rueful half-smile. "When did you become so confident?"

"When I started trusting myself."

His smile fell. One hand rose to rub the back of his neck, his eyes unable to meet hers. "Look, Cat, I mean, Cora." He sighed. "I'm sorry about what I said. It's been one hell of a few weeks. Losing Mother, worrying about Father, you... Liana."

Cora laid a hand on his arm. She watched him swallow, his eyes squeezing shut. Her thumb swept over the crook of his elbow soothingly.

"I know." Her voice came out hoarse. "We've both been through a lot. You kept so calm when Mother died. I didn't even

332

stop to think about how hard it was for you. I've had time to reflect, to grieve. And I realized, without her, I felt so…relieved."

The confession sat heavy on her tongue. Arik's brows rose, pain flashing in his eyes.

Cora pushed on, swallowing the bitterness that threatened to infect her words. "I could breathe, could think for once. And as much as I loved her, I finally feel like I've found my place, without her here."

"Is your life really that miserable?"

Cora closed her eyes against the pain lacing Arik's words. He couldn't—or wouldn't—understand her perspective. She forced her face into neutrality, giving his arm a squeeze before dropping her hand.

"Forget I said anything. I have a mission for you." She waited for him to nod before continuing. "Go with Gray to the palace. Help him navigate the security and find Father. Make sure he's safe, and get him away from Callan."

Arik nodded again, giving her a quick salute before going to join Gray. She watched him go, a weight settling in her chest. She knew then that he would never see her the same again.

It wasn't long before the cars were loaded, ready to take Cora's team as far into the tunnels as they could fit. She stood next to Makari, watching them all cram into the vehicles.

One tall brown figure stayed back to watch with her. Theo threaded his fingers with hers, staring down at her in a way that set her soul on fire.

"I'll be waiting for you at the palace." Theo's voice was barely audible over the rumbling engines. "We'll do this together."

Cora stepped closer, one hand sliding over the body armor covering his chest. "Stay in one piece until I get there."

Theo's eyes flicked up to stare at Makari. "Keep her safe."

Makari's tail lashed as a low grumble vibrated deep in her chest.

Cora brought his eyes back to her with a gentle hand on his cheek. One muscled arm wrapped around her waist as his other hand slid into her hair. He kissed her deeply, pulling her even closer as cheers and wolf whistles shot from the cars behind them. They lingered longer than they probably should have.

When they pulled apart, Cora was grinning. She brushed one spiral curl away from Theo's forehead before he trailed off to squeeze into the nearest car.

She nearly started as Phaendar materialized next to her.

"I have something for you, kid."

Cora turned a curious eye toward the elf as he unscrewed the lid on a small metal pot. Deep red liquid shone in its depths like oil.

"When your ancestors showed up, they had their faces painted. They looked like a pack of demons," Phaendar muttered. He dipped three fingers into the paint, struggling to fit them all inside the lip of the little pot. "I'll skin you alive if you ever repeat this, but I nearly wet myself when I first saw them."

Phaendar paused with his painted fingers facing her, waiting for an invitation. Cora swiped a few stray hairs off her face, then closed her eyes.

The paint was cool against her skin as he dragged his fingers from her hairline to her chin, leaving long streaks across her right eyelid and nose. She stayed perfectly still until Phaendar declared the paint dry. When she opened her eyes, he was saluting her again.

Cora climbed onto Makari as Phaendar entered the last vehicle. Makari couldn't fit down the tunnels they were taking, so Cora watched as the cars drove off. She waited until the last set of headlights faded before letting Makari go back the way they entered the tunnels.

The silence pressed against her ears like a physical weight. She'd gotten so used to being surrounded by people that she couldn't remember the last time she had been so utterly alone.

Her mind turned the plan over and over again as they trekked back through the tunnels and caves. She had some time to spare before they could fly to Narous.

They almost made it to the hidden entrance when a side shoot caught Cora's attention. A warm breeze drifted past her face, just enough to push a stray hair out of place. Makari froze, nose twitching in the direction of the breeze.

334

Cora slid down from Makari's back. Her boots tapped softly against the stone floor as she entered a short side tunnel.

Just a handful of feet off the main path was a cave big enough for two or three people. Inside was a stone statue of a woman with a dragon curled around her feet, a phoenix on her shoulder.

Cora dug into the small pouch at her waist for an offering. She managed to find a half-mangled protein bar and placed it at the foot of the statue.

"Great goddess Elidi, accept my offering."

Makari snuffled behind her, nose as far into the shrine as she could reach.

Cora sighed, sinking into a cross-legged position on the cold floor. "I don't even know why I'm giving you an offering. I still haven't decided if I believe in you. If you are real, then where have you been? When the Nine Guards took power? When they fell? When my uncle died, and my father became king? When I was nearly smothered in my own bed? When Callan killed my mother?"

The words tumbled out of her like a waterfall. They came faster, louder as she went on. A roiling current of emotions came with them, surging through her.

"And now I'm supposedly gods-blessed? I don't know if it was chance or the gods that sent me Makari. If I'm worthy, or lucky, or if you just need something from me, but I guess I should say thank you. Thank you for sending her to me and showing me what I could be. Something more than anyone ever showed me before, more than a piece in a political game, more than a pretty face or a polished speech. And I'm going to be more than I ever was before, but I'm choosing it for myself. Not because you or anyone else chose for me. But because I chose it."

Cora stood, dusting off her backside. She was ready to turn away from the shrine when the protein bar on the floor burst into flames. She watched, stunned, as the fire flared into the shape of a rising phoenix. Almost as quickly, it died down to a smoldering ember.

A warm breeze blew past her again, carrying a whisper.
Go forth, blessed one.

335

33

Theo knew what it was like to be one of the bottles in Sloan's storeroom. Every bump in the tunnel floor sent him banging against his neighbor and set his bones rattling like glass. They were packed in tight, Orym's bony elbow digging into his ribs. At least he wasn't sitting with Arik again.

Theo lost track of the minutes in the monotonous dark. Eventually, they pulled to the side as the tunnel ahead branched and narrowed. They piled out of the cars, grateful to have room to breathe again.

They broke into groups efficiently, hardly waiting for everyone before trekking down the various tunnels. Theo led Siraye and Barden toward the Dragon Slayer. Sloan was already waiting in the storeroom for them.

"I was hoping you'd show up soon," the barkeep rumbled. "The city's been chaos since early this morning. I just had a Watcher friend come warn me that the Galtans are nearly organized. They're going to start firing on civilians."

"We're not going to let that happen," Theo said. "Siraye, what do you need to get into the network?"

"I need a few uninterrupted minutes in a Watcher station."

Sloan gave them directions to the nearest one before holding the back door open for them. Barden poked his head through first, glancing up and down the dim street before giving the all-clear. Siraye slipped out after him, her long braid nearly swinging into Theo's face. He made to follow when a large hand landed on his shoulder.

"You be careful out there, eh?" Sloan said quietly. "And tell the princess we're here to support her."

Sloan gave his shoulder a squeeze before he disappeared to the front of the bar. Theo wondered if Cora knew just how many people in Narous cared about her. He shook off the distracting thoughts, hurrying to meet Barden and Siraye in the alley.

They followed Sloan's directions, picking their way through narrow stone streets toward the Watcher station. They'd only gone a few blocks when they ran into a group of dark-clad people. Theo caught sight of bottles stuffed with rags passing hands. The group whirled around as they approached, brandishing knives.

"Hey, we're here to help," Theo said soothingly, hands up. "We're with the Dragon Riders."

The mood shifted immediately. They were clapped on the back and ushered into the circle. The sting of alcohol invaded his nose as they got a better look at the bottles getting distributed. It didn't take much to convince the group of rebels to help them. Within just a few minutes, they were in position around the Watcher station.

Theo crouched in an alley across from the station, eyes scanning the street in front. A soft chime from his wrist broke the silence around him.

Good morning, Theo. I know I promised you I'd stay a little longer, but I can't stay with your sister any longer. I'll tell you about it next time I see you. For now, I'm heading back to Narous and I'm going to take that job at the hospital.

Theo stared in horror at his mother's message. It took him a full minute to realize that someone was speaking in his ear.

"Theo!"

"Sorry, I'm here."

"Are we ready?"

Theo dropped his hand from his comms to scan the street again. All of the Watchers they'd seen were in the station, and there were no civilians in sight. He gave the all-clear, then began furiously typing as a Watcher vehicle went up in flames behind him.

Where are you right now?

I'm on the train back to Narous.

337

Get off in Peora. Stay there for a while. Whatever you do, DON'T come home! Narous isn't safe right now. Promise me, Mom.

Theo didn't have time to see if she responded or not.

Watchers poured out of the station, weapons drawn. Barden tossed a smoke bomb into the street, filling it with yellow vapor and the smell of rotting eggs. Theo pulled the rifle off his back and shot into the air a few times, driving the Watchers back, toward the palace. Their group of rebels joined in, shouting and yelling, throwing rocks. Theo spared a single glance over his shoulder to watch Siraye slip into the empty station. She gave him a thumbs up, then motioned for him to keep going.

He gave her a quick nod before chasing after the retreating Watchers. It was time to get to work.

Gray usually embraced silence. He'd spent many a quiet day in the field, observing. But the silence stretching between him and Arik skittered against his skin like a persistent itch. Maybe it was the disdainful glance the prince had dragged over Gray. Maybe it was the way he'd completely ignored Nova's attempts to befriend him, sending her into an irritated mood. Or maybe it was the way he charged ahead as if he had any idea where they were going. In any case, Gray knew without a doubt who his favorite twin was.

"We need to keep heading straight," he said, stopping Arik from taking the tunnel to the right. "That will take us to the university."

Arik didn't say a word, simply corrected course with a huffed exhale. Gray sensed rather than saw the tiny spines on Nova's back bristling. A tiny growl echoed against the stones, and Arik's head whipped back.

"Keep that thing away from me."

"Her name is Nova."

"I don't care."

Gray caught himself sizing up the prince. He shook his head, shoving the thoughts away. It didn't matter that they were roughly the same size, or that Gray probably had more training. What mattered was reaching the palace. Without fighting among themselves.

338

Gray trailed his fingers down Nova's neck to soothe her. She didn't understand why Arik was so clearly hostile, but she responded to Gray's soft touch. Her hackles fell, and her wings tucked close to her sides as she relaxed. Gray fought the urge to scratch his arms as they fell back into silence. Blessedly, they reached the tunnel exit closest to the palace.

Not as fortunately, the tunnel led straight into the sewers. Nova hissed at the dark water, barely managing to balance on the narrow ledge of dry stone along it. Gray led them to a metal ladder and shoved aside the manhole cover at the top. He offered a hand to Arik, which was ignored. They both stepped back as Nova scrambled up and out of the hole, her claws clicking noisily against the metal.

Arik took the lead again, walking boldly down the streets near the palace. Gray and Nova skulked behind him, keeping to the shadows. A gnawing pit grew in his stomach the closer they crept to the secret tunnel.

He darted next to Arik, keeping his voice low as his eyes scanned the streets around them. "Shouldn't you be a little less conspicuous? Anyone in the city could recognize you."

"That's what I'm hoping for."

Gray froze, his stomach dropping to his toes. Nova followed as he ducked into a side street to reassess. He'd barely had time to take a breath before a voice called out to Arik.

Gray peeked around the corner as a man with neatly trimmed dark hair and a black suit met the prince. A handful of palace guards surrounded them, hands on their weapons. It took him a second to realize they were facing outward, away from the prince.

"I'm glad to see you in one piece," the dark-haired man said, clapping Arik on the shoulder.

"Good to see you too, Nolan. How's Father?"

"He'll be better now that you're home. I'll take you straight to him."

Arik's fingers twitched, barely noticeable. Gray tracked the movement, watching as his fingers pointed subtly forward. He was pointing to a metal gate sitting unevenly on its hinges.

The secret passage.

Gray pressed himself against the wall of the street as Arik and the palace guards passed. He waited a heartbeat after they were gone before darting to the gate, Nova on his heels. They were past the metal bars in a moment, then they were swallowed by yet another dark tunnel.

Narous grew bigger with every wing beat. Cora clung tightly to Makari's neck, anticipation growing with each passing minute. Smoke rose from several streets, staining the sky like spilled ink. Makari swept over the buildings, letting out a bellow loud enough to shake the cobbled streets below. Cora caught sight of several heads peeking out of windows as they rushed by.

She tapped her comms with a finger. "Testing, testing. Can you hear me?"

"I hear you, Cora," Siraye's voice practically sang in her ear. *"I'm playing operator to keep the line chatter to a minimum. Call out anything you see, and I'll pass it along."*

Makari circled past the Middle Ring, low enough for Cora to get a look at the streets below. She relayed what she saw to Siraye, calling out Galtan positions as she passed. Their advance had stalled. Galtans and Watchers hunkered behind crowd control barriers, weapons out. They hadn't opened fire. Yet. She could taste the tension all the way from Makari's back.

Her dragon circled the entire city once before Cora urged her lower. Makari's wings nearly clipped buildings as they swooped down. She spotted what she was looking for.

A wet sheen coated the middle of the streets. Cora reached down the bond, and Makari obliged, setting the trail of oil on fire.

The oil was in the middle of the widest streets, hopefully far enough way to keep the entire city from catching ablaze. It was a risk Cora had agreed to down in the caves. Makari ignited another line of oil, forcing the Watchers and Galtans further into the city to escape the heat.

They swept down the last section wide enough for oil, yells and cries of alarm echoing in their wake. Makari flamed again, but the Galtans were ready this time. She barely managed to ignite the oil before shots rang out. She climbed out of range, her wings beating hard enough that Cora was afraid she'd lose her seat. Makari leveled off above the city, still low enough for her to watch the chaos they'd unleashed.

"Good work, you two," Siraye said. *"Now, I need you up by the night market. Theo's team needs help."*

They were moving before Siraye finished speaking. Cora shoved down the anxiety coursing through her mind. Theo could handle himself. At least until she got there.

34

Theo's team managed to push their way up to the night market, just a few blocks away from the palace towering overhead. They'd held the street for a few minutes now, pushing up just a few feet away from the hastily erected barricade.

But reinforcements had flooded in shortly after Cora's sweep of the city. They were pinned down, and Theo was running out of bullets.

He checked his mags once more, mouth pressed into a thin line. He had to make each shot count. For just a second, he wondered if this was how his dad felt on the Galtan front. Maybe he'd been counting his bullets at the end.

Theo pushed the thought aside. They weren't there yet, and besides, Cora would kill him if he died.

"How much do you have left?" Barden's quiet voice crackled in Theo's earpiece.

"Less than I'd like."

"We need to keep moving. Getting bogged down only helps them."

Theo agreed. He peeked around the corner of the building he was using for cover. More Galtans had come since he last looked. Their black and red uniforms filled Theo with disgust. He wanted to rip the phoenix insignia off each and every one of them.

A plan was forming in his mind. A reckless plan, but a plan, nonetheless. He had just about finished it when a sound made him freeze. Wing beats.

Makari crashed into the barricade across the street, flinging barriers and soldiers alike. Her teeth flashed as her head shot

342

forward like a viper. She grabbed and tossed men, not bothering to look as they crunched into the walls around them.

A flood of Galtans poured from a nearby street, as if they'd been waiting for this moment. Theo and his team were there, defending Makari's back. Cora clung to Makari's neck as the dragon rampaged.

Theo emptied his mag in a few seconds, then stopped to swipe a full mag from a fallen soldier. He leaped into an alley as Makari's claws swept out, clearing the street where he'd just been standing.

Theo raised his arm, swiping it across his wet forehead. His holo lit up, showing him two unread messages. He glanced back at Makari, then stepped further into the alley, away from her rampage. He hurriedly opened the first message. It was from Mom, time stamped thirty minutes after his last message.

I'm already home.

Fighting the rising panic, Theo opened the second message, desperately hoping it was also from Mom. He didn't recognize the contact code.

Glad to see you and your mom are back in town. Let's all catch up together. You know where to go.

All the blood drained from his face. His fingers shook as he dismissed the message.

He stepped out of the alley, his eyes finding Cora's. Concern flooded her face at his look, and she opened her mouth as if to call out to him.

Then they both heard the whirring. Like a thousand birds flapping their wings all at once.

She glanced to the sky, then back to him.

"Go," he mouthed, too far away for her to hear.

She nodded grimly, clutching Makari as they launched upward.

Theo watched until they disappeared, then he caught up to Barden. He handed over his weapons and told him to keep going.

Theo disappeared down the winding streets without a second glance.

343

Callan surveyed the city from the wide balcony. He wasn't sure when he'd decided to claim the old throne room, but he found himself here more and more.

Footsteps crossed the stone floor behind him. He knew it was Daen before his lieutenant passed the first throne behind him. When had he started alerting Callan to his presence?

"I assume you've already seen her?" Daen nodded toward the city.

"Yes, I've seen."

As they spoke, the dragon rose over the city. She circled high above like a vulture. Callan tracked her movements, hands gripping the railing tightly. He caught movement from the corner of his eye. He didn't turn, already knowing that Daen was fiddling with something in his hands.

"Sir." Daen paused to take a breath. Callan had never heard him hesitate before. "Are you certain you want to do this? You've made this personal. In my experience, that's when men get sloppy. When they fail."

Callan spun slowly, working to rein in his anger. A part of him knew that Daen spoke as his friend. That part was quickly losing ground against the part of him that wanted to watch that dragon fall from the sky.

"It was personal for me in Galta, too," he murmured. "Wasn't my passion an asset then? Isn't it what kept our men pushing forward, even when they wanted to pull back?"

"Yes."

Callan snatched the glass jar from Daen's hands and knocked it back. He swallowed, then held it as it fought to come back up. His stubbornness won out, and the foul mixture remained in his stomach.

He thrust the empty jar back at Daen. "Send out the Shrike. It's time to show the princess who the new lord of the sky is."

"And what of the researchers? We've combed every piece of data they had."

"Take them to the university, then dispose of them. Make it look like an attack."

"Understood, sir."

344

Callan didn't hear Daen's footsteps as he left. He flexed his fingers, a building tension lurking underneath his skin.

He hoped Catarina survived the Shrike. If only so he could show her the real power granted by the gods.

Callan watched from the balcony as the Shrike rose into the sky.

Cora banished the image of Theo clinging to her mind. She shook her head to clear it. Theo could handle it. She trusted him.

Makari cleared the tops of the buildings, the whirring growing louder. It rounded the palace like a giant black insect.

A round nose, dark glass covering a single pilot. Spinning blades attached to the sleek body, tilting as the aircraft banked. Makari growled beneath her, rage surging across the bond. It looked sleeker in the sunlight, but they both remembered it.

The Shrike.

"That's not possible," Cora found herself whispering. "We destroyed the only one."

The Shrike shot forward, closing the distance between them.

Cora tightened her grip on Makari, moving by instinct. *Dive!* She wasn't sure if she yelled it out loud or only in her mind.

Makari rolled, narrowly avoiding getting shot. They plummeted down to street level. The Shrike followed. Makari took a sharp turn, brushing the buildings to either side. The Shrike banked, its tail smacking into a building. The Shrike dropped briefly, then leveled off again.

Cora looked over her shoulder. She could barely make out the pilot's face through the tinted glass.

Makari took another sharp turn, and the craft hardly managed to follow. The pilot fired. Makari dodged, hissing as it grazed her wing. Cora ducked as a nearby window shattered, raining glass shards on top of them.

He's going to end up shooting the people hiding inside.

She urged Makari upwards, out of the city streets. Makari's powerful downbeats made the air behind her turbulent. The Shrike was buffeted, nearly slamming into the side of a building.

Makari climbed higher. The aircraft followed. Cora pressed

345

onto Makari's mind. The dragon followed her lead, spinning in the air. She brought her wings together, sending a powerful gust of wind directly into the Shrike. It lost control, spinning out.

Makari lunged forward, grabbing the side of the Shrike. She ripped one of the wings off, sending it flying into the palace courtyard. Cora heard the cockpit warnings blaring. She clung to Makari. Cora didn't draw her weapons for fear of hitting her. The dragon was relentless in her fury. She ripped and grabbed anything her teeth or talons could reach. The front glass cracked, drawing their attention.

Good job, Cora thought to Makari. *Now let's go before this thing crashes.*

Makari pushed off the aircraft, launching herself into the air and it towards the ground. The pilot managed to point the Shrike at them as it plummeted.

He fired a single shot.

There was a heartbeat before Cora's senses were overloaded by searing pain. Makari shrieked, spinning as they fell. Cora nearly blacked out, head spinning with the sudden change in altitude.

Makari's wings flapped weakly at first. Then more powerfully, slowing their fall.

It wasn't enough. Cora could only watch as the ground rushed towards them, fingers white where they held Makari. Her bones shook as they connected with the ground.

Then she was in the air again, moving sideways. By pure instinct, she tucked her head into her arms.

She didn't know how long she lay stunned. She sat up, wincing as her head swam. Warmth trickled down the side of her face and into her ear. She reached up a shaking hand and pulled back red fingers.

She reached for the bond, desperate to check on Makari. She bounced off a wall of solid blackness in her mind. She pushed against it, straining to reach her dragon.

Makari keened, a piercing sound that nearly shattered Cora's heart.

"Makari!"

Cora shoved herself to her feet and ran to her dragon. She

346

stared at the bloody remains of Makari's rear leg. She fought the urge to vomit as she ran feather-light fingers across the intact skin. Makari yelped, pulling away from her touch.

"Easy! Don't hurt yourself more."

Cora ran her hands along Makari's side until she reached her snout. She couldn't see or sense any other injuries. She brushed against the mental wall again, hissing as pain lanced through her skull.

Cora glanced around, coming aware of her surroundings. They were at the base of the palace steps.

The doors cracked, and a few Galtan soldiers eased out. Makari snarled at them, smoking curling between her teeth. The soldiers raised their rifles, fingers already on the trigger. Makari let out a burst of flame, driving them back.

Cora stared into the deep red fire. Makari was injured and nearly spent; it would only keep the soldiers at bay for so long. Heat built inside her veins, growing even as Makari's fire dimmed. Even in agony, her dragon protected her. She looked up at the palace, to where she knew Callan waited. To where the soldiers stood between her and him.

In seconds, her swords were in her hands. She ran through the flames and up the palace steps. The soldiers saw only the flash of her blades before they dripped red. Three more soldiers ran out the front door. They also met her blades.

Cora turned away from the carnage. She knew she'd see those soldiers' faces again in her dreams. But right then, all she cared about was Makari.

Her dragon's eyes clouded as she pushed onto shaky feet. Makari stumbled, crying out. Cora rushed down the steps toward her, but Makari righted herself before she reached the fourth stair. Makari found her balance on three legs, head rising to meet her.

Cora brushed the bond. Pain shot into her mind, but also determination. Makari wouldn't stay down.

She nodded, gesturing to the door behind her. A question went down the bond.

In response, Makari climbed up the stairs in a few bounds. Cora followed her dragon into the palace.

35

Gray followed Nova through the dim tunnel, her nose keeping them from wandering down side shoots. He wasn't even sure if Cora knew there were other tunnels under the castle. Most of them were hidden beneath piles of debris, only noticeable when Nova paused to sniff, then moved on.

The tunnel was silent aside from their own footsteps. No guards, not another soul. He wasn't sure if it was because there were no guards down here, or if Arik's distraction was paying off. Both twins had a habit of acting first and explaining never.

Nova slowed as they neared the end of the passage. Her pointed ears swiveled, picking up sounds too faint for Gray to hear. He crept to the door as silently as possible, pressing his ear against it. He recognized Arik's voice on the other side, faint though it was.

"I'm not going to my room like an errant child," the prince snapped. "I'm going to see my father. Now."

"His Majesty is in a meeting," a low voice responded, barely audible. "He isn't available—"

"To see his son? I think he'll make an exception."

There was a long pause. Gray could almost see the stubborn set to Arik's jaw. He pressed his ear closer, afraid they'd moved away.

"Very well, Your Highness. We'll have to go the long way, so it will take some time."

"Why can't we just go through the guest quarters?"

"We have a few civilians there right now."

"What are they, refugees?"

"No, they're researchers from the university. There was a

348

potential link to your sister's disappearance we were investigating."

"I don't think they'll mind if we walk past." Arik's voice dripped with disdain. Gray felt sorry for whoever was arguing with him. "I'm not delaying for *anyone*."

Heavy footsteps stomped past the hidden door, then the hallway was silent. He looked to Nova, who sniffed at the bottom of the door. When she didn't react, he eased it open far enough to peek out.

The hallway was empty. They slid out of the secret tunnel, door closing silently behind them. Gray had only a vague idea of the castle's layout, but he was certain he could find the guest wing.

They padded down the palace halls, Nova's keen nose alerting them before someone got near. They managed to hide, Gray hardly even breathing until they were along again. It took them ten minutes before he was certain they were near the guest quarters. He could hear an increase in activity just around the corner. He and Nova crouched behind a tall potted plant while he considered what to do next. He needed a distraction.

A tremendous boom shook the castle. Chandeliers rattled, and pictures frames vibrated against the walls.

Gray crouched lower as boots rushed past. He didn't hesitate. As soon as the Galtans passed, he darted out from his hiding place and around the corner.

Nova snuffled, nose close to the floor. Gray kept a step behind as she criss-crossed the hall, finally stopping three doors down. She stared at the door expectantly. He took a breath and threw the door open wide.

Dr. Lander and all of their interns jumped at his sudden entrance.

They stared at each other for a long moment before Ophelia launched herself across the room and into Gray. His arms circled her, a flood of relief washing through him at her warmth against his chest. He hadn't realized how much he'd missed her.

The others gathered around, each giving him a quick squeeze before peppering him with questions. He held his hands up in surrender, a laugh bubbling up from his chest.

"Slow down! We don't have time to talk right now." Gray sobered. "We're here to get you out."

Nova let out a loud purr, drawing everyone's attention. She twined between their legs as they stared open-mouthed at the young dragon.

Ophelia's eyes welled with tears. "Is that…?"

"The egg you saved. We bonded."

Ophelia's head whipped to Gray, pale pink hair swinging. "You're a Rider?"

He opened his mouth to answer, but approaching footsteps cut him short. He eased the door closed, motioning for everyone to sit down. He bolted across the sitting room, Nova at his heels. He slid the last foot into the bedroom, spinning to close the door to nothing more than a crack. He peered through it as his team scrambled into their seats. Nova growled softly at his knees.

"Shh," Gray whispered. "Not yet."

A barrel-chested blond entered the room. Gray didn't know what the patches on his uniform meant, but he gathered that he was some sort of officer. Four soldiers entered behind him, blocking the exit. Gray's eyes snagged on the pistols at their hips. No fingers reached for them, but the message was clear.

"We're here to escort you back to the university."

Not a single member of his team moved. Dr. Lander scanned the waiting men. She kept her head raised, but he caught the subtle bobbing of her chin.

"Lieutenant Daen," she said coolly. "Why have we had to stay here so long?"

"We were waiting for your last team member to arrive," Daen said smoothly. "He's waiting at the university for you."

His blood ran cold. If the armed soldiers hadn't been enough of a warning, the detached look in Daen's eyes said enough. He looked over Daen's men one more time, already certain of what he had to do. He swept a hand through his hair and straightened his shirt. Then he threw the door open wide.

"Funny, considering that I'm right here."

Four sets of hands reached for weapons. Daen's only reaction was a stiffening to his shoulders. He gave Gray a bland smile.

"Then you'll be coming with us as well."

Gray caught movement in the corner of his eye. He kept his gaze trained on Daen, barely catching the subtle nod from Ophelia.

He returned Daen's smile with one of his own. "Not a chance. Now!"

Ophelia chucked the pillow off her chair, smacking a soldier in the head.

Gray ran, sliding the last few feet into the legs of another soldier as Nova leaped from the bedroom, nothing more than a shadow with teeth and claws. Cries of pain pierced the air as she tore her way through Daen's men, snarling and growling.

Gray rose to his feet only to take a fist to the jaw. He stumbled back, head ringing from the impact. Daen made to swing again, his thick arms darting forward with impossible speed.

Gray leapt back, keeping just out of reach. Daen's men were recovering as well, remembering the weapons they kept on their belts.

Gray's pulse pounded in his ears. He was going to fail. Just like when he was a kid, when his parents came to save him. But there was no one else coming. Just Gray keeping his team safe. And just like last time, they were going to end up full of bullet holes.

A wave of despair rose up, threatening to swallow him.

Daen landed another blow, sending pain shooting down Gray's arm. He couldn't do it. He was alone.

There was a touch on the bond, sending a ripple of calm through his mind.

He wasn't alone anymore.

Gray ducked Daen's next hook, catching Nova's eye as he did. Her amber eyes seemed to glow, and something snapped into place in his mind.

Gray's senses burst to life. Smells flooded his nose, sounds pounded against his ears. Vibrations in the floor echoed through his bones with every movement. It was like he was in two places at once. Sensing his own body, and a small, lithe body.

He stood up straight to face Daen. The soldier drew back, staring in shock. Gray knew from the power thrumming through his veins what the man saw.

He and Nova moved as one. Gray's fist shot out, sending Daen to his knees. Nova was on him next, teeth closing around his throat. She ripped and pulled, leaping off him as he fell face-forward.

They ran to the next soldier. He too went down in mere seconds. They were nearly finished with him when the other two had the sense to run.

Gray had never moved so fast in his life. The soldiers had no chance of escape.

The last one tried desperately to point his weapon at them, but his hands shook. His one and only shot went wide, leaving a hole in the hall window.

Nova bellowed her victory, then licked the blood off her dripping claws. Their minds separated, and Gray swayed.

The world around him dimmed, the colors less vibrant, the scents muted. He looked around at their handiwork and had to swallow down bile.

He'd been so consumed in their combined instincts. A predator's instincts.

He shoved the thoughts aside. For now, his team needed to get out of this gods-cursed palace. He whirled around, ready to go back, only to find his team edging out of the room. They gave the bodies a wide berth, Dr. Lander particularly pale.

He felt the sudden need to wash his hands.

Ophelia materialized next to him. She laid a gentle hand on his arm, tearing his focus away from the carnage. She gave him a half smile.

"You saved us."

Ophelia's hand slid down his arm, twining with his. She gave it a squeeze.

Gray clung to her as he led his team back to the secret tunnel.

The path into Red Gryphon territory was burned into Theo's brain. He was certain he could reach the converted office building in his sleep. He'd certainly visited it enough in his nightmares. He forced himself not to look up as he ran through Narous. If he did, he wasn't sure he'd be brave enough to keep going.

The thought of Mom in the hands of the Red Gryphons propelled him forward. It was only a few minutes before he found himself in front of the awful gray building again. He didn't allow himself to pause at the front door. He pushed inside, surprised to find the main level empty. The stairwell was also empty, his footsteps echoing noisily as he climbed. Up and around, again and again. He didn't see another soul until the top floor.

The blond man in the pressed suit was waiting, Rolph and Gregor at his side. Theo knew now that his name was Matteo. He doubted it was his real name, not that it mattered. Five other gang members stood guard in the room, their faces half covered by red masks. His mom was nowhere in sight.

"Where's my mother?"

Theo didn't bother keeping the anger from his voice. He had no intention of playing games or exchanging pleasantries. This ended now.

A wicked smile curved Rolph's mouth. Theo looked between him and Matteo, his gut sinking to the floor.

"I haven't the faintest idea," Matteo answered. He picked a stray hair off his pants, looking bored. "But we'll make sure she finds you when we're done."

The gang members around the room pulled in, surrounding him.

His hands curled into fists, his voice shaking with unrestrained fury. "What, you're not going to toy with me? No warm-up match to make me think I have a chance?"

"Not this time." Matteo leaned forward in his seat. "Your death has been paid for, and I intend to deliver on my promises."

Theo started to respond when movement caught his eye out the window. Across the city, near the palace, Makari was ripping apart a flying machine. The other eyes in the room followed. They stared as the aircraft went down.

Theo's heart swelled with pride. He made to face Matteo when a flash of light speared through the sky. Then Makari was falling, and his heart along with her. He waited for an agonizing minute for Makari to get back into the sky.

She never did.

"Perhaps your girlfriend is not as intimidating as Chancellor Byrne supposed."

Theo stared out the window. Cora was alright. She had to be. Makari was tough. They'd pull through.

Matteo flicked his fingers, and the Red Gryphons approached, Rolph in the lead.

Theo stared as his smug face drew closer. He had to get to Cora, had to know if she was hurt.

Quick as an adder, Theo struck. Rolph slumped to the floor, unconscious.

Gregor came next, pummeling his arms and torso. Theo sent him stumbling back with a powerful kick. He had a single second to enjoy his victory before the others were on him.

His world became nothing but fists, and feet, and pain. He tried to fight back, to throw a single punch. But the onslaught was relentless. He fell to his knees, hands still guarding his head. He was going to die on this floor, just like Lane.

The door behind him opened and snicked shut again. A faint hissing filled the space, then thick smoke billowed through the chamber. Theo's attackers slowed, heads whipping around to find the source of the disturbance. The only warning they had was a slight swirl in the smoke.

A knife cut through the smog, slashing at the men surrounding Theo. They cried out, clutching at deep gashes on their bodies. Theo stared, the pounding in his head making it hard to process.

Long fingers wrapped around his arm, yanking him to his feet. He stumbled along as he was dragged back out to the stairwell.

Siraye practically shoved him down the stairs, braid swinging. Theo gaped at her, nearly tumbling down the stairs in their rush.

"Hurry, Theo. It won't take them long to come after us."

"How did you find me?"

"I saw you run past on the station camera." She herded him down and around at breakneck speed. "I knew wherever you were running, it wasn't good. So I followed."

"Thank you." He swallowed around a lump in his throat. "You saved my life."

354

"Why were you here in the first place?"

"They said they had my mom."

"Sick bastards," she spat.

They hit street level and sprinted. Theo held a hand to his throbbing side, wheezing as he ran. He was certain he'd broken some ribs. Siraye made to head back to the Watcher station, but he shook his head.

"I'm going to the palace. I have to help Cora."

"I'll come with you," Siraye panted, catching up to him. "Cora will kill me if I let you die after saving you."

Theo nodded, unable to reply. He was slowing, his body begging for rest. He let the adrenaline coursing through his body carry him forward. He'd pay for it later, when the pain hit him, but he didn't care. All that mattered was getting to Cora.

They passed the palace gates. Theo's legs protested as he pumped them up the steep drive. Siraye kept pace with him, face red. They were nearly to the palace steps, so close.

Theo heard Makari roar from deep within the castle. His foot hit the first stair when Siraye cried out.

"Watch out!"

Theo ducked instinctively. Siraye's knife sailed past his shoulder to bury itself in a Galtan soldier. He grunted, his finger squeezing as he fell. The shot made Theo's ears ring.

He froze, waiting for pain. None came. He let out his breath, then he heard the thud behind him. He whirled around, a guttural cry ripping out of his throat.

He ran back to Siraye, pressing his hands against the blossoming wound. She shoved him aside to press her own hands against her side.

"Don't worry about me." Her voice was strained. "Get to Cora."

"I'm not leaving you here," Theo growled. "We're getting you help."

"I'll be fine," Siraye hissed. "The others will catch up soon enough."

His instincts warred with each other. Cora was behind him, facing gods knew what. But Siraye was losing far too much blood.

Her hands were already soaked.

"Theo! Siraye!"

His head whipped up as Barden barreled into the courtyard. A narrow gash wept near his collar, but he looked otherwise intact. He skidded to a halt, dropping to his knees next to Siraye.

"See?" She grunted. "I have help. Now, *go!*"

Theo nodded, spinning to race up the palace steps. To Cora.

Makari was panting before they'd made it three hallways deep. Spears of pain sailed across the bond as she hobbled along. Cora did her best to send calm, soothing feelings back to Makari. The black wall still sat between them, shielding her from the worst of Makari's pain.

The palace was eerily quiet. Cora had never seen it this empty in her entire life. It sent shivers down her spine. They wound through the palace's main corridors without seeing a single soul. Cora turned into the royal family's private wing, her unease growing.

She paused at an intersection, ears perked. Footsteps tapped against the floor ahead. She pressed herself against the wall, waiting. Makari followed her lead, tail swishing against the stone floor. They shared a look as the footsteps grew closer. Cora swept around the corner, sword leveled.

Nolan's hands went up, eyes wide.

"Princess!" He took a small step back, avoiding her blade.

Cora pressed forward, Makari limping into the hall behind her. "Where is everyone?"

She didn't lower her sword. Her eyes flicked over the head of security, taking in the unbuttoned jacket, the mussed hair. There was a wildness to his eyes she'd never seen before, so unlike the man she thought she knew.

"Most of the staff were evacuated a few hours ago." His eyes kept darting over her shoulder. "All that's left is a few security officers."

"And Chancellor Byrne."

"Yes."

Coincidences were adding up in her mind, building to a

356

sickening outcome. A bead of sweat trickled down Nolan's temple.

Cora edged closer. "When did you betray us?"

"You can't betray what you were never loyal to."

Makari growled, her talons dragging along the carpeted hallway as she stalked closer. Nolan jumped, backing into the wall. Cora followed, hand tightening around her blade.

The edges of her vision ran red as she stared at the man her family had trusted. The man in charge of their safety. In charge of Arik's training. How many times had her brother sung Nolan's praises? How many confidential meetings had Nolan overheard?

Makari growled again, egging her on.

He looked between Cora and Makari, face white.

He held up shaking hands. "Wait! I can tell you where Callan is."

Cora let her sword drift closer to Nolan. "Why should I trust you?"

"Callan has come unhinged," he whispered. "I should have seen it coming, should have stopped him long ago. I've never seen my brother like this."

"Your *brother?*" Her blade dipped.

Nolan met her eyes steadily. "Yes."

"Why should I believe you would turn on him?" Her sword made its way up to Nolan's neck.

"Because Callan is not the man I believed him to be."

Warm breath blew across her shoulder as she considered. Makari tugged on the bond, growling again. Her dragon was ready for blood. Her lips parted, flashing her dagger-like teeth.

"You do realize that when I find Callan, I will kill him."

Nolan's head dropped, but not before she saw the tears streaking his cheek. "Yes."

Cora let her sword drop to her side and stepped back.

Nolan's hands fell. "He's in the throne room. The old throne room."

She nodded, rolling her shoulders. She walked down the hall, Makari at her side.

Nolan's voice made her pause.

"He's waiting for you," he warned. "Don't underestimate him."

"I know," she replied. Now it was her turn to stop Nolan. "If I ever see you again, I won't be as kind."

Nolan nodded once, then disappeared around the corner.

She pivoted back, taking a deep breath. "Are you ready for this?"

Makari let out a short roar in answer, smoke curling from her nostrils. They set off, into the depths of the castle. The silence clung to Cora like a cloak.

She crept closer, the hair on the back of her neck rising. The air felt oppressive, her lungs heavy. She shook her head, trying to push off the feeling. She stopped in front of the tall chamber doors, heart squeezing.

Makari nudged her shoulder, hot breath blowing through her hair. Cora's lip lifted, nodding to herself. She shoved open the doors, swinging them in with a resounding bang.

Callan sat at the head of the arc of thrones. The only light came from the window behind him, looking across the city. He had left it open to the stone balcony, fresh air blowing through the chamber.

Cora approached slowly, passing through the rows of empty chairs to either side.

"Nine stone chairs," Callan's voice carried across the chamber. "I thought the Bjorns would have changed this room, but it's almost the same as it was hundreds of years ago."

"It's a nice room."

Callan chuckled, shifting in his chair. "It's a symbol of power."

Makari hissed quietly, her mind pressing against Cora's. Cora glanced around but couldn't see anything. Makari pressed closer, and a scent filled her nose. She recognized Callan's scent, but it was wrong. It mingled with the reek of death and decay. She swallowed, fighting back a wave of nausea.

"The symbol of the oppressor," Callan continued, ignoring Makari.

Cora's eyes snapped back to him. "How fitting that you would be here."

"I am no oppressor. I am the great unifier!"

"You are only a great fraud."

Callan shot up from his seat. He stepped forward, no longer

shadowed. His eyes had turned silver. "How dare you!"

His clothes were ragged, as if he'd torn them. His hair stuck up at odd angles, his face haggard.

"I am the chosen one!" he continued, his face reddening. "I am the favored of the gods!"

"According to who?" Cora shot back, anger flaring. "You are nothing but a murderer."

"No!" A vein throbbed on Callan's forehead. "No! It's me! I'm the one, not you! How dare you bring that creature here!"

Cora glanced at Makari, confused. The dragoness sat on her haunches, gaze fixed on Callan. He became more hysterical with every sentence.

"For years, I have sought the gods' favor! I have pursued my destiny!" Callan pulled at his hair. "And then you! No! The Dragon Riders are through! I am the chosen of the gods!"

Callan grabbed the front of his shirt and ripped, releasing a guttural yell. Cora took a step back, her grip tightening around her weapons. His crazed silver eyes locked onto her, hands curled into claws.

"I have hunted dragon nests for years." The air in the room warmed as Callan spoke. "I have tried hundreds of potions and been denied my power again and again. But no longer. Now the only thing in my way"—his eyes bored into Cora—"is you."

Callan's arms exploded in flames.

Cora lifted a hand to shield her eyes from the sudden brightness.

Fire. She could handle fire.

He threw a fire ball at her. Cora barely flinched, taking a step toward him. He threw again. The flames grazed her arm, singing her clothes.

She continued forward. Her swords gleamed in the firelight.

Another fireball. Another step.

Callan roared in frustration. He brought his hands together and pointed them at Cora's feet. A wall of flames grew in front of her, rising above her head. She paused, staring into the flickering flames.

Go forth, blessed one.

Cora stepped through the flames. It felt like a warm summer breeze caressing her from head to toe. She emerged perfectly intact, not a thread or hair so much as singed.

His face was a mask of rage, the vein on his forehead nearly popping out of the skin.

Cora moved into her sword stance. "I carry Elidi's Blessing. Fire can't hurt me."

She reached Callan. Her blades flashed, heading for his chest. He caught her wrist, stopping her first blade before it could reach his skin. Her second sword followed. Callan dropped his elbow into her wrist, sending her weapon to the floor.

A maniacal grin lit up Callan's face. "Then it's a good thing I have more than fire."

Callan kicked her across the room. Her side exploded with pain as the breath left her lungs. Her remaining sword fell to the ground with a *clang*. Warmth dripped down her face again as she struggled to push to her feet.

Makari leaped over top of her, bellowing. Callan stumbled back, fists clenching. Makari slammed back down, mouth open wide. Callan dodged, and her teeth snapped around air. The room rumbled as the stones beneath Makari's feet began to quake.

She fell onto her torn stump of a leg, crying out. Agony tore through Cora's head. She slammed to her knees, her vision darkening.

"Your pet is no match for me."

Makari glared at Callan. She tried to push to her feet, snapping at him. The stones shifted under her, and she fell again. Makari roared, and Cora fought to stay conscious. She forced air into her lungs. Her head cleared enough to shut out the pain from Makari. She shoved herself to her feet and darted to her discarded swords.

She straightened into her sword stance as Callan stepped down from his throne. He brought his hands together, water gathering along his fingers. A chill emanated from him as the water expanded into a massive sword of ice.

Cora stepped back, a shiver racing along her skin. She brought her swords up, deflecting the long blade. She grunted, teeth grinding together. Her arms moved furiously, countering the blows, keeping his blade from her flesh.

Callan drove forward, pushing her back. He laughed, sending his weight forward. She stumbled back, her stance breaking.

Makari cried out, surging forward. His attention shifted to the dragon, face darkening. The wind coming through the window intensified, funneling directly into Makari. She beat her wings, fighting against the force.

Cora lurched forward, aiming for Callan. The wind kept her pinned in place.

Callan grunted, straining. Makari hissed as she thrashed against the furious wind. It backed her into the corner. Callan's hand swung toward the wall, and the stones around Makari shifted, creating a barricade. Makari bellowed, tearing furiously at the stones. Cora felt it in her own hand when Makari's claw broke against the unyielding prison.

"Makari!"

She lunged forward.

He easily batted away her strike. She danced back, light on her feet. Callan held his sword in a two-handed grip, the blade sailing towards Cora. She jumped to the side. Again the icy blade swung towards her. And again she dodged, sweat beading on her forehead. Her swords smacked into the ice blade, chipping the edge. Callan thrust, trying to catch her off guard. Cora twisted, hissing as her arm was met with bitter cold.

She barely glanced at the gash in her arm. The cold numbed the pain, but warm blood wept down her arm.

Callan pressed forward. She parried, keeping his sword away from her neck. She couldn't stay on the defensive. His reach was longer, his sword heavier. He'd wear her down soon.

Cora tripped over one of the stone chairs. The stones beneath her shifted. She rolled once, then again. She barely made it to her feet before the blows rained down.

The force of Callan's swings vibrated her arms. Her muscles screamed as she held him off. Callan kept advancing, forcing her back with every move. She blinked against the sudden brightness as he drove her out to the balcony. Cora swept her swords out in front of her. They fell to the stones. Instinctively, she thrust her hands up, catching Callan's wrists.

Callan bore down, her back bending as she struggled to hold him off. She slid one foot back, trying to gain purchase. Her heel found the edge of the balcony.

She started, nearly losing her grip on Callan. He pressed closer, straining her arms to their breaking point.

I'm sorry, she thought to Makari. *I'm not strong enough.*

Callan's sword crept closer to her neck. Her arms would give at any second. Sweat dripped into her eyes and down her back. Makari's whimper echoed in her mind and her ears.

"I am the champion of the gods," he declared, bearing down.

Cora gasped. The cold of the blade kissed her skin, the sharp ice nearly touching her. Her arms shook as she fought. She ground her teeth, holding on. Her strength was almost spent.

Desperately, she reached across the bond for Makari. That black wall separated her from her dragon. Cora ran mental fingers along its surface, looking for breaks. A tear slid down her cheek as she pushed against it.

Please, Makari. We're better together.

Makari stilled. Her claws stopped ripping against the stones, and the wall between them fell. The bond snapped into focus, and strength flooded Cora's limbs.

She shoved Callan back, sending him stumbling away from the balcony. He stared at her in horror.

"You will never know true power, Callan." Her voice reverberated across the stone. "Because it has to be given, not taken."

The silver in Callan's eyes had faded to a mere sliver. He backed away from her, shaking his head.

Makari burst through her stone prison, sending him into a throne. He shrank away from them, throwing his hands out. A white-hot stream of fire poured from his hands.

Cora walked straight through it, Makari at her side. When it died, Callan's eyes were blue again and staring down the barrel of her handgun.

Callan glared at her, lifting his chin defiantly. Makari simmered in Cora's mind, urging her to spill his blood. She could practically

362

taste it coating her tongue. She stared into those piercing blue eyes and extricated herself from Makari's mind. Separated from her dragon's bloodlust, she found her own fury cooled.

Cora lowered her gun. "I have no desire to kill you, Callan. And I have no interest in starting a war with Galta."

Callan surged upward as if to lunge at her. Makari's front paw slammed down. He let out a shriek as a single claw pierced his shoulder.

Cora ignored the trickle of blood running down his chest. "Makari, on the other hand, has no such qualms. So if you'd like to make it out of here in one piece, I suggest you cooperate."

36

Theo wasn't the first one to find Cora. He had to step aside as a pair of palace guards led a bandaged and cuffed Callan out of the throne room, Arik leading the way. The prince gave him the barest of nods before barking orders at the guards.

Theo rushed in behind them, taking in the damage before spotting Cora on the balcony, Makari at her side. She turned as he ran across the room. He threw his arms around her and lifted, ignoring the screaming pain in his sides. She laughed, squeezing his shoulders.

"Are you alright?" he breathed.

"Exhausted, but mostly unscathed. What happened to you?"

Theo set her down carefully, his body protesting at the movement. He must look awful. He gave her a shortened version of what happened. He glanced over at Makari, only just noticing how she slumped to one side.

"What happened to Makari?"

Cora's levity dissipated as she told him about the Shrike. She had to pause more than once, her eyes shining. He pulled her close as her shoulders began to tremble.

He stroked her back, letting her tears soak his shirt. "We need to get Makari some medical attention."

Cora nodded, taking a shuddering breath before pulling back. He watched as her spine straightened and determination filled her eyes.

Within an hour, they were sitting in plush armchairs above the hospital's largest operating theater. Cora leaned into the observation window, her nose nearly touching the glass.

"She'll be fine," he murmured.

"She's going to have to relearn how to do everything," she whispered. "I don't even know if she'll be able to hunt on her own."

"Then we'll make her the most pampered dragon in Liskow. And, if you want, a friend from tech school works with prosthetics. I could reach out to him."

A ghost of a smile touched her lips. Theo leaned over to rest his hand on her knee, tracing slow circles with his thumb. They watched for several minutes as the surgery team stitched Makari's skin closed. The head surgeon turned and lifted his thumb skyward.

Cora relaxed, her hand coming to rest on top of his. "Will you stay here with Makari for me?"

"Where are you going?"

"I'll be back in a few minutes. I need to do something."

Gray blinked against the sudden brightness as his team exited the hidden tunnel. Nova chirped, her tail lashing as she looked back at the palace.

"I'll make sure our students get home," Dr. Lander said, following the hatchling's gaze. "You're needed elsewhere."

She began herding the wide-eyed undergrads before Gray had a chance to protest. Ophelia bumped his shoulder, squeezing the fingers still clasped in hers.

"I've always wanted to see the palace."

"Are you sure you want to stay with me?" Gray asked, his voice hoarse.

"Let's see, you're hot, brilliant, *and* you have a baby dragon? Oh, and you just saved my life," she tapped a finger against her chin, pretending to consider. "Honey, there's no *way* you're getting rid of me."

As if in agreement, Nova wound around Ophelia's legs, purring loudly. Gray laughed, a deep, genuine sound. He stared at Ophelia, at her disheveled hair and ripped pants. He'd never seen anyone more beautiful.

"Then I think it's time you met my friends."

"Why am I not surprised that you wanted to meet here?" Arik said from behind her.

Cora gave him a thin smile over her shoulder. He joined her at the balcony railing, watching the sun sink towards the horizon. They stayed like that for a long time, drinking in the quiet.

"I'm leaving," she whispered.

"What do you mean, you're leaving?"

"I mean that we both know this is never what I wanted. And now that I have Makari, I can't stay."

Arik spun around to lean back against the balcony. He exhaled slowly, folding his arms over his chest. His voice shook with barely controlled anger. "So you're just going to make a mess of everything, then disappear? How am I supposed to explain that to the Council?"

"Tell them the truth." Her eyes flicked up to meet her brother's. "Princess Catarina died. You've always wanted the throne. So take it."

"If you're caught, you'll be tried for treason."

"I know."

Arik let out another slow exhale. He ran a hand through his hair, leaving the golden strands sticking up at odd angles. "As your Protector, I really shouldn't be encouraging this."

"Just take the crown, Arik."

He nodded, then straightened. The setting sun sent arcs of orange light around his body like a crown.

Cora's breath snagged as she looked up at her twin. He was every inch the monarch she was not. She wrapped her arms around his torso.

Arik froze for a beat before returning the hug. He pressed a kiss to the top of her head. "Say goodbye to Father before you go."

"Yes, Your Majesty."

He shoved her shoulder, his mouth twitching up into a smile. Cora gave his arm one last squeeze before walking through the debris of the old throne room.

It didn't take her long to get to her father's office. She paused in front of the door to trace the carved dragons with her fingers.

She eased the door open and slipped in.

Father looked up from his desk, beaming. He threw his arms out, nearly sloshing his drink out of the short glass he held. Cora eyed the line of empty bottles lining his desk. She gently pushed a stray bottle out of the way with her toe.

Father wrapped her in a bear hug, pulling her close to his chest. Cora fought the urge to gag at the sharp scent of liquor.

He pulled back to look her over with bloodshot eyes. "Catarina! I'm so glad you're safe!"

"Hello, Papa," Cora said softly. "I see you've been busy."

"It's all I have left," Father slurred, his words morphing into a sob.

She wiped the tears from his face as she sat on the edge of his desk. She took the glass from his hand and set it down. Then she told him everything, all that had happened to her since the gala. He listened intently to her story, reaching out now and then to touch her, as if to make sure she was real. Cora wasn't certain if he'd even remember what she told him tomorrow.

"So now, I'm taking my dragon to get a prosthetic."

"Look at my daughter," Father said, more lucid than he'd been before. "Become a woman before my eyes. And a warrior."

Cora blinked away the prickling in her eyes. She hugged her father again, wrapping her arms around him tight.

"I love you, Papa. I'll come see you again."

"I love you, too, my little Dragon Rider."

Theo made sure Makari was in recovery before leaving her. He wasn't about to slack on his dragon-sitting duties.

He had to weave through a labyrinth of equipment that had been shoved against walls and into spare rooms to make room for her. The hospital had been renovated only a decade prior, but they'd kept the extra-wide hallways leftover from the old Riders. Theo hated to think how they would've fit the dragon in otherwise.

The halls beyond where Makari laid were buzzing with activity. Patients in varying degrees of distress occupied chairs and stretchers in every available space, while nurses darted between them like angry hornets.

Theo pressed himself against the wall as a middle-aged nurse in stained scrubs barked at him to *move*.

Even with all the chaos, it didn't take long to find her.

Siraye was perkier than the last time he'd seen her. Color had returned to her cheeks, and she sat up. She smiled as he poked his head into her room.

"Theo! Is Cora alright?"

"Yeah, a little banged up, but she's fine," he said, sliding into a chair next to Siraye's bed. "What about you?"

"I got lucky," Siraye shifted in her bed, then winced. "The bullet didn't expand, so the damage wasn't too major. I did have to have two blood transfusions, though. I have a feeling I'm not the only one."

"The halls out there are crazy," Theo said, glancing out her open door. "There's so many injured."

"It could have been a lot worse."

"You're right," he sighed. He stared down at the bed, unable to meet Siraye's eyes. "Siraye, what you did for me…"

"You would have done the same in a heartbeat," she interrupted. "You and Cora. And I would gladly do it again for either one of you."

Theo swallowed the lump in his throat. He breathed deeply a few times, blinking against the prickling in his eyes. Siraye reached over and gave his hand a quick squeeze.

"What are you going to do after they release you?"

Siraye shrugged. "I don't know for sure. I'll stay in Narous for a while, explore the city. Then, we'll see where the wind takes me."

"What about Stony Hollow?"

"They can learn to do without me," she replied, a bit sharply. "I think it's time I figured out exactly what I want, for a change. Just, promise me one thing?"

"Of course."

"Invite me to the wedding?"

Heat rushed into Theo's face. Siraye shrieked with laughter, then winced and laid a hand against her bandage. Theo gave her a gentle hug and a promise to keep in touch. Then he left to return to his Dragon Rider.

368

When Cora returned to the hospital, Makari was in a recovery room, Theo the only one with her. He pulled in two armchairs from the waiting room. Cora smiled, settling in next to him. He offered her a snack.

"They said everything went well." Theo kept his voice soft.

Her shoulders relaxed. "Good. Where did everyone go?"

"The surgeons have a lot of patients to see. I ducked out for a few minutes before they left."

"You *left* her?" Cora's voice rose in pitch.

"I wanted to check on Siraye."

Cora settled back into her seat with a forceful exhale. "Lead with that, next time. How is Siraye?"

"Recovering," he replied, pulling open their snacks with a pop. "She should be released from the hospital in a week or two."

"Good," she sighed, then glanced toward the door. "I feel like I should be helping them."

"You did help them. The princess saved her people."

Cora looked down, picking at the corner of the package in her hands. Her heart rate kicked up. "About that." She paused to clear her throat. "I'm not crown princess anymore."

Theo froze next to her, hand halfway into a bag in his lap. "What do you mean?"

"I abdicated."

"But you can't!" Theo cried, spilling crisps onto the floor. "It's against the law! You'll be prosecuted."

"I'm not too sure about that. There will be a very touching funeral for Princess Catarina."

His brow furrowed, food forgotten. "What are you saying, Cora?"

Her face broke into a smile. "I'm free, Theo."

She reached out and took his hand. He leaned into her touch, face softening. She looked up into his face and pulled him to her.

His lips crashed into hers, warm and soft. Her hands roved, needing to touch him, to make sure this was all real. One long arm wrapped around her waist, the other sliding beneath her knees. Then she was in his lap, her hands tangling in those silky, perfect curls.

They broke apart, breathing ragged. Cora pressed her forehead to his, one hand on his chest, over his wildly beating heart. Theo brushed her hair behind her ear, hand lingering at the back of her neck.

"I think it's about time I left my hometown," she whispered. "Do you want to come with me?"

"Yes."

Soft purring from the side of the room brought both of their heads around. Makari watched them with sleepy eyes.

Cora crossed over and threw her arms around Makari's scaly neck. The purring grew louder. Makari pulled away, pushing clumsily to her feet.

"Don't!" Cora cried, hands out to help her. "You aren't ready to stand yet."

Makari hissed defiantly. She rose onto wobbly legs, swaying until she found her balance. She sniffed at her amputated leg for a long time. Satisfied, she brought her head up proudly, balancing on three legs. She pressed an image of the sky across the bond, and Cora frowned.

"What's wrong?" Theo murmured.

"Makari wants to leave," she explained. "I'm not sure that's a good idea, considering she just got out of surgery."

"Maybe she's right. If you're supposed to be dead, hanging around could put you in danger."

Makari snorted in agreement, pressing more firmly on Cora's mind.

She frowned, stroking Makari's neck softly. *Only until your pain meds wear off.*

Cora didn't even like that compromise, but she knew better than to argue with a dragon.

Makari swelled in satisfaction, blowing hot air across Cora and Theo. Theo smiled, twining his fingers with hers.

They waited for dark. Gray had found them not long after Makari woke, Nova and a lovely sprite in tow. They spent the hours until twilight talking and reveling in the fact that they were

370

alive.

All four people and two dragons crept through the dim city, keeping to the shadows. Most people were holed up at home, still shaken from the attack. The few people that were out didn't dare glance into the alleys as they passed. It didn't take long before they were on the plain surrounding the city.

"You could come with us, you know," Cora said to Gray.

The four of them watched as Makari flexed her wings, testing her balance on three legs. Gray glanced down at Ophelia, his hand clasped with hers. Cora hadn't seen him let it go once since they'd reunited.

"Not yet," he said. "I'm going to teach my class this semester, first. Give the university enough time to find a replacement. Besides," he tugged Ophelia closer, a smile curving his lips. "I have a date."

Ophelia's flush was visible even in the dark. She stared at him with round eyes.

Cora swallowed a laugh, finally understanding how Gray saw her and Theo. Theo wrapped his arms around her from behind. She leaned into his warmth, soaking in the rise and fall of his chest.

They all stood in comfortable silence for as long as they could, unwilling to break the moment.

At last, it was time.

Cora squeezed Gray, then Ophelia, promising to see them soon. Theo and Gray embraced tightly, murmuring something to each other that even Cora's keen ears couldn't hear. Nova bounded to Gray as they pulled apart, whining as she separated from Makari.

Makari shifted her weight, testing her balance. She was adapting to three legs remarkably quickly. Theo checked to make sure their packs were secure, then gestured for Cora to go first. She flashed him a smile, hopping easily into her place on Makari's back. Theo settled behind her more warily.

"This is your last chance to back out," she teased.

"I wouldn't dream of it," he replied. Then swallowed hard.

Cora laughed softly. She stole one last look over her shoulder at the city. She memorized the pattern of neon lights, shining like constellations in the dark.

"Are you ready for your first ride on a three-legged dragon?" she asked.

Makari spread her wings, leaping into the air forcefully. They soared above Narous, and Cora said one final silent goodbye to her home, waving to Gray and Ophelia. She directed Makari away from the lights, away from her old life.

Makari found a pocket of warm air, rising ever higher. Her rumbling purr settled into Cora's bones as they soared toward new adventures.

Epilogue

Callan's shoulder throbbed. He'd been given painkillers before he was thrown into a dark, cold cell, but they hardly touched the pain. Callan shifted on the hard cot, wincing as his shoulder twinged. He was drained, exhausted from using his powers, but sleep evaded him. All he could think of was Catarina's dragon sinking her claws into him.

Soft footsteps padded down the hall. Callan didn't bother to sit up. Why should he care what happened now?

"Well, the prince certainly treats his guests poorly, doesn't he?"

Callan pushed himself upright to glare at Stellana. Her white pantsuit nearly glowed in the dim dungeon. She smiled at him, a feline expression that made him want to squeeze his hand around her throat.

"What are you doing here?"

"We've reconsidered."

"Excuse me?"

Stellana stepped forward, tapping long red nails against the bars of his cell. "Come work for my organization, and I'll get you out of this cell."

"Your organization abandoned me," he growled. "Why should I listen to you?"

Stellana leaned her head forward until her forehead pressed against the bars. Her expression was feral. "What if I told you that Elidi is not the goddess you should be so devoted to? I can get you power, *true* power. Enough to put your little bonfire to shame."

"I know of the other elements. I had all of them at my control today."

373

"A parlor trick compared to what I'm offering. The power of the gods themselves."

Callan gaped at her, mind whirling. He had no reason to believe her, and yet… He recognized the hungry gleam in her eyes. It was the same one he saw in the mirror.

Callan rose from his bed to meet her at the bars. "What would I have to do?"

End of Book One

Acknowledgements

I can hardly believe I'm here, writing this now. This book has come after years of dreaming, learning, writing, and rewriting. I couldn't have done it alone, and so I wanted to take a moment to say thank you.

First of all, thank you to my wonderful husband, Matthew. Thank you for letting me bounce ideas off of you, even when all you did was listen. For helping with the kids, for giving me time and space to write. And for being the inspiration for so many little moments between Cora and Theo.

Thank you to my best friends, Ella and Sierra. Your unwavering support has carried me through so many moments of doubt. Thank you for reading my hot mess of a first draft, and for continuing to read, even when life was chaotic. Your feedback and encouragement is why this book even exists in the first place.

Thank you to my parents for your constant support through every phase of my life. And a special shoutout to my mom for telling everyone she knows that I wrote a book, and that they should buy it. Love you both.

Thank you to my DnD group - Matthew, Hunter, Nate, and Kacey - for being so supportive and encouraging. And for letting me prattle on about my book before far too many of our sessions. Your enthusiasm has truly meant so much to me.

Thank you to Clara Abigail, my editor, for your wonderful feedback. You were such a joy to work with, and I love how much you love my characters. You made my words and characters shine.

Thank you to my talented cover artist, AK Westerman. You brought my vision to life in the most gorgeous way. You took my word soup of ideas for the design and made something stunning. Thank you for all the care and time you put into my cover.

Thank you to my readers: Ella, Sierra, Julia, Charlotte, and Kacey. I cherish every tiny piece of feedback you've given me, and for just being a listening ear while I geek out about my world and characters. You all gave me the confidence to keep going.

I have to express thanks to everyone on the Lit Service, Your Mom Writes Books, and Intentionally Blank podcast teams. Thank you for providing content for new writers like me. Studying craft from all of the incredible authors on these podcasts helped not only bring my spark back, but hone my skills as a writer.

A special thanks to Brandon Sanderson, and every member of his team who made his university writing lectures available on YouTube. The ability to virtually attend a university level writing class was such a tremendous blessing, espeically during a phase of my life where attending a class in person was impossible.

I could not finish these acknowledgements without thanking my Heavenly Father. Thank you for the talents I've been given, and the skills I've developed. And for the spark that grew to a burning flame of passion for this project. I never would have made it without that fire in my chest urging me on.

And finally, dear reader, if you've made it this far, I thank you. For taking a chance on a new author, and for coming along on my character's journey. I hope you've come to love this story as much as I do.

About the Author

Elle Winters is a novelist, former zookeeper, wife, and mom of three humans, two dogs, and one snake. She started Brigham Young University as an English major, but graduated in 2019 with a degree in Wildlife and Wildlands Conservation. During the pandemic, she became a mother and rediscovered her love for fantasy and fiction. Now, she jots down her stories while caring for her family at home, bringing her love for nature and animals into her fiction.